...

ONCE WE
WERE
BROTHERS

...

...

ONCE WE
WERE
BROTHERS

...

Ronald H. Balson

St. Martin's Griffin
New York

ONCE WE WERE BROTHERS. Copyright © 2010, 2013
by Ronald H. Balson. All rights reserved. Printed in the United
States of America. For information, address St. Martin's Press,
175 Fifth Avenue, New York, N.Y. 10010.

www.stmartins.com

A different version of this book was previously published
by Berwick Court Publishing Company, Chicago, Illinois.

Library of Congress Cataloging-in-Publication Data

Balson, Ronald H.
    Once we were brothers / Ronald H. Balson.—First edition.
        pages cm
    A different version of this book was previously published by Berwick
Court Publishing Company, Chicago, Illinois
T. p. verso.
    ISBN 978-1-250-04639-0 (trade paperback)
    ISBN 978-1-250-04812-7 (hardcover)
    ISBN 978-1-4668-4670-8 (e-book)
    1. Philanthropists—Fiction.   2. Holocaust survivors—Fiction.
3. Nazis—Fiction.   4. Chicago (Ill.)—Fiction.   5. Poland—History—
Occupation, 1939–1945—Fiction.   6. World War, 1939–1945—
Atrocities—Fiction.   7. Jewish fiction.   I. Title.
    PS3602.A628O53 2013
    813'.6—dc23

                                                            2013026247

St. Martin's Griffin books may be purchased for educational,
business, or promotional use. For information on bulk purchases,
please contact Macmillan Corporate and Premium Sales
Department at 1-800-221-7945, extension 5442,
or write specialmarkets@macmillan.com.

First Edition: October 2013

10   9   8   7   6   5   4   3   2   1

To my wife, Monica,
with whom I dance through life

I

...

THE
CONFRONTATION

ONE

. . .

BEN SOLOMON STOOD BEFORE his bathroom mirror fumbling with his bow tie. He was eighty-three years old and getting dressed for Judgment Day. Years had come and gone since he had last worn his tuxedo, but then, Judgment Day was a black tie affair.

He uttered a Polish phrase to the man in the mirror and reached into his pocket to reexamine his pricey ticket.

Lyric Opera of Chicago. Opening Night Gala, September 26, 2004. La Forza del Destino. Main Floor, Aisle 2, Row kk, Seat 103—a seat he did not intend to occupy. Truth be told, he didn't care much for opera. The ticket had set him back five hundred dollars, a goodly sum for a pensioner.

He pulled back the cuff of his shirtsleeve to check the time on his watch, a silver-band Citizen given to him when he retired from the Chicago Park District eight years ago. Four thirty—still two hours until the doors would open. He walked into his living room.

The windows of his modest one-bedroom apartment faced east, toward Lake Michigan and the row of condominium towers that stretched north in a line from the Loop to Thorndale Avenue like a stand of Midwest corn. The late-afternoon sun laid a track of shadows across Lake Shore Drive and onto the lush grass of the Waveland Golf Course, where he'd worked as a starter for almost fifty years. To his right, in the mirrored calm of Belmont Harbor, the luxury cruisers rested comfortably in their slips. He lingered. How he loved that view. He conceded that he might be looking at it for the last time.

Once more he checked his appearance in the mirror. He asked Hannah if he looked all right. Was he dapper? He wished she were there to answer.

Underneath his sweaters, in the bottom drawer of his bureau, lay a cardboard cigar box. Setting the box on the bureau top, he lifted the lid and removed a German P08 Luger, World War II vintage, in mint condition, purchased at an antique gun show for $1,250. Another hit to his savings account. He stuffed the pistol in his belt beneath his cummerbund.

Five o'clock. Time to walk to the corner, flag a southbound taxi, and join up with the glitterati at the "undisputed jewel of the social season."

Two

...

I N HIS DRESSING ROOM on the second story of his Winnetka mansion, a generous four-acre estate set high on a bluff overlooking the lake, Elliot Rosenzweig stood fumbling with his cuff links. "Jennifer," he called out, "would you come help me, please?"

The young medical student, sparkling in her formal evening gown, breezed into the master suite and to the side of her grandfather, who was grappling with his French cuffs.

"Popi, we're going to be late if we don't hurry."

He watched her hands easily fasten the gold links. So supple, so young. Soon to be a surgeon's hands, he thought.

"There," she said.

Beaming with profound adoration, he kissed her on the forehead. "I'm so proud of you," he said.

"For fastening your cuffs?"

"For being my angel."

"I love you, too, Popi." She twirled and headed for the closet door.

"That's a beautiful dress," he called after her. "I like it."

"You should," she said over her shoulder, "it cost you a fortune. Nonna bought it for me at Giselle's. It's an original. Is Nonna going tonight?"

"No, I'm afraid not. She has another one of her headaches." He winked. "She hates these public events."

Jennifer lifted his Armani jacket from the hanger and held it for him as he slipped his arms through the sleeves. Smiling, she gave a short tug on his lapels and took a step back.

"You look very handsome tonight." She kissed him on his cheek. "Now we need to go. All our friends are waiting."

Together, hand in hand, they joined the rest of their entourage under the pink stone portico where the group filed into two limousines that would carry them downtown to the Civic Opera House. The iron security gates parted and the white limousines glided forward onto Sheridan Road and toward Chicago's Loop.

THREE

...

FESTIVAL BANNERS HUNG FROM the art deco columns of the Civic Opera House's mezzanine and multicolored buntings looped from the balustrades, all gaily surrounding the opera celebrants gathered in the foyer below. Costumed servers carried champagne and hors d'oeuvres on silver platters. In the corner, a subgroup of the Lyric Orchestra played selections from Rossini overtures.

Raising her voice to be heard above the din of conversations, Jennifer asked, "How many years have you been coming to opening night, Popi?" She smiled as she accepted a canapé from an Elizabethan palace guard.

"Since 1958, angel. Although in those days they didn't pay so much attention to me."

"You mean you weren't a Platinum Grand Benefactor?"

"I always gave what I could to support the arts, but . . ." His answer was interrupted by the approach of Chicago's mayor and first lady, who were being shuttled about by Lyric's artistic director.

"It's nice to see you again, Elliot. You're looking well."

"Thank you, Mr. Mayor. I think you know my granddaughter, Jennifer," he answered in the noisy hall. "It always brightens my day to see you and Edith." Rosenzweig flashed a congenial smile as he warmly took the hand of Chicago's first lady.

"Quite an event, the Lyric opening, thanks to you and the

board," said Mayor Burton. "The city owes you a great deal, Elliot. You're a priceless resource."

"Maybe *not* so priceless, John." And the two of them laughed.

While they continued to exchange flatteries, Ben Solomon quietly wound his way through the crowd toward the Grand Benefactor. He was oblivious to the music. He heard no conversations. He saw only his target. Making his way across the floor, he declined a flute of champagne from a seventeenth-century Italian peasant girl and felt for the Luger in his belt. The Lyric quartet pizzicatoed through the delightful strains of *La Gazza Ladra*.

He paused until the mayor and his wife had moved on to the next grouping and walked directly to Rosenzweig, his heart pounding like a pile driver.

"What did you do with all that jewelry?" he said inches from Rosenzweig's face.

"Excuse me, sir?" said the esteemed donor with a smile, unsure if this was part of a staged repertoire. Perhaps an opera joke?

But there was no sign of frivolity. "Just curious," Solomon said. "I asked you what you did with the jewelry—you know, the watches, diamond bracelets, wedding bands. You had a whole chest full. Don't you remember?"

Rosenzweig looked to his granddaughter and shrugged.

"I'm afraid I don't know what you're talking about, sir."

In a flash, Solomon drew the polished Luger and pressed the barrel hard against Rosenzweig's forehead. A woman screamed. The crowd immediately backpedaled into a large ring.

"Popi!" screamed Jennifer.

"Recognize this gun, Otto? Should be real familiar to a Nazi officer," Solomon said, waving the crowd away with his left arm. "Look at me, Otto. It's Ben Solomon. Here we are, together again, just like when we were kids. Never thought you'd see me again, did you, Hauptscharführer Piatek?"

Rosenzweig held up his hands in conciliation. The room was silent except for the words he delivered, slowly and evenly.

"You've made a mistake, sir. My name is Elliot Rosenzweig. It's not Otto. Or Piatek. I've never been a Nazi. In fact, sir, I am a camp survivor."

Very slowly, he held out his left arm. "Jennifer, undo my cuff link and roll up my sleeve."

As she did, his forearm displayed the blackened tattoo: A93554.

The gunman considered the offering, and then sneered. "You're a lying Nazi murderer and I can see the fear in your eyes, Hauptscharführer. Scream and cry and beg, Otto, like the innocent women and children who cowered before you. Mothers and fathers and grandparents. People who never hurt a soul. And the babies. All the children." He gestured wildly to the stunned crowd. "Tell them who you really are. Look at them all. They're listening. The masquerade is finished."

From out of nowhere, Solomon was blindsided and knocked to the marble floor. The gun slid along the tiles and came to rest against the staircase. Tackled by a Chicago Bears linebacker in formal attire, Solomon lay curled on the floor, weeping, his head shuttered in his forearms.

As he was pulled to his feet by security guards, Solomon screamed, "He's a Nazi. He's a murderer. He's Otto Piatek. He's Otto Piatek." The screams melted into sobs as they led the old man away. "He's Otto Piatek."

Four

...

ELLIOT ROSENZWEIG AGREED TO appear live on Monday morning's local news program. Three television cameras were positioned in his paneled library where Elliot sat confidently on his leather couch beside the fireplace. Though into his eighties and a little fuller than in younger days, he showed no signs of wear. His shoulders were square and his posture erect. Frequent sojourns kept his complexion bronzed.

Over his shoulder, the leaded bay windows framed a riparian vista: a velvet lawn leading to the bluffs and the Lake Michigan shore fifty feet below. Guests often remarked that the overlook was magnificent.

He had given television interviews in his library many times over the years and as recently as six weeks earlier, when he announced plans for one of his foundations to support an exchange of young musicians from Beijing.

Behind the philanthropist sat a wall of books and mementos, pictures with the high and mighty, gifts from foreign dignitaries, and in the center, a framed key to the city of Chicago, presented to him in 2001 by the mayor and the City Council. There were no religious symbols in his home. He once commented that he abandoned God after God abandoned him in the concentration camps. He no longer practiced his faith.

"Elliot, thank you for agreeing to come on with us this morning," the newswoman said. "What a frightening experience that must have been for you last Saturday night. I know it was for me. I was standing just across the hall."

"Yes, it was, Carol." He smiled warmly. The cameras panned to capture the choppy lake through the library windows. Sailboats tilted in the late September winds. "I was scared to death for my granddaughter, who was standing right beside me."

"Do you have any explanation for why this man assaulted you or shouted such a wild accusation?"

"None whatsoever. The poor, disturbed fellow obviously has me confused with someone else. A man named Otto, who apparently was, or is, a Nazi."

"We've learned that Mr. Solomon was a prisoner in a concentration camp. We know that you were as well, but I think it was quite a surprise for most people when your granddaughter exposed your arm. I don't think that part of your life is something you've chosen to share with the public."

"It's not. Once liberated, I never really wanted to discuss it again. It's behind me. I've been in Chicago now for fifty-six years. I've made my life here, I have my businesses here and my family is here. I've been very blessed in many ways."

"Otto Piatek. Does that name mean anything to you?"

"Nothing at all. I've never known anyone in my life named Piatek."

"You've been a prominent Chicagoan for so many years, on the boards of many civic organizations, yet you came here as a refugee after the war. Have you ever thought about writing a book? I think it would be inspirational."

"I'm too old for that. I'll be eighty-three next month." He chuckled and took a sip of coffee. "I was fortunate. I made acquaintances and invested money wisely. Business is a boring subject to most people, especially the insurance business. Would that fascinate you, Carol, to read a book on mergers of insurance underwriters? I don't think such a book would sell too many copies."

"What's going to happen to Mr. Solomon now? Have they told you?"

He shook his head. "I really don't know. It's quite obvious he needs help. He's very troubled."

"He's been charged with attempted murder."

"Yes, well, that's up to the prosecutors and the police. I pity the poor fellow. I hope he gets help."

Carol leaned forward and extended her hand. "Thank you, Elliot Rosenzweig, for joining us this morning. We're all glad that you weren't hurt."

"You're welcome, Carol," he said and unclipped the microphone from the panel of his silk shirt.

WHEN THE TV CREW had left, Elliot remained in his study, awaiting his secretary of twenty years. Soon a tall man, graying at the temples, conservative in his dark pinstripe suit and polished wingtips, entered the room and closed the door.

"You sent for me, sir?"

"Brian, do you know anything about this Otto Piatek? Do you know who he is?" said Elliot quietly.

"No, sir, I do not."

"Nor do I, but I have been publicly accused of being him."

Brian took a seat, crossed his legs, and set his writing pad on his lap. "Nobody believes him. Everyone thinks he's a crazy old man. That's what the papers say."

Elliot nodded and hesitated. "Still . . . it's an accusation delivered by a man who passionately believes it to be true, and it's hanging out there. It's a cloud on my reputation. Do you suppose there are people, maybe even friends of mine, who are now wondering, even if just a little, whether or not I could be a Nazi?"

"No, sir. Not at all."

"Hmm. I'm not so sure. Makes for great party talk. People love scuttlebutt." Elliot leaned forward and hit his palm with his fist. "I want to squelch it. Quickly. Permanently. I want you to find out who Otto Piatek is—or was."

Brian jotted a couple of notes.

"Contact that fellow over at Regency, the investigation firm we used last year on the DuPage industrial park. He's got a lot of local contacts."

"Carl Wuld?"

"That's him."

"Why do you want a local guy, if I may ask?"

"I think it's very possible that Mr. Solomon has been tracking this Nazi and has determined that he resides in Chicago. Maybe he does."

"Anything else, sir?"

Elliot pondered for a moment. "Yes. I also want you to find out whatever you can about Solomon. Use Wuld if he can help you. I want to know why this man would focus on me, of all people."

"Maybe he has ulterior motives."

"You think he wants money?"

Brian shrugged.

"No," Elliot said. "He stood inches from me. I saw the look in his eyes. They were filled with fire." He shook his head. "It's not for money."

Brian stood to leave and Elliot added, "Brian, let's keep this whole thing under wraps. Whatever information is uncovered, I want it to come directly to me. This has to be tightly managed. No leaks. If there's news, I want to be the one to break it to the media. If we should be lucky enough to find this Piatek and flush him out into the open, I want to personally release it. That will certainly remove any doubts about who I am."

Brian gave a sharp nod and left to do his work.

FIVE

...

A TELEPHONE BUZZED ON A desk in the Chicago law offices of Jenkins & Fairchild. Catherine Lockhart, her elbow resting on a stack of 7th Circuit appellate decisions, her desktop cluttered with graphs and financial statements, lifted the handset.

"Miss Lockhart, it's Mr. Taggart on line three."

She smiled.

"Hi, Liam. Did you locate George Crosby?" she said.

"Not yet. He's not at the bank anymore. But that's not why I'm calling."

"Do we have something else going on?"

"Only in my dreams, Cat."

"Ah, Liam. You wouldn't want to be anywhere near me today. Let's just stick to business. What are we doing besides Crosby?"

"Nothing. That's the only assignment I have from you, but I called to ask whether you have any free time for me this afternoon."

"Not today, not this week. I'm literally buried in work. So why don't we talk . . ."

"It's personal," he interrupted. "Can you spare a little time?"

"Seriously?"

"Can I come by about two thirty? I'll tell you about it when I get there."

"Of course," she said and set down the phone, concerned that her old friend might have stumbled into some trouble.

Two hours later, Liam appeared at her office door carrying a paper bag and two Starbucks cups. He paused at the doorway and shook his head at the sight. The credenza, side table, and desk were covered with file jackets, groups of papers, yellow pads, open casebooks, and empty water bottles. Banker's boxes, filled with sheaves of documents separated by color-coded tabs, lined the walls.

"You weren't kidding," he said.

Catherine looked up from her desktop. A lock of straw-colored hair freed itself from her barrette and flopped over her forehead. Her shirt sleeves were rolled up to her forearms. Her wool jacket lay draped over a side chair. Dark circles were forming under her eyes. She looked tired. He set the coffee on her desk. "I brought us some nourishment."

"Thanks," she said and took a sip. "So, what's up? Are you okay?"

"I had a visitor this morning," he said. "Do you remember Adele Silver?"

"No." She shrugged.

"You should, you represented her, although it was several years ago. She's that sweet old lady that lives around the corner from me on Kimball—in the redbrick bungalow. Remember?"

Catherine shook her head.

"Years ago she had this noisy beagle that kept getting out of her yard. I'd help her catch him and she'd bake me a cake or bring me some butter cookies. When her husband died, I brought her to you to help her through probate. Still don't remember? It was back when you were at Drexel, before . . ." Liam caught himself and bit his lip. "Well, it was about six or seven years ago, about the time you left."

He lifted a stack of clipped papers from a chair, sat down, unwrapped a turkey sandwich, and held it up. "You mind?"

Catherine nodded her head and responded solemnly. "I remember the butter cookies. Her husband's name was Lawrence?"

"Right."

"I had a lot going on in those days," she said to no one in particular.

Liam was silent for a moment. He tore the crust off his sandwich and took a bite from the corner. "Well, Adele came by my office this morning. She wanted help."

"From a private detective?"

"She wanted help for Ben Solomon."

She tapped her lips with the back of her pen. "Ben Solomon. Isn't he the lunatic who tried to kill Elliot Rosenzweig at the opera?"

"He didn't try to kill him."

"Liam, he's charged with aggravated assault and attempted murder. It was all over the papers. He had a pistol in Rosenzweig's face, and who knows what he would have done if that football player hadn't knocked him down."

"There were no bullets in the gun."

"You know that doesn't matter."

"It was an antique gun. The firing pin had been removed."

"Then he truly *is* a lunatic."

Liam shook his head. "Adele doesn't think so. She wants me to go talk with him."

Catherine rocked back in her chair. "And I'm involved . . . how?"

"Adele asked me to talk to you. He doesn't have a lawyer."

"Not a prayer. Look around. Where would I put another file? I don't have any more flat surfaces. Besides, I don't handle that kind of work. You know the firm's client base, it's institutional."

"Whether you represent him or not, will you go with me to see him at the jail this afternoon? If you come along, they'll let us use the attorneys' conference room. I promised Adele. She's such a nice lady and she pleaded with me to help him. Apparently, she's known him for a long time. Besides, she brought me some chocolate chip cookies."

She sighed. "Liam, a thousand people saw this old man put a gun in Elliot Rosenzweig's face. What could I possibly do for him?"

"You could listen to him." He took another bite of his sandwich and blotted the mayonnaise from the corner of his mouth. "And get me into the attorneys' room."

She shook her head. "Why do I do these things?"

"It's me Irish charm."

She shifted her eyes from her stack of work to her glib investigator, a man who had always been there for her, even in her dark days. He sat angled in his chair smiling, his right leg hitched over the armrest, his green Ulster rugby shirt flopping over the belt of his worn jeans. His face had miles on it, more than his forty-one years would suggest. His hair, with still a tinge of dusty red, gave him a boyish accent as it flopped over his forehead.

"All right. I'll go with you, but I'm not taking his case."

Six

...

CATHERINE SAT OPPOSITE LIAM drumming her fingers on a square metal table in the middle of a windowless room on the second floor of the Cook County Jail. They waited in silence, staring idly at the chipped linoleum floors and dented metal door. Catherine fidgeted and smoothed the lap of her wool skirt.

The rattle of dangling keys announced the arrival of a female deputy who escorted Solomon, a thin old man in an orange jumpsuit, into the interview room. She unlocked his handcuffs and motioned for him to take a seat at the table.

"I'll be right outside," said the deputy, pointing to a phone on the wall. "Just call me when you're finished." She left and locked the door.

Liam stood and offered his hand to the prisoner. "My name is Liam Taggart. I'm a private investigator, and this is attorney Catherine Lockhart." He gestured. "Adele Silver asked us to come and meet with you."

Solomon inventoried his visitors. His expression displayed no emotion. "I don't have any money."

"I didn't ask you for money."

"Lawyers and private investigators don't work for free."

"Well, not on purpose anyway. Ms. Lockhart happens to be an excellent attorney, but she's just come along as a favor to me. The clock's not ticking. No one's obligating themselves to do any work. We're just here to talk."

Solomon nodded and after a while said, "His name is Otto Piatek. He's a Nazi and an SS executioner."

"Mr. Solomon, no one can accuse you of aiming low," Catherine said. "You picked one of the most honored men in Chicago society. What makes you think that Elliot Rosenzweig is a Nazi? Most people would find that very hard to believe. He might be the most charitable man in Chicago."

Solomon defiantly stuck out his chin. "'The bigger the lie, the more the people will believe it.'"

Catherine shrugged her shoulders. "Meaning?"

"Do you know who said that?"

"No."

"Adolf Hitler, that's who. Your Grand Benefactor, this Mister Charitable—he's a fraud. He's a Nazi and I should've killed him."

"Is that why you took an unloaded gun?"

Solomon averted his eyes. He looked around the room, at the filmy lime-green wall and the soiled tabletop. Silent moments passed. He gazed upward and nodded his head, concurring with voices no one else could hear.

"Who are these young people, Hannah?" he said quietly to his voices. "It's never been their struggle. To them it's all ancient history. Like the Egyptian Pharaohs. Why should I expect them to care? Besides, Otto's covered his tracks too well."

Liam and Catherine exchanged glances. "Excuse me?" she said.

The old man focused his eyes across the table. "They tell me I'm being arraigned Wednesday. Attempted murder. I guess I don't have a defense. I might as well plead guilty. The cards are stacked. I'll read a prepared statement at my sentencing. That way at least it'll get to the papers and the television reports."

"There are defenses you could assert, Mr. Solomon. Perhaps you're not well enough to appreciate the consequences of your conduct."

Solomon laughed sardonically. "Insane? Should I plead insanity?

You have no idea what insanity is, young lady. I've known insanity and it can happen again; the next rip in the fabric of humanity. And if it does, the minions of evil will crawl through it—incomprehensible evil—the next Auschwitz or Cambodia or Bosnia or Darfur. This generation's Himmler, or Pol Pot or Milošević. The next *Aktion Reinhard*."

The old man straightened his body and shuffled to the door. "Aah, what's the difference? You can't put the pieces back together." He rapped his bony knuckles on the metal frame. The deputy returned and replaced his handcuffs. He turned his head and said, "Thank you for coming. Tell Adele Silver I'm grateful for her concern."

"WHAT DO YOU THINK?" Liam said on the drive back to the Loop.

"If he pleads guilty, he'll spend the rest of his life in jail. If he prevails on a plea of insanity, he'll spend it in a hospital. Either way, he'll be institutionalized until he dies. He's a very sad person, but Chicago's safer with him off the streets."

"I don't know, Cat, he didn't harm anyone. He had an inoperative weapon. He's lived here for fifty years and he's never hurt a fly. Chicago won't be measurably safer because Ben Solomon's behind a locked door."

"He may not have hurt anyone—yet—but he sure fits the description of an obsessed stalker. Anyway, what can I do? You heard him; he doesn't want our help. He's going to plead guilty."

SEVEN

...

"Cat, it's liam. did you see the paper this morning?"

"No. What should I have seen?" The telephone handset was clamped between her cheek and her hunched shoulder while she thumbed through sheaves of papers on her desk.

"Ben Solomon. They released him today. They dropped the charges."

"Why would the state do that? It's a slam-dunk conviction."

"Rosenzweig. He asked the state to dismiss the case. He said Solomon had suffered enough in his lifetime, that he'd been interned in the concentration camps and should never be interned again. He said he didn't want to testify against Solomon. He's a man of considerable influence, you know."

"I don't believe it. Is Rosenzweig a saint? Solomon assaulted him in front of a thousand people."

"Nevertheless, he's a free man. Rosenzweig said it was a case of mistaken identity and he felt safe from any future confrontations."

"Liam, I don't think Solomon believes he made a mistake."

There was a pause on the phone. "Cat, I got a favor to ask."

"Uh-oh. I don't like the sound of that."

"Can you meet with Adele and me this afternoon?"

"Come on, Liam, you saw my office. I'm under enormous pressure here. I don't want to get involved in this. Why is she focusing on me?"

"Because she thinks you're the best lawyer in Chicago."

"You probably told her that."

"Many times."

"Solomon's been released, so why does she want to meet with me?"

"I'd rather let her tell you."

"Damn it, Liam, I'm under water and I don't have time for pro bono work. They watch my hours like a hawk. If I don't bill two hundred hours this month, Jenkins'll be sitting on my couch lecturing me about law firm finances."

Silence.

"I'll take you to dinner, Cat. Anywhere you'd like. You'd be doing me a big favor."

"It's not fair to put it on that level." She sighed and stared blankly at the telephone. "All right, bring them in at three o'clock. Forget the dinner."

"Cat?"

"Yes."

"I think Adele is bringing Ben Solomon."

"Then I changed my mind. I want dinner at Ambria."

"Done. Dinner at Ambria. We'll see you at three o'clock."

JENKINS & FAIRCHILD OCCUPIED the top three floors of the Marquette Building, sixteen stories of brick and terra-cotta sitting kitty-corner from the U.S. Courthouse. Built in 1895, the landmark building still had the original bronze panels above the entrance depicting the life of Jacques Marquette, the French Jesuit missionary who explored the area in 1674. Colorful mosaic panels of Marquette's encounters with the Calumet, built by the Tiffany firm, adorned the circular lobby.

Liam, Adele, and Ben Solomon stepped out of the elevators into Jenkins & Fairchild's reception area. In his poplin golf jacket, khaki pants, and knit shirt, Solomon was nondescript, like any retiree waiting for an open seat at the North Avenue Beach chess tables.

Catherine's secretary ushered the group to a conference room where they settled into soft leather seats around an oblong table.

"It's nice to see you again, Mr. Solomon," Catherine said. "I understand the charges against you have been dropped."

He nodded and folded his hands before him on the polished slate table.

Silence.

"How can we help you?" She smiled.

Solomon fumbled for a starting point. He shifted his weight and tapped the tips of his fingers together.

After an awkward moment, Adele broke in. "May I?" she asked Solomon.

He shrugged and gestured for her to begin.

"I've known Ben for many years. He's a respected member of our congregation, very learned, very well read. I've never known him to be irrational. He has idiosyncrasies, but," she tilted her head, "who doesn't?"

Solomon interrupted. "I want to sue Rosenzweig."

Catherine studied the gaunt man with the wispy white hair. "According to the newspapers your case was nolle prosequied. It was dismissed by the state without prejudice," she said. "If you sue Mr. Rosenzweig, for whatever theory you think you have, it's possible the state will reinstate the charges and prosecute you for aggravated assault and attempted murder."

"Rosenzweig'll never testify. He'll never take the stand. That's why he let me go."

"If you sue him, he may not remain so gracious. He'll testify to defend himself."

"Gracious? Ha. He'll never expose himself to testimony. Believe you me, he'll never show up in a court."

"Mr. Solomon," said Catherine slowly, "a thousand people saw you put a gun to his face. Any one of them could testify against you."

"It wasn't loaded."

"It doesn't matter; you could still go to jail. And, if you don't mind my asking, what was the point of threatening Mr. Rosenzweig with an unloaded gun?"

Her tone of voice unnerved Solomon. "Well, maybe I *do* mind."

Catherine stood and extended her hand to bid him goodbye. "I'm sorry, Mr. Solomon, but I don't think I can help you."

Solomon lowered his head. Tears welled in his reddened eyes. He mumbled softly, words ostensibly meant for no one but himself.

"Please, Ms. Lockhart," Adele said. "I know his story. Sit down, please." She tapped the table lightly. "If you would listen for just a little while. Please."

Catherine sighed and returned to her seat. "Mrs. Silver, I'm willing to listen, but I don't think that Mr. Solomon is ready to talk. To be perfectly frank with you, I'm not aware of any legal basis to bring a civil lawsuit against Elliot Rosenzweig. Even if Mr. Solomon believes him to be a Nazi, even if he *was* a Nazi, and Mr. Solomon was imprisoned and tortured, I don't think there's an existing private cause of action that's still available in 2004. I think it's called a suit for reparations, but to tell you the truth, I've never done any research on claims by Holocaust survivors. In any event, because of the passage of time, fifty-odd years, wouldn't the claims be time-barred?"

"Not the claims I want to file," Solomon said. "If I sued Germany or any of the corporations that willingly did business with the Nazis, you're right, the claims'd be dismissed. And they'd be dismissed if I sued for imprisonment or torture. Treaties and settlements have put those cases to rest. The doors are all closed. As you may surmise, I've done a bit of research."

"Then, I'm confused. If the doors are all closed for private lawsuits, how do you plan to sue Rosenzweig?" Catherine said.

"I got it all figured out," Solomon said. "And Rosenzweig will have to answer for his sins."

Catherine pursed her lips and shook her head. "I can't be a party to a groundless lawsuit imposed solely for the purpose of harassment or torment. After all these years. And why Elliot Rosenzweig, of all people?"

"Catherine," Adele said, gently placing her hand on Catherine's arm, "let me tell you about Ben and why we're here." She placed her purse on the table and folded her hands in her lap. "Ben came to America in 1949. After the war. When he . . ."

"No, Adele," interrupted Ben again. "If a lawyer is going to hear *my* story, it should come from me." He paused and stared into the ether of the conference room.

The group waited patiently while Ben Solomon gathered his thoughts.

"Like I said, Elliot Rosenzweig is a fraud," Ben said. "His real name is Otto Piatek, and many years ago he was my best friend in the world. We grew up together in Poland. A triumvirate we were; Otto, me, and Hannah. Inseparable. I never knew he survived the war until I saw him on TV a couple of months ago. For some odd reason, probably Hannah's idea, I tuned into a public television special on patrons of the arts and there he was, sitting in his fancy office, calling himself Elliot Rosenzweig."

"Could you be mistaken, Ben?" Catherine said. "It's been fifty-nine years since World War II ended. Maybe he resembles Otto Piatek, or what you suppose Piatek would look like at age eighty-two."

"Mistaken? No. I recognize his features. I know his voice. The camera zoomed in on his face and I jumped to my feet. I ran to the TV and watched the balance of the show inches away from the screen. Oh, it's him all right. It doesn't matter how many years have passed. It's Piatek."

Adele lifted her eyebrows and nodded, as if to say, "You see. I told you so."

"There are look-alikes," Catherine said. "Some people think I look like Beth Stone, the newscaster. I've been stopped on the street for an autograph."

"I can see that," said Adele. "Except you're much prettier than Beth Stone. More classic looking." She punctuated her opinion with a quick nod of her head.

"I don't know about any Beth Stone, but that was Piatek on the TV," Ben said flatly. "So I went to the library. I looked up some newspaper articles about Elliot Rosenzweig. It's him. There's no doubt in my mind. I read how he immigrated to Chicago after the war. A penniless camp survivor. So how does he find the money to set up some million-dollar insurance company?"

"Doesn't he say he met people and invested wisely?"

"You're right, he met people. He met them in Poland and took everything they had."

He spread his hands. "Anyway, so now this Nazi bastard is a multimillionaire, with a grandiose estate in Winnetka, and he's prancing around in the costume of respectability."

"All these years in Chicago, why didn't you make the connection?" asked Liam.

"Well, of course I'd heard of him. Everyone knows about Billionaire Rosenzweig, but I never had any reason to give him a second thought. I certainly never met him. We don't exactly run in the same circles. I worked for the Park District, a starter at a municipal golf course; he's the country club sort. Our paths never crossed.

"Anyway, after I recognized him on the TV show, I read in the newspaper that he would be at the Lyric Opera on opening night. He's on the board of directors, you know, and one of the largest contributors, maybe *the* largest. So I made a plan. I bought a German Luger, standard issue to the Waffen SS, a weapon he knows very well, and I went to the opera to publicly confront him. Deep down, Otto's a coward. I thought if he feared for his life, he'd confess to everyone and admit that he's Otto Piatek. Of all the people in the world, Otto would fear me the most. He would be shocked to see me standing before him with a gun in my hand. I expected him to blubber a confession, and I think he would have if that Neanderthal hadn't knocked me down."

"Why don't you go to the U.S. Attorney's office?" Catherine said. "The Justice Department has the responsibility to investigate claims of Nazi war criminals. There's no statute of limitations. If he's really a Nazi, he'll be deported for trial."

"Otto's too clever. And wealthy. He's purchased a throne in Chicago society. What chance is there that the federal authorities would believe a lowly pensioner against the word of Elliot Rosenzweig? They'd never consider the case."

"But you have a plan to sue him in civil court?"

"Correct. I couldn't get him to confess at the opera, but I figured out a way to get him into court. Not for reparations or personal injuries, because those cases are barred, but I have the right to sue him for stealing my family's property. My parents gave him all our valuables to hide for us during the Nazi occupation. Otto agreed to bury them under the floor of my grandfather's barn until the war was over or until we were settled in America or wherever we ended up. All our money, our jewelry, my mother's silver."

He pointed his finger. "So, we make a demand for him to return the property and when he refuses, we sue him for replevin or conversion. I want the court to order him to return our property or pay me the value of what he stole, which of course he will never do. We're within our time limits. The statute of limitations does not commence to run until demand and refusal."

Catherine paused and raised her eyebrows. "Replevin or conversion?"

Solomon quickly added, "Right. The return of property wrongfully taken from me. There's legal precedent, you know. Plenty of it. Mostly concerning stolen artworks. Courts recognize the right to sue for return of specific property stolen by the Nazis. There's a case against an Austrian art museum. There's one against Sotheby's. There's a terrific case against a New York gallery to recover a Chagall. As long as the lawsuits are brought against individuals and not foreign sovereigns, they'll survive."

Catherine rocked back in her chair and folded her arms across her chest. "I guess you *have* been doing some research."

"Right."

"Impressive. But even if you could prove what you say, the cost of the litigation would more than exceed the value of anything you could recover."

The old man shrugged.

"I sense here, Ben, that you don't care one way or another whether you make money on this lawsuit, do you?"

"Not really. I want to bring him to justice and expose him for what he is—a cold-blooded Nazi killer. I want to get him on the witness stand and confront him with all of his murderous deeds."

Catherine lowered her eyes and slowly shook her head. "Well, I can understand your passion for justice, Mr. Solomon. I just don't think that Jenkins & Fairchild is the right place for you. We really don't handle such cases. We're a business firm. Our clients are financial institutions, hospitals, insurance companies."

"But you're a lawyer, right? Adele said you're the best lawyer in town. You go to court, don't you?"

"I do, but not on cases like this."

The wizened old man swiveled his chair and stared through the window across the street at the Dirksen and Kluczynski federal buildings—the two glass-and-steel Mies van der Rohe structures that anchored the concrete expanse of Federal Plaza. "Dead end, Hannah," he said to the window. "I guess I had no right to get our hopes up."

With noticeable effort, he lifted his body out of the black leather chair. "Thank you for your time, Miss Lockhart." And he left the room.

EIGHT

...

SOMETIMES IT PAYS TO play *Let's Make a Deal*," said Catherine, examining the menu in Ambria's gracious dining room. Full-length draperies, tied back with gold cords, framed a view of Lincoln Park on a warm October night. Fresh flowers and small shaded lamps adorned each table.

"That's not nice. I feel bad for the old guy," Liam said.

"Oh, don't get me wrong, I do too."

"What if he's right, Cat? What if Rosenzweig is really Otto Piatek?"

"Just because I feel bad for him doesn't mean I believe him. It's far more likely that Mr. Solomon is delusional. Did you notice that he was holding conversations with imaginary people?"

"I noticed."

"Nobody believes this wild story, Liam. The papers, the TV, they all treated it as the ravings of a madman. None of them followed it up."

The sommelier interrupted with the wine selection. Liam swirled the wine, took a sip, and gestured for him to fill the glasses.

"Cat, I don't think Solomon's insane. Since our meeting, I've done some poking around."

"I should have figured."

"Adele introduced me to several people who know Ben. He's very active in his synagogue life. He's the congregation librarian.

They say he spends hours reading and studying the Bible. He even teaches an adult class on Tuesday nights. On the Zohar."

"The Zohar?"

"I'm not very knowledgeable here, but I've been told that the Zohar is one of the central books of the Kabbalah, a spiritual, mystical commentary on the Old Testament. Divine energy. It talks of secrets and codes." Liam waggled his fingers.

Catherine shot him a hard look. "I'm not taking his case."

"Did I ask you to?"

"Well, I'm not."

"It may interest you to know that everyone I talked to, without exception, admires and respects Ben."

"I'm not taking his case."

"I know. You said that."

The conversation was interrupted by the service of a smoked salmon terrine. The two ate quietly for a time, with just the sounds of fork tines on the china.

Finally Catherine broke the silence. "So, who are you dating these days? Are you still with Donna Talcott?"

"I wouldn't say I was *with* her. We see each other off and on. She's fun to be around, but . . . I don't think it's ever going anywhere."

Catherine broke her sourdough roll in half and put a small pat of butter on the bread plate. She took a sip of wine. "Do you have any idea what it would be like to litigate against someone like Rosenzweig, to accuse him of being a Nazi?"

"Why do you care? You're not taking the case."

"Right." She took a small bite of her roll. "Why are you so invested in this, Liam?"

Liam laid his fork down and turned toward Catherine.

"Adele is good people. Just an ordinary lady who cares about her neighbors, who brings soup over to Mrs. Delevan's when she's sick, who pays the eight-year-old kid next door a quarter to bring her the Sunday newspaper from her parkway, who has a nice greeting for every passerby when she's out sweeping the leaves from her sidewalk. People like this, like Adele and Ben Solomon, they have no access to lawyers and courtrooms. They don't know any big-time litigators like you." He picked up his fork. "But they're good people."

"The fees and expenses would run in the hundreds of thousands of dollars. Rosenzweig would hire a team of lawyers. I couldn't staff the case, even if the firm would let me take it on. It'd never get past the management committee."

"It's not your choice to decide whether or not to take a case?"

"Are you kidding? I'm just an associate, not even a junior partner. I've only been with the firm for two years. Remember? I came out of early retirement."

Liam nodded. "Of course I remember. I'm sorry."

"If I wanted to bring a case in, I would first have to submit it to the practice group chairman for approval. The chairman decides what cases to accept and what to assign to me. That's how it works. They're all commercial cases. All on behalf of mega-institutions. This bank versus that. A zoning petition to allow a heavy manufacturing plant to locate where it should never be. A battle between insurance goliaths to see who stands the loss for last year's tornado in Lewisburg. Companies that don't blink at billing rates that exceed nine hundred dollars an hour. Cases like Ben's, against prominent defendants, would have to be approved by the management committee."

She shook her head. "People like Adele Silver and Ben Solomon—the firm doesn't want them. I don't like it, but that's big-firm economics."

"So why do you stay at Jenkins?"

"After I came back from my absence, Jenkins was happy to have me. You ought to know." She took a sip of wine. "And the money's good."

"He was happy to have you because he got a damn good lawyer for an associate's salary."

"He bought damaged goods, Liam."

He shook his head and took a bite of scallops. "Anyway, did you ever stop to consider how this so-called survivor of the concentration camps comes to America after the war, penniless, but within a very short time he's one of the richest dudes in town?"

She nodded her head. "You have a point."

"What if Ben could prove Rosenzweig stole his property? What if Ben had some proof?"

"Other than his recognition of Rosenzweig on the television? What kind of proof could he have, Liam? After all these years."

Liam shrugged. "I don't know."

"Even if there were proof and a pot of money at the end of the rainbow, it's not the kind of case my firm would ever let me take on. It's political suicide. Rosenzweig's an icon. For Solomon to build a case, one that can withstand the blizzard of motions Rosenzweig will bring, he'd need a crusader, with strong financial backing and eager young minds—like a law school clinic." She took another sip of wine. "Kids have no fear. I have a career."

"What kind of proof would he need?"

Catherine counted the elements on her fingers. "First, he'd have to prove that Otto Piatek actually existed and was a Nazi. Second, he'd have to come forward with some kind of evidence identifying the specific stolen property. Third, he'd have to show that Piatek appropriated and converted that property in derogation of the rights of the Solomons. And finally, he'd have to make the connection—prove that Elliot Rosenzweig is in fact Otto Piatek."

"Can I bring Ben to see you again?"

"Liam, please. I told you we can't take it in."

"Not to take it in, just to evaluate it and see if you can find him someone to represent him. Will you listen to his story? See if there's a case?"

"You're putting me in a tough spot, Liam. I have a job and partners to answer to. I submit my time records at the end of each day. How do I account for hours spent with Ben Solomon?"

He nodded his head in resignation. "I understand. Never mind."

Three servers wheeled a linen-draped cart to the table and set silver-domed dishes before Catherine and Liam. On cue, the covers were raised, revealing an almond-crusted rack of lamb on one side and a plate of wild striped bass on the other. "Bon appétit," they chorused.

After a few bites, Catherine said, "Mmm. Divine." She looked at Liam expecting to see a similar reaction, but noticed that he hadn't even tasted his dinner.

"You really care about this Solomon, don't you?" she said.

"I do. I don't know why—'cause he's a little guy—'cause maybe I think he's telling the truth, and no one will listen to him. Cat, nobody would invent such an accusation. It's just a feeling I have, that maybe . . . ah, never mind."

"Why do I let you do this to me?" Catherine said, setting down her fork. "Stop looking like a scolded puppy. I'll talk to him, okay? You can bring him by next Wednesday afternoon. I'll find some time and I'll evaluate his case for you. If there's anything there, I'll call Richard Tryon at the U.S. Attorney's office or I'll try to find a clinic to help him. But, bottom line, I want him to tell me what kind of proof he has. Proof, Liam. Solid proof. The kind you could bring into court."

Liam beamed. "Thanks, Cat."

II

...

BEN SOLOMON'S STORY

NINE

· · ·

IN THE EARLY 1930S, I was a child growing up in southern
Poland, in a town called Zamość. I had a warm and loving
family. My father's name was Abraham. My mother's name
was Leah. God rest their souls. We lived in a three-story home in
the Jewish quarter of the city."

Ben sat at one end of the conference table with his hands wrapped
around a mug of steaming tea. At the other end sat Catherine, tilted
back in her chair taking notes on a yellow pad that rested on her
crossed legs. Liam and Adele sat quietly to the side.

"Zamość was the jewel of prewar Poland, a gingerbread city
built by an Italian architect in the sixteenth century and modeled
after the Italian city of Padua. So colorful, so magical it was, you
would swear you woke up in Renaissance Italy," Ben said.

Catherine looked up from her notes and smiled. "Sounds lovely.
Now I'd like you to tell me about your property, Ben, what you
think Mr. Rosenzweig took and how you can prove it's yours."

Solomon resumed his narrative. "Although he was an educated
man with a business degree from the university, my father was ap-
prenticed as an engraver in the family's glass factory, founded by
my great-grandfather in 1861. The plant produced fine lead crystal—
wine glasses, goblets, stemware, vases, and bowls, much like the
Waterford crystal you see in the local department stores. By the

time I was born, my father was running the factory, and his products, handcrafted by Polish artisans, were being shipped all over Europe.

"Abraham Solomon was a rock, a man of inner strength. Sometimes he'd take me to the plant and walk me around with great pride, his only son. He'd say, 'Did you ever see a handsomer boy?'

"My father was also a man of great respect in Zamość. Townspeople would come to him, to consult and seek his advice. Many an evening, he would sit in our front parlor and take tea with visitors and I would sit on his lap or fall asleep with my head on his chest."

Catherine laid her pen down on the table and rested her chin on her folded hands.

"My mother was a beautiful woman, Miss Lockhart. Gentle. Elegant, in the ways of the Old World. Well mannered. Modest. Yet she was strong in her constitution and clear in her purpose. Her home and her children were her whole life. Do you follow me, Miss Lockhart?"

"Yes, I do, Ben," she answered, but her pen and yellow pad remained untouched on the table.

"There were linen doilies on polished tables, Miss Lockhart. Each piece of furniture in our home was special. It had significance. Not like today, when women buy groups of mass-produced generic furniture from warehouse sales on credit terms. Each of my mother's pieces was a treasure to her. Some were heirlooms, passed to her from her parents and their parents, to be passed on to her children and their children. Do you understand what I'm saying? Her home was a reflection of who she was."

"Mr. Solomon, there's no need to be confrontational. We're not enemies. I'm patiently waiting to learn about your legal claims against Mr. Rosenzweig. I'm certain that your mother and your father were extraordinary people, but I'd really like us to focus on the issue of the stolen property. After all, that is the foundation of your case."

"I'm not an attorney, Miss Lockhart, but as I understand a lawyer's function, it's to represent clients, to stand up for them, to give expression to their interests and to further their claims. Is that not so?"

"Well put, Mr. Solomon. That is a lawyer's function. But attorneys also have responsibilities to their practice and to the bar, to investigate the bases for a claim before charging another with a liability."

"Then perhaps we're on the same page. I'm trying to give you a sufficient background to understand not only the claim but the client. If an attorney is going to speak for me, then she needs to know who I am. If you're going to advocate my claim, then you need to know the circumstances. Please don't shortcut me."

Catherine smiled. "Go right ahead."

"I had a sister, Beka, the apple of Mama's eye. Her real name was Rebecca. She was blessed with the same lovely features as my mother: rich black curly hair, green eyes, and a soft, classic profile. She was a real beauty and smart as a whip.

"Before the war, Zamość was a multicultural city—Greeks, Armenians, Scots, Hungarians, Russians, Italians. And so there were Greek neighborhoods, Russian neighborhoods, Jewish neighborhoods. But we all got along. The mystery of other cultures was something we were taught to respect. In those days, Zamość was about forty percent Jewish.

"Zamość was also blessed geographically. The surrounding countryside was like an impressionist's canvas, with thick forests, clear rivers, and rolling hills. Farmlands lay to the north and east. And in the middle, our little pastel village. All in all, Zamość was an idyllic place to live. That was before the Germans decided we were a subspecies to be exterminated like a colony of ants.

"A few hundred miles to the south, in the Carpathian Mountains, my Uncle Joseph had a cabin nestled in a valley surrounded by the peaks of the High Tatras where the whole family would gather once or twice a year—uncles, aunts, cousins."

Ben paused. "There were fields of yellow flowers, tall pines, juniper berries hanging on the bushes. When I close my eyes, I see Beka and me running to poke our toes into the icy cold waters of the mountain stream." Ben smiled at the vision. "What an infectious laugh she had. What joyous days those were, especially for us children."

When he opened his eyes they were tearing. His facial muscles twitched. He took a sip of tea.

"I apologize and I don't mean to rush you, Mr. Solomon," Catherine said, "but I have a meeting in a little while. When you were here last week, you said there was a triumvirate. Otto, you, and . . ."

"Hannah."

"Ben's wife," said Adele softly.

"We were all close friends from high school." Ben wiped his eyes with the back of his hand and turned his head from the group. His lips were tightly clamped. "Please understand, I've never . . ." He stopped and started again. "There are very few people who know the whole story. It's not an easy thing for me."

An uncomfortable silence pervaded the room. "Forgive me," he said and he walked quickly to the windows.

"Why don't we take a few minutes?" Catherine said. "Let's stretch our legs and get some fresh coffee in here."

During the break she pulled Adele and Liam aside.

"Is all this worth it? For the price of some jewelry and watches? For the sake of an accusation?"

Adele answered in a whisper. "Miss Lockhart, surely you must realize it's not about the jewelry or the property. It's about his family and Otto Piatek. It's about a betrayal."

"And Ben is convinced that Rosenzweig is Piatek."

"He is certain."

"I'd like to get to the details of that betrayal. Will he tell me?"

She shrugged. "He will try."

They reassembled a few minutes later and Catherine resumed her questions.

"Ben, you were saying that the three of you were close friends from high school. Is that when you met Otto Piatek?"

"No, I met him earlier, when I was about twelve."

"Did you meet him at school?"

"No. He was left on our doorstep, in a manner of speaking. My family took him in. In the late 1920s the Depression hit Poland pretty hard—like the United States, only worse. Many families lost everything. I was very young, but I remember my father forming a council of businessmen. Through the council, efforts were made to help keep families afloat. As the Depression worsened, visits to our study became more frequent and visitors more desperate. I think my father would have given them all jobs at the plant if he could, but truth be told, his sales were down, too. Nevertheless, my mother made extra food and no one ever went away from our home hungry.

"One bitter cold evening in 1933, there was a knock on our door. We were in the middle of dinner and my father got up to answer the door. Otto, skinny as a rail in a threadbare coat, stood silently by his father, Stanislaw Piatek. They hesitated at the doorway, Stanislaw's head bowed, his soiled cap in his left hand, his right arm around his son. I remember how dirty and foul-smelling they were. Stanislaw held a piece of stationery from the Holy Cross Church in his hand, an introduction, which he gave to my father.

"'Father Xavier sent me to you. He said you help people.'

"'Come in,' my father said.

"Stanislaw did not move. 'I am not a Jew,' he announced.

"'And I am not a Christian,' said my father. 'And now that we know what we're not, why don't you come in and have a cup of tea.'

"So they sat in the parlor and talked. Stanislaw cried. He had no way to care for his son. He had lost his job as a woodcutter in the forests outside Zamość and he'd been evicted from the workers' compound at the lumber company. He had no place to live and no money. Otto's mother had abandoned them and run back to her family in Leipzig, Germany. 'My son is freezing,' Stanislaw said. 'I cannot keep him warm.'

"There were newspapers stuffed in the soles of Otto's shoes to keep out the snow. Stanislaw cursed his German wife who had run off. Even if he could find a job, what was he supposed to do with Otto? He'd been told that my father had helped some people get back on their feet.

"It took my mother but a second to see that Otto needed dinner and a bath. She took him by the hand and walked him straight into the bathroom where she filled the tub with hot water. Afterward she asked me to sit with him at the kitchen table where she fed him roast and potatoes.

"Otto and I were about the same size, so we gave him clean clothes. I remember that night like it was yesterday. He sat at the table, staring straight ahead, eating two helpings of everything. And never said a word.

"My mother returned to the kitchen with the news that Otto would be staying with us for a while. My father had found a room for Stanislaw on the south side of town, and while he tried to find work and get himself settled, Otto was to live with us and share my bedroom. I was less than thrilled, but my mother had laid down the law."

"How long did Otto live with you?" Catherine said.

"For the better part of six years. After leaving him with us, Stanislaw dropped out of sight. We came to learn that he was a drinker. Although my father found him a job, a couple of jobs, he couldn't hold them."

"Did he visit Otto?"

"Rarely, and only in the beginning. When he did, it was mostly to ask my father for money or to help him get another job."

"And Otto's mother?"

"For all we knew, she was in Germany. So in their absence, my parents cared for Otto. When he arrived at our home, his soul was empty. His spirit, like an old car battery, was dead and wouldn't hold a charge. But my parents, with infinite patience, filled him with warmth and love. They nourished his soul. Little by little, they taught him to trust and brought him into the fold.

"At our home, Otto received equal portions and was given equal responsibilities. Beka and I had chores, so Otto was given chores, too. My mother knew that taking on responsibilities would give him pride and self-worth.

"She did everything to treat him fairly. When I got new clothes, so did Otto. When we took our winter vacation at Uncle Joseph's and I got new boots, Otto did too. I think my parents became resigned to the fact that Otto would grow to manhood in our home.

"Beka and I attended school at the Jewish academy, but Stanislaw, in one of his few early visits, said he thought it best that Otto go to the public school. I don't know whether Stanislaw ever went to church, but Otto was baptized a Catholic. My parents respected his wishes and sent Otto to public school."

"And you shared your room with Otto?"

"I did, and eventually Otto and I became fast friends. We were the same age, we had similar interests and enjoyed the same activities, although Otto was much stronger than I—he was the athletic type, I was more of a bookworm. My Grandpa Yaakov had horses on his farm and we would ride on Sundays. We would pretend to be American cowboys. Tom Mix, Gene Autry," he said with a slight grin.

"Six years and his parents never came to get him?"

"Not exactly," Ben said. He leaned back and stared at the ceiling as though it were a window to visions of the past. "The spring of 1935," he said quietly. "Otto has been with our family for two years. We're fourteen now. Without warning and out of the blue, Stanislaw shows up at our front door. Standing right next to him is Ilse, Otto's mother, and the two of them are dressed to kill. In the midst of the Depression, she has a mink stole around her neck. Father invites them in, but they don't cross the threshold.

"'We come for Otto,' Stanislaw says. Just like that. Matter of fact.

"Meanwhile, Otto and I are in the bedroom, doing homework. Father calls us out. Otto sees his mother standing there and says to her, as cold as ice, 'What do *you* want?'

"'We're here to take you home,' she says softly, and then she starts to sob. 'We have a beautiful new home for you in Berlin. So get your things. And say thanks to the Solomons.'

"'*This* is my home,' says Otto, and he spins around and walks back to the bedroom.

"'What have you done to our son?' shrieks Ilse. 'You've turned him against us.'

"'I've done nothing, except to provide for him in your absence,' Father says. 'Who knew when or if you would ever return? I haven't heard from either of you in over a year.'

"'We've been extremely busy. We have very important jobs in Germany,' Stanislaw says with his nose in the air, trying to look official, pulling on his coat lapels. 'We have positions in the National Socialist Workers Party and we're quite capable now of caring for our own son. We don't need you anymore. And we don't want him raised here in the home of Jews. Too dangerous.'"

Catherine interrupted. "What were their important jobs?"

Ben leaned forward, resting his elbows on the table. "Ilse was a secretary in the Reich Ministry. Somehow she got assigned to Reinhard Heydrich. Maybe because she was a looker. Of course at the time, we didn't know much about her position or her boss. Heydrich happened to be the first deputy to Reichsführer Heinrich Himmler. Himmler was the second most powerful man in Germany, Hitler's right hand. Reinhard Heydrich was a ruthless man who held many offices and became head of the Gestapo and Ministry of the Interior. When they decided to kill all the Jews in Poland, they called it *Aktion Reinhard*, Operation Reinhard.

"Anyway, as Heydrich's secretary in 1935, long before the war, snippets of secret information would come across her desk daily. Piecing them together, she had a pretty good idea of what was going on. She knew about the plans for the Final Solution—she took notes in the meetings and typed the memos. She knew that Heydrich was drawing up death lists with Hermann Göring and she knew that a concentration camp had been set up by Himmler at Dachau in an old powder factory. She knew that plans for mass exterminations were taking form. She knew stuff that nobody knew—that the rest of us wouldn't learn until much later.

"Stanislaw was nothing but a low-level policeman. He had somehow become involved with the Brownshirts, and was roaming the streets of Berlin with the rest of the uniformed thugs, rounding up intellectuals to send to Dachau.

"In the 1930s, anti-Semitism was running rampant in Germany, and that's one of the reasons they came for Otto. They didn't want him to be mistaken for a Jew."

"Why did they say it was dangerous in Poland?" asked Catherine. "Were there Nazis in Zamość in 1935?"

"German Nazis? No. But there were Nazi wannabes in some Polish towns. The devastating effects of the Depression motivated people to search for blame, for the cause of their misfortune. Germans offered up the Jews as the sacrificial lamb. Here's the reason for the worldwide Depression, they said. Here's the cause of all your misery: it's the Jews! Hatred of the Jews had become a national policy in Germany and it was seeping slowly into Poland. What had once been a delicate fabric, community cooperation and tolerance among the diverse ethnic groups, began to unravel. Like a virus, colonies incubated in Poland, mostly among the disenfranchised youth. They called themselves Radical Nationals or National Democrats, patterned after the Nazis, but they were nothing more than bands of young thugs."

"For many years Poland had a history of tolerance towards Jews, the most hospitable country in all of Europe," Adele added. "Lublin was the seat of Jewish learning. There was a yeshiva, a school for Talmudic study, located there and scholars were turning out pages of biblical commentary. And Lublin was just north of Zamość by a few hours." She sat back and smiled. "Ben told me."

Ben paused to take a sip of tea and nodded. "The Jewish community was allied with leaders of the Polish government. Józef Piłsudski was the premier and leader of Poland following World War I, and until his death, Marshal Piłsudski protected the Jews.

"Piłsudski was a conservative and, like most Poles, distrusted Russia above all. We all feared the Bolsheviks. Piłsudski felt that he couldn't count on England or France to come to our aid if Russia attacked, so he signed a ten-year nonaggression treaty with Germany in 1934. Hitler was promising to protect Poland's borders."

"If the Jewish community was supported by Piłsudski, why didn't he contain the anti-Semitism?" Catherine asked.

"Ah. Piłsudski died of cancer in 1935," Ben said. "In the four years between his death and World War II, anti-Semitism grew much worse. For example, in the 1920s, one out of every four university students was Jewish, but by 1938, before the war, it was down to eight percent.

"Getting back to my story, Otto's mother stood in the foyer and begged Otto to go with her to Germany, but Otto turned his back on her and walked into the bedroom. She stood there sobbing.

"My mother, God bless her heart, took pity on Ilse. 'Come in, please,' she said and led her to the couch. Stanislaw followed her in.

"Minutes later, my father fetched Otto from our bedroom. He stood stiffly before his mother, his arms folded across his chest. Ilse looked at him, at his icy cold stare, and broke down.

"'Otto,' she cried. 'You can't understand what it's been like for me. I was beside myself. I never wanted to leave you and I curse all the forces that tore us apart. But not a single day has gone by that I haven't seen you and talked to you.'

"Otto was clearly puzzled by her statement and narrowed his eyes. 'What are you talking about? I haven't heard from you in over a year.'

"She fingered a gold locket she wore around her neck, clicked it open, and held it up. 'Look, Otto, I talked to you every day.'

"Inside the locket was a little black-and-white photo of Otto taken when he was very young. Ilse reached out for Otto, pulled him close, and combed his long blond hair with her fingers. 'My Otto,' she wept, 'you could come with us. I can take care of you now. We could make up for lost time.'

"Otto shook his head.

"'I have influence, Otto. I could get you a leadership position in the Hitler Youth. You could be very important.'

"'Could you get Ben a leadership position, too?'

"'No, *liebchen*, I'm afraid I can't. Ben is a Jew. There are no Jews in the Hitler Youth.'

"'That's what I thought. I'm sorry, but I live here now.'

"'You don't understand, Otto,' she said. 'You should see what's happening to the Jews in Germany. Soon, I think, the Jews will be driven from all of Europe. Please come with me.'

"'You left me in the care of Jews two years ago. It didn't seem to bother you then.'

"'Things are different now, Otto. Even here in Poland.'

"'Not for me,' he said. 'I'm staying here with Aunt Leah and Uncle Abraham'—that's what Otto called my parents. He turned his back and walked into the bedroom. Stanislaw led Ilse from the house. We didn't see either of them again until much later."

Catherine looked up from her pad. "Was she right? Were things different for Jews in Poland in 1935?"

Ben nodded. "It was getting dangerous to walk alone, especially after dark. It was just a year later that the Radical Nationals called for a Day Without Jews. It was planned for the date on which the Jewish academy students took their exams throughout Poland. Gangs gathered around the schools and in the Jewish neighborhoods.

"That very afternoon, Beka came running into the house screaming. Young punks carrying canes topped with razor blades had chased her from the school. Otto went berserk and ran outside with a broom handle, swinging it like a baseball bat, ready to take on the whole gang. I followed after him. Most of the gang took off, but a couple of them stayed behind and stood their ground. In the fight, Otto got sliced on his forearm. Deep cut too, almost to the bone.

"Instantly he became Beka's hero. The doctor stitched him up and Beka waited on him hand and foot for a week. My father reported the incident to the police, but nothing came of it. From then on, Otto walked Beka to and from school every day. Always with a broom handle and a knife."

Catherine looked up from her pad. "And yet, you say this is the same Otto who ultimately became a Nazi and betrayed your family?"

It took a long time for Ben to respond. "Things changed, Miss Lockhart. And so did some people."

"I'm afraid we have to wind this up," Catherine said. "I have a meeting in fifteen minutes."

"When can I come back?" asked Ben.

She glanced at Liam, who sheepishly grinned and shrugged.

"Well, it does seem as though we'll need another session," she said. "Maybe Tuesday. I have hearings the rest of this week. Call me tomorrow. I'll check my schedule." She smiled and ushered them all to the elevator.

* * *

FOUR BLOCKS WEST OF Jenkins & Fairchild's office, on the eighty-third floor of the Sears Tower, in the corner office of the Columbia Indemnity Corporation, Elliot Rosenzweig sat behind his desk, talking to his secretary Brian and a barrel-chested man with a ruddy face and a buzz cut. Carl Wuld, the owner of Regency Investigations, wore brown slacks and a tan-colored, checkered sport coat over a cream-colored polo shirt.

"There's not much on this Piatek guy," Wuld said. "Apparently, there really was a Nazi named Otto Piatek. German records mention him in passing. Nothing on his activities that I can find. He was some kind of officer. I don't think he was any big deal. He wasn't stationed at any of the concentration camps as far as I can tell."

"What happened to him after the war?" Elliot said.

"I don't know. Like I said, there's not much about this guy. Probably died."

"Carl, how long have you and I been doing business?"

"A long time, Mr. Rosenzweig, and I'm very appreciative."

"And I pay you well?"

"Oh, yeah." He smiled sheepishly. "No complaints."

Elliot swiveled back and forth in his oversized leather chair, first to the windows and then back at Wuld. First to the view of the Michigan shoreline forty miles across the lake and then to the flushed face of Carl Wuld across his desk. "This is important to me, Carl. I need to know everything that can be known about this Piatek person. Not just during the war but afterward. If he survived, I need to know where he went. If he's dead, I want to know when and how he died. And I want proof. Is Regency going to be able to do this for me?"

"Oh, yes, sir. You can count on me."

"Please don't come back and tell me that there's *not much* on Otto Piatek."

"No, sir."

"What about Solomon?"

Wuld looked uneasy and hung his head. He spoke in mumbles. "Not much on him either. Sorry."

"Tell me what you know," Elliot said with obvious irritation.

"He came from Poland after the war. Immigrated in 1949. No criminal record in Illinois. No arrests. I can't find anything through the secretary of state's office, you know, no DUIs. I guess he pays his bills on time—there's no judgments against him. No bankruptcies. Rents a place on Bittersweet." Wuld shrugged. "That's it."

"That's it? That's it? The man lives in Chicago and that's all you can tell me?"

"Sorry."

"I need to know more," Elliot said. "Maybe I've made a mistake hiring you, Carl."

"No, sir. You have not. I'll get more. Don't worry."

"Why did this man put a gun in my face, Carl? Are you following me? I want information. I want to know why this man linked me up with some Nazi."

"I'll get right on it, sir. I won't let you down."

TEN

...

Chicago, Illinois, October 2004

THE DEDICATION CEREMONY FOR the new Rosenzweig Pavilion for the Performing Arts took place beneath the ribbons of brushed steel that framed the band shell in Chicago's new Millennium Park. A chilly northeast wind blew in off the lake and across the Great Lawn, shaking loose and scattering the season's last brown and yellow leaves. Only a smattering of sailboats remained in Monroe Harbor, tied to their buoys and bobbing in the whitecaps.

Elliot Rosenzweig was introduced by Mayor Burton, who referred to him as "Chicago's treasure." The ceremonial assembly included the usual government dignitaries along with members of the Fine Arts Council. The crowd, which had come more to listen to the symphony orchestra than to see a dedication, numbered about six hundred.

Elliot, his white hair tousled by the wind, accepted the silver plaque and leaned forward to speak into the microphone. "Mister Mayor, members of the City Council, Maestro Bernard, and all you wonderful people of Chicago, I thank you for the generous words that have been spoken about me today and for the honors given to me. I am deeply humbled." His words came out in echoes. "It has been my privilege to serve the cultural core of the finest city in the world and to play my small part in its ongoing development." The wind sent rumbling noises into the microphone, which were amplified throughout the Millennium Park sound system like rolling thunder.

While Elliot addressed the assembly, two elderly men stood at the back, watching from the promenade. The one on the left handed a pair of binoculars to the one on the right.

"It sure looks like him, but it's been so many years," said the man as he returned the binoculars. "I don't know if I could swear to it in a court of law."

"Back in Poland, before your family was shipped to Majdanek and you were sent to Auschwitz, do you remember Piatek standing in the square? Doesn't that man look like him?"

"Remember him standing in the square? He was directing deportations." Mort paused. "The worst day of my life, Ben. It's a vision that never leaves me. But this man, I don't know. He's standing so far away." He strained his eyes to focus through the binoculars. "There's a resemblance, I won't deny it. Of course, Piatek was young with a head full of blond hair. And that was sixty years ago. I don't know, Ben, maybe it's him. Maybe if I saw him close up."

"Back in Auschwitz, did you ever come across a man named Elliot Rosenzweig? Did you ever know such an inmate?"

"No, Ben, I didn't, but there were so many."

"You were there for two years, Mort. Until the liberation. You even worked on intake. You saw them all."

"No. No one saw them all. We only saw some of the ones they registered. A fraction of the many. Dead skeletons and walking skeletons. Only a small number survived. But, in truth, I never knew an Elliot Rosenzweig."

The crowd applauded enthusiastically as Elliot waved and the Grant Park Symphony Orchestra began its program with selections from Grieg's *Peer Gynt*.

ELEVEN

...

ARLY TUESDAY MORNING, LIAM unlocked the door to his small office on the second floor of a Dearborn Street brownstone, just north of the Loop. Yesterday's mail, delivered through the brass chute in the door, lay scattered on the wooden floor. There was a message from Catherine on his voice mail: "I've scheduled a meeting with Ben Solomon today at one o'clock. Would you please join us?"

He dialed her office.

"Ben's due to arrive in a little while," she said. "I want you to come and sit in with us."

"I'm sorry, Cat, but I'll have to take a pass. I have a meeting with Lawrence McComb on a new job. From what I understand it'll be a big project. Lots of witnesses, statements, pictures."

"Liam, you're the one that roped me into this. Solomon is not an easy interview—he's hard to keep on task and I'm worried about the time he's taking. Besides, he unnerves me a little, fading in and out of conversations like he does, and Adele can't come today. The least you could do is sit with us. Are you sure you can't get away?"

"I'll try to get there late this afternoon, maybe around five or six, if you think he'll still be there."

"The way he's going, he'll still be here next Christmas. Please. Whenever you can. By the way, did you see the news last night? The dedication ceremony?"

"You mean Rosenzweig? Chicago's treasure? I saw it."

"How can I support bringing a lawsuit accusing Chicago's treasure of being a Nazi?"

"Are you harboring thoughts of representing him?"

"Absolutely not. Right now, I'm merely doing a favor for you and Adele. Keep that in mind. It's a favor."

"And I appreciate it. Evaluate his case and then decide if you want to go further."

"Wait a minute. Let's clarify my role here. Evaluation only. There is no *further*. If there's sufficient evidence—*proof*—then I'll send him over to Tryon at Justice. If he insists on a civil case, I'll help him find an available civil lawyer. That's it, Liam, but I have to tell you, so far I haven't seen factual support to justify either. I can't even get him to focus on the relevant issues. He just wants to give me history lessons."

"Cat, please be a little patient. I know you're busy and I realize this isn't Jenkins & Fairchild's usual inventory, but Ben's a sweet old man and he's been through a lot. He just needs someone to listen to him. You never know. He may have something."

"Liam, you don't understand the kind of pressure that large law firms put on associates. They don't give me time to talk to sweet old men. And frankly, I have concerns about him. He holds conversations with ghosts. I think I'll rue the day you talked me into this. Get here as soon as you can."

" 'Rue the day'?"

"Just get here."

"I'll do what I can."

Catherine hesitated and then spoke quietly. "Liam, there's something else."

"What is it?"

"I'm not sure. But there's more to this story than a betrayal of his family and a theft of their jewelry."

"Why? Did he tell you something on the phone? What did he say?"

"He didn't say anything. He didn't have to. I just know it. Lawyer's intuition. There's something deeper involved here. No one would be driven like this if it was solely about money and property."

"Well, Adele said he betrayed Ben's family. They raised him and cared for him and he became a Nazi."

"There's more. You can bet on it."

"Keep on digging, Cat. You'll find out."

Shortly after 1:00 P.M., Catherine was informed that Mr. Solomon had arrived. She found him in the reception area shaking his head, wheezing and complaining about the buses and the traffic.

"I know you think I'm just an old fool kvetching about public services, Miss Lockhart, but two buses drove right past me. They didn't even slow down. Once you reach your eightieth birthday, young lady, you start thinking that whatever time is left to you shouldn't be spent waiting for buses."

Catherine walked him back to the conference room and opened the file she had started.

"Can I help myself to a cup of tea?" he said. Without waiting for a response, he filled his cup and took a seat at the head of the conference table, dunking his tea bag. "So tell me, Miss Lockhart, where do we stand in our case against Elliot Rosenzweig? Have you done anything yet?"

"Done anything?" She smiled. "I need a lot more information before I can make any referrals on your case."

"What do you mean, referrals? I want *you* to be my lawyer."

"We'll make a decision on how to proceed when you finish telling your story. Your case might be better handled by the U.S. Attorney's office or a law school legal clinic."

He wrinkled his face. "No, Miss Lockhart, you're the one. You were meant to handle this case. Besides, some young law grad would get his ears pinned back by Piatek and his power brokers."

"Not necessarily. But I'd like you to begin to tell me how Otto Piatek wrongfully obtained possession of your family's property. Really, the history of Poland is fascinating, but as a lawyer, I need to focus on the liability aspects. Can you jump ahead and tell me what property was taken and when?"

"I'll get there soon enough."

Catherine sighed, took up her pen and yellow pad, and rocked back in her chair. "The last thing you talked about was the increased violence in the streets of Zamość."

"That's right. After Beka was attacked, we were told to come straight home from school."

Zamość, Poland, 1936

"Everything in our world seemed to be influenced by what was going on in Germany, and everyone we knew was trying to keep abreast of the news. My father had a shortwave radio in a large walnut console that stood in the corner of our living room, and we gathered as a family, almost daily, to listen to broadcasts from Germany, England, and America.

"There was no TV back then, you know, so families would congregate around the radio. My father would sit in his armchair to the left of the console and work the dials, tuning in the foreign stations. Mother would usually sit on the couch, with her darning or her knitting. Beka, Otto, and I would lounge about on the carpet. I was a little conversant in German, I'd studied it in school, and so I could understand the German broadcasts pretty well. Because of his business dealings, my father spoke German, and, of course, Otto was fluent.

"We listened in bewilderment to the speeches coming out of Berlin, the rantings of the führer and Goebbels' propaganda. My father would shake his head and tell us that Hitler was blaming the Jews for the cold of the winter and the heat of the summer.

"As the Depression raged on, Polish street violence worsened and members of our community became increasingly alarmed. Finally, since most Poles were Catholic, there was a decision to send a delegation to the archdiocese in Warsaw. My father was asked to participate in the conference.

"'Rabbi Perelman and three other rabbis are going to see Cardinal Kakowski,' he said. 'We're hoping he'll take a stand and issue a pastoral declaration condemning the violence.'

"So on a cold winter morning, we all piled into the car and drove Father to the Lublin station where he met the other delegates and boarded the train for Warsaw. He was gone for five days.

"When he returned, he looked very disheartened. 'The cardinal was a gracious host,' he said. 'He warmly welcomed us and served us tea in his office where we detailed our concerns and presented our petition. He patiently listened to us, nodding his head in sympathetic agreement, assuring us that these gangs were inimical to all God-loving people, not just the Jews. But when we finished, the cardinal said, "If life in Poland is so dangerous, why don't the Jews leave? Why do you stay here in danger?"

"'We were dumbfounded,' my father said. 'This is our home, we told him. There are over three million Jews in Poland. Are we all supposed to leave, to run from the lawless violence? Cardinal Kakowski said he would take the matter up with his superiors and see what he could do. Unfortunately, he also cautioned us that Rome is fearful of antagonizing Hitler. Things aren't going too well for the church in Germany. There have been persecutions of priests and nuns. Church property has been confiscated. Besides, Cardinal Kakowski doubts that the street thugs are church-going Catholics anyway, so he reasons that pastoral declarations will have little effect.'"

Ben opened his hands. "But in the end it didn't matter. Nothing came of the visit. There was no pastoral declaration."

Catherine paused to refill her coffee and left the room to check her messages. When she returned, Ben was standing by the window, speaking aloud. He blushed, like a student caught daydreaming by his teacher. "Oh, don't mind me," he said. "It's just an old man's eccentricity."

She nodded and resumed her place at the head of the table. "So, you got information about Germany from the radio broadcasts?"

"Not just the radio. People who traveled to Germany would return with firsthand information. My father had a cousin, Zbigniew, we called him Ziggy, a big, thick man with a bushy gray beard. He was a salesman who called on customers in Berlin and Munich. From time to time, he would come to dinner and tell us bizarre stories about what was happening in Germany.

"Like one night in October 1935, about two years after Otto came to live with us, Ziggy returned from a trip to Berlin with a frightening report. 'The Nuremberg Laws on Citizenship and Race,' he said, 'that's the latest—another crazy law passed by Hitler. He just revoked the citizenship of all German Jews, no matter who they are—war heroes, city officials, doctors, you name it. No longer are they even citizens of their own damn country. Only people of German or kindred blood can be subjects of the Reich.' Ziggy punctuated his story with his fat finger. 'The law specifically states that a Jew cannot be a citizen of the Reich. It says a person of Jewish blood can't vote and he can't hold public office.'

"'What's Jewish blood?' my mother asked. 'As far as I know, we all have the same chemistry.'

"'That's a good question. The Germans look at your grandparents. If three out of four of them were members of the Jewish religious community, you got Jewish blood. If two out of four, then you got mixed Jewish blood. There's all kinds of goofy rules. A non-Jew, who has never been inside a synagogue in his whole life, has Jewish blood if one of his parents was Jewish and he was born after the Law for the Protection of German Blood and Honor.' Ziggy took a sip of wine and laughed. 'I guess Jewish blood flows through your veins with a Yiddish accent.'

"My parents shook their heads. It all seemed morbidly unreal. Otto, Beka, and I sat there at the dinner table looking at each other like we were hearing fantastic ghost stories. To us it was all fiction. It was happening in Germany and that was worlds away from Zamość. It might as well have been happening on the moon.

"'From now on,' Ziggy said, 'anybody's right to be a citizen of Germany depends on a grant of Reich citizenship papers. Papers are the big thing. Everybody's got to have them. And of course, no Jews are allowed to have papers.'

"Then Ziggy went on to tell us about the rise of the SS, the secret police. 'Himmler recruits his SS out of the German youth program, mostly from middle- and upper-class families,' he said. 'They dress all in black—black tunic, black pantaloons tucked into black boots, black helmets. They're called the Schutzstaffel, the guard echelon of the National Socialist Party.' Ziggy shivered and his shoulders shook. 'They're terrifying, I tell you. Everyone's scared to death of them, all the way down to the average German workingman. Scares the hell out of me every time I go to Berlin. I don't know how much longer I'll go there.'

"He pointed a fork at my father. 'As crazy as Hitler is, Abraham, that's how crazy this Himmler is. Maybe even more. He's got himself a castle in Westphalia, a big medieval fortress up in the mountains, and he calls it Wewelsburg. He runs it like King Arthur.'

"'Oh, come on, Ziggy.'

"'That's what I hear. My customers tell me. He sits with twelve of his generals around a big round table like they're the Knights of the Round Table. And they say that he has a crypt beneath the dining hall he calls the Realm of the Dead, encircled by twelve pedestals.' Ziggy opened his eyes very wide, leaned forward, and spoke in a whisper. 'If one of his twelve knights dies, then they're going to cremate him and put his ashes in an urn to sit on one of the pedestals in the Realm of the Dead.' He held up his hands and wiggled his fingers.

"My mother put her foot down. 'Stop telling this nonsense, these crazy horror stories, Ziggy, you're going to give my kids nightmares.'

"'It's nonsense, is it, Leah? It's crazy? Well, it's happening right now. The SS wear rings with skulls on them. They march through the streets and sing, "We are the Black Band." They've got this medieval caste with ranks and privileges and customs. They believe in dueling as a way of defending one's honor. *Honor*, mind you. These cutthroats think they have honor and Himmler's made it all legal.'

"Ziggy held a butter knife over his upper lip to mimic Hitler's mustache, waved a spoon like a sword, and screeched in a Teutonic accent, 'A German has the right to defend his honor by force of arms!' The kids all laughed, but not my mother or father.

"Then Ziggy grew serious again and pointed his finger. 'Here's the scariest part, Abraham. He has the support of the entire German economy. All the captains of industry and banking bow to him. Bütefisch from IG Farben. Schacht from the Reichsbank. The Deutsche Bank. Even German-American companies. Himmler writes his own ticket. I tell you, this is no longer just rabble.'"

"What was your father's response to all this?" Catherine said.

"Generally, my parents felt like most Poles, that this was German insanity and would be confined within the German borders. But there was an air of uncertainty, even back then.

"'These may be radical lunatics,' my father said, 'but once they have the banks and industry behind them, they have the might of the German economy, the strongest economy in all of Europe.' And that was all in 1935, four years before the war."

Ben took a breath. "I also remember a dinner discussion that took place a year later, in 1936. After the meal Father and Ziggy retired to the living room for a brandy while Mother and Beka cleared the dishes. Ziggy lit up his pipe, a big burled wooden thing that looked like a tree stump. I remember it quite well because my mother always complained that the smoke left a stale odor on her curtains.

"'Germany has eighty million people and their hatred is spilling over into Poland,' said my father. 'We have trouble in the streets right now in Zamość. My Beka was attacked just last month, Ziggy. I'm afraid there may come a time when we have to move from the city, maybe to Papa's farm in the country.'

"'Or leave Poland, Abraham.'

"My father nodded solemnly. 'Perhaps, but I don't think it will ever come to that. Hitler may be a maniac, but people in Poland are good people. They won't join with Hitler. This will pass.'

"'It isn't *joining* that frightens me,' Ziggy said. 'It's the good people of Poland being annihilated that scares the hell out of me.'"

"And Otto?" Catherine said. "His parents were members of the Nazi Party. He had German blood. What was his reaction to all this?"

"Same as me. We were kids. We were indestructible. If the Germans dared to come to Poland, we'd wipe them out. There were millions of Jews in Poland, and we wouldn't let that racial madness come into our country."

Ben emptied his mug and walked to the sideboard for a refill.

He turned to face Catherine. "But life went on, Miss Lockhart. Every day, life went on. People went to work, people went to school, mothers diapered their babies, shopkeepers let out their awnings. Life went on. For us kids, we were in high school and that's where I met my beautiful Hannah. Shall I tell you about my Hannah?"

Catherine pursed her lips a little, and Ben caught sight of her impatience. "It's important," he said.

"Don't take this the wrong way, Ben, because I don't want you to get upset with me and start to scold me about a lawyer's function, but we've been meeting for two hours, and I don't think we're getting any closer to filling in the blanks on your stolen property. Could we just focus on that issue, please?"

"I *am* filling in the blanks. You'll see. I know what the blanks are—you don't."

"I have time pressures, Ben. Please understand."

"Hannah's important to my story."

Catherine slowly nodded.

Ben smiled. "All right, then. I know you'll be quite fond of Hannah when I tell you about her. Everyone who's ever met her has fallen in love with her. Hannah's family moved to Zamość when I was almost sixteen. I was in secondary school and immersed in my studies. My parents expected me to go to the university and be a professional. I was a top student, you know.

"One day, there she is, a new student taking a seat in the back of the classroom. I think to myself she's the prettiest girl I've ever seen, but of course, I'm way too shy to speak to her. Days go by. I watch her out of the corner of my eye. She sits a few rows behind me, so I look for excuses to turn around in my seat. Sometimes I think she catches me and my face turns red. I smile. She smiles back. Whenever other boys talk to her or make her laugh, I'm ravaged by jealousy, but, again, I'm too shy to do a darn thing about it. I curse myself for my weakness and my social clumsiness.

"Otto, on the other hand, is just the opposite. He's Mister Popularity at his school. He's a big, handsome blond kid, and he knows how to talk to girls. He goes to all the school parties, and he always has a girlfriend.

"One Sunday afternoon, when I'm being exceptionally lazy, lounging on my bed and bouncing a ball off the wall, my mother walks in and announces that she has invited the new doctor and his family to dinner. When she says it's the Weissbaums, I nearly have a heart attack.

"'I hear they have a daughter, Hannah, and she's in your class,' my mother says. 'Do you know her?'

"I try to be nonchalant. 'Maybe. I think so.'

"All day long I work, helping my mother clean the house. I polish the silver. I dust her antiques and vacuum her oriental rugs. I cut flowers for the vases and prune the flowers in the window boxes. She's never seen me so enthusiastic, and it doesn't take long before she gets the idea.

"'I thought you were tired today, Benjamin,' she says. 'This Hannah, is she somebody special?'

"I must have blushed because my mother has a mischievous twinkle in her eye before she turns to go into the other room.

"When the Weissbaums arrive, I rush to open the door. Hannah smiles so confidently. She's dazzling. Otto, of course, instantly engages her in conversation, and I am hopelessly jealous. How does he do that? Damn him, he has enough girlfriends. This is *my* secret love!

"My mother serves hors d'oeuvres in the living room, cocktails for the adults, punch for the kids, and while everyone is milling about, Hannah says to me, 'Ben, did you understand this week's math lesson?'

"'Of course,' I say. 'It was easy.'

"She asks if I would help her—she's lost and can't follow the assignment. This is too good to be true! I dash into my room and grab my math book. Now I have something to talk about. I'll teach her all about geometry. Months later, she confessed to me that it was just her way of breaking the ice. In fact, she understood the lesson just fine. She'd wondered why I didn't want to talk to her in school.

"Mother seats the Weissbaums around the dinner table and makes sure that Hannah sits next to me. I'm midway through the dinner when I realize that I've been talking to Hannah all night. She's so easy to talk to. But now she must think I'm a jabber-mouth."

"I think I know how she feels," said Catherine with a smile.

"During dessert my mother drops a bombshell. 'There's a dance at the school next weekend, Hannah, and I'm on the organizing committee. Your mother says you don't have plans to go. Neither does Benjamin, and I'm certain he'd be happy to escort you, wouldn't you, Ben?'

"I want to crawl under the table. Hannah looks at my face, which must be frozen in shock. The rest of the table stares at me. Otto's biting his lip to keep from laughing.

"I stammer, 'S-sure. That'd be fine. I'd love to take Hannah to the dance.'

"'Oh, that's wonderful,' Hannah says.

"After the Weissbaums leave, I grouse to my mother that she's set me up for failure. 'I don't know how to dance, Mom. I'm going to spoil my only chance with Hannah, and she'll never want to talk to me again.'

"But Otto ends up coming to the rescue. Elzbieta, his girlfriend, who is a very good dancer, will teach me. According to her, in seven days they will transform me from Stumbling Ben to Fred Astaire.

"Every afternoon, I come home from school and practice dancing with Elzie while Otto plays records on the Victrola and laughs until his sides hurt. By the end of the week I know all the steps—I just can't get my feet to do them.

"The night of the dance, I take a pretty corsage and walk to Hannah's. I am so sure this will be the worst night of my life. I curse the muses for making me such a klutz."

Catherine smiled. "What kind of dances did you learn, Ben? Were they traditional Polish dances?"

"Lord, no. We listened to the big-band music coming out of America. The Tommy Dorsey Band. Benny Goodman. Ray Noble and his orchestra. They were playing swing music and it was very popular with the Polish kids. The school had hired a swing band for the dance and it played all the latest songs.

"What a dance that was." Ben's eyes glazed over and his face softened. Catherine realized that Ben was back in Zamość; it was 1937 and he was young again. His eyes saw the dance floor, his ears heard the music, and his arms held the prettiest girl in Zamość.

Ben continued his narrative, barely audible, staring straight ahead, describing what he saw. Catherine strained to listen.

"She's wearing a beautiful blue dress, square-shouldered, tight at the waist. That's the fashion, you know. We dance all night long. We don't sit a single dance, not even one. My Hannah, she's light as a feather. So easy to lead. So soft to hold. Her flowers, her perfume, her hair, they fill my senses. The warmth of her face next to mine—it's intoxicating. In the blink of an eye, the evening is over. The band is playing their final song, 'The Very Thought of You,' and she whispers in my ear, 'Ben, you are such a good dancer.'"

Ben returned from his reverie and looked directly at Catherine. "I fell in love that night for the rest of my life and, if my faith is correct, Miss Lockhart, for all eternity."

Catherine's eyes glistened and a lump formed in her throat. "That's so sweet. I'm sure you're right."

TWELVE

•••

Zamość, Poland, 1938

Y OU DESCRIBED YOUR FRIENDSHIP as a triumvirate:
you, Otto, and Hannah," said Catherine, following a break.
"What did you mean by that?"

"We were in our teens—sixteen, seventeen—and we were al-
ways together, the three of us. We did our homework together,
we double-dated, and generally, we just spent time together.
Otto went through many girlfriends: Elzbieta, Anna, Karolina,
Jolanta. I can't remember them all. But the three constants were
Ben, Hannah, and Otto.

"Otto was a ladies' man, good-looking, gallant, and charming.
But he never cultivated a deep relationship with any of his girl-
friends, except for Elzbieta. He preferred conquest to commitment.
The perfect Nazi."

"But ultimately the triumvirate dissolved, right?" Catherine said.

"Miss Lockhart, I get the feeling you're trying to steer me
again. Please let me tell my story my way. You'll come to know why
I spend time on the background."

"I'll respect your wishes, Ben, but by the same token, I ask that
you appreciate the daily demands that my law firm imposes. I have
time constraints. I'm responsible to the firm for my hours. And
Ben, since we're spending so much time together, why don't you
stop calling me Miss Lockhart. I'm Catherine."

Ben smiled. "Catherine it is. And I promise to be mindful of your time. One afternoon in early 1938, while the three of us were in the living room finishing our homework, there was a knock on the door. It was Cousin Ziggy and he was frantic. He gripped my arms. 'Your Uncle Joseph is in great danger in Vienna. Find your father, Ben. I need to talk to him.'

"I grabbed my jacket and ran to the plant. It was still winter and the streets were filled with slush and snow. The cuffs of my pants got soaking wet. I found my father on the second floor in his office, in the middle of a new design, and he didn't want to be disturbed. 'Not now, Ben,' he said.

"'Cousin Ziggy's at the house,' I blurted. 'He says come home immediately.'

"'What's the emergency?'

"'I don't know, it has something to do with Uncle Joseph and I think it's real urgent.'

"My father snatched his long woolen coat from the rack and we hurried home. Ziggy met us at the door and pulled my father by his coat sleeves into the living room. The family all gathered to hear the news.

"'War is coming, Abraham. It's coming *now*. Last year Hitler grabbed portions of the Rhineland. Now he's been screaming about the mistreatment of German-speaking people in the Sudeten mountains. Everyone expects that he will move against Czechoslovakia soon.' Ziggy spoke as though he were out of breath.

"'Ziggy, we know that—we've heard it all on the radio,' my father answered. He was perturbed. 'Is that why you pulled me out of the factory?'

"Ziggy shook his head. 'You know Hitler's Austrian and he's long had his sights on Austria. Well, now we're hearing the same old refrain. Protect the German people from persecution. Reunite the German people.'

"'We know,' echoed my mother. 'We listen too, Ziggy, but such reunification is prohibited by the Treaty of Versailles.'

"'Treaties? What does Hitler care for treaties? And who'll stop him? The League of Nations? France? England? No, Leah, mark my words, he *will* take over Austria—and soon. Chancellor von Schuschnigg is in Berchtesgaden right now trying to make peace with Hitler, but that's a pipe dream. I told your brother to get out now, while he still can.'

"'Joseph won't leave Vienna; he's lived there for years,' Father said.

"'Now you know why I'm here. You must prevail on him, Abraham. This minute. He'll listen to you. You must convince him to come home to Zamość. Now. While the roads are still open.'

"'Of course he's welcome here, Ziggy. But maybe you're panicking a little too much. Maybe such a move is premature.'

"'When the Nazis roll into Austria, and they will, Abraham, they'll brutalize the Jews the same way they do in Germany, or worse. They'll confiscate everything. Call Joseph and tell him to gather up his things and come here to Zamość. When the family is all together, we must make plans to leave Europe.'

"'Leave Europe?' Mother said. 'Where would we go?'

"'America. I've already applied for a visa and I have a sponsor.'

"Father put his hand on Ziggy's shoulder to calm him down. 'I agree the situation is serious, Ziggy, but we're in no danger yet. Maybe you're right about Austria, and I will call Joseph, but Poland is secure. We have a large army and I've heard no talk of invading Poland. In fact, Hitler just gave his word to Minister Beck that he will guarantee our borders. He doesn't want to risk a fight with Poland.'

"'Risk a fight? Large army? We have *no* army compared to Germany,' Ziggy said with a wave of his hand. 'Hitler's been arming for years; there's no stronger army in the world. He invents excuses to invade. You think there's no talk of invading Poland? He screams about Gdansk, the free city of Danzig. He screams about the Polish corridor. Right now, Abraham, he's building roads to Poland. Maybe you can answer me: why would he build roads to the Polish border?'

"My father just shook his head. The talk went on well into the night. Otto and I walked Hannah home, came back, got ready for bed, and they were still talking. My father wired his brother late that night, but Uncle Joseph only said he'd think about it. A few days later we learned that Chancellor von Schuschnigg had resigned and that a new chancellor, a National Socialist, had taken over in Austria. On March 12, 1938, the German troops marched into Vienna to a great celebration. This was known as the Anschluss."

"Did your Uncle Joseph get out of Vienna?" Catherine said.

"Eventually, but not in time. He came to us the following May with nothing but a suitcase full of clothes and a few pieces of hidden jewelry. His leg was broken. My Aunt Hilda had to help him walk."

The afternoon was waning and Ben was tiring when Liam arrived.

"We're just wrapping up," Catherine said.

"I'm sorry, I couldn't get here any sooner. Can I take you both to dinner?"

"Ben is probably very tired—we've worked all afternoon," Catherine said, poking Liam with a hidden elbow. "We should let him go home."

"What kind of dinner did you have in mind, Liam?" Ben said.

"I thought maybe we'd grab a steak at the Chop House."

"Oh, that's perfect. I could eat a horse," Ben said.

Catherine shot Liam a look from a squinted eye. "You two go on without me, I need to finish up some work."

"We wouldn't think of it," Ben said. "We'll wait for you. How much time do you need?"

"Excuse me a minute, Ben," Catherine said as she pulled Liam aside. "I've been working with Ben for four hours, listening and taking notes for a lawsuit I doubt will ever be filed," she whispered to Liam through clenched teeth. "I admit he's very engaging and his story has captured my interest, but do you have any idea what this is doing to my practice? I worked until midnight last night. I have an unfinished motion sitting on my desk. I have Jenkins breathing down my back, and I've only billed twenty-one hours this week."

"Can you meet us at seven?" asked Ben from across the room.

Catherine's eyes sent darts of fire at Liam, who grimaced. She turned away and sighed. "Make it eight thirty."

* * *

BEN AND LIAM SAT by the windows on the second floor of the Chop House overlooking Ontario Street. The westbound traffic was heavy and the gridlocked taillights cast a red hue throughout the room. Catherine was now thirty minutes late.

"She doesn't like me," Ben said. "I'm not her kind of client."

"I think you're wrong," Liam said. "Don't be so quick to condemn."

"She's not a very happy woman. She rarely smiles. Maybe it's just me."

Liam shook his head. "It's not you, Ben. She had a meltdown a few years ago, and she's having a hard time getting past it. I've known her for a long time, since high school. She used to have a spark, a flash of light when she smiled." He shrugged. "It'll come back one day."

Ben nodded. "I'd like to know more about her."

"Maybe someday. She doesn't open up to many people."

Ben was staring out the window when Catherine arrived.

"How'd it go?" asked Liam, helping Catherine with her chair.

"I'm playing catch-up but it's coming along." She picked up the menu. "Really, though, Ben, if we could move ahead a little faster . . ."

"I was just at the part where my Uncle Joseph left Austria and moved to Poland," Ben said.

Catherine responded flatly. "He had a broken leg."

Ben shook his head. "Once again, Catherine, it's not so simple. It wasn't just a broken leg." Turning to Liam, Ben said, "She's such a good listener, but I wish she wasn't in such a rush. How can a person understand something when she's only interested in getting to the last paragraph?"

"She knows her business, Ben. Give her some credit."

"I'm sorry," Catherine said. "I'm trying to keep us on task, that's all."

"Well, it wasn't just a broken leg or I wouldn't have brought it up. To me, it was a critical part of the story." Ben stood up. He turned to Liam. "Earlier today Catherine and I made an agreement. But we didn't shake on it, so I guess it's not official. So now, we'll make a formal agreement and you'll witness it." He held up his right hand to take an oath. "I promise to be mindful of the demands of Catherine's law practice, and in return, Catherine has to give me credit for knowing what's important in my story. Okay? Do we have a deal?" He leaned over the table and stuck out his hand.

Catherine smiled and took his hand. "Agreed. I promise." She lifted her menu to study the entrees but Ben wasn't quite finished making his point.

"What happened in Austria was a precursor to what happened in Poland. What happened to Uncle Joseph would eventually happen to the people in Zamość. We should have known, Catherine. Cousin Ziggy warned us and Uncle Joseph would tell us, and yet all of us went about our daily routines as though nothing was going on, trapped in denial."

"What happened to your Uncle Joseph?"

Vienna, Austria, 1938

"The day of the Anschluss, the Nazis staged a military parade along Vienna's main thoroughfares. It was pure propaganda, intended for the movie theaters. Uncle Joseph and Aunt Hilda were not allowed to stay in their home because no Jews were allowed along the parade route. They were ordered to leave the area for the day.

"Neighbors later told them that the Nazis had assigned a make-believe family to their house—healthy, blond, and smiling character actors to be filmed cheering the German occupiers. Huge red-and-black Nazi flags were draped up and down the boulevards. As the parade of soldiers passed, some in cars, some on motorcycles, some on foot, their black heels hitting the pavement in goose-stepping rhythm, there were shouts of *Heil Hitler!* and *Sieg Heil!* coming from the balconies. Great jubilation, you know. Welcome to Austria, you wonderful conquerors. At the end of the day, when my aunt and uncle were allowed to return to their home, they found it ransacked and defaced with swastikas.

"Almost immediately the Germans instituted new rules in Vienna. Uncle Joseph and Aunt Hilda were issued identity cards stamped with a J. *Jude* was painted on the windows of my uncle's grocery store, and soon after the Anschluss, the store was taken from him. It was Aryanized. No Austrian Jew was allowed to own a business. They gave my uncle's store to an Austrian municipal worker, actually a plumber, and my uncle was forced to run the store as an underpaid employee.

"Then one night, after midnight, the Gestapo came through Uncle Joseph's neighborhood with a sound truck. 'All Jews are to assemble on the street. Now!' My aunt and uncle hurried down the stairs to stand on the cold cobblestones with coats wrapped around their bedclothes. Finally, hours later, they received instructions to report to the city hall at 8:00 A.M. to turn in all their valuables: jewelry, furs, silver, musical instruments. And radios. The Nazis didn't want Jews to have radios. Failure to comply would be met with dire consequences. Everyone knew what that meant.

"Uncle Joseph and Aunt Hilda stood in line at the city hall for most of the day. No one was permitted to leave the line for any reason, not for food or drink. Not even to go to the bathroom. No one was allowed to sit. Anyone who fell out of line was beaten. Nazi soldiers walked up and down the lines, slapping at people with their batons and screaming insults. After the valuables were handed over, they were allowed to go home. People who turned in a modest amount were accused of secreting valuables. Some were whisked back to their homes, where soldiers would tear the place apart looking for more."

"After their belongings were taken from them, did your aunt and uncle leave Vienna?" Catherine said.

"No. They stayed in their home."

"I don't understand that," Catherine said. "After the Anschluss, why didn't your aunt and uncle leave Austria? Certainly, I can understand why Jews didn't resist armed German soldiers. But after the confiscation, when they were allowed to go home, and when the soldiers weren't around, why didn't they escape? Why would they choose to stay in Austria and live in subjugation?"

Ben took a deep breath. He looked around the upscale restaurant, at the flocked walls, at the oil paintings in their golden frames, at the well-dressed diners enjoying their bone-in rib eyes and California cabernets, at the fireplace glowing warm and comfortable, and he said with a pained expression, "You're sitting here tonight in the lap of luxury, in a realm of comfort, a prominent lawyer, secure in every facet of her life, in a country where such madness seems inconceivable. Today, we look back at the Nazi scourge and shake our heads in disbelief. How could such a thing happen? Why were the Jews so meek? It's incomprehensible. Miss Lockhart, don't ask me, with all your presumptions, to explain why the Viennese Jews didn't leave their homes, their community, everything they knew and loved, and respond rationally to a world bereft of reason."

Catherine sat back. "I apologize. I have no right to judge."

Ben nodded. "They chip away and they chip away, taking your rights and your dignity a piece at a time, and you think, 'God, give me strength and I can endure this until the world is righted, until evil is vanquished, as it always is.'"

"I'm sorry," Catherine said.

"They broke his leg. One day, without any warning whatsoever, German soldiers burst into the store and grabbed my uncle from behind the counter. They yanked Jewish doctors out of hospitals, Jewish professors from the schools, old women from their homes, it didn't matter, and corralled them all out on the street. The Nazis gave them toothbrushes and pails of cold water and ordered them to scrub the cobblestones on their hands and knees, standing over them with automatic weapons, laughing and tormenting them. You see, Miss Lockhart, torture was amusement to the Nazis. Humiliation, battery, and even murder were acceptable forms of entertainment.

"One young thug in a shiny, creased uniform screamed at my uncle. 'That's not scrubbing,' he barked in German. 'Scrub harder, you Jewish swine.' My uncle cowered, like the others, scrubbing as hard as he could, waiting for the madness to pass and the storm troopers to withdraw so he could return to what was left of the normalcy of his home. 'After all,' he later said to us, 'we weren't enemy soldiers. We had no weapons, we made no threats, and we had declared no wars. This was supposed to be a peacetime annexation.'

"Nevertheless, this young sadist, who probably never had a job in his life before joining the Nazi army, pushed my uncle to the ground with his rifle butt and stomped on him with the heel of his boot, shattering his tibia. Then he turned his attention on some other poor soul and left my uncle lying on the street. After the Nazis left, neighbors carried my uncle home in a cart."

"It makes me sick that a man could do such a thing to another human being," whispered Catherine.

Ben leaned forward and stared into her eyes. "This was not a man, Miss Lockhart. This was a demon."

Catherine shifted uncomfortably. "I suppose you could call them demons. Anyone who could treat another so cruelly, without regard . . ."

Ben's lower jaw quivered. "They were demons in the *literal* sense, Miss Lockhart. Humans are incapable of planning and propagating mass genocide unless prompted by external evil. There is inherent goodness in the soul of man. God put it there. These Nazis were minions of the devil, recruited among the weak and those inclined to evil."

He leaned back in his chair and paused for a moment. "These monsters weren't just bad humans, Catherine, they had become missionaries, dispatched to spread the most heinous evil the world has ever seen."

Catherine said, "Dispatched by . . ."

"The archangel Samael. Satan. The devil. Whomever you choose. At the base of Mount Moriah there is darkness, wherein evil dwells. For me, there is no other explanation."

Catherine raised her eyebrows.

"Doubtful, Catherine? Too allegorical for you?"

"You have a right to believe such a theory."

"Not a theory. I have seen it."

Liam asked the waitress for the check.

"Well, anyway," Ben concluded as he stood and placed his napkin on the table, "eventually friends arranged for Uncle Joseph and Aunt Hilda to travel to Poland. They had to leave everything behind. That was the price of freedom. They were driven to the Polish border, where they caught a train to Lublin.

"By the time Uncle Joseph arrived in Zamość, infection had set in. It was a bad compound fracture. My father immediately sent for Doctor Weissbaum, but despite the care that was given to him, Uncle Joseph lost his right leg."

"Did they move into your home?" Catherine asked.

"Of course. There was some talk of their going to live in their mountain cabin, but with his disability it was out of the question. They had lost everything except each other."

Catherine folded her napkin, laid it on the table, and stood. "Excuse me, please," she said and walked in the direction of the ladies' room.

Ben and Liam watched her walk away. "She's upset," said Liam.

"Honest emotion. That's not a bad thing," Ben said. "She's dropping her barriers and maybe this case is just what she needs."

"Are you a psychologist now, Ben?"

He smiled. "Just an old man who reads too much."

Liam paid the check. They waited for Catherine, and then they all walked down the street to where the car was parked. "Can we drop you at home?" Liam said.

"If you're going my way; otherwise, I'll take the bus."

"Hop in, Ben. It would be my pleasure."

Thirteen

. . .

Chicago, Illinois, October 2004

THEY DROPPED BEN AT the entrance to his apartment building, a twenty-four-story blond brick structure on Bittersweet Place, a block off the lakefront in the Belmont Harbor neighborhood. Built in the 1930s, the building still had outdoor fire escapes and indoor radiators. Room air conditioners protruded from the windows. But despite its age, the proximity to the harbor and the twelve hundred acres of Lincoln Park made the rental units desirable and vacancies were rare.

Liam and Catherine said good night to Ben and drove off in the direction of Catherine's townhome. No sooner had they turned onto Marine Drive than Liam's cell phone rang.

"It's Ben. I got a big problem."

"You need me to come back?"

"Yeah. Apartment 1708."

The doorman buzzed them through and they took the elevator to the seventeenth floor, where they found Ben standing in the hallway outside his open door.

The apartment had been torn asunder. Bureau drawers were overturned, their contents scattered. Kitchen appliances and pots and pans lay on the floor. The bedroom closet had been emptied of its contents and piles of hangers and pants and coats were tossed about in rumpled heaps.

Thirty minutes later two investigators and an evidence technician from the Belmont district headquarters arrived and surveyed
the mess. They dusted for prints and took pictures. One of them
took a statement from Ben as he leaned against his kitchen wall,
shaking his head at the disarray.

"Are any valuables missing?" Catherine said.

"Like what? What's a valuable to you?"

"Jewelry. Money. Silver. Collectibles."

"Nothing that would attract burglars. Anything in this apartment has value only to me. These weren't thieves; they were Nazis
looking for evidence."

"Evidence?"

"Of course. That I might have on Piatek. Or something they
could later use to discredit me in my lawsuit."

"Are there such things? Do you have such evidence?"

"I have notes." Ben picked up the open cardboard box that had
previously held his gun and showed it to Catherine. "They're gone.
The notes are gone."

"Tell me about the notes, Ben," Liam said. "Where did they
come from?"

"I made them from my memory over the past several days, to
help me tell my story. About twenty pages or so."

"Were there any references to Catherine or her law firm? Did
you write about a lawsuit?"

"I think so. I probably noted that a certain person would make a
good witness or that we should seek out evidence of my property from
Rosenzweig's house or something like that. I'm pretty sure I did."

"Did you make a copy?"

"No."

Ben stood in the midst of his wrecked apartment. "Damn. They
sure beat the hell out of this place."

A Chicago Police Department evidence technician approached
them. "There's no sign of forced entry. We lifted some prints, we
have some fibers, but I don't know if anything'll come of it."

He handed a CPD card to Ben on his way out. "Sergeant Quinlan will be following the case."

"We'll help you put your apartment back together, Ben," Catherine said.

"No, thanks," he said, slowly shaking his head. His bearing seemed to wither. "I'd prefer to do it alone."

He righted a tipped chair and sat down with his face in his hands. "You two can go now. Thanks for coming back."

"Double-lock the doors, Ben." Liam started to leave and stopped at the door. "One more thing. How many ways are there to get into this building?"

"Well, there's the front desk, the way you came in, and there's a back door with a delivery dock that the maintenance guys use."

"Do the tenants have a key to the back door?"

"No. There's no reason to go out the back. There's no parking or anything."

T HEY DROVE FOR A while, Liam drumming his fingers on the steering wheel. Finally, he broke the silence.

"Well, what do you make of all of this, Cat? Do you still think he's crazy?"

"What do I make of it? I know his apartment was ransacked, but I'm not going to jump to any conclusions that Nazis were responsible. It could've been anyone. It could've been kids, drug addicts, or petty thieves."

"Or Otto Piatek?"

"Oh, come on. An eighty-three-year-old man drove over here, slipped by security, broke into the apartment, and tore it up without being noticed?"

"Rosenzweig is wealthy enough to get it done."

"And so is Bill Gates. But I have no more proof that it was Elliot Rosenzweig than I do it was Bill Gates. Which brings me to another issue. I've listened to Ben for days, and I grant you, it's an absorbing story, but I have yet to hear a single piece of evidence that would tie Rosenzweig to Piatek. And I've repeatedly raised the subject. All it does is unsettle him."

"You have to be patient. I'm sure he'll get there."

"Oh, I'm certain that if I devote enough time and listen long enough, he'll eventually finish his story, but you know what? At the end of that time, it still comes down to proof. What *proof* can he muster, what evidence is there that Rosenzweig is Piatek? What *proof* that Rosenzweig has the Solomons' property?"

"You know as well as I that his apartment was torn up because of his accusations. This was no coincidence. These weren't kids or addicts, Cat. They were professionals. They were looking to see what he had. In your heart you know he's right. We just have to help him get the proof."

"You saw his apartment. There's nothing there. How does he find proof from sixty years ago when he doesn't have anything?"

"He had notes."

"That's not evidence, that's his memory. And even if his notes weren't taken or weren't misplaced somewhere, they wouldn't be admissible in any U.S. courtroom."

"Please hear him out. Just a little longer. Like you said the other day, there's something much deeper here. Do it for me. I'll get you the proof, Cat. After all these years, they're still violating him."

Catherine stared straight ahead. "I can't do it much longer, Liam."

FOURTEEN

...

B EN SPOKE SOFTLY WHEN he arrived the next morning. "I spent most of the night trying to put my home back together."

Catherine nodded sympathetically and poured him a cup of tea. "I'm sorry," she said. "But before we get started, I need to tell you that I have a hearing scheduled today at two o'clock that may continue through tomorrow. We can work until noon, and if we don't finish, we can get together on Friday."

Ben shook his head. "I can't meet on Friday. I have somewhere I have to be."

"Is that because it's the Sabbath?"

"Well, it is *Erev Shabbat*, but that's not the reason. I have a standing commitment on Friday afternoons."

"Then we only have a couple of hours, and if you're up to it, I'd like to forge ahead. Perhaps we can focus on how Otto took your property and how we can prove that Mr. Rosenzweig is really Otto Piatek."

Ben took a sip of tea. "I don't know if I can do that in two hours. I'll do the best I can."

Zamość, Poland, 1939

"It was the summer of 1939, a warm Saturday evening, and we were enjoying dinner with friends and family—Hannah and her parents, my aunt and uncle, Beka, Otto. We had just finished dessert and were sitting in the living room when we heard a knock on the door, a soft knock, like whoever it was didn't want to alert anyone but us. My father looked at us, shrugged his shoulders, and went to open the door. There stands Otto's mother, Ilse, dressed in a dark cotton cloak. The hood is pulled up over her blond hair to hide most of her face. She's a pretty woman, with her curled hair and her high cheekbones. Dark red lipstick.

"'May I come in, please, Mr. Solomon?' she says softly. 'I need to speak to you.'

"Father brings her into the living room and introduces her to the group. Ilse is unnerved. She doesn't expect to encounter so many people. She backs up a step or two, pulls my father's sleeve, and leans over to whisper to him.

"'I really shouldn't be here,' she says. 'May I speak to you in private?'

"'Whatever you have to say to me you may say to all of us. This is my family.'

"She looks around the room, at each of us, and realizes she has no choice. She removes her cloak and hands it to my father. Her surprise visit knocks Otto a bit off-balance. He is mute as he stands and offers his chair. Everyone is quiet. Why does Ilse come to speak to my father? We haven't seen her in over a year. As far as we know, she's still working for the Nazis in Germany.

"'You must let me take Otto back to Germany,' she says. 'And as for you and your family, you must leave Poland immediately. You don't have much time.'

"She says this like a pronouncement. It's a fait accompli. Like she knows what's best for us and she's made the decision and we should obey without question.

"But Otto says, 'I'm not going anywhere. I've just finished school and I'm preparing for the university.'

"Ilse pauses. She purses her lips and ponders whether or not she should continue. Finally she speaks. 'Let's not deceive one another, Mr. Solomon. I have no love for you or for the Jews. I care only for my son. I also know you have no reason to believe that

I'm telling you the truth, but be assured I've come here at great personal risk.'

"My father stands in the center of the room with his arms crossed on his chest. 'I think you should leave now, Mrs. Piatek. Otto is free to make his own choices. We heard what you had to say. Certainly Otto may go with you if that's his wish.'

"'Why would I go with her?' Otto says. 'Everything I care about is here in Zamość. Thanks to you and Aunt Leah, I have the opportunity to go to the university and become a professional. I'm going to stay here, in Poland, where I belong.' He walks over to my father. They stand side by side, two strong men, standing tall. And I'm so proud.

"Ilse scoffs. 'Listen to me. You are all fools. Poland is history. Germany will overrun Poland within months.' She waves her arm at all of us. 'If you insist on staying here, you're already dead.'

"'Oh, such nonsense,' Dr. Weissbaum says, passing it off with a shake of his head. 'This is just more German arrogance. We are not Austria. Poland will live for a thousand years.'

"Father, as usual, is more prone to reason, and he responds with diplomacy. 'We've listened quite regularly to Hitler's broadcasts. We're trying to be ready for any eventuality, and this is a situation we continually reassess, but right now things are stable here and the children are preparing to enter the university in Lublin.'

"Ilse wrings her hands and begins to sob. 'There will be no university. There will be no Poland. Why won't you listen to me?' Her emotional breakdown softens the timbre of the room and melts some of the antagonism. Mother hands her a handkerchief, but Otto is unmoved. He shakes his head and starts to leave the room. Father stops him.

"'Mrs. Piatek,' Father says, 'we'll listen to you, but I'd like to know what brings you to our home on this particular day? You've been absent from Otto's life for so long and Europe has been on the brink of conflict for many months. So why come to Poland at this time, and why do you say you've come at great personal risk?'

"'I'm here to save my Otto,' she says through her tears, 'and to make amends. None of you can know the anguish of abandoning your only child. Six years ago, I had hit the bottom. I fled from my senses. I left the only thing I loved and returned to Germany, to the home of my relatives. After a while, they helped me find work as a secretary for the National Socialists.

"'I worked my way up the ladder, doing whatever I had to, and was eventually assigned to Reinhard Heydrich. I'm sure you know who he is. Well, I am his personal secretary. I get information every day, tiny swatches, you understand, but I put them together and when I do . . . all I can say is: it's urgent to get Otto out of Poland.'

"Otto doesn't buy into her remorse. 'Uncle Abraham asked you: what is your great personal risk?'

"She looks directly at my father. 'If I am discovered here, if Reinhard had the slightest idea that I came to Poland, I would be tortured for the information I gave you and then killed. Without a second thought. And so will all of you if you stay here.'

"'What do you know, Mother, about the Nazi plans for Poland?' asks Otto.

"'I should not say, both for your protection and mine.'

"'Then get out.'

"She begs, she pleads, but Otto is steadfast and refuses to listen unless she is willing to divulge what she has learned. Finally, in her hysteria, she relents.

"'In April, I helped prepare some of the documents that were later called Case White. They were top secret and I did not see them all, nor have I seen them in final form. But I know that Case White calls for a surprise invasion of Poland with sudden, heavy blows. The high command of the armed forces, the OKW, has been instructed to draw up plans to carry out the operation at any time after September 1.'

"We are all stunned. 'That's two weeks away,' Father exclaims.

"She nods. 'Hitler's waiting for Stalin to assure him that Russia won't come to Poland's aid. Reinhard believes that assurance will come next week. Ribbentrop is in Moscow now. There are telegrams daily. Hitler expects a nonaggression pact to be signed and announced by next Wednesday, and if it is, Poland will be history by the end of September. Otto, please, you can't be here when the bombs fall. As for you, Mr. Solomon, I am indebted to you for the kindness you've shown to my son, and so I warn you to get out of the country. You've seen the fate of Jews in German-occupied lands.'

"'I'm not going,' Otto says. 'If they come, I'll stay and fight.'

"Otto's rebuff is too much for Ilse. She covers her face with her hands and weeps loudly.

"'Where can we reach you, Mrs. Piatek?' Father says. 'Let us all think about what you've just said.'

"She jots a Berlin address and phone number on a piece of paper and leaves. Two weeks later, before the sun rises on Friday, September 1, 1939, a million and a half German troops cross the Polish border in the most ferocious, deadly attack ever known to man."

FIFTEEN

...

ON THE CORNER OF Belmont and Western, next to a
shopping mall built on the grounds of the old Riverview
Amusement Park, sits a glass-and-concrete structure housing the Chicago Police Department's 19th District. Belmont District. Liam entered a little after noon and made his inquiries at the
front desk.

Walking out to greet him, a plainclothes detective said, "I'm
Jack Quinlan. How can I help you?"

"Liam Taggart," he replied, shaking Quinlan's hand. "I called
earlier about the burglary at Ben Solomon's apartment."

"Right. You're the PI."

"I'm also a friend of Ben Solomon."

"Well, come on back and I'll grab the file."

Quinlan's desk sat near the windows, one of a dozen desks in
the common area on the second floor. He opened a metal file cabinet, took a manila folder back to his desk, and spread out the papers.

"B and E of an apartment on Bittersweet," he read from the
report. "Nothing missing but some papers. This is not your high-
priority crime."

"It is to me. We think it has larger implications."

Quinlan studied the pink carbon copy. "No prints. No lab work.
Nothing."

"I'd like to find the guys who broke in. I'll help any way I can."

"Listen, Mr. Taggart, and I don't mean any disrespect, but right here in the Nineteenth we had twelve hundred burglaries and four thousand thefts last year. And that was an improvement over the previous year. I don't know what we can do. I'm not going to canvass over a petty burglary."

"Do you care if I look into it?"

"Suit yourself. Until I get a complaint."

Sixteen

...

Zamość, Poland, 1939

THAT FIRST DAY OF September 1939, the Germans attacked Poland from the north, west, and south, destroying everything that lay in front of them. Their tanks and bombs did not reach Zamość that day, but news of the invasion did, arriving through radio broadcasts. Everyone took to the streets. Even though it was the Sabbath, newspaper boys were on the street hawking extra editions. All that night there were meetings among the community leaders. My father didn't come home until morning, and that was to take us to the synagogue."

"May I ask a question?" Catherine said. "Friday you told me that Ilse revealed the existence of Case White, which I understand was a top-secret document."

"True. And you want to know why my father didn't immediately inform the Polish government?"

"Exactly."

"He did."

"Oh? They didn't listen to him?"

"In the days before the invasion, rumors were as common as butterflies and just as diverse. Hitler was cleverly giving speeches about peace-loving Germany and protecting borders. Our politicians wanted, *needed*, to believe in peace. Father gave Ilse's information to our local senator, who sent it on to Warsaw, but nothing came of it."

"Your father apparently believed it. Why did your family stay in Zamość?"

"That's a good question. Why did any of us stay? Obviously, if we had known the future, we'd have left. But as it was, our destiny was uncertain, and abandoning one's roots without anywhere to go is a leap into the abyss. As I mentioned to you at the restaurant, no rational person could have conceived of the unbounded evil, of the genocide and the slaughter.

"For Poland, even at the eleventh hour, there was reason to hope. We knew that Britain and France had warned Germany not to threaten Polish independence. England had sworn to use all of its power to defend Poland in the event of a German attack. I guess we all believed the world would not permit Germany to annihilate a peaceful country."

The conference room phone buzzed and Catherine excused herself to take a phone call. Solomon refilled his tea and stood by the window, gazing into the gray October sky.

"It was sixty-five years ago, Hannah," he said softly to the window. "So many years ago. Remember? It was a gloomy, cloudy day just like this one. The world was coming apart, but we had each other, and we had plans to escape."

"I'm sorry," Catherine said from behind. "Did you say something?"

Ben shook his head and took his seat at the table.

"That was a call about today's court appearance," Catherine said. "It's been continued. So let's make an effort to finish your story by the end of the day."

Ben nodded. "After Sabbath-morning services on September 2, the men assembled at the town hall to be given defense assignments. Otto and I built embankments with sandbags. Some built bomb shelters, some laid traps in the forest. In retrospect, we were naïve to think we could even put a speed bump in the way of the German advance, but our mood was optimistic, full of youthful exuberance, and we worked throughout the day and well into the night.

"Hannah and the other girls brought us sandwiches and told us how proud they were of their Polish soldiers. Otto and I sweated in the September sun, side by side, cursing the Germans and everything they stood for, swearing upon our souls to defend our motherland."

"The same Otto who would later . . ." started Catherine.

"The same. Elliot Rosenzweig. Piatek. Whatever you want to call him."

Catherine shook her head.

"Two days later, the first of the refugees began arriving in the predawn hours. Just a few at first, some pushing carts loaded with their clothes and possessions, or their babies in quilts. By midday there was a steady stream. They spent the night on their way to eastern Poland and the Russian territories. From them we learned about the horrors of the invasion and how we were hopelessly overmatched.

"You know, Catherine, *blitzkrieg* means 'lightning war.' Germany unleashed twelve hundred war planes. Bombers, fighters. Much of our air force never got off the ground. We had thirty-five divisions against a million and a half well-armed troops. In short order, the Polish army was decimated.

"To put this all in perspective, in 1939 Germany had two and a half million well-trained ground troops. England had a small professional army. The U.S. had less than half a million ground troops and would not reach one and a half million until mid-1941. Poland had less than three hundred thousand land troops that were initially called the frontier defense force. Poland had a single mechanized brigade, while the Germans committed six Panzer divisions, which were combined with motorized infantry and motorized artillery. I only bring this up to point out the enormous disparity in the strengths of the two armies. Germany went through Poland like a hot knife through butter.

"Krakow fell in seven days, and we knew that the bombs would soon come to our town. The Polish defense plan was based upon the expectation that England and France would provide a second front. Our only hope was the West. Every day we heard reports that England and France were sending troops. One afternoon, Otto ran up to our bunker shouting that sixty thousand English troops had landed in Danzig. Of course, it was only a false rumor, nothing more than a wish.

"On September ninth, again on the Sabbath, the bombs began to fall on Zamość. We were on our way to our synagogue when we heard the drone of the Stukas and the thunder of the bombs. Hundreds of dive bombers strafed the streets, bombs fell everywhere, like a meteor shower, destroying buildings, shops, churches, and schools indiscriminately. On Harowajszowska Street, in a poor neighborhood, a bomb exploded on a synagogue and hundreds of worshippers were incinerated."

"Was there no defense for Zamość?" Catherine said.

"We had practically nothing to use against aircraft or armored vehicles. People gathered their hunting rifles and shotguns. We were throwing pebbles at the apocalypse. The bombers flew at us without any countermeasures. It was target practice for them.

"One Stuka flew very close to the ground, maybe to see the fear in the eyes of the people he was slaughtering, but his wings clipped a steeple and his plane twirled and crashed in a field. The pilot was thrown from the cockpit and lay in a potato farm, broken and bleeding, awaiting his turn in line at the gates of hell, when one of our elementary school teachers, Mr. Kazmierecz, reached him. 'We're not soldiers; there's no army here,' he yelled at the dying pilot. 'Who are you trying to kill?' And with his last breath the pilot answered, 'Poland.'

"People scattered in every direction, many of them to the woods to hide. But for me, all I could think about was Hannah. I had to get to Hannah. I dashed through the rubble in the streets, past the frantic women and children who ran every which way ducking their heads, past the injured who lay bleeding. And the noise—the screams, the bombs, the planes, the guns—it was deafening. I found Hannah outside the school, grabbed her hand, and ran back to my house. If this was to be the end of the world, we would face it together. We held tightly to each other as the bombs rained on Zamość.

"Five days later the German army rolled into Zamość without any resistance. We watched their black convertibles, their tanks and canvas-covered trucks, from our living room window. My mother and father cried."

SEVENTEEN

· · ·

Chicago, Illinois, October 2004

THE UNIFORMED DOORMAN BEHIND his granite counter in the lobby of the Bittersweet apartment building pursed his lips and shook his head. "I don't know of anyone going up to Mr. Solomon's that day except you and the lady. But this is a busy place. We got a hundred sixty units here. I can't remember every visitor who comes in. And people could get buzzed in when I'm not at the desk."

"It would have been before 8:00 P.M. It could have been any time in the afternoon. Were there any unusual visitors that day, anyone who wasn't a guest—maybe a delivery man?" asked Liam.

"Nothing that sticks out in my mind."

Liam looked around the lobby. A bank of steel mailboxes lined the west wall adjacent to the glass entrance door.

"I assume the door to the elevator lobby is always locked?"

"Right. Either a tenant or I would have to buzz you in. Of course, the residents all have keys."

"How does someone get in the back door?"

"By the loading dock? Only the maintenance guys open the door. I suppose there are times when it's open and somebody could get through, but the door from the dock to the apartment elevators is always locked."

"Do the maintenance guys have keys to each of the apartments?"

"Of course. Fire regulations."

"Who was on duty last Tuesday?"

He thought for a minute. "That would be Stefan Dubrovnik."

"Is he here today?"

"Supposed to be."

"Where can I find him?"

The doorman reached behind his desk and pulled out a black walkie-talkie.

"Stefan? Can you come up to the lobby? I got a detective here who wants to ask you some questions."

"I don't have no information for detective," the handset belched in an Eastern European accent. "I just do my job. I don't get mixed up in no trouble."

"It's not about you, Stefan. It's about the break-in on seventeen."

"I don't know nothing about break-in. I go now."

"Stefan? Stefan?"

The doorman shrugged. "He turned off his two-way."

"Where is he?"

"Probably the basement."

"Will you buzz me in?"

"Can't do it. You're just a private guy."

Liam took out his cell phone. "All right, I understand. Let me call Belmont District and get a squad over here. Maybe if enough cops go through the building, talk to all the residents, I'll get some answers."

"Hold on, hold on," the doorman said. "Jesus, don't do that. I'll buzz you in."

Liam quickly descended the concrete steps into the boiler room where a small, thin man was hurriedly packing his duffel bag in the corner. He had close-cropped hair and wore a long-sleeved black T-shirt.

"Stefan Dubrovnik?"

"Yah."

"I'm Liam Taggart. Can I ask you a couple of questions?"

"No. I'm in big hurry. I know nothing about no break-in or nothing what's missing."

"I didn't say anything about something missing. How do you know something is missing?"

"I don't. I just figure. They break in, they take."

"Who'd you let in the apartment, Stefan?"

"No. No. I go now." He tried to angle by and head for the stairs, but Liam blocked his way, holding the man's biceps in a tight grip.

He spoke quietly, inches from Stefan's face. "Stefan, let me say something to you. Dubrovnik is a city in Croatia, on the Adriatic Sea, very pretty as I recall. I doubt that's your legal name. I also doubt you have a green card and the right to work as a super in this building."

Stefan swallowed hard.

"But I don't care about your legal status. All I care about is finding out who ransacked Ben Solomon's apartment, and I think you know."

"I lose my job."

"That's right, Stefan. You're probably done at this building. But if you tell me what happened, I won't turn you in, you won't go to jail, you won't get deported, and you'll likely find another job in Chicago."

Stefan dropped his duffel bag and nodded his head. "I never see them before this time. They come to my house. They know I have no visa. They say they need to go into Mr. Solomon's apartment. They threaten me: open Solomon's door or we call INS." He shrugged. "I got kids in the school."

"How many of them and what did they look like?"

"Two. White, your height, big shoulders. One have short hair, one have shaved head. That one have tattoo on his neck. Like a barb wire. I let them in back door, we take service elevator, I open Solomon's door for them, then I go home. I never see them again. I go now."

"One more thing, Stefan. Did they have a car?"

He nodded. "They wait outside my house when I come out to catch bus. They tell me get in. A gray car, maybe a Camry. I have no choice, I get in backseat. They drive me to the building."

"What did you notice about the car?"

"Tan inside. Cloth seats. On the floor was couple beer bottles and magazines."

"What kind of magazines?"

Stefan shook his head. "I don't know. I don't pick up magazines."

"Give me a number where I can reach you."

BEN RETURNED FROM A short walk and put his jacket over the back of his chair. He was sipping a cup of tea when Catherine entered the room.

"That's a pretty sweater you have on," he said. "Looks very nice on you."

"Why, thank you, Ben. I put it on this morning because there's a chill in the air, don't you think?"

"Maybe a little. I spent so many years out on the golf course, I'm used to the morning cold."

"I spoke with Liam. He said he'd try to stop by later, if you don't mind."

Ben smiled. "Trying to speed me up, are you?"

Catherine blushed. "I'd like to finish evaluating your case against Mr. Rosenzweig. I'm not trying to rush you."

"Yes, you are, but that's okay. I'm getting there, and when I do, you'll understand why I've given you the whole story."

Zamość, Poland, 1939

"The first thing the German army did after arriving in Zamość was to round up fifteen hundred of the town's men and hold them hostage, threatening to kill them if the town didn't follow orders. They took my father and they took Dr. Weissbaum. They were held at city hall and at the high school.

"No one knew what to expect; the Germans weren't exactly informative about their plans. With Father and Dr. Weissbaum gone, Hannah and her mother moved in with us. Mother made room;

she always found room. She and Beka bunked together and we gave Beka's room to Hannah and her mother."

"That's a lot of people in your house, Ben. Were your uncle and aunt still there?"

"Of course. And Otto."

"Your mother must have been going out of her mind."

Ben nodded and then shrugged his shoulders. "All of us. But it's a funny thing, Catherine, that even in the midst of a world gone mad, you can find hope to hold on to—things to look forward to. The human spirit is enduringly resilient. Hannah and I spent evenings sitting on the flat roof of our home, beneath the stars, planning a life together. Our world was crumbling, yet we were dreaming of a beautiful future."

Catherine watched as Ben shut his eyes and once again journeyed back to Zamość.

"The autumn nights are cold in Zamość. On the roof, Hannah and I huddle together, wrapped in a blanket. We talk about how we'll buy a home and raise our children, how they'll have Hannah's rich auburn hair and beautiful hazel eyes, and how they'll have my inquisitiveness and stubborn tenacity. Our love deepens on those quiet fall evenings as we look out over the stillness of Zamość. 'Dance with me,' she says, and I hold her in my arms. Her head rests on my shoulder and we waltz around the rooftop humming a song."

Ben paused. His eyes remained closed, and he rocked from side to side to the beat of the music in his memory. "You'd call them old standards today. Back then, they weren't so old. 'Dancing in the Dark' was a favorite, for obvious reasons."

Ben opened his eyes and smiled at Catherine. "Even in the midst of the war, those nights were sweet for us. We were young and enchanted with each other. We believed that no matter how these invaders oppressed our lives, it'd only be temporary. We'd endure the occupation by the strength of our love.

"'I don't know where we'll end up, Hannah,' I say with my arms tightly wrapped around her little waist. 'We may be scattered to the winds like cottonwood seeds.'

"'And you're worried about where I'll be when you find yourself at some other corner of the world?' she says.

"'Yes.'

"'I'll be standing right next to you,' she says. 'You just look for me. Wait for me. No matter what these monsters have in store for us, I'll always be there. I'll never leave you.'

"And I pledge the same to her."

Ben looked at Catherine. "And we've kept that promise."

He took a deep breath and continued. "The Germans held the hostages for four days. Then they let them all come home. The Weissbaums went to their home, and my father returned to his duties at the factory. People who had been hiding in the woods and on the farms came back into town. It was joyous relief for Zamość, but a tinge of sadness for me, because Hannah returned to her home as well.

"Some of the stores and houses had been looted, and some folks who left to hide in the woods found that they'd been victimized, but no one was being held hostage and no one was being shot, and for that we were grateful. We started thinking: we can make it until the end of the war. It's not so bad.

"Then the most curious thing happened. A week later, the whole German army withdrew—they drove right out of town, just like that. No one knew the reason, and radios were no help. We thought maybe England and France had mounted their offensive or Hitler had changed his strategy. We didn't know the real reason: Hitler and Stalin were still posturing over how to split up Eastern Europe. So the Germans left and a little while later the Russians rolled into town. Then we had the Russian army to deal with."

"Were the Russians in the war already?" asked Catherine. "Didn't Germany attack Russia?"

"That came much later. In the beginning, there was a treaty between Germany and Russia, the Ribbentrop-Molotov Nonaggression Pact. But in the fall of 1939, Hitler and Stalin were still trying to figure out how to carve up the roast. The Russian army came into

Zamość and appointed some of the townsmen as administrators. My father was appointed as a clerk at city hall."

"I confess, Ben, you've got me confused. I guess my history classes weren't thorough enough."

"Catherine, if you think you're confused, imagine how confused we were. We were a volleyball on the European map. But we felt that the Russians would treat us better.

"The Russian army instituted no pogroms, and there were no restrictions placed on Jews in Zamość. People started believing that life during the war would be manageable.

"Again, we didn't know that Hitler had no intention of giving Poland's riches to Stalin. He saw our country as a bountiful bread-basket for the fatherland. Hitler intended to resettle Poland with German citizens, and so he made a second deal with Stalin, giving Lithuania and the far eastern portions of Poland to Russia and keeping Lublin, Krakow, Zamość, and all of Warsaw for himself.

"The Russian soldiers stayed for one week and then they left, and for a while there were no soldiers at all—no Germans, no Russians. Not knowing what would happen next, we tried to get our lives back together. Men and women worked to clean up the rubble left from the bombing and to find housing for those whose homes were destroyed. Hannah worked at a nursery. Otto and I helped with the cleanup, loading bricks and bomb debris into carts to be wheeled to a refuse dump on the edge of town. It was only the eye of the hurricane, Catherine, but we didn't know it."

Ben paused and once again stared at the ceiling. His lips were taut.

"In early October, the Germans return, this time with the Gestapo. This time with the legions of Satan and his unbridled evil. Within hours, we feel the chill of their presence. The nightmare has come to Zamość.

"Not long after the Gestapo arrives, an elegantly uniformed officer appears unannounced at our home, accompanied by two German soldiers. He comes at the dinner hour. My father opens the door and they enter without a word. The officer struts into our living room and takes off his hat and white gloves. I estimate him to be in his late thirties, but his skin is pasty. He has beady eyes and a fleshy double chin. His slicked hair has receded deeply on the sides of his head and what's left comes to a point in the front. I watch as he surveys the room. No one speaks. He sits in Father's chair and crosses his legs. The polish on his black boots shines like a mirror. Helmeted soldiers stand on each side, like bookends with stone faces. We wait in silence while he lights a cigarette in an ebony holder.

"'Do I speak with Abraham Solomon?' he says at last. He's extremely well-mannered but as cold as a corpse.

"My father answers in German. 'I am Abraham.'

"'Herr Solomon, I have learned that you are a respected leader among the Jews, and so you are to be appointed to the Judenrat, the council of Jews. That is a much honored appointment for you and your family. The Judenrat will report to me, or to my assistant, and will implement the führer's orders on Jewish affairs.'

"'I seek no privileges, sir. I am no more or less than any other member of our community.'

"'You will address me as Dr. Frank, Herr Solomon. My name is Dr. Hans Frank, and you will not forget that, please. And I suggest you reconsider your declination. There *will* be a Judenrat, of that you may be sure, and it will consist of the most influential of the Jews in Zamość. You cannot help your people if you are not present.'

"All of us are seated in the room, barely breathing, not daring to say a word. Dr. Frank looks us over, points at Uncle Joseph, and says, 'Who is the crippled man?'

"'That is my brother, a well-educated and prominent man. He has had an accident.'

"Dr. Frank purses his lips and nods. He crushes his cigarette on a dish, slaps his gloves on his leg, and rises to leave. 'I will see you at the town hall tomorrow morning at ten.' On his way out, he stops at the door and points at Beka. 'Who is the young Jewess?'

"'My daughter, Rebecca. She is only seventeen.'

"'Yes. Seventeen.' He gestures for the soldiers to precede him through the doorway and turns to my father. 'You will be at the town hall at ten.' Then he bows slightly and leaves our home."

"Did your father go to the meeting?" asked Catherine.

Ben nodded. "At ten o'clock. When he came home his face was drained of all color. He kept repeating, 'We should have listened to Ilse, we should have left Zamość.'"

Ben's narration was interrupted by a knock on the conference room door. Catherine opened the door and Liam walked in the room.

"Hi, Ben. Are you driving my old friend crazy?"

"That's not fair," Catherine said. "I've been very attentive. I haven't rushed him at all. But, in fairness to me, we're not getting any closer to Rosenzweig, and if we don't steer our discussions to the relevant issues before the partners start bellowing about the time I'm spending on nonbillable hours, I'll be in hot water."

"It's true, she is a good listener," Ben said. "And she's kept her fidgeting to a minimum. But she's wrong about one thing. We're closing in on Otto. Soon you'll know the whole story."

Liam took a seat at the table, Ben refilled his tea, and Catherine picked up her notes.

"Ben was just at the point where the Gestapo had occupied Zamość and Dr. Frank had visited his home."

"Hans Frank?" Liam said.

"Yes. You know of him?" Catherine said.

"Wasn't he executed for war crimes at Nuremberg?"

Ben raised his eyebrows. "That's correct. His elegant manners belied his unspeakable cruelty. He was a monster. For a time during the early stages of the war, he was the governor general of all of Poland. How do you know about Dr. Frank?"

Liam flashed a sheepish smile. "I've been reading."

Catherine looked surprised. "Really?"

"I figured since I got you involved in all this, I'd better know something. Just in case I'm needed."

"I'm proud of you," Catherine said. "You might be useful after all. Ben was just telling me that Dr. Frank appointed Ben's father to the Judenrat, a committee to administer the town."

"Not exactly, not the whole town," Ben said. "The Judenrat was formed to implement the Gestapo's orders to the Jewish community, not the Christian part of Zamość. So, on the evening of the next day, we gathered in the living room to listen to my father when he returned from his first Judenrat meeting.

"'We've been ordered to take a census of every Jew in Zamość, by age, sex, and occupation,' he said. 'They're going to use that census to choose six hundred workers a day for forced labor. Essentially, we are to be slaves to the Germans. If we leave anyone off the census and they discover the omission . . .' He stopped and cradled his forehead in his hands.

"Mother came over and sat next to him, her arm around his shoulders. My uncle, my aunt, Beka, and Otto all sat speechless.

"Father continued, 'We are also ordered to collect money from Jewish families. They call it a tax to pay for their administration of our town. They have also decreed that they will soon decide which of our houses are needed for German officers and which of our businesses they will own.'

"Aunt Hilda jumped to her feet. 'Just as it was in Vienna. They take everything you own, and then they torture you and shoot you and break your legs.' Mother walked over to comfort Aunt Hilda, and then Beka started crying and Mother didn't know who to help first.

"The census that my father spoke about took several days; there were more than five thousand Jews in Zamość. During that time my father and the other members of the Judenrat were harassed and urged to complete their assignment quickly or face the consequences.

"Each week saw more Gestapo arrive from Berlin. They established quite a bureaucracy in Zamość. Dr. Frank would come and go; his travels took him all over Poland.

"It seemed like every week the Gestapo would institute a new restriction. Our liberties eroded bit by bit. One afternoon my father returned home with a bag of armbands. 'Jews are ordered to wear white armbands with yellow stars. You may not go out without it,' he said. 'They have threatened severe punishment for violation of their rules.'

"A few days later he told us that Jews were banned from using any vehicles, and none of us were allowed to exit the town, except in work details."

"What happened to your car?" Catherine said.

"It was usually parked in front of our house. One day German soldiers came and demanded the keys. And that was especially devastating to my father. He loved his car and kept it polished. It ran like a dream." Ben shrugged. "It was a German car. It broke his heart to hand over the keys.

"The loss of Father's car was another slap of reality. As long as we had a car, we had mobility, a way out, a chance to escape. Now we were trapped."

Ben stopped. He stood, put his palms on the table, leaned forward, and looked directly into Catherine's eyes. "And now, Catherine, we will focus on the metamorphosis of Mr. Otto Piatek." He pointed his finger at her yellow pad. "Get ready to write."

"It is the night after they took our car. We are clearing the dinner table when there is a loud knock on the door. My father opens it to find Ilse and Stanislaw standing there, she in a long tan raincoat and he in the khaki uniform of a minor SS functionary. They don't wait to be invited in; they just brush past my father and demand to see Otto.

"I fetch him from our bedroom. He takes one look at his mother and father and makes a spitting noise.

"'You are not permitted to stay in the house of Jews,' declares Ilse. 'You are a German citizen, here are your papers.' She holds out a folded identity card, but Otto refuses to take it.

"'Otto, take your papers,' she says. Otto shakes his head.

"'Do what your mother says, you ungrateful little snit,' says Stanislaw.

"'Or what?' Otto says belligerently.

"Seeing that Otto won't budge, Ilse softens her demeanor. 'I have help for the Solomons, but you must listen to me.'

"'Can you get us all out of Poland?' Otto says.

"'That I cannot do, not at this time. But I have arranged an appointment for you here in Zamość. You'll be an assistant clerk and work in the offices of the German administration, part of the group that reports directly to Vice-Reichsführer Heydrich's office in Berlin. You are to help administer the Jewish work details for the Zamość region.'

"'Oh, really? Send my people to do slave labor? How gracious of you. No, thanks,' Otto says and he turns to leave.

"Ilse pleads, but Otto shows no interest.

"'Wait a minute, Otto,' Father says. 'Maybe we should talk this over.'

"Otto is surprised, but he's not about to question my father, especially in front of others, so Otto nods and says to Ilse, 'I'm going to talk this over with Uncle Abraham. In private. I'll let you know later what I decide.'

"'*Liebchen*, there's a war going on,' Ilse says. 'Look around the room. These people are declared to be enemies of the Reich. Without your help, they may all be casualties of the war.'

"'Come back tomorrow night and I'll give you my answer after I talk to Uncle Abraham.'

"'I've had enough of this,' Stanislaw says, pushing aside Beka and making his way toward Otto. 'No Jew is going to make decisions about my son. You listen to your mother, you Jew-loving punk.'

"Otto, who is much younger, taller, and stronger than Stanislaw, steps forward and blocks Stanislaw's approach. 'Don't you ever push anyone in my house,' he says. 'Ever. Or I'll break you into little pieces.'

"Ilse turns to her husband and says through clenched teeth, 'Shut up, you fool.' Then, turning back to Otto and squeezing his hands, she pleads, 'Please think about your opportunity here, Otto. You'll be an officer of the Reich in an administrative position. And you'll be able to help your friends. Just think about it. I'll come back tomorrow night.'

"She gives him a kiss on the forehead and walks to the door. Stanislaw follows, and as he reaches the doorway, he turns, gives a Nazi salute, snaps his heels, and barks '*Heil Hitler!*' He laughs and slams the door behind him."

Catherine shook her head. "The Otto you're describing in your story, he's . . ."

"Once we were brothers," said Ben sadly.

Chicago, Illinois, October 2004

"You have information, Carl?"

The private investigator stood meekly before Elliot's desk, shifting from one foot to the other. Brian sat to his left.

"Well, sort of, Mr. Rosenzweig," he said. "Otto Piatek was born in Germany. In Leipzig. I guess that's how he ended up becoming a Nazi officer. I can't find out much about his early life; there's no records on him in Germany. He's not mentioned in the records of the Hitler Youth organization. I've checked the major German cemeteries, especially those where German soldiers are buried. Again, nothing. I also checked the immigration records after the war. No Piatek. That's not surprising, they change their names. But I got an idea."

Elliot raised his eyebrows. He glanced at Brian, who was taking notes.

"I got a contact, Mr. Rosenzweig. He's like a friend of a friend. You know what I mean?"

Elliot shook his head. "What's the point, Carl?"

"Yes, sir. Well, he belongs to the Liberty Crusade. It's a Teutonic group. You know, some people would call them neo-Nazis. They have a lodge and hold meetings out on Mannheim Road. They network with a lot of those kinda groups."

Elliot stood. "You mean, Piatek is a member of this group? You have that information?"

"No. Not yet." Wuld winked. "Some of these guys are, how shall I say, former German citizens. Maybe sons of National Socialists or German soldiers. They have ways of keeping in touch and finding out what happened to their people. My friend's friend, he's always in financial difficulty. I'm thinking he could be a source. You know, for the right price?"

Elliot smiled. "Good work, Carl. Let Brian know how much you need. And get back to us as soon as possible. What about Solomon?"

"I've obtained some additional information, and I'm putting it all together for you. I should have a report by tomorrow."

Wuld left the office and Elliot glanced over at his secretary. "Who's he kidding, Brian? 'Friend of a friend'? Indeed."

"Sounds like he's looking for an extra payday, sir," Brian said. "But I've always been a bit wary of his political inclinations. Shall I discharge him and engage another firm?"

"Hell, no. Let's see what he digs up. Besides, I want to see his report on Solomon."

"May I ask, sir, why are you still concerned about this Piatek fellow? The unpleasant episode at the opera has come and gone. It's all but forgotten by the public. I doubt that anyone ever thought you were a Nazi anyway."

"I'm not so sure. Brian, I was publicly accused of being someone else, and not just someone, but according to Solomon, a murdering Nazi. It doesn't get much worse than that. And I don't know why he would single me out. Maybe Piatek found his way to Chicago and maybe Solomon spotted him somewhere. Maybe he looks like me and Solomon got confused. I know it's a long shot, but if that's the story, I want to find Piatek. You know, Brian, if this guy does exist, if he was a Nazi murderer and he's still around, then he ought to be caught. We'd be doing society a favor. And it would put to rest any suspicions that anyone could have about me."

"Very good, sir. I'll see that Wuld gets the money he needs for his friend of a friend."

"When we get information on this guy, dead or alive, I want to make sure that all the papers and the TV stations understand that I spearheaded this search. That will clear my name. When you give Carl his money, have a talk with him. Make sure he knows that all the information is to come directly to you or me and to no one else."

EIGHTEEN

•••

Chicago, Illinois, October 2004

LIAM AND BEN SAT on wrought-iron stools at Bernini's, leaning their elbows on the stained, cigarette-burned oak, sipping beer, and waiting for Catherine. Located on a tree-lined side street in Chicago's Little Italy, the tiny trattoria had been in operation since the 1920s and was rumored to have been a haunt of the old prohibition gangs. The daily menu was written on a chalkboard over the bar and featured specials like fusilli carbonara, manicotti al forno, and steak Vesuvio.

"She seemed tense to me today," Ben said.

"Well, to be frank, you've taken a pretty good chunk of her time recently, and she had to meet with her department heads after we left. I'm sure her time records will be addressed. They're going to want justification for the time she's spending with you."

"She has to understand how it was."

Liam lifted his frosted mug. "Does she really? In such detail? In order for her to evaluate your case or to be an effective advocate, does she need to know any more than the strength of your evidence? Does she really need to have all the historical background?"

"It's about passion, Liam. For a lawyer to take on a case like mine against a monster like Piatek, she has to have no reservations. She has to attack like a bulldog, with a fire that burns from within, not because it's another piece of legal inventory or a case assigned to her by a department chairman."

"Maybe you're not giving her enough credit. She's very dedicated."

"Oh, of that I have no doubt. But to take on Rosenzweig and all his wealth, and prevail in a lawsuit that accuses him of participation in Nazi atrocities, will take more courage, more heart, more dogged determination than this young woman has ever had to muster. That's why she must know the whole story, piece by piece, day by day. She has to have a true feeling for what happened. And that's also the reason that she can't farm it out to some clinic or some inexperienced lawyer."

"And what if Rosenzweig isn't Piatek after all? Have you considered that possibility? What if Piatek ended up dead in the war? Or exists somewhere as a retired plumber? You've got to have proof of the connection. That's what she's looking for."

"Rosenzweig *is* Piatek. And I will have the proof. I just need Catherine to believe in me and be strong."

"Don't sell her short, Ben. She's a good person and a great lawyer. You can believe in her, even if she doesn't believe in herself. Sometimes she's her own worst enemy."

Ben turned to Liam. "I've come to notice that. How well do you know her?"

"About as well as two friends can know each other."

"Who is she, Liam? Tell me about her. After all, I'm entrusting quite a lot to her."

Liam pondered the request. "I guess you're entitled," he finally said. "Cat was two years behind me in high school. Prettiest thing you ever saw. A buddy of mine was dating her and that's how we met. She was part of our social group. After a while we came to be very close friends. I became her confidant. She'd call me at night and talk to me like a girlfriend."

Liam stared at the condensation on his beer mug. "I always had a crush on her, but you know how it is, they never date their best friends. So even after she broke up with my buddy, I stood on the sidelines as she passed through her high school ups and down—the boyfriends, the true loves, the breakups.

"After graduation, she attended UCLA and I went downstate to Illinois on a football scholarship."

"Football?"

Liam nodded. "I played tight end. Started every game until I blew out my knee in the last game of my senior year. I had aspirations of playing on Sunday, but a Wisconsin strong-side linebacker ended those dreams. Anyway, even though we were thousands of miles apart, Catherine and I stayed connected. We'd get together on the breaks and the vacations. Just best friends hanging out.

"After she got her undergraduate degree, she enrolled at Northwestern Law School and moved back to Chicago. Every so often we'd link up for dinner or a movie. We'd still have our 'girl talk.' 'Who are you seeing,' she'd ask me. 'Is it serious?' It never was. I'd tell her I was still waiting for the right one to come along."

Ben smiled. "So how come you didn't tell Catherine she was the right one?"

"Hey, wait a minute. We're talking about *Catherine's* life story, not mine. Don't twist this around, you sneaky old coot."

"Well, I'm just thinking, maybe they're connected."

"Yeah, well, quit thinking."

Liam finished his beer and ordered another. "Cat was a great law student and finished near the top of her class. She had offers from all the top firms. She ended up taking a job at Drexel Youngquist and was soon on her way up the ladder. She was a rising star.

"It was in her seventh year, she had just made partner at Drexel, when she met Peter Goodrich. He was a trader at the Mercantile Exchange in the high-flying 1990s. Good-looking and glamorous. Fancy car, fancy clothes. Mister Rush Street."

Liam shook his head. "I never liked the guy. I knew he was wrong for her. I told her, too. 'You're just like my mother,' she said one day, giving me a kiss on the cheek. 'Always trying to protect me. But I'm a big girl, so don't worry.'

"She fell head over heels for this glamour boy, and within six months they'd moved into a condo off Michigan Avenue. A year later they were husband and wife. He was big time at the Merc, pulling down seven figures, spending money like a rock star. It was a train wreck in the making, but she couldn't see it. God bless her heart, she gave herself completely to the bastard. She believed all his bullshit.

"The sky fell three years ago. The feds showed up one night with a warrant and a forfeiture notice. The government froze all their property, including their joint bank accounts and their condominium. Goodrich was arrested two days later in the home of a girlfriend, one of several, it turned out."

"What'd he do?" Ben said.

"Fraud. Theft. Ponzi scheme. He ran a fund and used the trust assets to fund his commodities trading. He was way over the edge in corn futures, and when the market dipped he couldn't make the margin call. It was a big swing, millions of dollars. He borrowed what he could from everyone they knew, and what he couldn't borrow, he swindled with more phony securities. He'd even talked Cat's mother into loaning him her retirement fund. Cat never knew any of this was going on.

"When the shit hit the fan, she was devastated and went into a tailspin. She couldn't concentrate or handle her caseload. She quit her position at Drexel so she could cash in her profit sharing and give it to her mother. The disillusionment knocked her for a loop. She couldn't deal with the betrayal or the shame. Even though they didn't blame her, she couldn't face her friends. Deep depression set in. A total breakdown."

Liam paused for a moment, sifting through his memories. "When I think of all the people affected by her breakdown, it was Mickey Shanahan who took the biggest hit. She has never forgiven herself for what she did to Mickey. He was her supervisor and mentor at Drexel. Probably the best trial lawyer in the state. A legend in Chicago. Cat was his prized associate. He took her under his wing and taught her how to practice law—the stuff they don't teach you in law school. And she worshipped him. When she fell apart, Mickey tried to cover for her. He handled her overdue assignments, he appeared in court on her cases, and he supported her in the stormy partner meetings.

"But in the end, Mickey was left picking up the pieces. There were angry clients and the firm lost a lot of business. Not to mention the malpractice claims. Mickey ended up taking the blame and caught a six-month suspension from the disciplinary commission for a case that Cat blew.

"To make matters worse, Mickey was going through a bad time himself. He had lost his wife tragically a few months earlier, a loss from which Mickey has never recovered. Cat felt terrible that she wasn't there for Mickey, but then, Cat wasn't even there for herself.

"She had a sister in Iowa City who finally came in, bundled her up, and brought her out to Iowa to rehabilitate. Weeks later, she recovered enough to take a job waitressing in the evenings and babysitting her nieces during the day. Seems like a big comedown, but it was all she could handle. It was almost a year and a half before she could regain her balance enough to come back to the city.

"I was doing work at the time for Jenkins & Fairchild, and I asked Walter Jenkins if he'd talk to her. I told him all about her problems, but I also told him that she was the best lawyer I knew. Of course, when he interviewed her, he liked her and hired her on the spot. She's been in their litigation section for a little over a year and a half. And that's her story. She's still back on her heels a little bit, but she'll come around."

Liam took the last swallows of his beer and set the empty mug on the bar. "I've loved her forever, and I'd kill anyone who'd hurt her, including Goodrich, if he ever gets out of the federal pen."

"Is she happy working at Jenkins & Fairchild, because I don't get the feeling she is."

"No, in truth, she's not. When she and Mickey were working together, they were doing some terrific public-interest work. Stuff to be proud of. J&F is an institutional firm representing large corporate interests. Very unsatisfying for Cat."

"So, why does she stay there?"

"Do you know what the job market's like? She's got a job. She gets up every day, puts her shoes on, and goes to work. She's well paid, enjoys the esteem of her colleagues, and has enough work to keep her conscience from reminding her how empty her soul is. But that's a story for another day."

"Okay," said Ben. "It clears up a lot of questions."

"Do me a favor, Ben. Let's just have an evening of pleasant conversation, no talk about Poland or Otto or Rosenzweig. Okay?"

"Deal."

"Hey, there, can I get some good-looking guy to buy me a drink?" said Catherine, breezing up to the bar.

"You must be talking about *me*," Liam said. "White wine?"

"That'll be fine. Hello, Ben."

Ben offered his stool. "Hi, Catherine."

They lingered at the bar for a bit. Catherine related a story from the staff meeting about a judge who threw a stack of motion papers at a young first-year associate earlier that afternoon. She took a sip of wine and laughed. "It's a rite of initiation. We all went through it."

Soon they were escorted to a small table covered with a red-and-white checkered tablecloth. In the center was a wax-covered Chianti jug with a glowing red candle. Catherine folded her coat, set it on the empty chair, reached down into her briefcase, and pulled out a notepad. "Can we do a little business? Would you mind? This afternoon you told me about Ilse and Stanislaw's visit. Did they come back the next night?"

"I'm under orders," Ben said. "Only small talk. Pleasant conversation."

"Don't baby me, Liam," Catherine snipped. "If I didn't want to bring up the subject, I wouldn't have asked. If you don't mind the questions, Ben, I'd like to use the time because I have a busy office schedule this week."

"You caught shit in the meeting, didn't you?" Liam said.

She tilted her head from side to side. "I defended what I'm doing with Ben. I told them I need to see this through, but I promised to watch my hours. So could we do a little right now?"

Ben looked at Liam, who shrugged back at him. He took a sip of his water and resumed his narrative.

"After Ilse and Stanislaw left the house, everyone caucused in the living room—my father, my mother, Uncle Joseph, Aunt Hilda, Otto, and me. Beka was there too, she had just turned seventeen." His voice caught in his throat. He paused and lowered his head. It was clear to Liam and Catherine that some powerful memory had suddenly entered his mind and bowled him over. His words came out in short phrases. "Just had her birthday. My mother baked a big cake. Whipped-cream-filled. It was her favorite. With a big seventeen on the top. In pink. Beka was so beautiful, so full of life, so good and honest. So innocent." His eyes reddened and he suddenly stood up. "It was my fault," he said to Catherine. "Damn it. It was all my fault. I'm so sorry, Beka." He turned and rushed toward the door.

Watching him dash outside, Liam shot an astonished look at Catherine. "Jesus. I wonder what that was all about. Maybe we should give him a break."

"Maybe both of us need a break," she answered.

"I'm sorry, Cat, I didn't know he'd go on so long. He says you have to know the details. He wants you to have an emotional investment. I'm not sure what I can do."

She shook her head. "It's okay. I'm just getting frustrated." Then she leaned over and said quietly, "Can I tell you something. You'll think I'm nuts."

Liam smiled and leaned forward. "I already think you're nuts."

"Sometimes when Ben's telling his story, he spaces out. His eyes gloss over and he goes into a zone. It's like he's gone into another dimension or something."

"Cat. He just has powerful memories."

"No. It's more. Really. There is something surreal about it. He'll be describing a scene and it's like he's actually looking at it, not just remembering it. He speaks in the present tense." She paused and tightened her lips. "Don't give me that skeptical look, Liam. I'm a little creeped out by this. You know how he always talks to Hannah? Well, I think he sees her. I think he's really talking to her."

"You're right."

"What?"

"I think you're nuts." He smiled.

Catherine smiled. "Maybe you're right."

"Is he eventually going to tell you that his best friend becomes a Nazi, betrays his family and community, and ends up with the family's fortune? Is that what you expect?"

"Without question. I know that's where he's going, but it's more than that. It's deeper. Piatek did something. Something terrible. I don't know what it is, but I'm going to find out."

Ben returned to the table. "I'm sorry. Please forgive me. I'll be all right now."

"Let's just have our dinner, Ben, and we'll talk tomorrow."

He nodded. Food was brought to the table and the conversation remained light.

During coffee, Ben said suddenly, "If you wouldn't mind, would you please take out your notepad, Catherine. There are a few things I wanted to tell you while I'm still thinking of them."

She looked at Liam and back to Ben. "Are you sure?"

"I want to file my lawsuit. I want to get on with this just as much as you do."

Catherine pulled out her notepad.

"After Ilse left, we gathered in the living room, all of us, and Otto kept shaking his head. 'I'm not going to become a Nazi,' he said. 'I'm not my mother's good little German soldier and I won't select people to be slaves for the Nazis. I'm standing with you; I'll wear the armband. Whatever they have in store for you, it goes for me too.'

"Aunt Hilda praised him. She said, 'You're a good boy, Otto. Don't get into bed with those animals.'

"My father, however, surprised us all when he urged Otto to reconsider.

"'Let's not dismiss this so quickly. You're not a Jew, you don't have so-called Jewish blood, and you haven't been branded. You don't have to wear an armband, and you're not subject to restrictions on where you can go and what you can do. There may come a time when we need someone who can move about freely.'

"The room was quiet. We all deferred to Father's wisdom. 'You can't live in a Jewish household anymore,' he said. 'They've made that clear. And I fear things will get worse before they get better. I think you should accept your mother's proposal, take the appointment, and move out. You can help us all by being on the inside.'

"'Where would I go?' Otto said. 'This is my home.' He was on the verge of tears.

"Father put his hands on Otto's shoulders. 'I don't know. They'll find a place for you. They're confiscating buildings and houses all over town.'

"'How can I do that? How can I displace a Zamość family?'

"'Someone is going to take that appointment, Otto. If you turn it down, they'll appoint someone else. I'd rather have you choosing a work detail than some sadist from Germany. You can do us a lot of good on the inside. Take the appointment, and do what you can to help our people until the war is over. Sooner or later, England and France will come to our aid.'

"So that's how we left it, Catherine. Otto agreed to take the posting and he informed Ilse the next night. Until they found a home for him, they moved him into the Maria Hotel, just off the square. He had an office in the town hall."

NINETEEN

. . .

A CHILLY RAIN BEAT AGAINST the conference room window and fog obscured the view of the federal plaza. Ben's umbrella lay open in the corner. His dripping jacket hung from the coat rack, and he sat hunched forward sipping hot tea to take away the goose bumps as he commenced another day's narrative.

Zamość, Poland, 1940

"After Otto moved out, it became kind of tricky for us to meet," he said. "I couldn't visit him at his office or at the Maria—no Jews were allowed in the hotel. If you ended up at the town hall, more than likely it was because you were taken there in the custody of the Gestapo. Otto and I arranged to meet regularly at Belwederski Park, around the corner from our house, and sometimes he'd bring us food."

"Food?" said Catherine.

"Jews were issued ration cards stamped with a J, and over the months the rationing became severe. We were denied access to many of the shops. One by one, signs were posted in the shop windows telling us that they wouldn't sell to Jews. Otto helped us out from time to time.

"Not long after the occupation, the Nazis imposed a curfew

requiring us to be off the streets by 8:00 P.M., so Otto and I arranged to meet twice a week, early in the morning. It was essential to keep our meeting place near the house. Not only did they take our cars, but they restricted our use of the bus. It was Hitler's plan to compress the Jewish communities into small areas and cut them off from the rest of the population. We had no right to use the public telephones, and soon we lost our home phone as well. Little by little we lost all communication with the outside world.

"After they took his car, my father had to figure out how to visit Grandpa Yaakov on Sundays. The only bus he was allowed to take would drop him at the end of the line, at the very outskirts of Zamość, and he walked an additional six kilometers to the farm. The curfew restrictions made it impossible for him to visit and return the same day."

Ben took a deep breath, leaned back in his chair, and once again appeared to lapse into a zone. He nodded to the voices in his head and stared at the light fixture.

"It's now a bright, clear morning and Otto meets Beka and me at the park. I can tell that he's upset. 'There'll be an order in two days,' he says. 'They're making plans to confiscate all your valuables. Every Jewish family will be ordered to turn over its money, jewelry, valuables, and radios at the town hall. They're going to send everything on to Berlin.'

"'This will devastate Mother,' Beka says. 'What can we do?'

"'I have a plan,' he says. 'It's common knowledge among the German staff that I'm dating Elzbieta, so no one will think twice if I drive off into the country with my girlfriend. Tell Uncle Abraham to gather some of your most precious things, like jewelry and gold, like Aunt Leah's diamond bracelet, and give them to me. I'll take them out to Grandpa Yaakov's and hide them. Select only the very most valuable, because if you don't turn in enough property at the town hall, they'll know you're cheating and they'll tear your place apart.'

"'Do you want me to go with you?' I say. 'I'll help you hide the stuff.'

"Otto shakes his head. 'If they found us together with a bag of jewelry, they'd shoot us both. Don't worry, I'll take care of it. I'll put everything in the treasure chest.'"

"Treasure chest?" Catherine said.

Ben nodded. "An old wooden box we kept buried in a hole in the corner of Grandpa Yaakov's barn. Years before, when we were young, Otto and I hid our secret stuff in the box and buried it in the last horse stall, beneath the floorboards. I know what he's talking about.

"So I arrange to meet him that evening before the eight o'clock curfew. Beka and I carry two pillowcases of valuables to the park and hide them in the bushes. And it's a good thing we do, because two German SS guards walk by and yell at us to get off the streets. We duck into an alleyway and when we see Otto's car we run out and give him the pillowcases."

Catherine perked up. "Exactly what was in the pillowcases?" She wrote "List of Stolen Property" on her notepad.

"My mother's jewelry, my great-grandmother's tea service, my father's silver menorah, and sixty thousand złotys—it was equivalent to about fifteen thousand U.S. dollars in 1940. I don't know how much that would be today—a pretty handsome sum, I expect. It was practically all the cash my father had."

"I need you to be specific," Catherine said. "Everything you can remember putting into those pillowcases, described in as much detail as you can recall. We'll need to have an expert give an estimated appraisal."

"My mother had a diamond brooch; it was surrounded by silver filigree. She had drop earrings with diamonds, a strand of cultured pearls, a beautiful cameo on a gold chain, and . . . I'll try to remember the rest. I'll work on it at home."

Ben took a sip of tea and continued. "Before he pulls away, Otto says, 'Tell Hannah to get her parents' valuables and give them to you. Meet me here tomorrow night and I'll hide their stuff, too.'

"Beka and I visit the Weissbaums the next morning and tell them about Otto's plan. They haven't heard about the confiscation order and they're skeptical, but they trust my father, and if he thinks it's a good idea, they'll go along with it. They pack a pillowcase with jewelry and money and give it to us."

"Do you know what was in the Weissbaums' pillowcase?" Catherine said.

"I know Mrs. Weissbaum put her wedding and engagement rings in there. Hannah may have told me about other things, but I can't remember right now."

"I want you to search your memory. Especially for the property that belonged to your family."

"I'll ask Hannah. She'll help me to remember."

Catherine winced at the response and then asked, "Do you think that Otto ever took the property to Grandpa Yaakov's farm?"

"Oh, I know he did. I saw it there some time later."

"Did the Nazis order everyone to turn in their valuables as Otto had predicted?"

Ben nodded slowly. "Not everyone, just the Jews." He settled back into his unfocused gaze. "The very next day sound trucks drive through our neighborhood screaming at us and ordering us to report immediately to the town hall with our valuables.

"We stand in line for hours, waiting to hand our property over to German soldiers sitting behind long tables. It's just as Uncle Joseph had described. The same as it was in Vienna. Guards walk up and down the lines, shouting insults, slapping at people with nightsticks or jabbing them with their rifles. My father, as a respected member of the Judenrat, is afforded a modicum of dignity: he isn't called a dog or a swine—that's a favorite word for them, *Saujude*, Jewish swine.

"Dr. Frank is there overseeing the whole process. He walks back and forth behind the tables, slapping a horse crop against his pantaloon. When it's our turn, he comes over to the table. 'May I see the Solomon property, please,' he says. I am frightened. I'm sure he'll remember everything he saw in our house and he'll know we've withheld valuables. He'll say, 'Where's that antique tea service?' I think about what I'll do if my family is attacked. How will I act? Will I be brave? I'm worried for my mother and Beka.

"Dr. Frank sifts through our belongings, moves them around on the table to examine them, and purses his lips, just as he did in our home. Then he looks at Beka, smiles, and says, 'Rebecca, seventeen,' and walks on.

"Mother, like many other Zamość women, leaves the town hall weeping, asking what right the Germans have to take her belongings. They are her special treasures. They're not weapons, we're not combatants, and there is no threatened insurrection. The Germans say that we are paying for the war effort.

"'They're twentieth-century Huns,' Father says, 'pillaging and raping our village. And like the Huns, they'll be defeated.' He tries to comfort Mother by saying that England and France will make them give back our property when Germany is overthrown, but we've heard the news reports: no armies have been sent to help us and there is nothing going on but a war of words. England's prime minister, Chamberlain, is pounding his fist in Parliament. The French premier, Daladier, is laying down ultimatums about 'real peace,' and Hitler is assuring the world that he has no interest in the West. I think historians now agree that the Allies missed a golden opportunity in not attacking immediately.

"In any event, on the way home from the town hall, I hear a girl's voice call out, 'Hey, Fred Astaire.' I turn around to see Elzbieta coming up to meet us, cute as a button with her bouncy gait. We walk together for a while but not for too long, because it isn't a good idea for Elzbieta to be seen in the company of Jews. I ask her about Otto and how they're doing.

"'I guess it's all right,' she says, 'but things aren't the same. He's a little full of himself these days, hanging around with the snooty Germans, dining in restaurants, drinking fine wines, always in a smartly pressed uniform. I liked the old days when the four of us went to the movies.'

"I agree with her."

"Wasn't Otto helping you out?" Catherine said. "Didn't he just hide your property?"

"That's true, but I knew he was starting to enjoy his privileged status. Elzbieta also warned me that he had been appointed to Dr. Frank's staff, but I already knew that. He'd sent me on an assignment."

"Really? When?"

"It was in early 1940. Otto and Hans Frank stood side by side in the square along with a businessman from Düsseldorf who wore a long wool coat with a fur collar. They selected four of us to travel with them to inspect and survey some property west of Krakow.

"We sat on benches in the back of a truck and followed Dr. Frank's car to where the Vistula and Sola rivers joined. The property was swampy farmland just outside of Oświęcim near the railroad tracks. We were ordered to make notes about the terrain, especially the part that was wooded."

"Oświęcim? Was this to be the Auschwitz concentration camp?"

"It was, although we weren't told anything about the reasons for our trip. Frank and the other guy, I think his name was Glucks, walked off and wouldn't speak in our presence.

"Anyway, right after we leave Elzbieta and turn the corner onto Belwederski Street, we see Hannah running toward us. She's hysterical.

"'Ben, we have to find Otto. They've taken my mother!'

"'Who took her?'

"'The Gestapo. Dr. Frank. He looked at our property when we set it on the table. "You must have forgotten your wedding band and your engagement ring," he said to my mother with a wicked smile. Then he grabbed my mother's hand, slammed it on the table, and looked at her ring finger. Of course, there was a mark where the rings had been. Mother was flustered. She said she'd lost them. "Oh, I'm sure you did," said Dr. Frank, ever so politely. "But don't worry, we'll help you find them." Then he ordered two guards to take us home to find the rings. We couldn't give them the rings because we'd already given them to Otto. The soldiers tore up our house.'

"'Where is your father?' I ask her. 'Where did they take your mother?'

"It's hard for Hannah to answer. She's crying convulsively. 'After they finished searching, they knocked my dad to the floor and took my mother away. She was screaming, Ben. I don't know where she is. Help me, Ben. We have to find Otto.'

"We run all the way back to the town hall, but there are still lines of people standing with their suitcases. There's no way to get into the building. We aren't allowed to enter the Maria Hotel, and we doubt Otto would be there anyway. We decide to find Elzbieta and ask her to help us. She lives in an apartment building near the center of town. Since there are no Jews allowed in the building, we enter through the rear door and go up the back stairs. Elzbieta isn't home.

"We can't wait in front of the building, we'd be arrested for loitering, so we walk around and around the block, hoping that no one notices us. Finally, in the early evening, we see Elzbieta walking down the street with a grocery bag. As soon as she sees us she knows something is wrong.

"'We need to find Otto right away,' I say after filling her in about Miriam Weissbaum. 'Can you tell him to meet us at the park tonight?'

"'Curfew's in twenty minutes. I don't know if I can find him that fast.'

"'Don't worry about the curfew. I'll be in the alleyway across from the park. No matter what time it is, I'll be there. Find him for us, Elzie.' Hannah leaves to care for her father, and I make my way to the park.

"I hide behind the garbage cans until later that night when I see Otto drive up and stop his car. I dash out and slide into the passenger's seat. 'You've got to go to Grandpa Yaakov's and get her rings. Dr. Weissbaum will say he found them in the house.'

"Otto shakes his head. 'That won't work. Dr. Frank will know he's lying—that the rings were never lost. He'll take the rings and then he'll imprison the Weissbaums.'

"'What can we do? We have to rescue her.'

"Again Otto shakes his head. 'There's nothing I can do.'

"'I don't believe what I'm hearing! This is Hannah's mother! You're a big shot. You can go anywhere you want. You can release her.'

"Otto won't look at me. He stares straight ahead, through the windshield onto the darkened street. He is dressed in his spotless Nazi uniform and his cap with its gold braiding. 'And what would

I say to Dr. Frank? How do you propose I persuade him to release a Jew, especially one that he's arrested for dishonesty?'

"'You have to try. You have to find a reason.'

"'No. If she's still alive, I'll try to get her assigned to a work detail. Maybe afterward she can return home.' He turns his head to me. 'It's always dangerous to lie to these people, Ben. They're very sharp.'

"'What are you talking about?' I shout. 'You're the one who told us to hide our most valuable possessions. It was *you* that suggested it.'

"'I didn't tell her to hide her wedding rings; that was stupid.'

"That's all I can take. I bolt from the car. It's well after curfew, but I don't care. I slam the door and walk all the way home in plain sight. As I approach the house, I see Hannah and her father waiting in the window. Hannah bursts out the door, jumps down the steps, and grabs me by the shoulders. 'What did Otto say?'

"'I don't know if Otto will help us. He doesn't know where she is, and he's afraid to confront Dr. Frank.'

"'Why? Why is he afraid? He's one of them.'

"I nod. 'That's why.'

"'What can we do? We have to help my mother.'

"'Otto said he'd look into where they took her, try to get her on a work detail and bring her home.'

"We wait for two days without any word. My father tries to locate her through the Judenrat, asking for a conference with Dr. Frank or any of his officers, but he doesn't get anywhere. Hannah's father reaches out to his former patients, many of whom are not Jewish and have greater mobility, but he is equally unsuccessful. Hannah stays with us. We try to comfort her and give her hope.

"Finally, we receive a message to meet Otto at the park. Hannah, Beka, and I meet him early the next morning.

"'I'm afraid I've had no luck,' Otto says. 'Dr. Frank has returned to Berlin, and no one seems to know what happened to Mrs. Weissbaum. You understand, I can't appear to be too concerned or they'll suspect me of befriending Jews.'

"'Won't you please contact Dr. Frank in Berlin?' Hannah begs. 'Can't you tell him that you need to talk to my mother about something important—that she has vital secret information or something?'

"'Are you serious? Dr. Frank is the governor general of all of Poland. Are you suggesting that I contact him in Berlin and bother him about some Jewish woman he arrested for concealing valuable property belonging to the Reich? And what kind of vital information, Hannah? What sense does that make? Why, right now Dr. Frank could be meeting with the führer. What would they think of me?'

"'Otto, who cares what the Nazis think? We're talking about Hannah's mother,' I say. 'Have you forgotten who you are?'

"'I can't risk it, Ben. I've done what I could. She's not in Zamość.'

"'Where could she be?' cries Hannah.

"Otto just shakes his head. 'I've got to go. I'll keep my eyes open. If I find out anything I'll contact you.'"

"Was Mrs. Weissbaum ever found, Ben?" Catherine said.

"Nope. Never found." He took a sip of tea.

"From then on we saw less and less of Otto. He was becoming quite the partygoer. We'd hear reports of him boozed up with other young Nazis, sometimes with his arm wrapped around some blond groupie. Ilse made sure he was promoted up the ladder and got all the benefits."

"What about your early-morning meetings at the park?" Catherine said. "Did he stop meeting with you?"

"He joked that it was hard for him to get up so early, that it was important for his career to socialize with the other officers late into the evening, and he had to sleep off his hangovers and clear his head for the next evening's revelries. Even so, every now and again he'd meet us at the park and give us a bag of food. 'How's everybody holding up?' he'd say.

"'We're making it,' we'd tell him, but to be truthful, the situation was deteriorating badly throughout the summer and fall of 1940. There were no jobs, no money, restrictions on every movement, and constant German brutality in the streets.

"In June, the Judenrat was ordered to conduct a public registration of all males between the ages of fourteen and sixty for special work details. The registration took place in the town square, and as usual, Otto and his superiors were there to supervise. There were over two thousand men selected, and we were marched to the town of Janowice, several miles away. Upon arrival, five hundred were chosen and sent directly to Wysokie, ten miles farther. Those five hundred men and boys were never seen again. The rest of us were sent back to town.

"Almost daily, Otto requisitioned workers through the Judenrat to be sent to labor camps the Germans were building, some near Lublin, some to the east. Most of the time, the workers returned in the evening. Sometimes they didn't. Everyone feared assignment to labor details, but if you didn't show up, the Nazis would take two, sometimes three members of your family and send them in your place or publicly execute them."

"Were you or your father assigned to these details?"

"Because he was on the Judenrat, Father was spared from the work details and remained in the town. Otto avoided sending me on assignments to distant labor camps, but there came a time in late summer when he met me in the park and told me that I would have to go. Some of his Nazi cohorts were pressuring him.

"'There's talk about my favoring the Solomons,' he said. 'In order to maintain credibility and protect the rest of the family, I've got to send you out.'

"'I understand,' I said.

"'The detail is temporary and scheduled to return to Zamość in a couple of weeks. You'll be chosen tomorrow.'

"The next morning I was sent with a hundred and fifty men to a construction site near Janowice, in a clearing on the edge of the forest. Long wooden buildings that resembled horse stables had recently been built, and we were housed forty to a building. We slept on the floor. They didn't even provide hay. Our daily rations were a piece of meat, a loaf of bread, a cup of tasteless water soup, and a cup of something brown they called coffee. The Judenrat tried to send shipments of food to the work details, but their requests were repeatedly denied."

"What work were you sent to do?" Catherine said.

"We built stables and riding paths for the SS. We cleared trails through the forest. We constructed fences and outdoor corrals. We worked on jumping and show rings. All those structures essential to the German war effort.

"We had been there about two weeks when we were rousted out of our sleep in the middle of the night and told to line up in the field. The SS commandant, a brutal man named Dolf, walked up and down the line, pulling men out to send to work at Belzec."

"Belzec, the camp?" Catherine said.

"It was to become one of the most ghastly of the death camps. Located in the forest between Zamość and Lublin, along the railroad line, Belzec's sole purpose was extermination. It was not intended to be a prison camp, so there were very few barracks constructed to house inmates. There was housing for the SS officers and there was housing for the kapos."

"Kapos. They were guards, right?"

Ben nodded. "They were prisoners—some Ukrainian, some Polish, even some Jewish—often brutal men, who were used by the Nazis to police the other prisoners, process the murders, and clean out the gas chambers."

Catherine shivered.

"Belzec wasn't operational until 1942, but workers were conscripted to clear the area and construct the site. The night we were rousted out of bed—it must have been three in the morning—Dolf took fifty men. They were loaded onto trucks and immediately driven out. The rest of us returned to our huts and slept. Our work detail lasted three weeks and we were marched back to Zamość. Eighty-two of us returned. The fifty taken by Dolf were never seen again. Eighteen never left Janowice. They died there or were kept by the SS to work the stables.

"I returned to my home, filthy from the work and weak from malnutrition. I hadn't had a bath since I left. Or a decent meal. My mother declared a holiday and broke out a bottle of wine she'd hidden in the back of the cupboard. There were tears and hugs from my family. It was so good to see Hannah again. And Beka.

"Grandpa Yaakov was there, too. While I was gone, he was

ordered to leave his farm, as were other Jewish farmers, and move into the city. My father had found a Catholic family to live at the farm with the understanding that Grandpa Yaakov would return once the war was over, but Grandpa Yaakov was distraught and couldn't come to terms with leaving his farm.

"'I'm not hurting anybody,' he said to me. 'Why do they care if I live on my farm? I already give them most of the milk and cheese, and they take all the grain.' I, of course, had no answer.

"Having been freed from the ordeal in Janowice, I was glad to return to the warmth of my home and Mother's good cooking, although the addition of Grandpa Yaakov to our already crowded home presented quite a dilemma for my mother. Grandpa was not just another mouth to feed when we were short of food, or a sleeping area to provide when we were short of beds, but we were running out of breathing room. People need privacy and dignity. These days we'd say they need their space. Overcrowding, even in a spacious home, breeds irritability, and that ran double where Grandpa Yaakov was concerned. He was not a city dweller; he'd lived on a farm all his life with his dogs and his cats and his horses. They were his family.

"Nevertheless, we tried to stay upbeat. We told ourselves that the conditions were temporary, that good would always triumph over evil, that God wouldn't let this madness go on much longer. We continued to wait for the Allies, listening to the rumors. Soon, we said, Poland will be liberated, the invaders will be repulsed, and prewar life will be restored.

"But truthfully, our hopes were dwindling. Hitler had already rolled into Paris, and he had conquered Denmark, Holland, and Belgium. Come autumn, we started to talk seriously about escape.

"'I want you to find Otto,' Father said one night. 'Arrange a meeting here at the house.'

"'I don't think he'll come,' I said.

"'Tell him that I am insisting upon it, Ben. He'll respect my wishes.'

"I met Otto in the park early the next morning. He handed me a bag of groceries and part of last night's dinner.

"'Father wants you to come to the house and meet with him,' I said.

"'It's too great a risk—someone might report me. They already accuse me of playing favorites, of being soft on the Jews. Tell him to meet me in the park.'

"'I think he wants you to meet with the whole family. He said you wouldn't refuse him if he asked you.'

"Otto took a deep breath. 'Very well. There's a rally Wednesday evening, and I'm sure everyone will go to the nightclubs afterward. I'll duck out and stop by the house. I can be there about ten.'

"We gathered all the members of the family and also Hannah and her father. Otto didn't arrive until eleven and he was nervous when he came in. His black leather coat was pulled up at the collar, covering most of his face. What a difference there was in his expression once he walked into the house. Gone was the smirk of the arrogant Nazi. It was like he felt he didn't belong anymore, but this was his family, all eight of us, and he hung his head.

"'We need to talk about getting the family out of Poland,' Father said.

"Otto shook his head. 'It's impossible. First of all, you can't ride the trains or the buses. They'll check your papers. Second, I can't get you a car, and even if I could, there are roadblocks at the entrance to every town. If you don't have the right papers, they'll arrest you or worse. Third, where would you go? Russia? Austria? Germany? There are no friendly neighbors. It would only end up getting you and me killed.'

"'What about getting us forged papers? We'll take our chances on the train, make our way to Turkey. Ziggy's in New York now and he'll sponsor us.'

"Otto pondered the request. 'I'll do what I can. I'll see if it's possible to doctor travel papers. It might take a while. But I better go now. The crowd will be looking for me.' He put his black billed cap on his blond hair and pulled his collar up. 'I'll get back to you.'

"Since my father had decided that we were all to leave Poland, we were in a continuous state of readiness. We waited throughout the fall and into the winter for Otto to get our papers and make arrangements for us to leave, but there always seemed to be a snag, some reason for another delay. Travel restrictions were changed, or escape routes were being closed.

"In December, a new commandant was appointed and Otto's duties were changed. He was made an adjutant to the SS commandant and given the rank of Scharführer, which was a staff sergeant. In his new post, he felt like he was under increased scrutiny. So there were more delays.

"Later that winter, in one of their numerous inspections, the Gestapo assembled all the Jews in the town square. Those with permits were dismissed to go to work, those without permits received a painted mark on their foreheads. Many of them were sent to Belzec."

"The concentration camp."

"No. It was a death camp."

"Aren't they the same thing?"

"No. Many people lump them together, but the Nazis had two different types of camps. Concentration camps were essentially prison camps. Some, like Dachau and Mauthausen, existed in Germany and Austria before the war. People were initially sentenced there by courts to serve out their terms, although the conditions were so terrible—malnutrition, disease, brutality, random executions—that most did not survive. While in the concentration camps, prisoners did slave labor for the Reich. During the war, new concentration camps were constructed, like Bergen-Belsen and Theresienstadt.

"Death camps, or extermination camps, like Belzec, Sobibor, and Treblinka, called the Operation Reinhard camps, were built for the sole purpose of killing as many people as quickly as possible. When the Nazis decreed in 1941 that mass murder, not expulsion, was the solution to the Jewish problem, they began to build death camps.

"Concentration camps had large barracks to hold thousands of workers. Death camps were located close to railroad lines and were small—just a short distance and a brief moment in time for a poor soul to be taken from a train platform to a death chamber. The worst death camp of all, Birkenau, or Auschwitz II, was a mixed camp and held about ninety thousand prisoners. Together with Auschwitz I and III, well over one hundred thousand innocents were imprisoned, awaiting their execution at any given time. And those were the lucky ones—they had a chance for survival. Nine hundred thousand were taken directly off the train and whisked immediately into the Auschwitz gas chambers.

"Auschwitz was immense. Over a thousand Polish homes were demolished to make way for the construction of the camp. The redbrick buildings and wooden barracks were surrounded by high-voltage barbed wire and guarded by over eight thousand SS. There was a twenty-six-mile buffer zone encircling the camp to hide it from the outside world. Beginning in 1942, Auschwitz was the principal center for the murder of European Jews."

"How many people were murdered at Auschwitz?"

"No one will ever know for sure. Those sent directly from the unloading platform to the gas chamber weren't registered or numbered. Their remains were incinerated or buried in mass graves. It is estimated that a million and a half people were killed at Auschwitz."

Catherine shivered and reflexively crossed herself.

"As horrible as those statistics are, we now know that the German high command planned to murder millions more all throughout Europe. Records show that Himmler, at a meeting in his Wewelsburg castle in 1941, told his generals that the German master plan for the East called for the slaughter of thirty million Slavs."

"Oh my God."

"There is no way to conceive of the ends of the German genocide had they not been stopped."

Catherine shook her head and sat perfectly still.

"Anyway, getting back to my story: in 1941 in Zamość, those without work permits were sent to Belzec to start building fortifications."

"Did your uncle and grandfather have work permits? Your uncle was disabled."

"Both of them had permits to work in my father's glass factory.

Of course, it no longer belonged to my father. It had been Aryanized, seized by the Germans and handed over to some German businessman, but the plant was being managed by my father's former plant supervisor, so we were able to get permits for Uncle Joseph, who did accounting, and Grandpa Yaakov, who helped in the shipping department.

"One morning in early spring, as Otto handed me a grocery bag in Belwederski Park, he said, 'Ben, bad orders are coming down. The whole community is to be resettled. Tell your father I'll come by at midnight. Tell him to get the family together. Get ready to leave.'

"My father had also heard rumors. 'We were informed today at the Judenrat that several thousand Jews from other regions are being uprooted and sent to Zamość,' he said. 'That may be what Otto is talking about. The Judenrat is to have the responsibility of absorbing these refugees into our community, although where we'll get food and shelter for them, I don't know.'

"Later that evening, with the family all gathered and nervous as hell, Otto came to the house. He pulled a chair to the center of the room. I remember it struck me at the time that he had the look of the quintessential German officer—a handsome, square-jawed, well-groomed man, in his creased Nazi uniform, white silk scarf, and polished boots.

" 'I have heard from Berlin,' he said. 'Reichsführer Himmler has selected Zamość to be the centerpiece of the new German territory, the General Government. He's very fond of our town—in fact, he intends to change the name to Himmlerstadt. It is to be the first resettlement area for German nationals. All the Poles, not just the Jews, will be removed to make way for German settlers. Initially, the plan calls for all the Jews to be rehoused in New Town. Eventually, they'll be moved to resettlement camps.'

"My mother gasped. New Town was the poorest section of Zamość, with dilapidated homes and buildings—a congested, blighted slum. Warehouses and factory buildings, many of them vacant or damaged in the bombing, added to the social disorganization. 'What about our home?' she asked.

"'It will be confiscated for use by others, mostly occupation forces, perhaps SS officers.'

"My mother stamped her foot. 'They can't do that! This is my house!'

"'When is this going to happen?' Father said.

"'Sometime in April.'

"'That's just days away. How do they expect us to move our entire home in such a short period of time?'

"Otto just lowered his eyes and shook his head.

"'Can you get us out of here, Otto?' Father said.

"'I think so. That's why I came. I have volunteered to take a shipment of wine and food south to an SS post in Debica tomorrow. I'll have a covered truck. I can hide three people behind the crates of wine. If I drive again, I can take three more. I'll keep trying to get the assignment and take all of you south to Uncle Joseph's cabin in the mountains. Because it's so remote, there are very few troops in that area. From there, you're on your own.'

"Uncle Joseph protested. 'This is not good. We want travel papers to take the train to Turkey or Greece, or maybe to Spain. The cabin is small and has only the little fireplace. The villages are several kilometers away and we won't have a car. How are we supposed to get food and supplies?'

"'You'll have to fend for yourselves. And you can forget about travel papers,' said Otto, irritated at Uncle Joseph's rejection of his offer. 'The train is out, don't you understand? You wouldn't get as far as Krakow. Right now, all the Polish borders are closed. There are armed soldiers at every border crossing. All trains are required to stop at the borders, and the passengers have to disembark to be examined for their identification. You'd be caught and shot.'

"'I don't like it,' Uncle Joseph said.

"'I don't like it either,' Grandpa Yaakov said. 'I was born here and I'm going to stay here. No Nazis are going to kick me out of my country.'

"'You tell 'em, Papa,' Uncle Joseph said. 'We have our work permits. We'll keep working at the glass factory. Sooner or later the Brits will come and these thugs will get the boot.'

"Otto looked at my father. 'Uncle Abraham, can you make them understand?'

"'Maybe over time they'll change their mind,' he said, 'but they have the right to make decisions about their own lives.'

"Otto shook his head. 'Well, let me take the women tomorrow. I can take Aunt Hilda, Aunt Leah, and one of the girls.'

"Aunt Hilda said, 'Not me. I'm too old and I won't leave Joseph. Take the young ones.'

"Mother agreed. 'Take Beka, Hannah, and Ben. They should be the first ones out. They have their whole lives in front of them.'

"The three of us immediately protested. None of us wanted to leave the family.

"'I'm staying with you,' I said. 'You'll need a strong hand to help you move and survive in New Town. I'm grown now, Father, and I can protect the family.'

"He put his gentle hands on my shoulders and looked into my eyes, and I knew, somewhere deep down, that he was casting me to sea and from then on I was to pilot my own ship. 'That's why you must go with Hannah and Beka. They'll need your strength and your wisdom. I'm needed at the Judenrat and my absence would be noted. If I didn't show up, they'd search for me. I should be the last of the family to leave Zamość.'"

Ben paused his story and swallowed hard. He shut his eyes.

"The girls are sobbing. Dr. Weissbaum holds Hannah in a bear hug, burying her face in his big chest. There are tears in his eyes, as well. 'Abraham and Leah are wise,' he says. 'Let's listen to them. As for me, there are only three doctors in our community and our existence worsens every day. I can't leave our people now. You go with Ben and Rebecca. If something should happen here, at least the three of you will have made it out.'

"'No, please,' Hannah cries. 'I don't want to leave you. Please, Daddy.'

"'It breaks my heart, *ziskeit*, but I know it's for the best. Mother's gone. We have no home anymore. You, my precious one, are all I have left. I've had a wonderful life. You deserve your happiness, a full and rich life. You and Beka and Ben, go and be safe. Go far from this town. I will stay and do what I can with Abraham.'

"She cries. He smooths her hair and wipes her tears.

"'Then it's settled,' says Father. 'Otto, you'll take the three children.'

"Otto stands to leave, positioning his cap on his head. 'I'll come by at daybreak and stop the truck in front of the house. I'll only pause for a moment, so be ready to jump in. Bring whatever you can carry in a bag, there's not much room in the truck.'"

Catherine looked at her watch and set down her pen. "I know you must be tired, Ben, because I'm exhausted. I'm anxious to know what happens next, but we have to stop somewhere. Let's pick this up tomorrow."

"I can't. It's Friday."

"Then let's meet Monday and try hard to finish."

TWENTY

...

Chicago, Illinois, November 2004

I BROUGHT YOU SOMETHING SPECIAL," Ben said, unloading a box of bagels and assorted cream cheeses on the sideboard. "Fresh baked from Meyer's Delicatessen. I took the El out there early this morning. Got 'em right out of the oven. You're going to taste heaven."

"You're wreaking havoc on my diet," Catherine said, lifting dishes from inside the cabinet and setting them next to the cups. She sliced a whole-wheat bagel and poured a cup of coffee.

"Ben, your story is taking its toll on me," she said. "I'm putting in fourteen-hour days trying to catch up with my caseload, and when I finally get home I can't sleep. I lie awake thinking about the death camps and the breakup of these families that I'm getting to know. Being immersed in your saga, it's truly unsettling to me. I'm not naïve, I know the world is full of racial hatred, but coming face-to-face with it in an intimate way, following your family, experiencing their persecution because of their race . . ."

"Nazi persecution didn't limit itself to race. Religion, national origin, alternative lifestyles, persons with disabilities—all were targets. How would you characterize the Slavs? Gypsies? Moors? All the lines get blurred. Even within Judaism, there are many races. There are Negro Jews in Ethiopia and Middle Eastern Jews in Iraq. There have been Jews in Japan since the 1860s. Poland was fractionally Jewish, but there were still three and a half million Jews living there in the 1930s."

"But still, today it all seems so incomprehensible."

Ben raised his eyebrows. "Incomprehensible because we're Americans? Land of the free and home of the brave? Let's not kid ourselves. We've authored our own chapters in the history of shame, periods where the world looked at us and shook its head. Early America built an economy based on slavery and it was firmly supported by law. Read the Supreme Court's decision in *Dred Scott*. We trampled entire cultures of Native Americans. 'No Irish Need Apply' was written on factory gates in nineteenth-century New York."

Ben shook his head. "We'd like to think we're beyond such hatred, but the fact is, we can never let our guard down. That's why this case is so important. To you and to me. It's another reminder of what can happen when evil is allowed to incubate. Find a reason to turn your nose up at a culture, to denigrate a people because they're different, and it's not such a giant leap from ethnic subjugation to ethnic slaughter."

Catherine nodded and picked up her notepad.

Zamość, Poland, 1941

"Beka, Hannah, and I packed our knapsacks in preparation for our escape to the mountains—a few changes of clothes, portions of meat, cheese, and bread—enough to keep us going for a little while after we got to the cabin. Early the next morning, before the sun rose, we waited by the window. We had stayed up through the night saying our goodbyes and assuring one another that we'd all reunite soon.

"We saw a covered truck drive slowly up the street and flash its lights. My father pulled me aside. 'Ben, you know how the situation is. We may not all survive this war.'

"'Don't talk like that. Please. We'll survive. We'll all make it. The girls and I will be waiting for you at Uncle Joseph's.'

"'Ben, if you're safe, if no one bothers you, and if the Germans don't come into the Podhale District, stay in the cabin. Wait out the war. But if you're threatened in any way and you get the chance, take the girls and make a run for it. The Tatras can be crossed in the summer into Slovakia and thence south through the countryside to the sea, although you must be mindful that no place in Eastern Europe is safe. Slovakia is no friend. We hear that the fifty-five thousand Jews in Prague are in as much trouble as we are. Stay clear of the Slovakian cities. Trust no one. Restrict your travel to the country roads. Make your way into eastern Hungary and down to Yugoslavia, to the coastal city of Split. Here is the name of a contact in Split who will help you get to America.' He handed me a folded letter of introduction.

"'Father, don't worry, we'll wait for you.'

"He smiled, gave me a kiss, stuffed some money into my pocket, and bid me goodbye.

"We climbed into the back of the truck, each of us with our small knapsack. With a gaping hole in my heart, I watched the only home I'd ever known fade into the misty daybreak. I can still see my mother with her hand on the windowpane.

"'Stay low behind the boxes and cover yourselves with the tarpaulin until we're out of town,' Otto said as the truck rumbled along the city streets.

"Once we left Zamość and were on our way through the countryside, we sat up to talk. Otto was paranoid, like a drunk driver trying to make it home on New Year's Eve. He gripped the wheel so tightly, his hands were white.

"'You don't know what I'm risking for you,' he said. 'I could lose everything, my position, my rank, even my life, if I'm caught.'"

"To be fair, Ben, wasn't that true?" asked Catherine.

"Would you say something like that to your brother and sister? Your position? Your rank?"

"No, I guess I wouldn't."

"We figured that the trip to the mountains would take about ten hours if we went nonstop. It was Otto's plan to drop us at the cabin and then double back to Debica, two hours away. We stopped only to relieve ourselves by the side of the road.

"We were a few miles outside Łysa Polana, about a half hour's drive from the cabin, and feeling pretty good when we suddenly encountered a roadblock. Two Wehrmacht soldiers walked up to the truck, one on each side. The girls and I huddled in the back under the tarp.

"'Good afternoon, Scharführer,' one of them said. 'Let's see your papers. Where are you headed?'

"'I'm headed to Debica,' Otto said in German, handing his papers through the window. 'I have a delivery for SS Sturmbannführer Kolb.'

"'Debica? You passed the cutoff to Debica a hundred kilometers ago.' There was silence for a moment and then we heard, 'Please step out of the truck.'

"'I was told to take Highway 12,' Otto said, stepping down from the driver's seat onto the gravel shoulder. 'I must have missed the turn in this pig-shit country.'

"'What are you delivering to Debica, Scharführer?'

"We heard Otto chuckle. 'You look like a nice fellow,' he said. 'I'll give you a little taste.' He climbed into the back of the truck, pulled two bottles of Riesling from the crates in front of us, and crawled back out.

"'Don't say where you got this or it'll be my ass,' Otto said.

"The soldiers thanked him profusely and said, 'Turn around and head back about two hours, my friend. Take the cutoff at Highway 23.'

"Otto turned the truck around and drove out of town, sweating buckets. Once around the curve and out of sight, he pulled over next to a stand of trees. He was breathing heavily.

"'Everybody out. You'll have to walk to the cabin. I can't risk going back.' We clambered out of the truck and I walked over to the window to shake his hand. 'I don't know how I'm going to get the rest of them up here, Ben. This is way too dangerous.'

"I thanked him, told him he'd think of something, and watched him drive away. The girls and I quickly got off the road and ducked into the forest. It was almost nightfall and there was a chill in the mountain air. As far as I could figure, the cabin was a two-day walk.

"Although it was April, there were still patches of deep snow in the high country, especially in the thick parts of the forest, and we hadn't prepared for such a hike. The snow caked in through the tops of our shoes, soaked our socks, and froze our feet. Our cuffs were heavy with snow, ice, and water. Nevertheless, we had no choice but to plow ahead, taking care to stay clear of the roads and the German patrols. Unsure of the countryside, we tried to navigate by the stars, stopping as little as possible. We knew if we were discovered, picked up without papers, knapsacks in hand, it'd all be over."

"How far was it to Joseph's cabin?" Catherine said.

"Maybe fifteen miles, but the terrain was wooded and hilly. Uncle Joseph's cabin lay in a valley just outside the village of Łysa Polana, a few kilometers east of Zakopane and just north of the Tatra peaks. The range divided Poland from Slovakia with rugged granite mountains that reached over six thousand feet. Today there are border crossings for the skiers and hikers. The town of Zakopane was then and still is a popular European ski resort."

"Ben, I'm wondering how your father thought your grandfather and uncle could make the passage?"

"It was a plan of last resort. I think all he was trying to do was to get them to the cabin to wait out the war, but in retrospect, I wonder whether he ever really believed they'd leave Zamość.

"Anyway, for the three of us, it was tough going in the dark. We twisted our ankles on the rocks, the brush scraped our legs, and the pine needles were sharp. Each of us stumbled several times and Beka had a bad fall. We made a couple of miles that night and decided to bed down in a small clearing until dawn, using our clothing for makeshift blankets and huddling together to share our body heat. By the morning, we were stiff and cold and ready to move on.

"The trek was easier during the day. We could navigate by the mountain peaks and the sun was warm. We followed trails through the pines until we hit the outskirts of Łysa Polana. From there, we found the old dirt road and reached the cabin by late afternoon.

"The wooden hut with the sharp peaked roof was a welcome sight. Naturally, it was shuttered and locked, but I knew Uncle Joseph kept a key on a shelf in the shed. I retrieved it and opened the creaky door. No one had been inside for a few years. There were cobwebs everywhere, and we could tell that small mountain animals, field mice, marmots, and chipmunks, had been tenants in our absence. The furniture was covered with sheets, but everything had a layer of dust. The girls immediately set to cleaning, while I went to gather wood and water. We boiled the water from the stream and kept a good supply in jugs.

"The cupboards held some canned goods, a jar of coffee beans and a grinder, and a few bags of flour, which we had to discard when we discovered the little mouse holes. We'd carried provisions, a small amount in our backpacks, enough for a few days, but we had no fresh food, and we knew we'd have to go to market sooner or later. There was an old rifle in the cabin, but I was no hunter. I had never hunted an animal in my life. I could fish, and there was a small lake a couple of kilometers through the woods, but we knew we'd have to buy food and that troubled me. Going into town would draw attention to our presence."

"Tell me about the cabin," Catherine said.

Ben smiled. "Euphemistically speaking, it was cozy. But there were good-sized bedrooms at either end of the large central room that served as kitchen, dining room, and sitting room. No bathroom, of course. We used an outhouse next to the shed. There was no plumbing or electricity, but there was an iron stove, vented through the roof, which served as a furnace. Remember, this was a wooden cabin and not very well insulated. There was a stone fireplace, but the stove heated the cabin much more efficiently and it used less wood.

"At the end of that first day, it was at least midnight, the three of us opened a can of food, warmed it up on the stove, and sat around the table, tired but proud of ourselves for having made the journey and forged a secure base as a haven from the world's insanity. I took a cup of coffee to the front porch and sat on the steps. Soon I was joined by Hannah and Beka and we all wrapped ourselves together under a thick woolen blanket. Sitting on that porch, sipping hot coffee, it was hard to tell the world was at war. We had each other and we felt safe."

Ben closed his eyes. "There we sat on that crisp, clear night, the moon illuminating the Tatra peaks, a thousand stars punching pinholes in the darkness, and the only sound was the wind rushing through the pines. And it struck me—the incongruity of it all—that in the most ungodly of times, I was bearing witness to indisputable evidence of God's work on the third and fourth days, a world he created in perfect balance."

Catherine wrinkled her brow. "Ben, I attended Catholic school through the eighth grade and I had to take catechism every year, but I wouldn't have a clue what happened on the third and fourth days. The nuns would not be happy with me."

He nodded and then recited:

"'And God said, "Let the earth sprout tender sprouts, the plant seeding seed, the fruit tree producing fruit according to its kind, whichever seed is in it on the earth." And it was so. And the earth bore tender sprouts, the plant seeding seed according to its kind, and the fruit tree producing fruit according to its kind, whichever seed is in it. And God saw that it was good. And there was evening, and there was morning the third day.

"'And God made the two great luminaries; the great luminary to rule the day, and the small luminary and the stars to rule the night. And God set them in the expanse of the heavens, to give light on the earth, and to rule over the day and over the night; and to divide between the light and the darkness. And God saw that it was good. And there was evening, and there was morning the fourth day.'"

He smiled. "If you want proof of God, Catherine, go to the mountains."

She put her pen down and folded her hands. "May I ask the obvious question? You don't have to answer if you don't want to. With such indisputable evidence of God, how did he let the Holocaust happen? Where was God?"

Ben responded straightaway. "That's a question I've pondered all my life, as has every person affected by incomprehensible tragedy. My answer is this: he was there, Catherine, weeping. Many see fit to explain it as free will, God's gift to mankind, freedom to do as one chooses, and so some choose to pursue evil. It's an explanation that has its roots in Deuteronomy. When Moses called upon the heads of all the tribes, the elders and the officers, and all the people to stand and receive God's laws, they learned that God had set before them life and good or death and evil. They were told they had the choice. They were told to choose good and not evil, but they were given the choice.

"Evil exists, Catherine, in the dark of Moriah where goodness does not dwell, and in the souls of those that can be seduced. And mankind as a whole must bear the responsibility for following or permitting the evildoers. Those who perpetrated the Holocaust, those who assisted and enabled the perpetration, those who profited, and those who turned their heads must all bear the responsibility." Ben pointed his finger emphatically. "The Holocaust was not God's will. It was the will of those who had become infused of the devil."

"Allegorically?"

"Maybe for some. Not for me. It is why we must remain diligent and relentlessly pursue men like Piatek. Evil is contagious. Much like a pathogen, it must be snuffed out at the source."

Ben shrugged. "Enough preaching. That first night in the mountains, we bedded down late, exhausted but pleased with our efforts. I took one bedroom and Beka and Hannah shared the other. I drifted in and out of sleep, and throughout the night I could hear sobbing from the girls' room. The separation was hard on them.

"The next morning, over coffee, we tried to assess our situation. We made an inventory of what we had and we parceled out the chores.

"'We're going to need supplies,' Hannah said. 'Basics: soap, flour, butter, oil for the lamps. Then there are items that won't store: vegetables, fruit, eggs. From time to time we'll have to get supplies from town. It's a long walk to Łysa Polana and even farther to Zakopane.'

"'We have no choice,' I said. 'But we should keep our appearances in town to a minimum. I'm sure the SS makes rounds, and I expect that sooner or later they'll descend on Zakopane like they did on Zamość. I was told there's a large Jewish community there.'

"'How much money did Father give you?' Beka said.

"'Five hundred złotys, enough to buy food and supplies for a few months.'

"'How long do you think it will be before the rest of the family joins us? I miss Mother and Father. And Grandpa Yaakov. I even miss grumpy Uncle Joseph.' Beka was homesick already.

"'I would hope no more than two or three weeks,' I answered, fearful that if my parents did not escape before long, the gates of opportunity would close.

"Suddenly there was a sharp knock on the door. I waved the girls into the back bedroom and stepped out onto the porch. A large, bearded man in mountain clothes and heavy boots stood before me, a single-shot carbine in his hands.

"'What are you doing in Joseph's house?' he demanded.

"'Who wants to know?' I said.

"'A man with a rifle.'

"'Joseph is my uncle.'

"'You are Abraham's boy? Little Benjamin, the piss-cutter?'

"I laughed as he shook my hand like a water pump. He said his name was Krzysztof Kozlowski and he lived farther down the valley beyond the pines. He had seen the smoke from the stove and thought there were poachers. I invited him in for coffee and called the girls out.

"'Do you remember Beka?'

"'The giggly one,' he said.

"'And this is my Hannah.'

"'She is your wife?'

"I blushed. 'Not yet.'

"'What brings you to the Podhale district and how is my friend Joseph?'

"I explained about our escape from Zamość and our plans for gathering the family and eventually making our way to the Yugoslav coast.

"'Who told you there are no Germans here? There's a garrison in Zakopane. The area is crawling with Nazis. There's also a Gestapo police school in the town of Rabka, up the road from Zakopane. The SS and Gestapo come from all over to train the recruits on how to be prison guards. And there's a villa nearby where the officers hold their parties. They call it a spa, but it's nothing more than a brothel with drunken Germans and young girls. Everyone knows to keep their daughters away from Zakopane and Rabka. There are stories about girls being snatched off the streets and taken to the villa.'

"He poured himself a mug of black coffee, took a gulp, opened the door, and spit it into the yard. 'This stuff's awful. I think Joseph must have purchased these beans in 1930. I'll bring some to you.'

"He handed his cup to Hannah. 'There are also German guards in Łysa Polana at the Slovak border crossing. You must be very careful if you go into the towns for food or supplies. As far as I know, they haven't come up here to the mountain valleys, but I hear stories about shootings.'

"'If we can't go to Zakopane or Łysa Polana, where will we get food? Will you buy some things for us if I give you the money?'

"'Your father and uncle are old friends, and I would help them any way I could, but please don't ask me to assist you in hiding or escaping from the Germans. If I were caught, they would surely kill me and my wife. I'm afraid you'll find that to be the general attitude of the people in the district. I don't think anyone would run to the Nazis and turn you in, but they will avert their eyes.'

"'I understand.'

"He clasped my arm. 'I'll tell you what I can do. I have an old horse and a wagon. Take them. On Thursdays and Sundays there is an open market in Nowy Targ, twenty kilometers up the road, which draws Slovaks and Poles from all over the region, many of them with a horse and wagon. You'll blend in with the crowd. So far, the Germans have not shut down our market, but go Sunday, it's safer. On Thursdays, many Jews come to buy for the Sabbath and there have been stories of harassment.'

"I tried to give Krzysztof money for his horse and wagon, but he refused. Later that day he came by with coffee, eggs, butter, and bread to hold us over until Sunday."

"We need to stop here," Catherine said. "I have a brief that's due Wednesday afternoon, and I'm hopelessly behind schedule. As much as you've snared me in your saga, I need to meet my deadlines."

"Does that mean we can't meet tomorrow or Wednesday?"

Catherine nodded. "I'm afraid so. Let's shoot for Thursday, bright and early."

TWENTY-ONE

• • •

Chicago, Illinois, November 2004

CATHERINE WAS AWAKENED SEVERAL times by dreams of Zamość and visions of the High Tatras. At 5:00 A.M. she gave up trying to sleep and dialed Liam.

"You're up early," he said in a whispered voice.

"I'm sorry to wake you, but I don't know who else to turn to. I'm caught up in Ben's story. I'm so disturbed that it occupies my thoughts, day and night."

"You'll have to fill me in. Do you want me to come over?"

"Thanks, but I'm going to head down to the office. I have a meeting with Ben later this morning."

"Are you going to file suit?"

"Not yet. I talked to him at the end of our session a few days ago and stressed the need for evidence before moving forward. I reminded him that this is a property case, not a personal injury case. We have to identify stolen property in order to file suit."

"He understands that, he's the one who brought it to your attention."

"I know. He said, 'I'm sure that bastard Otto has my mother's tea service sitting on his table, if I could only get into his house.'"

"Good luck."

"To file a replevin or a conversion case we have to specifically identify pieces of property, and in all of our discussions, we haven't even come close."

"But you're hanging in there?"

"He's such a compelling narrator, I've become engrossed in his odyssey. I keep trying to move him along, pry out the evidence, but he won't be rushed. He says I need the details to fully understand the case and I've come to think he's right. There's no doubt in my mind that eventually we'll reach the point where Otto Piatek betrays the Solomons and absconds with their assets."

"But you think there's more."

"Oh, I know it. There's a door to a dark room that Ben hasn't opened. I'm scared to death to see what's behind that door—something very horrible that has nothing to do with money and jewelry. "

"What makes you think so?"

Catherine took a deep breath. "Liam, I can feel it. If you sat with Ben you would know. You would see his determination. It's all rising in a crescendo."

"And when he finishes his story?"

"I don't know. Obviously Ben's motive is to file a civil lawsuit, publicly exposing Rosenzweig. He says that Nazis must always be exposed so the world will never let down its guard, but, again, I know there's something deeper. He's driven by his ghosts—they want retribution, retaliation, I don't know. Anyway, a civil suit may not be the best way to go about it. I think he'd be better served referring the matter to the government. When ex-Nazis are arrested in the United States, the government revokes their citizenship and sends them overseas to be tried for war crimes. I've half a mind to send the file to Richard Tryon at the U.S. Attorney's office now, but Ben insists that the government won't take on such a powerful man without further work-up, and he's probably right."

"How do you know Richard Tryon?"

"From law school. I can approach Richard, but we'd need solid evidence."

"Which we don't have?"

"I haven't seen it. All we have is Ben's uncorroborated identification. And let's face it, even if I filed a civil suit, I'd need more than Ben's testimony. I'd never get to the jury. The case would get thrown out on a motion. I need something more, and I'm waiting to see if it's there."

"Such as?"

"Well, another witness or two for starters. People who can eyeball Rosenzweig and swear that he's Piatek. Maybe Ben's tea service sitting on his table. Maybe a picture of Piatek in uniform taken during the war. Maybe some discrepancy with his immigration papers. I'd like to know something more about Rosenzweig's history."

"Aah, I got you. That's where I can help. I've already been doing a little digging. I can bring it by later this morning. I'm a pretty damn good PI, you know."

"I know you are, and I knew I could count on you." She lay back and stared at the ceiling, cradling the phone on her ear. "I'm terrified, Liam."

"About what?"

"About what I could learn. That maybe Elliot Rosenzweig, this pillar of Chicago society, was and is a monster, a ruthless Nazi who crawls about today living on the property he wrenched from his victims."

"You could be right."

"And then it'll be little ol' Catherine tilting at windmills, accusing a civic icon of being part of the most heinous atrocities ever known to man. Talk about nightmares!"

TWENTY-TWO

...

Uncle Joseph's Cabin, 1941

ON SUNDAY MORNING, BRIGHT and early, I hitched up Krzysztof's horse. I called her Buttermilk—after Dale Evans' horse, which was kind of a joke, because my Buttermilk was a swayback, a tired old lady."

"Dale Evans?" Catherine shook her head.

"Are you serious? You don't know Dale Evans? She was Roy Rogers' wife. Don't you know anything about Roy Rogers? The Sons of the Pioneers? 'Happy Trails to You'?"

She shook her head again. "I guess I may have heard the name Roy Rogers."

"From 1935 to 1940, Otto, Hannah, and I must have watched twenty Roy Rogers movies. I told you we pretended to be cowboys on Grandpa Yaakov's farm. Anyway, the horse Krzysztof gave me was a twenty-six-year-old mare missing several teeth and content to stand in the meadow and chew on the grass with the choppers she had left. I called her Buttermilk.

"That Sunday morning I left Hannah and Beka at the cabin, put on a straw hat I'd found in the shed, climbed up onto Krzysztof's wooden buckboard, gave a slap of the reins, and Buttermilk pulled me into Nowy Targ before noon. Just as Krzysztof had described, there were trucks and wagons from all over the area, loading up with food and supplies from the open market stalls. I didn't see any

Germans, but I trusted no one. When one of the vendors kindly mentioned that she hadn't seen me at the market before, I told her I'd been coming there for years with my parents and I'd be sure to say hello the next time.

"The provisions took at least a quarter of my money, and I knew that at that rate, we couldn't hold out very long. We'd need my father to join us with more money or start the journey to Yugoslavia. In the meantime, with the summer coming, we needed to learn how to supplement our food from the forest. Here, Krzysztof was a big help. He showed us how to find berries, mushrooms, and edible foliage. There were juniper bushes at the bottom of the hill and wild raspberry bushes by the stream. He was also a skilled fisherman, and the lake below the cabin had an ample supply of trout and pike.

"During the day, the girls would garden, gather plants, boil water, pretty up the cabin, and wash our clothes—we had only three outfits apiece. I'd fish, take care of Buttermilk, cut wood, and do repairs. We'd have a fresh meal in the evening and sit on the porch under the stars, talking until midnight. We were about as healthy as three people could get, but the thoughts of our families imprisoned in Zamość haunted us.

"As for Hannah and me, our love grew deeper day by day. I couldn't stop looking at her or keep from holding her hand. One night, three or four weeks after we had arrived, I was awakened by the squeak of my bedroom door. Hannah quietly tiptoed in and slipped into my bed. Curling up next to me, her body soft and warm, she whispered, 'Beka sent me to be with you. She said we should stop sneaking around, she knows all about us.'"

Ben blushed a bit. "We'd been stealing a little private time whenever we could. I thought we were doing okay, keeping our intimacy secret, or at least minimally clandestine, but I guess not. Beka was the one that finally put us together.

"The days passed by in our idyllic seclusion. We rarely saw anyone other than Krzysztof or the folks I'd meet going to Nowy Targ. Krzysztof never brought his wife to the cabin, and I respected his wishes not to involve her. In turn, we never went to Krzysztof's house."

"What about the Germans?" Catherine said. "Did they come around?"

"They never came to the cabin. On occasion I would see them walking around at the market, but they never questioned me. I heard that they were starting to force their presence on the Zakopane Jewish community, so I stayed away from Zakopane.

"In June, with my money running low, having heard nothing from my folks or Zamość, I sat down with Krzysztof to plan an escape route to the Adriatic. He had a tattered map of the Tatras that he spread out on our kitchen table.

"'Do not enter Slovakia at Łysa Polana—there are German guards at the crossing,' he warned. 'Take your Buttermilk, cross the border near Zdziar. There's a pass through the mountains there. It's rugged, but there are trails. Go down through the Bratislavska Dolina valley and follow the river. Stay clear of the Slovak cities, like Poprad and Košice. Remember, Slovakia is Germany's ally.'

"He traced a route through eastern Hungary, portions of Romania, and into Yugoslavia.

"'I do not know the Yugoslavs or their country. You're on your own when you get there.'

"We talked deep into the night about the trip. It would take weeks and cover many miles, but as long as we had Buttermilk and our wagon, I felt we could make it. Beka, however, was against our leaving the cabin. She wanted to wait for Mother and Father. 'We shouldn't leave without them,' she said. 'Let's stay another month.'

"'Beka,' I said, 'it's mid-June and we've been here for ten weeks. Father told us to make a break for it.'

"'No, he said to wait in the cabin as long as we were safe, and if we were threatened, then we should try to escape. We're safe here in the cabin, Ben. There have been no Germans in this area. We can wait a little longer.'

"'We're running out of money,' I argued. 'When it comes time to leave, have you thought about how we'll get food on the way to Split? Have you thought about how we'll pay our expenses on the way? What if we have to pay for passage to America?'

"Beka put her hands on her hips and stuck out her chin. She had our mother's stubbornness. 'Have you thought about where we'll sleep while we're traveling through Slovakia and Hungary?' she countered. 'Have you thought about how we'll make it through the mountains with your rickety wagon and a wheezing old horse? And if the family were to come tomorrow, after we left, how would they make it to Yugoslavia? They'd need us, Ben. We can't leave without them.'

"'I agree with Beka,' Hannah said. 'I'll leave the decision to you, but I'm for staying.'"

"So you stayed?" Catherine said.

Ben nodded. "Until July. Then our money ran out. I sat the girls down after dinner and said, 'I'm going back to Zamość. I'm going to see what happened to our family and try to get some of that money that's buried at Grandpa Yaakov's.'"

Ben paused. His eyes filled with tears. "They tried to talk me out of it, Catherine, they didn't want me to leave. 'It's too dangerous,' they said. But I was bullheaded and foolish. 'I can take care of myself,' I said.

"Beka and Hannah rightfully feared for my safety. They worried that once I went into Zamość, I'd never get out again.

"'Stay here,' pleaded Beka. 'Don't go back. Let's wait another week. Just one more week.'

"'We don't have any money,' I said. 'What if I can't find Father's contact in Split? Or what if he demands money for passage to America? We can't hold out here without money for the market.'

"'We'll make do,' she said.

"I shook my head. I had made my decision. 'I have a road map from Krzysztof, and I'll take Buttermilk back to Zamość on the country roads. I'll try to stay out of sight.'

"They protested, Hannah cried, Beka stomped her foot, but I wouldn't listen." His voice broke. He paused and looked hard at Catherine. "I didn't listen, Catherine." Ben stood up abruptly, trying to suppress his convulsive sobs. "Damn me all to hell, I didn't listen to them." He covered his eyes. Catherine handed a box of tissues to him and sat silently.

After a few minutes, his chin quivering, he said, "Forgive me."

"Ben, don't punish yourself because of your decision. It was perfectly logical."

"I had a bad feeling about what was going on back home. I felt I needed to check on my family. We were out of money. But it was the wrong thing to do, and I've had to live with that mistake ever since."

"Do you want to tell me what happened?"

Ben nodded. "I reasoned that since there were no German patrols in our area, and since Beka and Hannah were strong and fit and had become self-sustaining, I could return to Zamość and get back without putting them at risk. They knew the mountains and they were much safer in the cabin than back in Zamość. Besides, I'd only be gone a week.

"So early the next morning I started out for home. The weather was accommodating, warm and sunny, as Buttermilk clip-clopped along the country roads. We ate what we could find in the fields, hay for Buttermilk and vegetables for me, and I slept in the wagon. By the time we got to Grandpa Yaakov's a few days later, the good horse was ready for a rest. It was late afternoon and Mr. Zeleinski was in the field when I pulled up.

"'Ben? Is that you?' he said.

"'Mr. Zeleinski, it's good to see you.' I climbed down from the buckboard. 'Could I have a glass of water?'

"He quickly shuttled me into the barn. 'Ben, what are you doing here? All Jews have been ordered into New Town. It's forbidden to leave the city.'

"'I wasn't in the city. We've been living in the mountains. I came back to see my father. Would you mind if I spent the night in the barn? I promise to be gone first thing in the morning.'

"'Please, don't ask me that,' he said. 'I'm forever grateful to your father for letting me live on your grandfather's farm, but I'd endanger my entire family if I let you stay here. I have a six-year-old son and a wife. Please, don't ask me.'

"'I understand. May I rest for just an hour in the barn and then I'll walk to town?'"

"'Sure. Of course. You may leave your horse and wagon here, Ben. I'll take care of her for you.'

"He left me alone in the barn. When I heard the farmhouse door shut, I went directly to the last stall in the far corner and brushed back the piles of straw. Grabbing the iron crowbar we kept hanging on the wall, I pried open the board to our secret hiding place and pulled up the old wooden treasure chest. I was thunderstruck by what I saw. There were watches, rings, diamonds, and jewels of all description, twenty times more than the Solomons and the Weissbaums had given to Otto. I recognized my mother's jewelry. There were gold picture frames and lockets. There were pieces of sterling silver. But there was no money. I dug through the entire cache, but there was absolutely no money. My father's life savings, tied up in a brown envelope, were nowhere to be found.

"I set the chest back into the hole, replaced the floorboard, and covered it over with straw like I had found it, all the while cursing Otto. Full of rage and feeling betrayed, I left for Zamość."

Catherine's conference room intercom broke into Ben's narrative to announce that Liam Taggart was waiting in the reception room. He entered the room a few minutes later carrying a folder of papers.

"Hello all. I have some interesting news. Ol' Liam's been snooping around." He pulled the rubber band from around the accordion folder and laid his papers on the table. "Do you remember what Rosenzweig said about coming to America in 1945?"

"He said he came through New York, a penniless immigrant, after he was liberated from the camps," Catherine said. "Although he never said which camp."

"It had to be Auschwitz," Ben said. "That's the only camp that tattooed prisoners with numbers."

"Well," Liam said, "I've spent the last two days at the Chicago office of the National Archives and Records Administration, assisted by a wonderful woman named Bertha McKenzie."

"I'm not familiar with that agency," Ben said.

"Oh, I think you are. NARA's in charge of the National Archives in Washington, D.C., which houses the Declaration of Independence, the Constitution, and the Bill of Rights. It also maintains a huge collection of papers, photos, motion pictures, and sound recordings. Bertha told me there's more than eight billion pieces of paper."

"And where's this going?" Catherine said.

"NARA also maintains immigration records for arrivals to the United States between 1820 and 1982. Passenger lists for arrivals through New York are available on microfilm. You can view them at NARA's office on South Pulaski Road, where they're happy to assist anyone doing genealogical research. They don't get many visitors."

Liam sat back with a broad grin and laced his fingers behind his head. "There's no record of Elliot Rosenzweig coming to the United States in 1945."

"Well, what does that prove?" said Catherine flatly. "He could have entered the United States through some other port or border crossing. Some came through Canada."

"Nope. NARA would have the immigration records."

Ben looked at Liam and cocked his head. "There's more here, isn't there, Liam?"

"There sure is. Elliot Rosenzweig entered the United States through the port of New York in November 1947 aboard the *Santa Adela*, which sailed from Buenos Aires. From Argentina, not Europe."

"How can you be certain that this is the same Elliot Rosenzweig?" asked Catherine.

"He was given permanent resident papers in Chicago in 1948, and naturalized in 1954, both showing his birthplace as Frankfurt, Germany. He listed his 1948 residence at a posh address on North Lake Shore Drive. He's in the 1948 Chicago phone directory, but not in the 1947 book or before."

Ben slapped the table. "Argentina. That's where Nazi big shots went after the war through the ODESSA network. Eichmann was captured by the Israelis outside Buenos Aires and brought to Israel for trial in the 1950s. Mengele went there, too, and became a wealthy man owning a farm and a drug company."

"Cat," Liam said, "if Piatek escaped from the Allied forces and followed the Nazi underground to Argentina, he could have changed his name to Rosenzweig, emigrated to the U.S. in 1947, and drawn upon some overseas bank account where he stashed his wealth."

Ben stood and walked quickly to the windows. He covered his face with his hands. "Oh, my sweet Hannah, it's all coming together," he whispered. "Now he'll answer to the world. His past will finally catch up with him."

Catherine said softly, "That's great work, Liam. We're getting close. We still need more than immigration records, though. We need that smoking gun. We need a tie-in to Piatek. I wish we had some physical evidence." Turning to Ben, she said, "Like specific property. Let's talk more tomorrow afternoon."

"I can't. It's Friday and I have an appointment. I'll come back Monday."

TWENTY-THREE
• • •

Winnetka, Illinois, November 2004

THE FORMAL DINING ROOM was aglow with candles and the uniformed server carefully set the dinner entrees before the three family members. Elliot smiled at the lovely presentation of rack of lamb and said, "Thank you, Gwyneth. It looks delicious."

Rosenzweig's wife winked at her granddaughter, giggled, and announced in a singsong voice, "Elliot, Jennifer has something to tell you."

He sat back in his chair and folded his hands on the table. "Well, my angel?"

The pretty, young medical student blushed and held her crystal wine glass to her lips with both hands. She peered over the top of the glass at her beloved grandfather and said, "Popi. Michael proposed to me. And I said yes. We're getting married."

Rosenzweig beamed and clapped his hands. "Aah, congratulations." He pushed his chair back from the dining room table and bustled quickly around to hug his precious granddaughter. "We'll have the grandest wedding Chicago has ever seen," he said. "When?"

"We'd like to get married next June, after graduation."

"Isn't it wonderful," said Elliot's wife, "our little granddaughter will be a bride. And Michael's such a lovely boy."

"Imagine that," Elliot said, "a doctor and a lawyer, such a professional union. You'll be very successful."

Jennifer giggled. "He's only a third-year associate, Popi."

"But he's with a prestigious firm: Storch & Bennett. Soon he'll be a fancy partner. This calls for a celebration! Robert," he called, "would you please bring us a very good bottle of champagne."

The uniformed butler entered the room. "We have a chilled 1966 Dom Pérignon, Mr. Rosenzweig, would you like me to pour it?"

"Excellent, excellent."

Resuming his usual seat at the head of his lacquered dining table, Elliot said, "Have you thought about where you'd like to have the ceremony?"

"I'd like it to be here. At our home. We can have it on the back lawn. There's plenty of room for a dance floor, a lattice archway, and bunches of tables."

Robert brought out the champagne and filled the crystal flutes.

Elliot raised his glass. "This is the happiest day of my life."

As they rejoiced over their granddaughter's engagement, a solitary figure ascended the brick staircase from the beach and stepped out onto the Rosenzweig back lawn. The night was dark and he kept to the shadows. Every now and then he would sneak up to the back of the house, peer in a window, and move on. As he looked into Rosenzweig's den, the overhead security lights came on and a buzzer sounded in the main security station.

Robert promptly came to the table and whispered into Elliot's ear. "There's been a breach of security in the back, sir. Russell is checking it out." Elliot nodded.

Frightened by the lights, the intruder quickly returned to the staircase and descended back to the beach, blending into the darkness.

A few moments later, Robert returned to inform Elliot that Russell found nothing out of order, but they'd review the tapes.

"Probably an animal," Elliot said and returned his attention to the gaiety.

TWENTY-FOUR

...

Chicago, Illinois, November 2004

THE FOLLOWING MONDAY, CATHERINE unlocked the front door and entered Jenkins & Fairchild's still-empty offices before dawn. Ben wasn't due to arrive until noon and, despite working all weekend, she had a desk full of files screaming for attention. She hung her blazer on the back of her chair, rolled up her sleeves, and dug into the overflowing in-box. At nine o'clock, she was interrupted by the buzz of the intercom.

"Miss Lockhart, there are three attorneys from Storch & Bennett in the reception room asking to see you."

"I have no appointments scheduled."

"Yes, ma'am. They say it involves Mr. Solomon and that you'll want to talk to them."

Curious, Catherine walked to reception. She recognized the older of the three, E. Gerald Jeffers, past president of the bar association and a legal force in Chicago. The other two were much younger, clearly in their late twenties, and were introduced as associates.

"We'd like a few minutes of your time," said Jeffers. He wore an expensive hand-tailored blue pinstriped suit, Brioni tie, and contrasting pocket square. He carried a cashmere coat, folded over his arm. "It concerns your client and his recent activities."

Catherine led them back to the conference room. Jeffers carried no briefcase. He left the toting to his two juniors, one of whom carried a business case large enough to house a laptop and a projector, which he proceeded to unload and set onto the conference room table.

"What's this all about?" Catherine said.

"As I said, it's about your client. May I turn off the overhead lights?" Jeffers said.

A surveillance video began to play out on the conference room wall.

"You're looking at the rear of the Rosenzweig estate," Jeffers said. "The pool and cabana are on your right, the living room windows are on your left. The steps to the beach are directly ahead. The time is noted on the bottom—it's 9:00 P.M. This was taken Saturday night, two nights ago."

Catherine watched as a darkened figure approached the windows from the side bushes. It was Ben. He peered into one set of windows for a while, took pictures with a small camera, and then walked outside of the surveillance area. The video paused and then resumed with a different view. The scenario was similar: Ben peering into the windows and taking pictures. Three different cameras, all recording Ben snooping around the massive home, taking pictures, and then running to the steps.

The projector was switched off and the lights turned on.

"We understand that you represent Mr. Solomon," Jeffers said with a beneficent smile. "Stalking, burglary, trespassing, harassment— take your pick. Mr. Rosenzweig has had quite enough." He nodded to one of his juniors, who took a folder of papers from his briefcase and laid them on the table.

"Here are four copies of a proposed order of protection that we've prepared for Mr. Solomon to sign. After he affixes his consent, we intend to present the order to a judge and have it entered forthwith. As you can see, the order restrains Mr. Solomon from stalking, harassing, or bothering Mr. Rosenzweig or his family in any way. In fact, it prohibits him from coming within one-half mile of the Rosenzweig property. He may not contact Mr. Rosenzweig, confront him, speak publicly about him, accuse him, or denounce him in any way. As the order recites, violation of its terms will be punishable by contempt—a fine or punitive incarceration. If Mr. Solomon refuses to sign this order by tomorrow, we will immediately file an action against him."

Catherine was speechless.

Jeffers walked around the table and stood next to Catherine's chair, looking down at her and speaking solicitously. "Miss Lockhart, this is really not the kind of messy business that's good for you or your firm. How old are you? You look very young."

She responded meekly, as though she were being addressed by her elementary school teacher. "I'm thirty-nine."

"Well," he said in a sickly sweet tone, "to me that's very young, indeed. You have a long career in front of you, many years as a fine lawyer. But this matter, representing this deranged character, would surely brand you as a pariah in the legal community, if you know what I mean. The leaders of our profession, the judges and lawyers that I know, would not be receptive to one who risks her professional stature on such a man."

He turned to his junior and held out his hand. As though rehearsed, the young lawyer quickly handed Jeffers a DVD and shot a smug grin in Catherine's direction. Jeffers set the DVD on the table in front of Catherine.

"You may have this copy. Show it to your client. Get him to sign the order and then send him on his way. By the way, it may interest you to know that Mr. Rosenzweig has spent a considerable sum of money himself looking into this Nazi issue, this Otto Piatek."

Jeffers and his two associates walked to the door.

"Call me when the order is signed. You needn't get up, Miss Lockhart. We know the way out. Good day."

TWENTY-FIVE

. . .

BEN ARRIVED PUNCTUALLY AT noon carrying a paper bag.

"I stopped by the farmer's market at the Daley Plaza. I brought us some apples. Last of the season."

He smiled, but Catherine did not.

"What's the matter?" he asked.

"Sit down, Ben, I want to show you something."

Ben watched the video play out on a computer screen.

"I should've figured. Okay. I agree, that was dumb. I thought I'd get a picture we could use, maybe some of my mother's jewelry. Maybe the silver tea service. Maybe I'd find the physical evidence, the solid proof you're always talking about."

"Mr. Rosenzweig's attorneys brought this video over today along with a proposed order of protection. It's a restraining order, Ben, to keep you away from Rosenzweig and stop you from accusing him. They want to file this as an agreed order or they'll pursue it through the court," she said, handing the document to Ben.

He read the proposed order. "I'm not going to sign this."

"Ben, they have you on video. You have no defense."

"To get this entered by a judge, he'd have to go to court and testify against me, wouldn't he?"

"You mean Mr. Rosenzweig?"

"I mean Otto."

"Yes, he would."

Ben sat back with a Cheshire grin. "He'll never do it. He doesn't want to confront me in a courtroom. Remember, his life is built on lies and cover-ups."

"He's retained a powerful law firm. They're not afraid to battle it out in court."

"If I signed this order, the case would be over, wouldn't it? I'd be enjoined from accusing him."

"Essentially, that's correct."

"No way." Ben shook his head. "Let me ask the question a different way. If I don't agree to sign this order and Otto decides to take me to court, would the judge enter the order?"

"Partly. He'd certainly enjoin you from trespassing on the Rosenzweig property and from harassing him. I have my doubts as to whether he can enjoin you from accusing him in a lawsuit."

"Then I'd be no worse off than if I signed it, right?"

"I guess not. I might also tell you that Gerald Jeffers urged me to drop you as a client on the threat of ruining my reputation."

Ben looked concerned. "I'm sorry. Does he have that kind of power?"

Catherine shrugged. "Jeffers is influential."

"Are you dropping me?"

Catherine shook her head. "I don't take well to intimidation. My natural reflex is to say, 'Screw you.'"

Ben leaned forward, smacking the table with his palm. "I knew I was right about you. And I'm right about Rosenzweig. That's one issue you don't have to worry about. Rosenzweig is Piatek and of that I'm one hundred percent positive. And it will all come together. That I promise you."

"There's something else. Jeffers told me that Rosenzweig has spent considerable money looking for Piatek."

"He said that?" Ben wrinkled his face in a sarcastic smile. "Very clever, Mr. Rosenzweig. I suppose after he throws a few dollars around, he'll come up with a story that Piatek died in the war, or maybe disappeared in Casablanca. Nice try. He is Piatek and I will prove it."

Catherine sighed. "You won't sign the order of protection?"

"Nope. Don't you see, all this pressure, the baloney about trying to find Piatek, it's all about the lawsuit. They know we're planning to file a lawsuit and they're trying to scare off my lawyer."

Catherine shook her head. "I don't see that. They don't know that we're planning to file. *I* don't know that we're planning to file. At this stage I don't know what we can do. This is about them catching you trespassing on a surveillance video."

Ben smiled and shook his head. "Have faith, young lady. Hear me out, listen to my story, and you'll understand. I promise."

Zamość, Poland, 1941

"It was late in the afternoon when I walked from the farm to the outskirts of Zamość and took the bus back to our home on Belwederski Street. The July sun was high in the skies and the weather was warm."

"Why did you go back to Belwederski Street? I thought you said your family was being resettled to New Town."

"Well, I didn't know where they would be. Maybe they were still in the house. Maybe they hadn't vacated yet. I hadn't had any contact with them for several months. So I thought my home would be the logical place to start. I walked up to the door and rang the bell. A stout lady with a bulbous nose and tightly permed white hair answered and stood in my doorway. She had on a black wool dress, a formless thing that draped over her stocky body and hung down to her shins, and she stood with her arms folded across her chest in a defiant posture.

"'I'm looking for the Solomons,' I said.

"'They don't live here anymore. They're Jews. They're all in New Town now. Who are you?'

"'No one,' I said. She gave me a nasty look and slammed the door.

"I walked down the steps and headed for Kozmierski Street to catch the bus to New Town, but as I reached the corner I saw two German soldiers standing at the bus stop. I turned and walked across the street, melting into the pedestrian crowd. One of them saw me, followed me, and confronted me at the next corner.

"'*Dokumente, bitte,*' he said.

"'*Nicht verstehe,*' I replied. 'I don't understand.'

"He grinned at me and shoved me back against a building with his rifle. 'Papers,' he repeated.

"I just shook my head. I had no papers and I wasn't wearing an armband, so I was immediately arrested and taken to a warehouse near the town hall, where they locked me in a tiny windowless room. All during that dark night I was tormented by my bad decisions. Why did I leave the mountains? What was I thinking? If I were killed, who would care for Hannah and Beka? If they send me to a concentration camp, who will protect them? How I regretted my decision to return to Zamość. I should have budgeted our money more carefully and left for Slovakia when my parents didn't show up. I should have listened to Beka when she begged me not to go.

"After an eternity, the door was opened and two guards stood in the doorway silhouetted by a blinding light. They pulled me up by my armpits and shoved me down the hall to an office, where they sat me in a metal chair before a lesser-ranked SS officer.

"'What is your name, *Saujude?*' the SS corporal said. He was a beastly man, so fat he couldn't fasten the bottom two buttons of his tunic. His blemished forehead was covered in sweat.

"'Benjamin Solomon,' I answered.

"'Who sent you to Frau Maudsten's yesterday afternoon?'

"'Who?'

"A guard slapped me and the officer repeated the question.

"'The only place I've been to is my home on Belwederski.'

"The officer snorted. 'That's not your home and you know it. It belongs to Frau Maudsten. Your family has been resettled. Why did you go to Belwederski?'

"'It was an innocent mistake,' I said. I didn't want to tell him I had been out of Zamość. 'I was on a work detail. I forgot we had moved. Without thinking, I walked up to the front door, and then I remembered that it wasn't my house anymore and I left. I didn't cause any trouble, sir.'

"'You have no papers and no work permit. You have no armband. You're not permitted outside of New Town. Did you forget all that, too?'

"'No. I lost my work permit and my armband, or maybe I left them at my new apartment.'

"'I thought you said you were coming home from a work detail?'

"'That's right. I'm very tired. I get confused.'

"He gestured to a guard to take me out. 'Too many mistakes, *Saujude*. You are to be sent with the next group to the new camp at Majdanek.' I was grabbed again and hustled to the door.

"'Wait!' I said quickly at the doorway. 'I didn't tell you the truth. I was on a special assignment.'"

"Special assignment? Why on earth did you say that?" Catherine said.

"I was a dead man anyway. Either he'd kill me for lying or I'd be sent to Majdanek, and nobody ever returned from there. I had nothing to lose.

"'Oh. I'm sure.' He laughed at me. 'And what was this special assignment, *Saujude*?'

"'I can't tell you,' I said.

"'Oh, you'll tell me, I promise you that.' They closed the door and brought me back to the chair. The corporal took a knife from his desk. 'You'll tell me right before you die.'

"'Then you'll be the one sent to Majdanek,' I said. 'My orders came straight from Scharführer Piatek.'

"The SS officer laughed heartily. His fat belly shook. 'Where did you hear that name?'

"'Scharführer Piatek gave me my assignment and warned me to keep it secret. If you don't believe me, take me to him.'

"The officer hesitated. 'You're lying.'

"'Can you take that chance?'

"He unholstered his pistol and waved it at me, directing me to proceed out of the room. 'I'll take you to Scharführer Piatek, and if you're lying I'll shoot you on the spot.'

"We left the prison and walked to Otto's office at the town hall.

Thank goodness he was still there. I hadn't heard from him in months, since he dropped us at the side of the road. The corporal said, 'This Jewish pile of shit tells me he is on secret assignment from you, Scharführer.'

"Otto showed no recognition and looked down at his papers. Finally, he looked up and said, 'The Jew is correct. I sent him on a mission. Leave us.'

"The fat man bowed. 'Yes, sir, Scharführer. That's why I insisted he be brought directly to you.'

"Otto waved him away with the back of his hand.

"When he had left and shut the door, Otto said, 'What are you doing back in Zamość? I took you out of here.'

"'Where is the rest of the family? You were supposed to bring them to Uncle Joseph's.'

"'They won't leave. Your father's serving on the Judenrat and Hannah's father is running a clinic. I tried to get them to leave. I warned them that if they stayed here they'd have to move to New Town and probably to a resettlement area after that. Maybe you can talk them into leaving.'

"I felt it was time to bring up the money. 'Otto,' I said, 'I went to Grandpa Yaakov's.' He showed no reaction. 'Where's the money?'

"'Is that what you have to say to me? "Where's the money"? Go to hell, Ben! I risk my life to get you to the mountains. I risk my rank and position bringing your family food. I even offered to get the rest of your family out and you have the ingratitude to accuse me, saying, "Where's the money?"'

"'My father gave you over sixty thousand złotys, our life savings. I know the Weissbaums gave you money, too.'

"'I had to move it, Ben. I didn't trust Zeleinski. It's all in my apartment, under lock and key. Well, almost all of it. I had to use a little. These Germans have a ritzy lifestyle, and if I want to stay connected I've got to be a big spender.'

"'What about all that jewelry I saw? The box was filled to the brim, like a real treasure chest, and it didn't all come from us.'

"'I've helped other people, Ben. The Solomons and Weissbaums aren't the only families in Zamość. But let's not argue,' he said, getting up from his desk and putting his arm around my shoulders. 'Let me take you to the family.'

"He drove me into the New Town ghetto. I couldn't believe my eyes. First of all, many of the buildings had been damaged or destroyed by the German bombs. Second, there were people everywhere. So many. And in such a sorry condition. The worst poverty you've ever seen. Otto pulled up to the side of a large warehouse, stopped his car, and let me out. 'The family lives here now. They're all on the second floor.'

"In its prewar days, the brick building had been a grain warehouse with loading docks and offices on the first floor. Now it was a giant dormitory. I climbed the stairs to the second floor and asked a young girl where I might find the Solomons. She led me down the hall to a large warehouse space that had been partitioned into living areas by hanging blankets and sheets from the ceiling. The degrading conditions gave me a sick feeling in the pit of my stomach. My mother was straightening up a small corner area that held a bed and a few pieces of her furniture.

"'Benjamin,' she cried. 'I prayed that I would see you again, but not in here.' She hugged me and kissed me and we both shed tears. With my arms around her, I could tell she'd lost a lot of weight. Once she was an elegant dresser. Now her cotton dress hung straight from her shoulders like it was on a hanger. In the four months since I'd left, she had aged considerably.

"'Is this your home now?' I asked.

"She nodded sadly. 'We're allotted this corner of the floor. The Judenrat is under enormous pressure to find living space for each of the families in the ghetto. There are so many here, Benjamin. Jews from all over the region have been sent here.' She shrugged and smiled. 'But we make do. We share a kitchen on the first floor, we take turns in the bathroom, and we try to be respectful of special needs. Sit down, my handsome boy. You're so tan and healthy. How are Rebecca and Hannah?'

"'They're fine. Just as healthy, thanks to the mountain air. We've been very lucky, living at Uncle Joseph's.'

"Sitting there talking to my mother, I felt guilty about my

condition. What right did I have to good health while my mother was wasting away in the corner of a rat's hole? I vowed to get her out.

"Holding my hands, she said, 'Why did you come back? You were free. Things here get worse every day.'

"'I came back for you.'

"She hugged me and sobbed. 'Oh, Benjamin, that's so like you, so foolhardy. But your father is very involved. We cannot come just yet.'

"'Where are the others?'

"Her expression turned grave. 'I'm so sorry to tell you. Grandpa Yaakov has died.'

"A cold shiver shot through my spine. 'What happened?'

"'You know what a strong, independent man he was and how outspoken he could be. It happened during one of their incessant roll calls. We were told to line up outside the building. The Germans with their rifles and their savage dogs walked up and down the line screaming insults and pushing and slapping. For no reason. Grandpa Yaakov protested. He said, "Why do you treat people like this? Were you brought up as animals?"'

"'Oh my God.'

"'Benjamin, they set their dog on him. They laughed as the dog tore into Yaakov. Mr. Leibman, who was standing beside him, tried to help, and the dog attacked him too. Both of them died from their wounds. We buried Yaakov on May 22. Rabbi Gerstein gave a beautiful eulogy. He said such nice things about Yaakov. You'd have been proud.'

"'And Uncle Joseph?'

"'My mother shook her head and cried into her hands. 'Benjamin, Benjamin, it's all so inhuman, so ungodly. Joseph could not stand without a crutch. Sometimes in the assemblies, when we were forced to stand for hours, we'd hold him up. Finally, the Germans took everyone with such a disability and sent them away. We don't know where, but I've heard stories. Some even say they were shot in the woods.'

"'Aunt Hilda?'

"'She's here, but she's not well. We've had some sickness going through the ghetto. Dr. Weissbaum is treating her. She went for a walk. She should be home soon.'

"'We need to get you and the others out of here,' I said. 'It's safe at Uncle Joseph's.'

"She cupped my face. 'Talk to your father. If he leaves, I'll leave.'

"Later that day, I found my father sitting behind a desk in the Judenrat office, which was located in a part of the old synagogue. There was a line of people waiting to speak to him. He stood and embraced me but then repeated my mother's query, 'Why did you come back?'

"'We waited and waited for you. Beka and Hannah, they wouldn't leave without you. Finally, we ran out of money.'

"'Otto has our money,' he said. 'I gave him all we had.'

"'I know. I saw Otto this morning. I want to take you and Mother to the mountains.'

"Father shook his head. 'Do you see all these people here? They're desperate and in need. The Judenrat is all they have. We set up a communal kitchen and we're getting food from the Jewish Self-help Organization in Krakow. We help families stay together and find spaces to live. When you left Zamość there were fewer than five thousand Jews living all throughout the city. Now there are over seven thousand, shipped in from all over the region and crowded into a few city blocks. The Judenrat is their government. We intercede with the Nazis. How can I leave these people, Ben?'

"'What about Mother? I could take her back to the cabin.'

"'That would be fine, if she would go. She's working in the women's clinic, helping Dr. Weissbaum.'

"My father gave me identification papers and an armband. I decided to stay in New Town for a few days and convince my parents to leave. I'd get the money from Otto and take them all back to the mountains. That night I slept on the floor beside my parents' bed. Over the next few days I helped my father at the Judenrat office and tried to convince my mother to come back with me. But no matter how hard I tried, my mother was unwilling to leave Zamość without my father. 'Whither thou goest,' she said to me, and I understood the depth of the love that bound them. I was foolish to think they would part.

"She added, 'I'm needed at the clinic. We've had an outbreak of typhus and many are gravely ill. The Judenrat is opening a hospital in the school building. Right now we have forty beds.'"

"There was typhus in New Town?" Catherine said.

"Right. It's a nasty disease that occurs in poor areas where people are forced to live in crowded, unsanitary conditions. Typhus is spread by lice or fleas, especially in the cold weather. Anne Frank died of typhus. It was common in the camps. Now it can be cured with antibiotics. Back then, well, it was a terrible way to die.

"Anyway, after a few days, the time had come for me to go. I was worried about Hannah and Beka alone at the cabin. They were never out of my thoughts. Sitting with my parents, I said, 'I'm going to get money from Otto and return to the mountains. I'll take the horse and wagon. As long as we're safe, we'll stay at Uncle Joseph's. If things get worse here, or if they start shipping people out, have Otto bring you to the cabin.'

"My father nodded. 'If I can no longer help our people, Mother and I will join you. But you must promise me that if the Germans come into the Podhale, you'll take the girls and head south through the mountains.'

"I promised, kissed my parents, and left to find Otto."

"How did you get through the ghetto walls?" Catherine said. "Wasn't there barbed wire and weren't there armed guards to stop people from leaving?"

"No. Zamość didn't have a walled ghetto like Warsaw. People were free to come and go, but Jews were not permitted on the street after curfew. During the day, they could travel through Zamość, but they were subject to being stopped, harassed, beaten, or worse. If you didn't have a work permit, the Germans were likely to shoot you and leave your body on the street. I left the ghetto and met up with Otto at his office. We took a walk.

"'I need money,' I said to him. 'Would you please bring me some of my family's money?'

"He seemed annoyed with the request. 'What do you need money for?'

"'I'm going back to the mountains and I want to get a little extra money for my parents. But even if I wanted to burn it, it's our money.'

"'I know it's your money, Ben, you don't have to tell me that. How much do you need?'

"'I'll take two thousand złotys.'

"'Two thousand? Why do you need that much?'

"'Otto, that's my business. Would you please bring me two thousand złotys and help me get to Yaakov's farm?'

"'The money's locked up at home. I'll meet you here tomorrow morning.'

"'Tomorrow? I need to leave today. I was hoping to get the money and drive out to the farm. I'm worried about the girls and I want to get back to the cabin.'

"Otto shook his head. 'I can't get the money right now.' He looked around and came closer, like he was telling me a secret. 'You know Teresa Zumszka?' he whispered.

"I nodded. 'The buxom blonde.'

"'Right. She's staying with me right now. She's a wild tiger, I tell you. She has my little soldier saluting her all night long.' He laughed. 'I don't want her to see where I keep the money. And be sure not to tell Elzbieta about her.' He winked at me.

"'I have to leave today, Otto.'

"He reached into his pocket. 'I can give you a few hundred.' He pulled out a huge roll of bills. 'Here,' he said counting them out, 'here's five hundred. I'll give the rest to your father.'

"I looked at the roll and said, 'Whoa, that's a lot of money you carry in your pocket.'

"'Money's easy in Zamość if you're a German.'

"The statement disgusted me, but I said nothing. What good would it do?

"'Will you drive me out to Zeleinksi's farm?' I said.

"Otto agreed and we climbed into his fancy car. All the way to the farm he bragged about his escapades. Never once did he express any concern for the two people who took him in and raised him. Never once did he ask about Beka or Hannah. When he dropped me off he said, 'I gotta get back to the tiger. I bet she meets me at the door wearing nothing but her underwear.' He laughed and then sped away.

"Zeleinski was sitting on the porch of the farmhouse when I arrived. He helped me hitch up Buttermilk, gave me a loaf of bread, and I left immediately. The longer I stayed away, the more anxious I became. I'd been gone almost twelve days and it would take at least three more to get back to the cabin.

"I drove deep into the night until I started falling asleep in the wagon seat. Then I pulled over, caught a nap, and rested my muscles. Just before dawn, I started up again. Every time I saw a car, I'd head into the fields to make it look like I was farming. No one bothered me all the way to Łysa Polana, where I bypassed the town and the border guards. I couldn't wait to hold Hannah in my arms and see Beka's infectious smile. The closer I got, the more eager I became. Finally, at noon on the third day, I arrived at the cabin.

"'Hannah? Beka?' I called as I unhitched Buttermilk. 'I'm back. Hannah?'

"I walked into the cabin but no one was home. At first I figured they were out gathering mushrooms or greens, but then I noticed the stove was cold. The mountain nights were chilly and they should have been using the stove for heat. I started to worry, but I kept reassuring myself that they were just out for a walk or gathering food. I decided to sit down and wait on the porch.

"The time passed with agonizing slowness. Each minute seemed like an hour. I kept scanning the edge of the woods, focusing on the trails, and hoping to see the two girls walking up the hill. As the twilight settled in, my anxiety turned to panic. Something was wrong. Finally, I ran down to Krzysztof's and rapped on his door. His wife answered. I apologized for the disturbance and asked to speak to Krzysztof, who was eating his dinner. He came to the door with a napkin tucked into his shirt, and he shooed me out to the road.

"'I'm sorry, Krzysztof, but Hannah and Beka aren't at the cabin,' I said. 'I've waited all day. Do you know where they are?'

"He nodded solemnly. 'My friend, I have bad news. The Germans came through a few days ago.'

"I felt like I'd been kicked in the stomach. I could barely breathe. I could hardly stand. 'Where did they take them?'

"Krzysztof shook his head. 'Maybe to Zakopane. Maybe Rabka.'

"All my thoughts turned to how to get them back, and I knew I couldn't do it on my own. Otto was my only hope. I dashed back to the cabin and hitched up Buttermilk. 'Sorry, old girl, but we need to get back to Zamość in a hurry.'

"I traveled through the night and all the next day, blind with panic, pushing Buttermilk, hoping she wouldn't stumble from exhaustion, finally arriving at Grandpa Yaakov's farm two days later. Zeleinski's six-year-old son was playing in the front yard when I arrived.

"'Can you do a big favor for me?' I said with my hands on his shoulders. 'Would you unhitch Buttermilk and give her some oats?'

"'Sure,' he said, and as I gave him the reins, he added, 'Your friend, the German soldier man, was here again yesterday. He went into our barn.'

"I thanked him for his help and started off down the road to Zamość. Catching a bus at the edge of town, I went directly to SS headquarters.

"'I have a message for Scharführer Piatek,' I said to the young adjutant at the desk.

"He looked at his watch and laughed. 'It's only one o'clock. He hasn't come in yet today. It's too early for him.' I started to leave and he called after me, 'It's Hauptscharführer now. He's been promoted. What is your business here?'

"'Special assignment. I am to report directly to Hauptscharführer Piatek.'

"He nodded and looked down at his papers. 'Try again later.'

"I didn't know exactly where Otto was living and I knew he wasn't at the Maria anymore, so I decided to ask Elzbieta for help. I found her at home in the early evening.

"'Ben, you're out after curfew. It's very dangerous for you,' she said as she hustled me through the doorway and into her apartment.

"'Elzie. The SS—they've taken Hannah and Beka.'

"She was stunned. 'Where were they taken?'

"'I don't have any idea. They were taken from the mountain cabin. We have to find Otto.'

"She lifted the phone and dialed. Placing her hand over the mouthpiece, she whispered, 'Otto and I have been having some problems. He's Mister Bon Vivant these days.'

"'Hello, Otto?' she said into the phone. 'Ben and I need to see you right away.' She paused. 'He's here at my apartment. Yes, he's here. Please come over.' She paused again, and a look of strong determination came over her face. 'I don't care what you're doing, you come over here right now!' She hung up. 'He'll come,' she said with disgust. 'He said I caught him at a bad time.'

"Otto arrived a little while later.

"'Ben,' he said lightly, 'you keep coming back. You're like one of those Australian boomerangs.'

"'They've arrested Hannah and Beka,' I said. 'The SS took them from the cabin and I don't know where they are.'

"For all of his Nazism, Otto was visibly shaken. 'When were they taken?'

"'While I was here in Zamość. When I arrived back in the mountains two days ago, the cabin was empty and the neighbor told me the Germans had come by.'

"Otto sat down on the couch and pulled at his lip, deep in thought. 'They may know where they are at the SS office in Krakow—they should have records of arrests in the Podhale region. If there's one thing Germans do well, it's keep records. Krakow is headed by Obergruppenführer Krüger, who is a very unpleasant man, but I think Dr. Frank is presently in Krakow or at the resort south of there, I can't remember the name.'

"'Rabka?'

"'That's it. I'll go tomorrow morning. They'll give me access to the records. Elzie, I'll need two dresses.'

"'I'll go with you,' I said.

"'No. It's better I go alone. You'll just get in the way. How would I explain your presence?'

"'I have to go,' I said. 'I'll wear one of your old uniforms. I can pass for a Nazi.'

"Otto just shook his head. 'It's too risky and Dr. Frank knows you. You'll get us both killed.'

"I realized that I had no choice and I'd have to rely on Otto. We agreed that I would stay at Elzbieta's and wait for him.

"The next three days were unbearable. I didn't want to alarm my parents, so I didn't return to New Town. I figured that if Otto brought the girls home safely, and if everything was all right, I would have frightened my parents unnecessarily. So I sat at Elzbieta's for three days listening to the radio and going nuts. She was very kind to me and tried to calm my nerves. We had discussions deep into the night about our lives and how the world had changed. But every time we heard a noise, we panicked. I would duck under the bed or into a closet.

"Finally, on the third day, in the middle of the night, there was a knock on Elzbieta's door. When I heard Otto's voice I came out of hiding. There stood Hannah in Elzbieta's dress.

"She ran to me and I hugged her tightly for several minutes, afraid to let her go. Otto shut the door.

"'Where's Beka?' I said.

"Otto shook his head and held up his hand, as if to say 'I'll tell you later.'

"'Otto rescued me,' Hannah said. 'We were in Zakopane, at a hotel, being held prisoner with other women. So many women, some only fourteen years old. We were all kept in an empty ball-room, like penned-up cattle. German officers would come and go, look us over, and pick the ones they wanted, like a slave auction. They took Beka, but Otto's going to go back and get her.'

"'Tell me what happened, how did you wind up at Zakopane?'

"'Beka and I had just come back to the cabin from gathering berries, and there was a car parked in front. Three soldiers stood on the porch and shouted at us. We thought about running, but they had rifles, so we figured we'd try to talk our way out of it. They asked for our papers. We played dumb and coy and said we had never been issued any papers, that we just lived in the mountains and we didn't know anything. We said we weren't Jewish, and the two of us were living alone since the death of our father.'

"'They said something in German, but they were eyeing us, especially Beka. They told us that they would have to take us to Zakopane, register us, and bring us right back. But they didn't, of course. We were taken to the Palace Hotel and locked into the ballroom with dozens of other girls. SS and Gestapo were everywhere.'

"Hannah shivered and seemed unsteady. Elzbieta led her to the couch and gave her a glass of water. Hannah hadn't eaten much in the past several days, so Elzie made her a sandwich.

"'Even though it was a hotel, the conditions were terrible,' Hannah said. 'We were only allowed to use the toilet twice a day. Food was meager. We slept on the floor. From time to time the SS would come into the hall and take out a group of girls. We all talked about it. There were rumors that we were going to be sent to army camps to be whores for the Germans. I kept remembering what Krzysztof told us about Rabka and the parties that went on.

"'It was during the second day that Dr. Frank came into the ballroom with an older, creepy officer who stood there gazing at the young girls. It made my skin crawl.

"'It was like they were selecting pastries from the dessert cart. The nasty, lecherous old man who accompanied Dr. Frank pointed his fat finger, and one of the girls was pulled to her feet by a guard and hustled out of the room. Dr. Frank's eyes fell upon Beka. There was instant recognition. "Rebecca. Seventeen," he said, smiling, and motioned for the guards to bring her along. Beka cried as she was yanked away.'

"Hannah stopped and covered her face. Elzbieta sat next to her, put her arm around her, and let Hannah cry onto her shoulder. It took a few minutes for Hannah to compose herself. 'I never saw Beka after that,' she said. 'Two days later, Otto walked into the room, pointed at me, and said, "I want that one."

"'He led me from the hotel and out to his car. Then he gave me

Elzie's dress, told me to put it on and act like his girlfriend if we were stopped. We drove directly back to Zamość.'

"Hannah looked up, with a small, hopeful smile. 'Otto says he can go back and get Beka in a few days. I'm so worried about her, Ben.'

"Elzbieta poured us each a glass of wine, and we drank to Hannah's freedom and to Beka's impending rescue. But after a while, Otto took me aside and said, 'I can't get Beka.'

"My heart sank. 'Why?'

"'She wasn't with the others when I got there. Dr. Frank took her up to Rabka. The villa is filled with SS officers and it's heavily guarded. I'm not on the guest list. I'd be recognized and questioned. They would ask me what I was doing there.'

"The thought of Beka being used by those monsters sickened me. 'I thought it was forbidden for SS officers to have relations with Jews,' I said.

"Otto lowered his eyes. 'Don't be naïve. Besides, Hannah and Beka said they weren't Jewish and no one in the Podhale knows them. Rabka's a decadent resort where anything goes. The SS officers who train guards at the academy all stay at the villa. That's what makes the academy so popular. And they have a ravenous appetite for young girls.'

"Visions of those filthy Nazis violating my sister boiled my blood. 'Let's go,' I said. 'We need to get Beka out of there.'

"Otto waved his hand. 'We can't. There's a detachment of Ukrainian guards securing the villa. There are soldiers everywhere. You'd never get near her.'

"'I'll take the chance. Let's go.'

"Otto put his hand on my shoulder. 'You know I'd do anything for Beka. But we have to face reality. She's beyond our reach. There's absolutely nothing we can do for her.'

"'That's it? You're going sit by while she's abused in a whorehouse by fucking Nazis?'

"'The abuse is saving her life. She's alive because officers desire her. The girls at the Plaza Hotel, the ones that aren't chosen to go to Rabka, are sent to Majdanek.'

"'If SS officers can get into the villa, then you can get into the villa. I'll go with you. We have to get her out.'

"Otto shook his head. 'You'd just wind up getting us all killed. Give it up.'

"'You won't go?'

"'No, Ben, I won't.'

"'Well, I will. Give me one of your uniforms and some identification. Let me have your car. I'll go in and bring her out.'

"Otto turned to Hannah and Elzbieta. 'Can either of you reason with him? He's committing suicide. No, worse. He's implicating me. Maybe all of us.'

"Hannah stepped forward. 'I'm grateful for what you did for me, Otto, but I won't talk Ben out of rescuing his sister. In fact, I'll go with him.'

"'I will too,' Elzbieta said.

"'You're all crazy,' screamed Otto. 'I'm not giving you a uniform, I'm not giving you my car, and I'm not giving you my credentials. You have no chance of succeeding, and I've worked too hard to earn my rank and position. When they find out I loaned you a uniform, my career'll be finished. And that's the least of what might happen to me.'

"'Career?' I said. I was furious that he would consider his position as anything more than a temporary posting that he accepted to help his family.

"'Yes, Ben, a career. Like it or not, Germany is now ruling all of Europe. This is a new world, the world of National Socialists, the world of Adolf Hitler, and I have a very important position in the party.'

"His arrogance disgusted me. 'Mister Big Shot. An important position with a bunch of soulless murderers.'

"'Let's not forget that it was my position that rescued Hannah today.'

"I was angry, but I needed Otto's help. 'Find out what you can about the villa and the surrounding area. I need to know how it's run and how it's guarded. I'll handle the rest without involving you.'

"The girls looked at Otto challengingly, with their hands on their hips, and I think he was shamed into cooperating. 'Damn you all,' he said and left the apartment.

"'I have to get back to New Town,' I said. 'Mother and Father will want to know what's happened to Beka.'

"'Wait until daybreak, Ben,' Elzbieta said. 'There's nothing more you can do tonight and it's too dangerous to be out and about. You two stay here tonight.'

"I watched her bring linens out to make up the couch for Hannah. I figured I'd sleep on the floor.

"She finished and inclined her head toward the back bedroom. 'You two take the bed,' she said. 'I'll sleep out here.'

"I protested and declined. I blushed. I told her I'd be happy on the couch, but Elzbieta waved me off. 'She needs you tonight,' she said.

"Hannah hugged her. 'Elzie, you're such a good friend.'

"'Someday this will all be over and pigs like Frank will roast.'"

Ben paused his narrative and drifted away again, his eyes seeing Elzbieta in her Zamość apartment. "What a sweetheart she was," he whispered.

TWENTY-SIX

...

Zamość, Poland, 1941

IN THE MORNING, HANNAH and I made our way back into New Town. It looked even more crowded than I remembered. People were out and about, walking everywhere, but they had no purpose, no place to go. Employment, education, commerce, and professional activities were essentially nonexistent. Hundreds of uprooted families, newly arriving from other cities, were trying to assimilate and were wandering about, adding to the confusion.

"Hannah went to find her father at the hospital, and I walked directly to the Judenrat. Father was surprised to see me, but he was also very troubled over demands that had been passed on by the new SS commandant, Gotthard Schubert.

"'I need to talk to you, right away,' I said.

"'We've been ordered to fill large work requisitions daily,' he said to me as we walked out into the street. 'Hundreds per day are being lined up and marched out of here to Izbica. Those few who return report that the Germans are building another ghetto. Sadly, Ben, most do not return.'"

"Can I ask an ignorant question?" interrupted Catherine.

Ben smiled. "Is there any other reason to ask a question? If you knew the answer, you wouldn't have to ask."

"Exactly what is a ghetto?"

Ben nodded and wagged his index finger. "You ask a good question. It has a different connotation today than it had many years ago. Today we speak of a ghetto pejoratively, when we mean to address the poorer, depressed parts of town. It didn't always have such a meaning. There are many theories about the origin of the term. Some say it comes from the Jewish section in fourteenth-century Venice, which was located on the grounds of an iron foundry. *Ghetto* is Italian for 'foundry.' Others say it comes from the Italian word *borghetto*, which means 'small neighborhood,' and that's what we generally mean by ghetto.

"The European ghettos, into which ethnic groups were forced, were generally abolished following the Age of Enlightenment at the turn of the nineteenth century. There were no forced ghettos in Poland until the Nazis arrived.

"The Jewish ghettos that were established in Poland were the brainchild of Reinhard Heydrich, Ilse's boss. In September 1939, right after the occupation, Heydrich told the army that the first step would be to concentrate the Jews from the countryside into the cities and compress them into ghettos. That's why Grandpa Yaakov was forced to give up his farm and move into Zamość."

"Wasn't one of the reasons for concentrating the Jews to supply workers for the German war effort?"

"No, Catherine, the purpose was always elimination. Heydrich declared that the Jewish ghettos were to be located as close as possible to rail connections. Heydrich saw this as a temporary situation, until the Jews could be moved to extermination camps, because his stated goal was the elimination of all European Jews.

"Others in Germany, especially the industrialists, saw the ghetto as a source of free labor. They gleefully rubbed their hands together at the thought of increasing their profits by eliminating labor costs, having a free and motivated workforce. The productionists were sadistically clever. Jews were good workers because bad workers were transferred to the death camps. Ghettoization was essentially accomplished throughout Poland in 1941. The industrialists had their free labor force, but of course, it didn't last. Heydrich, Eichmann, and the mass murderers prevailed, and without remonstrance from

German industry. Even during *Aktion Reinhard*, when thousands and thousands of Jews were being carted off to die, there was little or no protest from IG Farben and the rest of the industrial community. It seemed to them that the stream of workers was inexhaustible."

"Didn't the German war effort benefit from Jewish labor?"

"Minimally. It could have been substantial, but that was one of Hitler's great blunders. Despite the availability of a huge slave workforce, the Germans starved the Jews and kept them on minimum subsistence. Thousands died of malnutrition and disease. But then, this was no unfortunate mistake. Death by attrition served Heydrich's mass-murder purpose, even though the by-product was to deprive the German industrialists of their endless supply of slave labor.

"There are many reasons to study and teach about the Holocaust, and maybe the most important reason is to prevent reoccurrences. We are sentries, Catherine. We stand on the wall, on guard against any hint that the minions of genocide are reassembling. As the 1945 Nuremberg trials would establish, crimes against humanity must never again go unpunished. That is why Otto must be exposed and publicly prosecuted. We must never allow the world to forget."

Catherine sat back and laced her fingers around her knee. There was a wistful tone in her speech. "I'm not sure how to say this, but . . . all of your zeal, your extraordinary quest for knowledge, it makes me feel inadequate. I look back at what I've accomplished in my life, and it has comparatively no significance. My legal work doesn't serve any social good. I represent big companies against other big companies in a commercial arena. Nothing I do has enduring worth."

"My, my. Aren't we hard on ourselves? First of all, you're not even forty. It seems to me that you don't have all that much life to look back on. Secondly, it seems to me that you took quite a moral stand a few years ago."

Catherine twisted her lips. "So Liam opened his big mouth, did he?"

"We had a short talk. It was my fault. I persuaded him to tell me a little about you."

"He told you what happened a few years ago?"

Ben nodded.

"What else did Liam tell you?"

"That you are a wonderful person. He's quite fond of you, you know. You could do a lot worse."

"I see. In addition to all of your other callings, are you also a matchmaker?"

"Would it be so bad? He's a very good man."

Catherine smiled and shook her head. "All right. All right. Let's get back to your story. You were telling me about your father when I interrupted you."

"Right. I was trying to tell him about Beka and he was upset over new orders he had received. The Judenrat was charged with supplying hundreds of Jews daily to be sent to do construction on the new camps.

"I told him again that I needed to talk to him and Mother privately as soon as possible. He said he'd meet me back at the apartment in an hour.

"I found Mother at the clinic. She looked so thin and tired, tending to other thin and tired people. We walked back to the apartment together. I didn't want to say anything until my father was present.

"'How is Aunt Hilda?' I asked as we walked.

"A sad look came over her pretty face. 'Oh, Benjamin,' she said with her hand on my arm, 'she has typhus. Dr. Weissbaum is treating her at the hospital, but he's overwhelmed. They have very few medicines and typhus is so hard to treat.'

"We arrived at the massive, crumbling building that my family now called home, walked up the darkened stairway and down the hall. As I looked around, the building appeared roomier than it had previously. No, I should say more empty. Some of the furnishings were gone. There was less clothing hanging on lines, fewer pieces of furniture.

"'What's been happening here?' I asked.

"'Food, Benjamin. We don't get enough food to keep us going. People trade their belongings to the townsfolk for food. A coat will bring bread and vegetables. A beautiful chair might fetch a roast. The Germans suspect that most of us have squirreled away a little money or jewelry. It wasn't all turned in to the Gestapo. So they reason, if they starve us, sooner or later, people will have to spend the money and cash in their belongings for food. The Germans will impoverish us one way or another.'

"Father arrived soon afterward. I gestured for them to sit in the chairs and I sat on the edge of the bed.

"I swallowed hard and began. 'There's no easy way to say this. When I got back to the cabin the girls were gone. Mr. Kozlowski told me the Germans had taken them.' My mother gasped. She held her hands over her mouth. 'I came back as fast as I could and asked Otto for his help. He went to Zakopane and was successful in bringing Hannah back last night, but not Beka.'

"My mother grabbed my arms and squeezed. I felt her fingernails. She put a hand on her mouth to stifle her hysteria.

"'She's alive,' I added quickly, 'and I know where they're keeping her. I'm going to get her myself. One way or another, I'll get her out.'

"'And Hannah?' Father said.

"'She's here. She's with Dr. Weissbaum.'

"'Where are they keeping Beka?'

"'In a place called Rabka.' I omitted the lurid details. 'It's like a compound.'

"'I'm going to see Otto,' said Father. 'He'll get her out if I have anything to say about it.' With that he stood and strode from the room, looking every bit like a father going to read the riot act to a teenager.

"Later that evening, Father returned to the apartment. 'It's worse than I imagined,' he said, choking back his rage. 'Beka is being kept prisoner at a bordello. She's being forced . . .' He looked at me and shook his head. 'Otto says you can't go there, Ben, the place is full of SS and Gestapo and there are Ukrainian guards patrolling the grounds. Since there are highly ranked officers at the villa, the security is airtight.'

"'What will Otto do for us?' I said.

"Father shook his head. 'He says there's nothing he can do. He'd be recognized, especially by Dr. Frank, if he went there. Frank will make the connection between Beka and Otto. Maybe they'll let her go when the officers leave.'

"'Otto's a coward!' I snapped. 'He's afraid to jeopardize his prestigious position.'

"'He did rescue Hannah. That took courage.'

"'How much courage? He's an officer in full uniform who walks into a detention area and takes a young girl. What kind of risk was he taking?'

"My father stood. That was his way of ending a conversation. 'We shall think about this for a while. Something will come to us.'"

"And did something come to you, Ben?" asked Catherine.

"An angel came to us. An angel named Elzbieta. She came to the ghetto a couple of days later and met with Hannah and me. We held a secret, whispered meeting in a stairwell—you could never be too careful, a starving person would sell his grandmother for food.

"'I have a car and Otto's extra uniform back at my apartment,' she said to us. I smiled and gave Elzbieta a big hug and a kiss.

"'When did Otto agree to do this?' I said.

"'Well, he didn't agree exactly,' she answered with a mischievous smile. 'I kinda took them last night in exchange for services rendered. He said to tell you, if you're caught, he won't help you and he'll say that his uniform was stolen. He also said to tell you that Dr. Frank is in the area and he may be at the villa.'

"'I need Otto to tell me where the villa is and give me a layout.'

"Elzbieta shook her head. 'He'll have nothing to do with this. But, truthfully, I don't think there's much he can tell you. He hasn't been to the villa. He told me it's on the River Raba, midway between Zakopane and Krakow.'"

"Don't tell me that you went alone to the Nazi villa," Catherine said, leaning forward on her elbows, forgoing her note-taking.

"I did. I left that afternoon with my money and a small picture of Beka. Wearing the uniform of an SS Hauptscharführer, I drove straight to Krakow and south to Rabka, a distance of about two hundred miles."

"Did you have papers? What would happen if you were stopped?"

Ben shrugged. "I had no Nazi papers. Otto wouldn't allow Elzbieta to lend me his identification, but I only faced a single roadblock east of Krakow. Thankfully, when they saw my uniform, they saluted and waved me through.

"It was early evening when I arrived at the villa, a gracious Polish estate set back several hundred meters from the road, reachable on a winding stone pathway built long before there were cars. True to the warning, there were several guards patrolling the estate and two sentries at the portico. As I pulled up to the columned entryway, I was welcomed by the guards, who deferentially gave me the *Heil Hitler!* salute and opened my car door. I had to leave my car with an adjutant to park in the grass field below. That worried me. If I needed to make a quick exit, I'd have to find the car and hope the keys were in the ignition. But I had no choice.

"The villa once belonged to a Polish aristocrat, a prince, I think. It was three stories of brick and stone with balconied windows and a pitched slate roof. In more congenial times it would have hosted Krakow's elite, but on this night it was crawling with Nazis. Some were passed out in overstuffed chairs. Others, running about in their underwear, were chasing women through the halls. I feigned intoxication and weaved unsteadily as I walked through the foyer, past the guard who was checking the guest list, pretending that I was already checked and had gone out for a breath of fresh air. I also figured if I appeared to be drunk I could get by with choppy German sentences and my accent would be less noticeable."

Once again Ben's eyes widened. He stared at the ceiling and settled into his zone.

"I wander around the first floor to get my bearings. Officers are sitting in groups, some arguing about military tactics, some about the impending Russian campaign, and some demanding service of food or alcohol from frightened waiters. I take a glass of wine from a server's tray and look for someone to talk to.

"Two young officers, obviously taking a break from the demands of their sexual exploits, their tunics unbuttoned, are lounging on a couch in the front room, laughing and swapping stories. I plop down on a chair opposite them and take a sip of wine.

"After a moment, one tilts his head at me and says, 'Did you just get here?'

"'A little while ago,' I say.

"'You better guard your pecker,' he says with a drunken slur, 'they'll suck it right off.' Then he and his compatriot double over in laughter.

"I smile and toast him with my wine glass. 'Where are the girls?' I ask.

"He gestures with his thumb, 'Upstairs. They're all over the place. But don't say I didn't warn you.' He spews a drunken giggle and downs a shot of whiskey.

"I leave them and walk up to the second floor. At the top of the grand staircase there is a sitting room where several girls in dressing gowns are seated on folding chairs, awaiting the attention of the visiting dignitaries. Most of them are young and all of them look frightened. I don't see Beka. A few of the girls force a smile as I walk in.

"I reach for the hand of a young blond girl, slight and fair-skinned, dressed only in a small silk nightgown barely covering her thighs, who dutifully rises and walks out into the hallway with me. Her hand is small and childlike. I judge her to be sixteen or seventeen. The villa has several bedrooms, maybe a dozen, and we hear orgiastic noise emanating from behind many of the closed doors. We come upon an empty bedroom. I lead her in and shut the door. She stands still, head down, waiting to be invited onto the bed or to be told what my perverted pleasures demand of her.

"'What is your name?' I say.

"Her eyes are lowered. 'Please, sir,' she says in Polish, 'what would you have me to do?'

"I repeat my question in Polish, 'What is your name, please?' She continues to stare at the floor."

Catherine said softly, "She doesn't want to personalize the experience."

"That's what I think, too, but I have to know who she is. 'Tell me your name and where you're from,' I say forcefully.

"'I am Lucyna. My home is in Nowy Targ.'

"'Are you Jewish, Lucyna?' I say.

"She swallows hard, averting her eyes, and begins to unbutton the top of her gown, exposing her breasts. Tears are forming and rolling down her face.

"'Stop undressing,' I say, taking out my picture of Beka. 'I'm looking for a girl. This one.'

"She doesn't know what to make of me. Taking the photograph, her eyes move back and forth between my face and the picture. She nods. 'I know her. She came with me last week. She's here.'

"'Where is she?'

"'Please, Your Honor, I'm just a peasant girl. I don't really know what others are doing. I will be happy to please you. Please don't ask me questions, for I have no information to give.'

"I grab her wrists. My face is inches from hers. 'She's my sister, Lucyna. Her name is Beka. I'm not a Nazi. I'm a Jew, like you. I've come to get my sister.'

"Tears stream from her eyes and she blinks several times. I let her hands go and she wipes her eyes. 'You're a fool,' she says. 'The only way out of here is in a wagon.'

"'Where is she, Lucyna?'

"She hesitates, then nods and says, 'I'm a condemned girl anyway.' She takes my hand and leads me into the hallway, whispering, 'She was taken earlier today by a young SS officer named Rolf. He has a bad reputation among the girls—mean and violent—he likes it rough. He's been in the corner bedroom for two days.'

"I open the door to the corner bedroom where Rolf is propped up on the bed, his back against the headboard. He's a stocky man with a massive hairy chest and powerful arms. He has close-cropped blond hair. He sits alone in his boxers and sleeveless undershirt, soaked down the front with what I assume is sweat and dribbled whiskey. He holds the neck of a bottle of brandy in his left hand. His uniform, boots, pistol, and knife lie in a heap on the floor by the side of the bed. He smiles broadly and holds up the brandy bottle as we walk in.

"'Hellooo, Hauptscharführer,' he slurs. Brandy spills from his lips and down his shirt. 'Did you bring me another tasty morsel?'

"'All in good time, my friend. I was hoping you could tell me about a pretty, young girl you were with earlier.' I show him the photograph.

"He snorts. 'This one,' he says, 'is gone. You wouldn't want her anyway. Fucking cold bitch.'

"Listening to him talk about my sister sends fire through my veins. It takes all my effort to restrain myself.

"'Do you know where she is, my friend?'

"He sits up, tries very hard to focus, and points at Beka's picture. 'Let me tell you about this one. She almost ruined my whole weekend. Fucking bitch,' he sneers, 'didn't want to be touched.'

"He snorts again. 'I could tell in a minute, she's a Jew, so I decide to teach this Jewish sow a thing or two about the Master Race.' He reaches down and picks up his knife from his pile of clothes. 'You'd be surprised how romantic they become when they feel the cold of my blade on their soft white tits.' He laughs and flips the knife up in the air. It lands on the end of his bed. He takes a swig of brandy. 'Besides, there's something erotic about debasing those arrogant Jewesses, don't you think? It gets me all excited. So, I grab this bitch by the hair, lean back, spread my legs, and point at my crotch. "Come and taste the German High Command," I say. "In your dreams," she says and then she spits at me. Can you believe it? This fucking Jew spits at a German officer. I let her go to wipe my face.'

"He tips another swig of brandy, wipes his mouth with the back of his arm, and slurs, 'She backs up toward the door, so I jump off the bed with my knife. "Oh you'll take it all right," I tell her, "all eight inches of it, and then I'm going to carve my initials in your lily-white ass." I grab at her, but she's quick and darts away. I swing my foot and manage to trip her and she goes tumbling across the floor. Now I've got her cornered, and I'm going to take her right there on the floor, but the wild beast spins away from me. She jumps up and looks at me with these crazy eyes. "This is one Jewish girl you won't violate," she says and she flings herself out the window. Two stories down. Stupid bitch. She hit the cement below and broke her skull wide open.' He snorted, laughed, and took another swig. 'Serves her right. I'm only sorry I didn't get to do it myself.'"

Ben paused his narrative. His jaw tensed. "Everything is a blur—I'm operating on animal instinct. I grab Rolf's knife from the bed and fly at him, my right hand tight around his throat, my left pressuring the tip of the knife over his heart. His eyes are wide with fear, his body is still. 'That lovely girl was my sister,' I say, inches from his vile face. 'You want romance? Here's a kiss from Beka Solomon.' I push the knife deep into his chest, twisting it up and then down, holding his throat until he stops convulsing.

"Lucyna stands frozen in the center of the room. 'We're dead,' she says.

"'Help me get him into the closet,' I say to her, 'and I'll take you out of here.'

"We pull him into the closet and cover him with bedding.

"'Your hands,' she says. I look down at my shaking hands. They're covered in red. I dash to the bathroom and wash his filthy blood down the sink.

"His pistol is lying on the floor. I stick it in my belt, grab Lucyna, and lead her from the bedroom to the staircase, pretending to stumble like two drunks, my arm around her waist, to all appearances my courtesan for the night. I take a bottle of vodka off a table near the door and, swinging it around, walk out the front door sauntering like I own the place, me in my uniform, Lucyna in her nightgown. Winking at the sentries, Lucyna and I wobble and giggle through the portico and out toward the woods, another sick Nazi off to get his jollies.

"We make our way down to the car, and thankfully, the keys are on the seat. I quietly drive down the stone pathway back to the road."

A lump in Ben's throat put a halt to the narrative. He placed his palms flat on the table and nodded his head. Looking into Catherine's eyes, he said, "And that's what happened to my sister. It's my fault, Catherine. I never should have left her."

"I'm so sorry," she said, gripping his forearms. Her face flushed, her eyes full of tears, Catherine put her arms around the wiry old man, hugged him tightly, and buried her head on his shoulder. He patted her on the back. They rocked together.

"It was never your fault, Ben. You can't continue to blame yourself. Please. If you'd have been there at the cabin, you would have also been arrested. Or shot." She gently lifted his chin. "I'm honored that you shared your story with me, Ben."

She gathered their coats from the brass coat tree, handed Ben his parka, pushed her arms through the sleeves of her camel coat, and wrapped a cream wool scarf around her neck. "Would you take a walk with me? I think we could use a breather."

In raw November winds, the Alberta clipper churned Lake Michigan like an agitator in a washing machine, lifting the whitecaps and slamming them down on the sandy shore. Park district workers busily constructed wooden snow fences along the edges of the beachfront to keep impending winter snowfalls from blowing and drifting over adjacent Lake Shore Drive. Catherine and Ben walked briskly and without conversation past the Oak Street beach and back again. By the time they finished their walk and returned to the office, it was dusk and Ben was breathing hard.

"Whew. That's more exercise than I've had in a while," he said.

"It was a therapy walk for me," Catherine said. "I needed a few degrees of separation. I hope you didn't overdo."

"I'll be okay. The years have taken their toll, I'm afraid. There was a time when I could walk, and did walk, for days." He poured a cup of hot tea and wrapped his hands around the mug. Ben shivered, making ripples in the surface of the tea. "But then, that's another chapter of my story."

"Do you feel up to continuing, because I'll go a while longer if you want to."

"Full speed ahead."

Zamość, Poland, 1941

"Leaving Rabka, I could barely contain my rage. I wanted to drive back to Zamość as soon as possible, gather Hannah and my family, and get out of Europe. Of course, now I had Lucyna with me. I offered to take her to her home in Nowy Targ, but she rejected the suggestion, fearing that she would be re-arrested and sent back to Rabka. Or worse. She felt that she was a marked woman, that she'd be sought as the woman who helped murder Rolf.

"We drove through the night, her head on my shoulder, and arrived in Zamość about 3:00 A.M. Dressed only in her nightgown, my tunic wrapped around her, she shivered in the night's cold. I parked the car a block away from Elzbieta's and walked with Lucyna up the back stairway. Elzbieta answered the door in her robe.

"'Come in quickly,' she whispered and inclined her head at Lucyna standing in the doorway, essentially asking me, 'Who the heck is this?'

"As she ushered us in and handed Lucyna a robe, I hurriedly recounted the details, leaving nothing out. Needless to say, Elzbieta was shaken by the news of Beka's death.

"'I've got to get Hannah and my family out of Zamość. One way or another we're leaving Europe,' I said.

"'What are we to do with Lucyna?' Elzbieta said, staring at us both. 'She has no papers and from what you tell me, the two of you are public enemies number one and two.'

"I shook my head. 'The drunken scum at Rabka don't know who I am. I figure I'll take Lucyna into New Town tomorrow morning. She doesn't have any place else to stay. My mother will find a home for her until we leave, and then she'll come with us.'

"Elzbieta hesitated. 'I heard rumors tonight.'

"'From Otto?'

"She nodded. 'Soon there are to be mass deportations from New Town. Railroad transports to Izbica. The Germans have built a large work camp there.'

"I knew that was the beginning of the end—I'd worked at Izbica. It was a small, primitive community with old wooden houses, barely any electricity, and mud streets. It was located in a desolate valley, near Belzec, farther from the Tatras and more remote. It was truly cut off from the rest of the world. 'Once they're transferred there, it'll be hell to escape.'

"'Take my car,' she said, 'it belonged to my aunt and she doesn't drive anymore. Get your family out of here.'

"I gave her a big kiss. 'Elzie, you're wonderful. Tell Otto I need to keep his uniform in case we're stopped.'

"'I will, but he's not going to like it,' she said. She led Lucyna back to her closet to find some clothes. I caught a short nap and awoke at daylight.

"The two of us made our way into the ghetto without incident. I carried Otto's tunic in a shopping bag covered with potatoes. Neither my mother nor my father was at the apartment. I hid the uniform and pistol under the bed, left Lucyna, and headed to the Judenrat, for I preferred to have my father with me when my mother learned about Beka. When I found him he was in the midst of an argument with several older men, trying to formulate a protest to present to Commandant Schubert, complaining about the lack of medicine deliveries.

"My father saw me and excused himself from the argument. He put his arm around me and walked me to the street.

"'Did you get Beka?' he asked.

"I could barely speak. I was always awed by my father, and in his imposing presence I couldn't bring myself to tell him right off that Beka had died. But intuitively he knew.

"'This will crush your mother,' he said. 'I don't know how much more she can take.'

"'We need to get out of Zamość,' I said. 'I have Elzie's car. We can leave tonight. We'll head straight for the southern border. Krzysztof showed me a route through the mountains into Yugoslavia. I have a gun and Otto's uniform—we'll bluff our way through.'

"Father didn't answer immediately, and that troubled me. We started walking to the clinic. After a short while he said, 'There is much to do before we can leave.'

"Hannah and Mother were both at the clinic when we arrived. Father pulled them aside and we stepped into a small office. He quietly closed the door and looked at them with a face that said it all. I stood next to Hannah, my arm around her waist. Father put his hands on Mother's frail shoulders. 'Leah, our beautiful Beka is gone. *Alav hashalom*—may she rest in peace.'

"My mother crumpled into his arms and wailed. Hannah wept. I held her tightly. It was the most profound sadness I had ever witnessed. The three of us stayed in the room for several minutes without talking. Finally Mother lifted her head from Father's chest and asked, 'When will this end?'

"'Now,' I said. 'We're going to leave Zamość.'

"We walked slowly, arms around each other, back to the apartment. I introduced my parents and Hannah to Lucyna, who was sitting silently across the room. Mother lay down on the bed, Hannah sat by her side, and my father and I walked out to the sidewalk to talk. He didn't want to know the details of Beka's death and I didn't offer.

"'I'll have to make arrangements for someone to take my position at the Judenrat,' he said. 'That'll be difficult because I dare not disclose my intent to leave. There are too many who would sell that information for a loaf of bread. If I can arrange it and if your mother is up to it, we'll leave tomorrow night.'

"'I'll contact Otto. We'll need money,' I said.

"'I suppose you're right, but I no longer trust Otto. Be careful.'

"I nodded and left for Elzbieta's."

Catherine held her hands up. "I need to stop here. I'm exhausted—physically and emotionally. I feel like I lost a friend today. I want you to finish your story, but I can't absorb any more today."

"I'm sorry. You're a good person, Catherine. Shall I come back tomorrow?"

"Tomorrow," she stammered softly. "Yes, tomorrow."

Catherine walked slowly back to her office and rocked in her desk chair staring through the window at Federal Plaza, below. The last of the season's open-air markets was folding up. Federal employees, finished with their workday, were filing past the orange Calder statue and dispersing through the plaza. There was a beehive of energy outside the window, but inside her office Catherine was drained. After several minutes she picked up the phone and dialed Liam.

"Are you busy?" she asked.

"Never too busy for you."

"Can you pick me up at the office?"

"Now?"

"Please. I'll meet you on the Dearborn Street side."

Jeffers stood by the window in Rosenzweig's corner office, looking out over the Chicago skyline on a clear, starlit evening.

"This view makes me feel like I'm standing in an airplane," he said to Elliot.

"Did Solomon sign the order?" Elliot said.

Jeffers shook his head and walked away from the windows. "Not yet. I just gave it to Lockhart today. You were right: she does represent him."

"That's what was told to me. Did she say whether or not Solomon would sign the order?"

"No. But if he doesn't, I'll bring him into court. We'll get the order entered one way or another."

Rosenzweig shook his head. "No court hearing, Gerry. It's bad publicity."

"I disagree. Solomon's a stalker, and a dangerous one at that. No one would blame you."

"He'd use the hearing as some kind of soapbox to accuse me. I don't want to give him a forum. The papers and TV stations would be all over it, and all of Solomon's rantings would get airtime. No, thanks, I don't need it."

"Well, he may end up signing it voluntarily. I threatened Lockhart pretty good. I even leaned on Walter Jenkins, her boss."

"If he does, fine; otherwise let it go. As I told you, I have an investigator on the trail of the real Otto Piatek. He told Brian this afternoon that he has a lead. Believe it or not, he thinks Piatek may actually be in Cleveland."

"You're kidding!"

Rosenzweig opened a walnut humidor and took out two cigars. He clipped the ends and handed one to Jeffers.

"How did he find him in Cleveland?" Jeffers said between puffs as he lit his Cohiba.

Elliot shrugged. "Friend of a friend. He's got friends in low places, as they say. I don't ask too many questions. The investigator's been spreading some money around in one of those neo-Nazi groups and seems to have come across information that Piatek was living in a bungalow in a Polish neighborhood somewhere in Cleveland. Who knows? We may find this guy. He's tracking it. Wouldn't that be something?"

"You trust this investigator?"

"Not entirely. But I'll spend a few bucks and see what he comes up with."

Jeffers examined his cigar. "Okay. I'll hold off on the order of protection. Damn fine cigar, Elliot."

Thanks," said Catherine, sliding into Liam's car. "I didn't want to go home alone."

"Rough day? Did Ben give you a hard time?"

"Liam, you have no idea. The story, the people, what they went through. I keep thinking, who am I to be given the responsibility for bringing this matter to judgment? How has it found its way into my lap?" She shook her head and tried not to cry. "I don't have his strength of character. This is too lofty an assignment for me."

"Don't beat yourself up, Cat. I have faith in you."

"I know you do. You always have. Keep telling me to be strong, Liam. I need it."

As Liam pulled up in front of Catherine's townhome, she said, "Do you have time to come in for a while? I could use the company."

"Sure," he said. They found a parking place a block away. The streetlights had come on and the November evening was blustery.

"I can cook us dinner," she said, unlocking her door. "That is, if you don't have plans."

"Don't go to any trouble. You've had a tough day. How about we order Chinese? Unless you're dead set on cooking."

"Chinese sounds perfect."

THEY SAT ON THE living room couch, eating moo shu pork on paper plates, while the stereo played softly. Catherine summarized the day's narrative.

"Poor Beka. Poor Abraham and Leah," Liam said. "How does anyone deal with a loss like that?"

"I have no idea. I suppose you carry the nightmare for the rest of your life. By the way, Gerald Jeffers and two of his young Storch & Bennett associates came by and threatened me today. They had security films of Ben sneaking around Rosenzweig's house taking pictures. They flung a court order at me and demanded that Ben sign it. Jeffers called him 'deranged' and they told me to send him on his way."

"What did you say?"

"I just sat there doing nothing, intimidated like a busted teenager."

"How did Jeffers know you represented Ben?"

"What?"

"How did he know? Have you filed anything? Have you sent any letters? How did he know to come to you, that you were Ben's lawyer?"

"I don't know. Maybe because I visited him at the jail?"

"Jeffers wouldn't have that information."

"Then I have no idea."

"Think about it, Cat."

She sat on the couch, looking at the floor. Then she turned and faced Liam with a look of surprise. "Ben's notes! They were missing after the break-in. He said there were notes about conversations he had with me."

Liam smiled. "It could be."

"Ben's right. Rosenzweig *is* Piatek."

"Whoa, hold on, Cat. That's a leap. But it raises interesting questions. Even if it ties Rosenzweig into the break-in, it doesn't necessarily connect him with Piatek. There's an alternative explanation. It could just be that he wanted to find out about the guy who assaulted him at the opera and what information he had."

Catherine snorted. "Hah! You don't believe that any more than I do."

She poured two glasses of wine, handing one to Liam. "Do you think you can find out about Rosenzweig's insurance companies? I'd like to know how some poor impoverished immigrant becomes a billionaire."

Liam nodded. "Now you're talking. I've been thinking the same thing. There are state insurance records I can access. I'll poke around."

They sat together until the wine was gone and Catherine's eyelids were heavy. Liam slipped his coat on. "Double-lock your doors, Cat. You can never be too careful."

"Do you think they'd try something?"

Liam shrugged.

"What about Ben?" Catherine said. "If Rosenzweig is Piatek and if he ordered the break-in, then he knows that Ben is telling the whole story to me. He might even kill Ben."

"I've been thinking about that. I don't think he'd want Ben to be found murdered. It'd be a media field day. Ben's death or disappearance following his public accusation and in the midst of his meetings with you would create an unmistakable presumption that Rosenzweig was involved. I don't think he'd take that chance. No, I think he has to continue to brush aside the accusations and treat Ben as a lunatic."

TWENTY-SEVEN

. . .

Chicago, Illinois, November 2004

EARLY THE NEXT MORNING, before Ben was scheduled to arrive, there was a knock on Catherine's office door. The firm's senior and founding partner, Walter Jenkins, nattily dressed in his three-piece wool suit and bow tie, walked into her office. His shoes were brightly polished, his nails were freshly manicured, and his thick silver hair was fashionably styled.

"Do you have a few minutes, Catherine? I'd like to talk to you about a matter I've learned you're working on."

"I know what you're going to say."

"Do you?"

Catherine shifted uneasily. "You're going to say my hours were down last week. I've been spending time interviewing a pro bono case, and I think it has a lot of merit. I know it's probably far too much time on a single case that hasn't even been logged into the system. But don't worry, I'll make up my time."

Jenkins took a seat on Catherine's couch and crossed his legs. He smoothed his trousers. "Gerry Jeffers came to see me last night. He said he paid you a visit yesterday."

"That bastard. So he went over my head?"

"I've known Gerry for many years."

"He waltzed in here unannounced with his two smug kids and put on a dog-and-pony show trying to scare me away from my interviews. He told me not to risk my professional future. I was supremely offended."

Jenkins nodded slightly. "Gerry tells me that you haven't returned the signed order of protection that he prepared for you. All he wants is for Solomon to leave his client alone."

"Mr. Solomon won't agree to the order, nor should he. Besides, it goes further than Jeffers told you. It prohibits him from talking about Rosenzweig in public or denouncing him or even accusing him."

"What's wrong with that?"

"It's a clear violation of Ben's First Amendment rights, his freedom of speech, among other things, and violations of that order of protection are punishable by contempt."

"He was videoed snooping around Mr. Rosenzweig's house, peering in the windows."

"He won't do it again."

"What's this all about, Catherine? Why are you spending so much time with this fellow?"

Catherine spent the next fifteen minutes outlining Ben's story.

At the end of her summary, Jenkins said, "What proof have you seen that any of this has any connection with Mr. Rosenzweig?"

"Well, none yet. Up to now, I'm just taking background notes. But Ben assures me that he is certain of the identification."

"I don't want it, Catherine. I can understand your emotional commitment to this saga, but we run a business and this case is bad business. You could never take on Elliot Rosenzweig without solid proof. It's insane. Hell, even with solid proof it'd be insane. It would cost us in money, time, and reputation. Unless we have the horses, we have no business in the race."

"What about all the contradictions in Rosenzweig's stories, like he immigrated in 1945 after being liberated from Auschwitz, when he really came in from Argentina two years later? And how does he come to America, a poor, penniless refugee, and take up residence on Lake Shore Drive?"

Jenkins shook his head. "I don't want it. The case would cost us six figures with no hope of recovery."

"What if we could prove he took Ben's property? Rosenzweig certainly has money to pay a judgment."

"You said you haven't seen any proof."

"Not yet."

"Catherine, what's the basis for a lawsuit? The case is sixty years old and probably time-barred in any event."

"The grounds would be misappropriation, conversion, replevin, return of the stolen goods, or a judgment for the equivalent amount of money. In a conversion case, the time commences from demand and refusal. The matter may not be time-barred. Ben has thoroughly researched the cases, and even given me a Ninth Circuit printout, recently decided, giving the heirs of Jewish refugees the right to sue an Austrian museum for the return of a valuable Gustav Klimt painting. It was affirmed by the Supreme Court. So there's precedent for this type of action."

"Can Solomon pay the ongoing costs of this lawsuit? You're looking at a big ticket."

"Of course not. If we filed suit for him, we'd have to take it on a contingency basis."

Jenkins shook his head. "I'm not putting our firm's money into this."

"Hold on, Mr. Jenkins. I'll work it in the evenings, in my spare time. Liam will do the investigation for free. I won't file anything unless there's solid evidence. I promise. I want to help him, Mr. Jenkins. I'm very serious about this. I believe in him. There's something about this man, this case, that impels me to continue."

Jenkins shook his head again. "I don't want a civil case filed by this office. It's a black hole."

"Well, even if we don't file a civil suit, if I can develop enough evidence to show that Rosenzweig is a Nazi, I can send the matter over to the U.S. Attorney for prosecution. There's no statute of limitations on Nazi war criminals."

Jenkins lifted himself off the couch and straightened his vest and jacket. "Pass on it, Catherine. Let him go to some charitable, pro bono outfit to wage this war. I don't want this firm involved civilly or criminally. I don't want you referring him to Justice. I don't want you involved at all! It's already causing trouble for me in the legal community."

"Are you backing off because of pressure from Jeffers?"

Jenkins turned quickly. "Excuse me, Miss Lockhart?" he said sharply.

He walked over to Catherine's desk, leaned forward on his fists, and said, "Have you ever stopped to consider that this crazy old man is probably wrong? What if it's a case of mistaken identity? What if Solomon is just plain wrong and Elliot Rosenzweig is exactly what everyone thinks he is—a pillar of society? Do you understand, you have no proof! You could assassinate the character of a good man! And furthermore, what if Solomon is truly delusional? What if he has fabricated this entire scenario? Have you considered that? How do you know that this lunatic hasn't come in here and made up the whole damn thing? Do you have any proof that he is who he says he is?"

"I need look no further than every fiber in my body. You might as well tell me that Lake Michigan is imaginary. I know he's genuine. And if I can gather proof that Rosenzweig is Piatek, I'm going to represent him. I'm either going to file a civil suit or I'm going to send it to the U.S. Attorney."

"Not in this office, you're not."

"Are you going to fire me?"

"Catherine, you're a damn good lawyer—that's why I gave you a break and hired you two years ago—but I'm going to tell you right now, this firm will not represent Ben Solomon. I won't let it past the committee."

"I'll take a leave of absence."

"I won't approve it. Besides, Catherine, face reality. You can't run this case on your own. Jeffers will throw multiple lawyers at you, dozens of motions, simultaneous depositions. He'll eat you up with discovery costs, travel costs, expert fees, and court time. And for what, Catherine? To prove that Rosenzweig worked for the Nazis sixty years ago and maybe to get some old man a few dollars?"

"Mr. Jenkins, I'm ashamed of you. For what? For *justice*, that's what! I'm not abandoning this case. I'll work the file out of my house if I have to. Fire me, if you want to. For now, I'm on leave."

Reeling from her confrontation, she grabbed her coat, left the office, and burst out the door onto Dearborn Street. She walked to the corner and stopped to take stock of what she had just done. She looked at the Marquette Building and up to the windows on the fourteenth floor. She turned and faced Federal Plaza across the street, which suddenly seemed more formidable. She swallowed hard, bit her lip, and called Ben to reschedule the morning's appointment. Her next call was to Liam.

"What's up, Cat?"

"Liam, I'm standing on the corner of Dearborn and Adams."

"Are you okay?"

"I just did something totally irrational."

"What happened?"

"Remember what we talked about last night? Jeffers and his threats?"

"Of course."

"Well, I just walked away from Jenkins & Fairchild. Probably the biggest mistake of my life. Jeffers put a full-court press on Jenkins, who ordered me to pass on Ben's case and give it to some pro bono outfit. When I told him I wouldn't back off, Jenkins gave me an ultimatum. I walked."

"I'm proud of you, Cat."

"This'll crater my legal career."

"Not a chance. There may be some firms that would consider you politically undesirable, but those firms aren't good enough for you anyway. Why don't you hang out a shingle?"

"A neighborhood lawyer?"

"Why not?"

"That's not me. I never had the nerve to fly solo. I need the support of a large firm."

"What about a small partnership?"

"I'm not going to make any of those decisions today. Want to take an unemployed woman to lunch?"

"Let me make a couple of calls. I'll meet you at Shaw's in thirty minutes. By the way, I started looking into the formation of Rosenzweig's Columbia Indemnity Corporation. I ordered some files and should have the results in a few days."

TWENTY-EIGHT

• • •

T HURSDAY AFTERNOON FOUND BEN walking to an address on a quiet tree-lined street in the Lincoln Park neighborhood, an area ten minutes north of Chicago's Loop.
Graystones, brownstones, and frame bungalows were neatly set
back from the parkways and nestled in abundant foliage, under-
scoring Chicago's motto: *Urbs in Horto*—City in a Garden.

He stepped onto the concrete stoop of a three-story graystone
with a large iron-framed bay window and rang the doorbell. He
was greeted by Catherine in her blue jeans and white bulky-knit
sweater.

"Nice-looking home," he said, taking off his jacket.

"Thank you, Ben. It was built in 1928 and actually belongs to
my aunt. I'm a renter."

"Tell me again why we're not meeting at your office," he said,
following her into the kitchen.

"It's an inner-office conflict. We'll need to meet here for a while."
She filled a red tea kettle and set it on the stove.

"Did I get you into trouble?"

"No, Ben. I make my own decisions." She walked Ben through
the dining room archway and into her front room. "I built a nice,
warm fire for us."

Ben sat in an overstuffed chair, at an angle to the fireplace, and
waited for Catherine to settle on the couch and pick up her pen and
paper.

"The last thing you told me was that you were going to Elzbieta's."

"They don't want you to represent me, do they? There's no economic upside for Jenkins & Fairchild, am I right? It's a political embarrassment, right?"

"Stop, Ben."

"Look, Catherine, I don't want you to do this. I'll figure something else out. Tell Jenkins that I'll find another lawyer. I'll call him, if you want me to."

"Stop."

"I don't want to see your career suffer because of me. You're a brilliant young woman. I couldn't handle the guilt. Jewish guilt—more powerful than the atom bomb, as they say."

"I appreciate your concern, Ben, and I know that you're sincere, but I'll handle my situation. It's mine to deal with. Right now, I believe the correct path for me is to do what I think is right. I've made a decision. We're finished talking about this. Now, tell me what happened when you went to Elzbieta's?"

"All right." Ben nodded and smiled at Catherine. "But don't ever try to tell me that you've never done anything significant or never felt impassioned. I have a world of respect for you."

"Thanks. Now, the story, please."

Zamość, Poland, 1941

"After I talked to my father about taking the family and escaping to Yugoslavia, I headed to Elzbieta's to get in touch with Otto. I told Elzie we needed his help. I didn't want to say anything to her about the money or get her in the middle of that dispute. She asked me to wait at her apartment while she tracked him down.

"It was just past midnight when she and Otto returned. He looked angry—no, put out was more like it. Irritated.

"'I'm sorry about Beka,' he said, and then quickly added, 'but you can't drive to the Tatras. That's out of the question. And you certainly can't drive there in my uniform.'

"'Why not?' I argued. 'Should we stay here until we're shot or die of typhus or starve to death? Or maybe we should be displaced again and sent to that shit-hole Izbica. I'd rather take my chances on the road.'

"'Are you going to drag your mother through the mountains? What about Aunt Hilda? Are you going to take her, too? Look, Ben, there are new orders coming down. No one is to leave the ghetto unless they're sent on a work detail. No more walking around town with work permits, not even here to Elzie's. I can't let you go.'

"'You what?'

"'I'm telling you, you can't go. You have to obey the law.'

"'Are you going to turn me in, Otto? Are you going to shoot the only real mother and father you ever had? We're going, Otto, whether you like it or not, and we're going tonight.'

"Otto placed his hat carefully on his head, tugged at the shiny bill, and turned for the door. 'Do what you want, but don't look to me for protection,' he said, closing the door behind him.

"I chased him out into the hall. 'Hold on,' I yelled. 'We need our money.' He kept walking away like he didn't hear me. I ran after him and halted him at the stairs. 'We need our money, the sixty thousand złotys my father gave to you.'

"'Can't do it, Ben. It's against the law for you to have it. If they change the law, then I'll give it to you. But mind this warning: you and your family must obey the laws or face severe punishment.'

"Part of me couldn't believe what I was hearing, and the other part of me knew it all along. I grabbed him by his black leather overcoat and swung him around, but he caught me with a sharp right that sent me back into the wall and down onto the floor. Before I knew it, he was down the stairs and out of the building. I returned to Elzbieta's.

"'I'm sorry, Ben,' she said. 'I can try to talk to him tomorrow and see if I can get him to change his mind.' I left Elzie's a little after two in the morning.

"My father just shook his head in despair when I told him of the previous evening's encounter with Otto. 'Power corrupts,' he mumbled and put on his hat to walk from his makeshift apartment to the Judenrat office. As we walked, I said, 'I still have five hundred złotys. Are we all set for tonight?'

"He shook his head. 'Aunt Hilda is very sick, close to death, and Mother doesn't feel right leaving her. I think we'll need to put off our travel for a little while.'

"I felt trapped, caged in, like a wild animal at the zoo. Every muscle fiber tensed. 'We need to leave *now!*' I said, raising my voice to my father, an act which surprised us both. 'There are more *orders* coming down. Things will only get worse!'

"'Take Hannah and go,' he said. 'I can't leave today and I don't know about tomorrow. Even if Hilda wasn't sick, these are my people. They depend on me. They depend on your mother. Should we abandon them, Ben? Just turn our backs and run away? Nothing stands between them and the Nazi miscreants but the Judenrat.'

"I was furious. 'The Judenrat is a collection of meek appeasers,' I screamed. 'You're not protecting your people, you're helping to exterminate them!'

"My father looked at me sternly, slapped my face, and walked away. I didn't know where to turn next. I was torn between my urge to escape and my loyalty to the family. Maybe Hannah would have the answers. I found her at the clinic.

"We sat outside on the curb, just the two of us. My emotions flipped between rage and despair. I couldn't accept what was happening—Beka's death, Otto's betrayal, my father's inaction, the deterioration of our lives. 'What are we to do, Hannah? Give me the answers,' I said.

"'If you want to leave tonight, I'll go with you,' she said. 'I can't speak for your father, but I know mine will never leave Zamość as long as there's a sick patient in the clinic. He knows the consequences; so does your father. They're making their choices and we have to respect them. But just as they make choices about their lives, so we have the right to make ours. Without guilt.' She leaned over, kissed me on the forehead, and whispered, '"All my fortunes at thy foot I'll lay, and follow thee my lord throughout the world."'"

Catherine smiled. "That's Juliet's promise to Romeo."

Ben nodded. "Exactly. Hannah was so wise—our future, our

escape, it all seemed to make sense. So we agreed to gather our things and meet at ten that night. We'd get in the car and drive south to Zdziar. Our plan was to ditch the car there and backpack south through the pass and into the Bratislavska Dolina valley, following the route Krzysztof had drawn. Meanwhile, I felt terrible about the blowup with my father, so I decided to find him and seek his forgiveness.

"I found him later that day at the synagogue, and I apologized for my anger. I never meant to demean him or the men who served on the Judenrat. He hugged me and held me close like I was six years old and said, 'I have never been disappointed in you, Ben. You have made me proud every day of your life. Go with Hannah and may God protect you both.'

"I told Lucyna of our plans. She was nervous about going back into the Podhale, but she was spunky and courageous. She said she wanted to go along. We each packed our bags, said our farewells, and walked from the ghetto at ten that evening. By now, Jews were forbidden to leave the ghetto and our presence on the street was illegal, so I wore the Nazi uniform I had hidden under the mattress, reasoning that at a distance we would appear to be German. If we were stopped, well, I had the gun and I wasn't afraid to use it.

"As I turned the corner on Dolna Street, my heart sank. The car was gone. Immediately I knew that Otto must have taken it. We quickly made our way down the block to Elzbieta's.

"'He was here earlier today,' she said to me. 'He knew you would be coming, and he said to tell you to go back to the ghetto, because if you're caught on the streets, he won't be able to help you.'

"I thanked Elzbieta for her help and started for the door.

"'What are you going to do now?' she asked. There was fear in her voice. 'Otto's coming back tonight. What am I going to tell him? He'll be here soon.'

"'I'm not going to involve you, Elzie. If I tell you, then I put you in the middle. Tell Otto the truth—you gave us his message and you don't know where we are.'

"We kissed her and left by the back stairway. 'Where *are* we going?' asked Hannah.

"'To Grandpa Yaakov's. We'll take some of my family's jewelry to use for barter. Then we'll hitch up Buttermilk and take her south. Are you still with us, Lucyna?'

"She put her hands on her hips, stuck out her chin, and said, 'Of course, I am.'"

The tea kettle whistled and Catherine walked into the kitchen to answer it. Ben followed.

"Wasn't it a long walk to the farm in the dark?" she said as she poured the tea.

"Six kilometers—three miles, more or less. We got there in the middle of the night. I entered the barn, and as you may have guessed, Buttermilk wasn't there. There weren't any horses. I cursed Otto. Then it dawned on me. If he had been there to take Buttermilk, he probably took the valuables from the cache. I ran to the corner, pried open the floorboard, and confirmed my fears. The chest was gone.

"I sat on the floor of the barn with my head in my hands. Finally, I said to Hannah, 'We'll have to go back. I need to make a new plan.'

"We spent the rest of the night in the barn and returned to my parents' apartment just as they were getting ready to leave for their jobs. My father was surprised to see us, but when I told him what Otto had done, he shook his head and said, 'He's been seduced by his position. I've misjudged his character, Ben. He's a much weaker man than I thought.'

"Hannah and I were exhausted and we lay down on the bed to rest. Sometime later that morning we were awakened by Elzbieta sitting on the edge of the bed. She had a bruise on her left cheek.

"'He sent me to get his uniform,' she said. 'He wants me to bring it to him right away. "*Mach schnell*," he said.'

"'Did he do that to you?' I said, pointing to her face. She didn't answer me. I pulled the uniform from beneath the bed and handed it to her. She thanked me and stood to leave.

"'He's not the same man that we knew before the war. It's all gone to his head,' she said.

"'I'm sorry for you, Elzie. I never meant for you to get hurt, and

I'm sorry I put you in this position. It's better if you don't see us anymore.'

"She shook her head, started to speak, but turned and left the room carrying Otto's uniform."

Catherine rose, walked into the kitchen, and returned carrying a tray with a plate of cookies and a tea service. Ben stood at the front window watching the activity on the neighborhood sidewalk. The sun was setting earlier now—dusk came shortly after 4:30. A child with a school backpack scampered by an old woman walking her dog. A mother pushing a stroller loaded with grocery bags glanced back at her toddler scurrying behind. Just for a moment, he was looking at Belwederski Street and Beka was toddling after his mother.

"Thanksgiving's just a week away, Ben," Catherine said as she set the tray down on a table. "Do you have plans?"

He shrugged.

"Then you'll dine with me?"

"Don't you have family? I don't want to butt in."

"Oh, there'll be a few relatives and I've invited Liam, but we have plenty of room and lots of turkey. Can we count on you?"

Ben smiled. "Sure. Thanks."

Catherine handed a mug of steaming tea to Ben and took her place on the couch beside the fireplace. Ben settled into the easy chair holding the warm mug with both hands.

"Our plans for escape to the mountains were tabled. We had no way of getting through the countryside, and even if I could get my hands on a car, I no longer had Otto's uniform. It was just too risky. Hannah and Lucyna went back to working at the clinic and I to helping Father at the Judenrat.

"The winter of 1941–1942 was particularly severe, and many of the buildings lacked adequate heat or had no furnaces at all. And even if there was an operable furnace, we had no coal deliveries. It seemed like we lost people every day to the unforgiving cold or to malnutrition or disease. Aunt Hilda finally succumbed to typhus in January. Yet more refugees arrived daily in the ghetto; as we would bury one poor soul, three more would arrive.

"It was in the midst of all this suffering that Hannah and I decided to get married. We could endure a lot but not living apart—we hadn't lived together since the mountains—and we wanted to be joined in the eyes of God. No matter what the world had in store for us, we would face it together.

"My mother and father were delighted with the news, as was Dr. Weissbaum. A wedding was planned for February, just enough time for my mother to make a dress and veil for Hannah and for my father to build a chuppah."

Catherine smiled.

"What'd you expect? We had to have a chuppah. Damn if those Nazis were going to deprive us of our traditions. Traditional Jewish wedding ceremonies are conducted under the open sky beneath a canopy called a chuppah, supported by four posts and open on all sides. The rings and the vows are exchanged under the chuppah. The groom gives his bride the *ketubah*, a marriage contract, his vow to honor and provide for his wife, which in Judaism symbolically affirms the wife's dignified status. Then there are seven blessings, and the bride circles the groom seven times and the groom breaks a glass with his right foot. It wouldn't have been a wedding without our traditions."

"With the ceremony taking place under the open sky, maybe that accounts for the abundance of June weddings," she said.

"Well, it wasn't June for us. It was February. But we wanted to do it the traditional way, so we planned to have it in the synagogue courtyard. Winters in Poland are harsh, but on our wedding day, the sun shone brightly, the winds calmed, and for a short moment, the horrors of the war were lands and eons away.

"Many of our friends had come, including Elzbieta and Lucyna. Hannah looked dazzling in her gown—my mother had outdone herself. The women had worked for hours on Hannah's hair and makeup. Her auburn hair was woven and covered with a veil. Everyone said she was the most beautiful girl they'd ever seen."

"My goodness, that sounds lovely, but I wonder, where did the women get the cosmetics?" Catherine said.

"In their time, before they were displaced, these were elegant ladies. Many of them squirreled away a little makeup for special occasions to make them feel like ladies, to remind them that they were women of refinement and not dogs in a cage. And where he got it, I don't know, but Dr. Weissbaum had scared up a tuxedo, and he looked so proud as he walked with Hannah.

"I was mesmerized by my bride as I waited under the chuppah, and I had to be prompted to speak my vows. The ceremony ended, I smashed the glass, the crowd yelled 'mazel tov,' I kissed my bride, and looked up at the happy gathering. There standing at the back, leaning against a brick wall in his black uniform, was Otto. He nodded at me, tipped his cap, and withdrew into the shadows.

"The guests cheered and hustled us off to be alone before the dinner party, a traditional time of privacy. Hannah was now my wife, my dream come true."

Ben stopped talking. He had traveled back to Zamość and was with Hannah once again. His lips formed words that only Hannah could hear. Catherine gave him his time and his privacy, as did his friends and family sixty years earlier. She sat silent and still until Ben returned to the present many minutes later. "Thank you," he said.

He took a sip of tea, regained his composure, and resumed his story.

"Rank had its privileges, even in Zamość, and my father found us a room in a nearby building. Our own apartment. Or should I say *com*partment. It was probably eight by eight, but it had a bed and a door. My mother and her friends found linens and we had a small chest of drawers. For a while that little corner was our marital abode, and it couldn't have been any sweeter if it was the Taj Mahal.

"It was later that spring, in 1942, following a meeting of the Judenrat, that my father and I were visited by Jan, a former high school classmate, who told us about a secret resistance movement in the Zamość region. He was tall and square-shouldered, a wrestler in his high school days. In a small anteroom in the synagogue, Jan quietly described his group and started my heart pumping.

"'We meet in the forest, in the old mill house on the river,' he said, 'and we need strong young fighters like you, Ben. We supply aid and arms to our brothers and sisters in Warsaw and do whatever we can to foil the Nazi pigs in their subjugation of our country.'

"As we talked, I realized that other young people were taking a stand and maybe making a difference. It excited me to think that I could have a role in battling these bastards until the end of the war. Following the meeting, I asked my father what he thought about my joining the resistance.

"'Ultimately it's your decision,' he said, 'but you should ask Hannah, not me.'

"That night when we went to bed, I tried to find the right moment to tell her all about my meeting. But lying with my Hannah, with her soft body curled around me . . . I confess I got a little distracted and decided to wait until a more appropriate time. In the morning, she said to me, 'You didn't sleep so well last night. Do you want to tell me what's on your mind?'

"I detailed the meeting with Jan and asked what she thought. Hannah was supportive, as always. She believed it was the right thing to do, though she feared for my safety.

"So that night I slipped out of the western side of town, into the woods and to the river a few miles away. I walked along the stone riverbanks as I had been instructed, my German pistol in my belt, until I met up with Jan. He led me toward the mill house, which at first seemed unoccupied, but as we drew nearer, I could see it was well fortified. The whole scene reminded me of Robin Hood in Sherwood Forest—you didn't know the men were there until they wanted you to. There were guards in hidden embankments and in foxholes dug into heavily wooded areas, covered with brush and undetectable to the casual eye.

"Inside the mill house, several partisans had gathered—both men and women. They welcomed me and gave me a code name—no one used his real name. I was called Lis—that's Polish for 'fox.' Why they gave me that name, I didn't know, but I liked it.

"When I arrived the group was making plans to steal a shipment of weapons from a railroad depot near Zamość in the village of Wojda. Before disbursing for the night, we gathered in a circle, put our hands together, and said *Nigdy się nię poddamy!*—never surrender!

"For the first time since the war began I felt like I could make a difference. I wasn't running to escape. I was standing up for my country and my people. The raid on the Wojda depot was to occur in seven days, on April 14, but before that, a major event happened in Zamość.

"It was on April 11, 1942, *Erev Pesach*, Passover eve, and my family was preparing for seder as was nearly every other family in New Town. At noon, without warning, the entire ghetto was surrounded by German soldiers with automatic weapons. Sirens wailed and megaphones announced that all Jews were ordered to assemble in the market square. Soldiers on horseback charged through the streets, shouting and whipping and trampling pedestrians. People were ordered to take a suitcase of clothing and go immediately to the square.

"Sadly, many of our older residents thought it was another registration, and they dressed in their best clothes to impress the Germans. Three men stood at the front of the square, standing on a platform: Commandant Schubert and Otto were joined by Bruno Myers, the head of the Zamość Gestapo.

"We crowded into that square, thousands of us, waiting for five hours without any food or water. Some collapsed, some fainted, and some were hauled away. Eighty-nine people were shot. While we stood there, the Germans searched the ghetto. They shot any person found hiding or remaining in his home. The sick and injured, too weak to come to the market square, were executed and their corpses flung out of the windows and left in the street for us to bury.

"Finally at 9:00 P.M., long after the time we would have been sitting down to our Passover seder, Otto and Schubert walked through the crowd, pointing at groups and families, instructing them to march directly to the railroad ramps and board the boxcars for deportation. We didn't know the destination, but there were announcements that people were to be resettled at a new work camp. Three thousand people were put onto the train that night, packed over a hundred to a car.

"During the selection process, Otto walked up to our family, looked us over for a moment, said nothing, and passed us by. At 11:00 P.M. those of us who were not selected were dismissed to go home.

"The next day was burial day. Over two hundred bodies had been left on the streets, in the buildings, on the sidewalk, and in the clinic. If anyone ever harbored a doubt as to who these Nazis were or what was in store for us, it was all brought home that day. Mournful cries were heard throughout the night. I saw the resistance as our only way to fight back.

"That evening I ducked out of town and made my way to the mill house, joining up with thirty others, mostly young, some Jewish but many Catholic, some from Zamość but many from surrounding villages, and all dedicated to Polish freedom. The leader, an older man known as Irek, was detailing the mission on a map nailed to the wall. A drawing of the arms depot near Wojda was also tacked on the wall. It was reported to be lightly guarded.

"There was a fierce debate over the raid, some claiming it would cause serious reprisals from the Germans. Irek countered that all Poland was condemned anyway, and why would death by reprisal be any different than death by extermination? The majority were firmly behind Irek and intent on doing whatever they could to disrupt the German occupation.

"The conversation then turned to Zamość and the mass deportation. I told them about the selection and what I'd seen the day before. 'The Germans told us the people were being transported to a new work camp,' I said. 'I believe it to be Izbica.'

"'There has been some construction at Izbica—it's a transit camp and some barracks have been built,' answered Irek, 'but the Zamość transport went directly to Belzec. I'm sorry to tell you this, Lis, but the entire group, all three thousand, were executed as soon as they arrived at Belzec.'

"I was stunned. I knew so many of them. 'Are you sure? They told them to take a suitcase, to bring their clothes. There were little children on that train.'

"'I'm sorry,' he said. 'Our information is accurate. They were all killed by carbon monoxide exhaust piped from a truck into locked chambers. As to their suitcases, that is a Nazi ruse—to make the victims more comfortable and compliant. Once at Belzec, the suitcases are taken by the kapos—money, jewelry, eyeglasses, and clothing are collected and supposedly sent to Berlin, although we know that much is stolen by the local SS. All the rest—the family pictures, the Bibles, the mementos—is discarded.'

"All I could think of was how Otto, a boy I had known and loved for so many years, could willingly stand shoulder to shoulder with these monsters and send his townspeople to their deaths. And to think, Catherine, that he lives today in a mansion, wealthy beyond imagination, all at the expense of the thousands he robbed and sent to die. He's living the life of a respected member of society, unblemished, loved by all Chicago."

TWENTY-NINE

...

THE FIRST SNOW OF the season, light fluffy flakes, floated about on the Saturday before Thanksgiving, like a Lincoln Park snow globe. Ben rang Catherine's doorbell just before noon. He brushed the snowflakes from his jacket and shook his wool cap before entering her foyer.

"I predict it'll be winter before it's summer," he said.

"That's a safe prediction," Catherine said. "Come on in. I've got a fire going and some tea brewing."

"Are you sure you want to work on a Saturday?" Ben said.

"It's as good a day as any. I don't have regular office hours now, anyway. Besides, we need to push ahead."

They walked into the living room and Ben took a seat in the overstuffed chair beside the fireplace. "I feel like I'm in therapy. Shall I take the same seat and confess my life's history?"

Catherine sat back with her pad and pen. "So, tell Dr. Lockhart, what happened next?"

Zamość, Poland, 1942

"Ah yes. The raid on Wojda. Irek's intelligence was flawless. There were six Germans guarding the arms depot with a couple of dogs. Our plan was to rattle the dogs, get them barking, and draw the guards out into the railroad yards. It worked perfectly. Half of them came snooping around the boxcars with their dogs. Having split from their group, we outflanked them and made quick work of the guards and their dogs. The rest of our group overtook the three guards at the depot and carted away dozens of weapons: pistols, rifles, machine guns.

"Unfortunately, as some of the partisans had warned, there were reprisals. We learned that German soldiers later descended on Wojda, indiscriminately grabbing people on the street, screaming at them, even shooting them. But we were not dissuaded from our cause and the raids kept up. Weapons seized were sent by underground to the Warsaw ghetto. Some of them were given to the AK, the Polish home army.

"Hannah continued to work in the clinic with my mother. Father continued to serve on the Judenrat. There were no further transports from Zamość in April, but many refugees were shipped into Zamość from other villages, other cities, and even other countries. A large group arrived from Czechoslovakia and the sheer numbers were difficult to absorb. Zamość became a transit location. People were collected in Zamość and then sent to other ghettos or to the death camps. It was like living in the middle of a crowded train station, with people coming and going all the time.

"As for me, I spent more and more time in the Zamość forests with the freedom fighters, sneaking back into the ghetto every few days to be with Hannah. I enlisted several more young people to join the resistance: friends from high school, kids I'd grown up with, even Lucyna, who became a tough little fighter.

"Despite the wretched conditions, my nights with Hannah were sweet. We would shut out the world and talk of a future, far from Poland and the Germans, where we would raise our family. Hannah would become a nurse, she announced one night as we lay together, her head on my arm.

"'What about me?' I asked her, lightly tracing the curves of her figure with my fingertips. 'What will I be when this war is over?'

"'You'll be a brilliant statesman, like your father. Or,' she said mischievously, 'maybe just a cranky old farmer, feeding hay to Buttermilk.'

"Moments like those were heaven itself. Even in the midst of our captivity, life was precious to me as long as I could hold my Hannah."

Catherine smiled. "I wish I had met her."

"I do too," said Ben. "She was a woman of strong resolve, just like you."

Ben stared into the fire, watched the flames dance, lingered with a memory or two, and then continued. "On May 17, the Judenrat received a directive from Otto's office containing a list of elderly citizens who were ordered to register for deportation and resettlement by May 27. We were shocked to see that Dr. Weissbaum's name was included. Hannah and I immediately went to my father and asked him to intercede with Otto.

"My father scheduled an appointment for the next morning.

"'I suppose you're here to argue about the old people's list,' said Otto to my father. 'There's nothing I can do. The orders were issued by Adolf Eichmann himself. They are to be resettled in barracks at Izbica to wait out the war. They're unfit to enter the workforce.'

"'They're not going to Izbica and you know it,' Father said. 'Stop lying to me, Otto. I want you to cancel the deportation.'

"'You're a fool, Abraham. Even if I wanted to, I don't have the authority to cancel Eichmann's order.'

"'Hannah's father is on the list.'

"'He's over sixty.'

"'He's a doctor and he's needed in the hospital.'

"'For what? To prolong the lives of dead men? To keep them alive for another few months?'

"'Take him off the list. He's needed at the hospital.'

"Otto rocked back in his chair and flipped a pencil. 'Is that your parental command? Your son is killing German officers with the so-called freedom fighters.'

"'I don't know what you're talking about. Ben is in Zamość.'

"'Now who's lying, Abraham? Bring Ben to me and I'll release Dr. Weissbaum from the list.'

"'You want me to turn in my own son?'

"'And then I'll release Dr. Weissbaum.'

"'What will happen to Ben?'

"'I just want to speak to him.'

"'You know I'll never do that.'

"'Then we have nothing more to talk about.' Otto summoned his orderly, who entered the room with a crisp Nazi salute. 'Go back to your Judenrat, Abraham, and stop causing trouble or I'll add you to the list.'"

Catherine took a deep breath. "What happened to Hannah's father?"

"On May 26 and May 27, all of the people on the list were taken to the ramp, put on the train, and transported directly to Belzec. Dr. Weissbaum was in the group."

Catherine put her hand to her mouth.

"He had said his goodbyes to Hannah the night before. He knew what was in store for him. So did Hannah. Mother stayed by Hannah's side throughout the next few days. It's impossible to imagine the anguish of having parents taken from you, when you know . . . you know that they're being sent to their death, that they're going to be murdered. They're going to be slaughtered. You can't imagine, Catherine, you'd do anything, you'd . . ."

Ben couldn't finish his sentence, and all Catherine could do was sit helplessly and nod her head. He walked to the window and gazed at the street. It took a while for him to compose himself. He stared at the neighborhood, calm and peaceful. The grassy parkways were covered by a thin blanket of white. Catherine tapped him on the shoulder and handed him a box of tissues. A few minutes later Ben returned to his chair and continued.

"The summer passed without any further deportations. My resistance unit was busy attacking German patrols, setting bombs at German fortifications, and capturing arms to be smuggled into the Warsaw ghetto. I was forced to spend longer periods away from Zamość. Many nights I could not return to New Town and I stopped going to roll call. A search was conducted and I was listed as missing. The official word was that I was killed in a raid. That meant I couldn't be seen in town anymore, not even by our own people. But now and then I'd sneak back in the middle of the night. For Hannah and me, our time together became less frequent and all the more precious.

"On one of my visits, my father informed me that I was a wanted man, that Otto believed that I was still alive and had offered a reward—food and an exemption from the deportation list—for information leading to my arrest, or the arrest of anyone else in the Zamość resistance. To protect my family, I had to stay away. I would slip into Zamość only on rare occasions, spend a few hours with Hannah, and be gone long before sunrise.

"In late September, Irek pulled me aside and told me that he had received word that the entire Zamość ghetto was to be demolished by the end of October, that every person was to be transported, probably to Izbica first and then to the death camps at Belzec or Sobibor. I knew I would have to get my family out before that happened. I made plans to get back to Zamość as soon as our raid in Zaboreczno was finished. Unfortunately, the operation took longer than planned and it was late October before I returned.

"I slipped into town after midnight and moved quietly through the shadows. Many of the apartment buildings were vacant and the ghetto was very still. As I walked through the halls to my little corner apartment, it was obvious the building had been emptied. My apartment was bare. Hannah was gone.

"I dashed to my parents' building and up to the second floor. Sheets still hung from the ceiling, but they only partitioned empty, silent spaces. I rushed down the hallway to their apartment. My heart sank. They too were gone. Only a few souls remained, hiding in the building, and they told me that almost everyone had been marched out days ago.

"Now I was frantic. I left the ghetto, ran to Elzbieta's, and knocked on her door. She answered in her robe and hurried me in. 'Do you know that half the German army's looking for you?'

"'I'm sorry to come here, Elzie. I know I said I wouldn't involve you, but Hannah and my parents are gone. The buildings are empty. I'm sure Otto knows where they are.'

"'I'm sure he does, too,' answered Elzbieta. 'There have been mass deportations. They're clearing out the ghettos, not just in Zamość but all over Poland.'

"'Would you take me to Otto, please?'

"'Now? It's the middle of the night—there's nothing that can be done tonight. And, believe me, Otto will not help you. He's the one who made the selections. He's the one who implemented the deportations.'

"'Will you drive me to his house? I don't know where he lives.'

"She grimaced. 'I will, but you cannot tell him that you talked to me.'

"'I promise. I won't mention you.'

"She nodded, grabbed a wool coat from her closet, and wrapped it around her night clothes. She drove me to the north edge of town, to where a large home lay nestled in a walnut grove, and stopped the car at the end of a long gravel driveway. 'That's where he lives. His bedroom is on the second floor at the end of the hallway. Be careful,' she said and drove away.

"The house, a three-story stone building with light blue shutters and a gray slate roof, was dark. I found a back window unlatched and climbed through. A winding staircase ascended from the foyer. I found Otto easily. He was sound asleep, loudly snoring off the evening's alcohol, and thankfully he was alone. I took the Luger from my belt, walked to his bed, and pushed the cold steel barrel against his neck. He opened his eyes, looked at me, and didn't move.

"'Where's Hannah? Where are my parents?'

"'You're a dead man,' he said in a gravelly whisper.

"I pushed the nose of the gun harder against the base of his skull and repeated my question.

"'They're no longer in Zamość,' he said. 'They were sent out last week with a group that marched to Izbica. You're lucky. I was good to you. I could have sent them straight to Belzec.'

"'Get up,' I said. 'We're going to get them.'

"He laughed. 'Even you can't accomplish that, *Fox*. The moment we enter Izbica, you'll be shot.'

"'Then so will you. You better pray that everyone's alive. Your life depends on it. Get up.'

"I opened Otto's closet and removed two uniforms. Each of us put on the uniform of an SS Hauptscharführer. We got into Otto's car and he drove the twenty-one kilometers to Izbica with my pistol sticking in his ribs, arriving just as the sun was coming up.

"Izbica was teeming with refugees, thousands more than could fit into the small wooden huts and barracks. The streets were muddy, and the primitive conditions were far beneath my most dreadful expectations. Izbica was a transit ghetto, just a stop on the way to Belzec, Sobibor, or one of the other death camps.

"We parked Otto's black sedan on the outskirts of the village. I approached a sentry and demanded in German to know where the group from Zamość had been housed. He didn't know. There must have been ten thousand people in a rural town fit for five hundred. With my pistol in Otto's back, we walked together through the filthy streets, our boots sticking in the mud, asking people about the Zamość refugees. It seemed to be an overwhelming task.

"'What will you do if you find them?' Otto said. 'Where will you go? All Poland is enemy territory to you. There isn't a town you can hide in, and as soon as you're caught you'll be shot or sent to Belzec.' He turned his head and looked at me with his steely eyes. 'If you drive me back to Zamość right now, I'll let you go.'

"I dug my pistol into his ribs and prodded him forward. 'Pray to whatever demon gods you worship that I find my parents and Hannah. Pray that they're alive and haven't been sent on to Belzec. Otherwise this mud will be your grave.'

"All afternoon we sloshed through the dirt of Izbica, looking into the crowded barracks, into the gaunt faces of the poor, uprooted families. 'Have you seen a group from Zamość?' we asked, but we were Nazis in full uniform and the people just cowered and shook their heads.

"As the October darkness settled in, we neared the edge of the town and my hopes were dwindling. We rounded a wooden barrack, and there, in the dim light of the setting sun, I saw my Hannah. In her cotton dress, standing in the mud, she was still the prettiest girl in all the world. It took her a moment to recognize us and realize what was going on. She inclined her head for us to follow her and led us into a long wooden building. Plywood bunks lined the walls, four rows high, slabs of wood without mattresses. My mother and father were sitting on the edge of a bunk.

"'Otto?' Father said. 'You came for us?' He started forward. Then he saw my gun and understood.

"'There. Now you have them,' Otto said to me. 'You see, they're just fine.'

"'Take off your uniform,' I said.

"'What? You found your family, now let me go.'

"'I don't think so, Otto. We wouldn't get far before you and your soldiers re-arrested us. No, you need to stay here awhile, but don't worry, you're among your people now. These are your Zamość townsfolk, the ones you grew up with, the ones who taught you math and history, the ones that served you sodas after school.' I waved my arm at the people standing in the barracks, watching us and smirking at Otto's comeuppance. 'Now, take off your uniform.'

"He stripped down to his underwear. 'I'm not safe here,' he said quietly to me. 'I got your family out, didn't I? You owe me. I'm begging you, Ben, these people are hostile to me.'

"'You've always made friends easily, Otto. Tell them all about how you grew up and rose to your lofty position with the Third Reich.' I handed Otto's uniform to my father and told him to put it on.

"With the laces from his boots, we tied Otto's hands tightly to the bunk with multiple knots and left him standing in the barracks, shivering in his underwear. The Zamość captives turned their backs and walked outside. But even if one of the townsfolk decided to help him, it would be a while before they could get the laces untied. We walked quickly back to Otto's car, saluted by the sentries and guards as we passed—*Heil Hitler!* to the Hauptscharführers and their women prisoners. We drove south out of Izbica, through the valley—Hannah, Mother, Father, and me."

Catherine whispered, "Bravo."

THIRTY

...

Chicago, Illinois, November 2004

Monday morning, a few hours before she was scheduled to meet with Ben, Catherine entered the offices of Jenkins & Fairchild to box up her belongings under the watchful eye of security personnel. After her argument with Walter Jenkins, the firm immediately locked her out of the system, confiscated her computer, and sealed her office. Now she was allowed a short period of time to gather her personal effects, submit them for inspection, and take them home.

She carefully wrapped each of her little mementos in newspaper—figurines, pictures, gifts from clients, all accumulated over the years and sitting on the office bookshelves—and placed them into a cardboard box. She took her diplomas from the wall, brushed the dust off the tops of the frames, and set them inside the box. A patchwork of nostalgia played out in her mind. Suddenly, she was shaken from her daydreams by a knock on the open door.

"May I come in?" Walter Jenkins said.

Catherine nodded. He dismissed the watchmen, shut the door, and took a seat beside her desk. The vest of his three-piece, dark blue suit was clasped with the gold chain of his pocket watch.

"You don't have to do this," he said quietly. "Why don't we talk this through?"

Her eyes filled with tears. She reached for a tissue and dabbed her running mascara.

Jenkins, thirty years her senior, spoke kindly and paternally. "You're a fine litigator with a bright future, and I don't say that lightly. I was lucky when Taggart recommended you after your troubles. I didn't know at the time what a top-notch lawyer I was getting, but I took a chance on you. Give me a little credit. I gave you a new start and it worked out well for both of us. Don't throw it all away. You're making a big mistake. I keep thinking you're doing this out of some professional stubbornness, because I demanded that you give up a case. Am I right?"

"No. It's your law firm and you have the right to decide what cases the firm'll handle, but . . ." She shook her head. "It's not stubbornness—but I think I have an obligation. I gave my word and I'm going to see it through. What's more, I've come to believe in him."

"I have news for you that just may change your mind. Gerry Jeffers came to see me this morning."

"Ah, the prominent Mr. Jeffers."

"Now wait a minute, Catherine. Wait till you hear what he told me. He said that Elliot Rosenzweig has invested a considerable sum of money trying to find Otto Piatek. He's hired a firm of private investigators, and they've found him. He's got a house in Cleveland. Are you listening to me? They found Otto Piatek and he's not Elliot Rosenzweig."

"Seriously?" Catherine looked stunned. "I . . . I don't know what to say."

Jenkins smiled. "Thought so."

"Where is he? Did they turn him in to the U.S. Attorney?"

"Well, they don't have him yet. Although they're sure they've located his home, the lights are dark. No one's been home for a few days. But they're watching it."

Catherine tilted her head. "They don't have him yet?"

"No, but Jeffers says it's only a matter of time. So, now you can let the government handle this matter and get back to your work."

"That's extraordinary," Catherine said. "I can't wait to tell Ben.

I'm due to meet with him in a couple of hours. He'll be delighted to learn the news."

Jenkins stood. "Excellent. Give the news to Solomon, close your file, and come on back to work. All's forgiven."

"Well, that's quite an offer. I don't know what to say. Except I need to finish what I'm doing. I haven't quite completed taking the history. No matter who handles this case, whether we do or the government does, they'll need my background notes. And I think I owe it to Ben to let him finish his story. We've spent a lot of time and it's been very emotional. It would be hard for him to do it all over again."

"Maybe I'm not making myself clear. There's no reason for you to spend your time, the firm's time, on Mr. Solomon's case. When Rosenzweig finds the guy, the government will take over. They're very good at taking notes."

"But I made a commitment to him. And he may still want to proceed civilly against Piatek."

"I don't want us to handle that case, or even take any more notes. I assured Jeffers that we, that you, would no longer be involved with Ben Solomon."

"Why did you do that?"

"Jeffers asked me to. For obvious reasons, Solomon is a pariah to Rosenzweig. Jeffers asked that we disassociate ourselves entirely from Solomon, and I agreed."

"You didn't even consult me and I gave Ben my word."

"Your word? You didn't give your word that you'd take a civil case to trial, did you?"

"No."

"Okay then, so pitch it. Cut him loose. There's no basis for a civil case against Rosenzweig anyway. Piatek has been found in Cleveland. Let some Cleveland lawyer bring a civil case."

"Well, to be precise, Walter, Piatek has not been found, nor has he been positively identified. Rosenzweig thinks he found his house. He could be wrong."

"He found him. Can't you accept that? What would be the sense in fabricating such a story?"

"I gave Ben my word I would see it through."

"This whole thing, Catherine, it's a waste of time. We'll never make a penny. And it's a huge embarrassment to me."

Catherine rocked forward in her chair. "What about the moral imperative, Mr. Jenkins?"

"What?"

"The moral imperative—doing it because it's the right thing to do. And because you gave someone your word."

"Am I missing something here? Do moral imperatives pay the rent? We have payroll due twice a month for one hundred and forty lawyers, eighty clerical employees, and twenty-odd paralegals. Have you thought about what would happen to this firm's gross income if we pissed off Jeffers and Rosenzweig and the rest of the legal community?"

Jenkins stood and raised his voice. "Some of our largest institutional clients, like Atlas Insurance, for example, would pull out on us in a second. Rosenzweig's a power in this town. Jeffers is a power in this town. They wield a hell of a lot more influence than any moral imperative I know."

Catherine dropped her eyes and shook her head. "I can't abide by those principles. I have a law license—a privilege to make a damn good living practicing a public profession. And it's a *service* profession, Mr. Jenkins. It's not just about the money and your books of business and how many institutional clients you can collect. It's about using that license to further justice. I'm going to do what I can for Ben Solomon. If it means helping him get to the U.S. Attorney, I'll do that. If it means bringing Piatek to justice for him, whoever he is and wherever he is, I'll do that. I'm not turning my back on Ben, and I'm not breaking my word just because it might piss off Rosenzweig, Atlas Insurance, Jeffers, or anyone else. Shame on you for asking me."

Unencumbered by misgivings, she picked up the box and left Jenkins standing uncharacteristically silent by her desk.

THIRTY-ONE

...

BEN WAS SITTING ON Catherine's front stoop, huddled in his winter coat, when she pulled up to the curb.

"I'm sorry to keep you waiting," she said, lifting the box from her trunk. "I hope you didn't catch a chill. It's bitter this morning."

"I'm okay, but you don't look so good," he said, pointing to her eyes. He took the banker's box from her and followed her to the door.

"It was a rough morning. Enough said. Why don't you build us a fire?"

Ben threw a few birch logs onto the fireplace grate and lit the gas starter. Catherine brewed a pot of tea and they sat across from each other, close by the warm fire, trying to take the edge off the raw November morning. Ben leaned back in the stuffed wing chair, holding a steaming mug. The fire crackled.

"That stuff I carried in the box, did it come from your office?"

Catherine nodded.

"I'm sorry."

"Ben, we're not going to revisit that subject. It's not the first time I walked away from a firm. It's my private business and I'd like to keep it that way. But I do have something to share with you. Jenkins told me this morning that Rosenzweig and some investigative agency have located Piatek. Apparently they found his home. It's in Cleveland."

"That's nonsense. Rosenzweig is Piatek."

"Gerald Jeffers came to see Jenkins today just to bring him that information. He said a detective was staking out Piatek's house and they expected to catch him soon."

"It's impossible, Catherine. Rosenzweig *is* Piatek. I'm one hundred percent certain of that."

"How can you be so sure? It was sixty years ago."

"When you live with someone, you don't ever forget their mannerisms. The way they laugh, the way they gesture when they speak, their facial expressions. And his voice—I'd know that voice anywhere. It hasn't changed. It's him. Unless the detectives are staking out his mansion in Winnetka, they won't pick up Piatek. Don't you see, this is a diversion. I bet they told you to drop the case, didn't they?"

"Yes."

"What did you tell them?"

"I told them no."

Ben slapped his leg. "That's my girl! Don't fall for their tricks."

Catherine shrugged. "We'll need more than gestures and facial expressions."

Kraśnik, Poland, 1942

"When I walked out of Izbica, I had no permanent solution in mind. My immediate plans were to drive south through the night to distance ourselves as far as possible from the Izbica transit camp. I knew I was a wanted man. Elzie had said that the Germans were looking for me. I had just kidnapped a German officer and stolen his car. For all I knew, Otto had connected me with Rolf's death at Rabka. I would have to find a way for my family and me to go deep underground.

"I suggested that we try to meet up with the freedom fighters at the mill house and seek advice from Irek, although I had some fear that our group had been compromised. Otto had called me Fox and it seemed likely that one of the partisans had been captured and forced to give up information. But then, I had nowhere else to turn. We couldn't go back to Zamość and the mountains were out of the question. They were too far and that's the first place Otto would try to catch us. All of Poland was crawling with Nazis. As Otto said, every town was enemy territory.

"We had other problems, too. We were driving a 1937 Mercedes, the quintessential German sedan. In 1942, no one in Poland would have such a car except a high-level Nazi. Although my father and I were each wearing Nazi uniforms, they were identical and his didn't fit very well. On top of that, we had no papers. Hannah and my mother were in the clothes they had been wearing for two weeks, and they looked like they'd come out of a resettlement camp. They wouldn't exactly pass as girlfriends of two Nazi officers. And we had only half a tank of petrol. So I decided to head for the mill house.

"I parked at the end of the logging road and started walking toward the river house when my father called me back.

"'If you go into the woods wearing a Nazi uniform, you'll make a dandy target,' he said. I hadn't even thought of that. So I left my tunic in the car and ran off toward the mill house with Hannah close behind. It was too dark and too difficult for my mother to make it through the thick forest. She and my father stayed with the car.

"As we came upon the encampment, we stopped short in our tracks. It was a macabre scene, too horrible to describe. Several of our companions lay dead on the forest floor. Irek's body was swinging by the neck from an oak tree. Jan's twisted body lay facedown in the dirt. The rest of the group, I was sure, had been taken away and executed.

"I cut the rope and lowered Irek to the ground. Hannah and I covered the bodies with leaves and pine boughs, said a prayer, and turned to leave when we heard a rustle. I pulled my pistol and stood in front of Hannah like a shield. From behind a clump of bushes came a small, dark figure. It was Lucyna. She was covered with mud. She ran to us and fell into my arms. Her whole body was trembling.

"'They came two days ago,' she said, 'with machine guns and

dogs. They jumped out of their trucks, set their guns on tripods without a word, and opened fire. We scattered into the woods, chased by the dogs. I managed to make it to the river and hide in the mud beneath a log until they were gone.'

"Hannah put her arm around her and walked her back to the car. 'Where have you been staying?' she asked.

"'In the forest,' Lucyna said. 'There are others, whole families—forest dwellers.'

"She slid into the backseat of the Mercedes and froze when she saw my father in his Nazi uniform, but then breathed a sigh of relief when she recognized him. 'Where are you all going?' Lucyna asked.

"'We don't know,' I said, slipping on my tunic. 'I had hopes that Irek could direct us to a safe route.'

"'Irek was brave to the end,' she said in a whispered voice. 'They tortured him for information. I heard his screams from the river. I still hear them.' She swallowed hard and shivered. Hannah and my mother tried to comfort her. 'There are no safe routes,' she added.

"We sat for a little while, but dawn was breaking and we needed to move on. 'There is a Catholic priest,' Lucyna said, 'Father Janofski. In a little town west of here. From time to time Irek would speak of him. He's assisted many Poles in obtaining forged papers and escaping through the Polish underground.'

"'Can you get us to this priest?' I asked.

"'I only know he has a church in Kraśnik. I don't know the name of the church or how to get there.'

"My father knew the road to Kraśnik. It wound around the forest and through open farmland. Fortunately, because of the early hour we were the only car on the road. By the way, Kraśnik was not so little. It was the size of Zamość and, because of the size, we were sure there would be SS offices there.

"As we approached the town, we came across a fifteenth-century church and monastery. We took a gamble and pulled into the courtyard. The wooden sign identified the complex as St. Mary's Ascension Church.

"With my Nazi uniform on, I knocked on the front door. A nun unlocked the heavy oak door and looked me over. 'Excuse me, Sister,' I said. 'Is Father Janofski available?' She nodded silently and withdrew into the darkness of the church. A few minutes later, an elderly man in a clerical collar and cassock came to the door. He had a full head of white hair and a pencil-sharp nose. The years had bent his posture.

"'What does the Reich demand of me today?' he asked.

"'Father, may I speak with you confidentially?' I said. He considered the request for a moment, eyeing me distrustfully. I decided to play my cards. 'I am not a German,' I said in Polish.

"'Hmph,' he snorted. 'Come in.'

"He led me into the old Romanesque building. It was designed in the shape of a cruciform with a large nave and rich stained-glass windows over the north and south transepts. A carved oak chancel held an ornate altar. The floors were stone blocks worn smooth over the ages. Candles burned at the entrances to small chapels at the recesses of the transepts.

"Father Janofski led me past the vaulted choir and into the sacristy, where he shut the door. 'What's this about?'

"As rapidly as I could, I explained our situation. I told him I had four others in the car and we had nowhere to go. 'I was told that you had helped some to find escape routes or safehouses.'

"'Where is the car?' he asked.

"'In the gravel drive by the quadrangle.'

"'We must dispose of the car immediately. It's a homing beacon.'

"'I'll drive it into the woods and ditch it.'

"'No!' He shook his head. 'They'll trace that car. The Gestapo will know you're in Kraśnik and they'll turn the town upside down. No, it must be returned to Zamość. Leave it there and they'll have no reason to come here.'

"We walked back into the nave, and he called out for Sister Mary Magdalena. The three of us quickly returned to the courtyard where my family was waiting in the Mercedes.

"'Sister, take the three women inside,' instructed the priest. Turning to my father he said, 'You come with me, sir,' and he preceded him in the direction of the church. He stopped a few yards before the door and called out to me, 'You must take the car back to Zamość.' Then he and my father disappeared into the church."

Catherine put her notepad down on the small end table and stood to stretch her legs.

"Another cup of tea? Soft drink?" she said, walking into the kitchen.

"How about I take you to lunch?"

"You got a date," she answered. "What do you have in mind?"

"Rocco's. Fullerton and Clark. Great meatball sandwiches."

Catherine grimaced. "Do they have non-meatball sandwiches?"

"They got it all. Anything you want."

The gloom of November had settled in and heavy gray clouds hung low over the city. Lincoln Park had lost its summer green and autumn orange. Colors had migrated south for the winter, like the Florida snowbirds, not to return until May.

"I feel so bad that you quit your firm," Ben said, stepping over chunks of cracked sidewalk.

"I didn't quit. I'm on leave."

Ben stopped and faced Catherine. "I know what you've done. It took great courage and I'm so proud to have you as my lawyer. I can only assure you that when you do the right thing, goodness will come to you."

Catherine's lips quivered. "I hope to hell the evidence comes to me along with the goodness."

Ben held the door for Catherine and the two entered Rocco's.

THIRTY-TWO

• • •

Kraśnik, Poland, 1942

I BACKED THE BIG MERCEDES out of the courtyard onto the road and headed for Zamość. I was a nervous wreck. I had left my family again, this time with total strangers. Both the car and I were on the most wanted list. I had very little gas, no money, no papers, and no way to get back to Kraśnik after I dumped the car in Zamość. And on top of all that, I was hungry and thirsty and tired.

"I made it almost all the way to Zamość before I ran out of gas. I ditched the car on the outskirts of town, pushing it into some bushes, and stuffed the SS tunic underneath the front seat. I didn't know if Otto was alive or dead or who might be looking for us, but at least there'd be no trail for anyone to follow back to the church."

"How far were you from Kraśnik?" asked Catherine, sitting across from Ben in Rocco's at a white Formica table and nibbling on the meatball sandwich she'd been talked into.

"Forty miles or so. The return route to Kraśnik wound partway through the woods, but most of the trip was through open farm country. My plan was to walk at night to minimize the chance I'd be spotted. Traveling through the woods that first day I came upon some of the forest dwellers that Lucyna had mentioned. They gave me food and water and, more importantly, encouragement."

Ben wiped his mouth with his napkin and pointed his finger. "These people were living amongst the trees and bushes, trying to wait out the war in makeshift shelters. Some of them had little children. I thought about the impending winter, the days of ice and snow and cruel winds, the loss of foliage and cover. How were they going to care for these kids? But as feral as their existence was, they were a lot better off than on the cattle cars to Belzec. What courage and determination those forest dwellers had.

"They led me into a thick part of the woods where they had constructed lean-tos out of pine boughs. I slept a few hours and awoke at sundown, refreshed and ready to start my journey back to Kraśnik. One of the men warned me to stay away from certain areas and described a trail to get me to the farmlands. As I was leaving, a little girl handed me an apple and wished me godspeed."

Ben paused his story and faded out of the conversation. His eyes saw the girl and he smiled at her. His distraction lasted only a moment, and he picked up his meatball sandwich. "By the way, Polish apples are very tasty.

"I followed the trail and reached the farmlands by morning. From there, I walked through the wheat fields and potato fields, staying clear of farmhouses and roads. Along the way I picked a few potatoes, some vegetables, and even a few eggs from a henhouse. It took me four more days to get back to Kraśnik.

"I arrived at St. Mary's late at night. The door to the church was locked and no one answered my knock. Adrenaline was pumping through my veins. I had the feeling that something was wrong. I ran around to the courtyard building and tried the door, but it was also locked. I was about to try a window when the side door opened and a woman bade me to be quiet. She had night clothes on, but I took her to be a member of the order.

"'I'm looking for the Solomons,' I whispered. 'They came here five days ago.'

"'There are no such people here; this is a convent,' she answered and started to close the door.

"I was shocked. I held my hand on the door. 'What happened to them? Where is Father Janofski?'

"'I don't know what you're talking about. Leave or I will call the authorities.'

"'Where is Father Janofski? Let me talk to him.'

"'I'm afraid that is not possible. He is on sabbatical. Now you must leave or I will sound the alarm.' With that she pulled the door shut.

"Now I was frantic. I ran to the side of the church, looking for an open door or window. I found a small, locked casement window at the rear of what would have been the north transept and cracked the upper pane with a rock. Once inside, I tried to find the priest's apartments. The interior was pitch black and I lit a candle to find my way.

"The old complex used to be a monastery and there was a maze of hallways leading from the church. I turned to follow one such hallway when I heard a gruff voice order, 'Put out that candle.' I spun around to come face-to-face with Father Janofski. He's the only man I've ever known to sleep in a nightcap and a night-gown, like the drawings for *The Night Before Christmas*.

"'Where is my family?' I demanded.

"'Asleep. Where I was until a few minutes ago. Are you trying to raise the dead?'

"'I just asked one of your nuns about my family and was told that no such people were here and that you were on sabbatical.'

"He chuckled and motioned for me to follow him down the hall. 'You can't be too careful. That was probably Sister Bonicja. She's a tough cookie.'

"He interrogated me about where I left the car, how I got to Kraśnik, and who I might have talked to along the way. When he was satisfied that I hadn't been followed, he opened the door to a small bedroom.

"'Get some sleep,' he said. 'We'll talk in the morning. After you fix my window.'"

THIRTY-THREE

...

Chicago, Illinois, November 2004

U PON THEIR RETURN TO the townhouse, Ben and
Catherine were greeted by Liam.

"Out for a walk?" he asked.

"I was treated to lunch at Rocco's," Catherine said.

"Ah, the meatball capital of the world. Do you have an ample
supply of antacids?"

"Cut it out," Ben said. "We're talking haute cuisine."

"I confess, it was a pretty tasty sandwich," Catherine said.

"I've got some information for you," Liam said, pulling up a chair
to the kitchen table and taking out a file folder. "Columbia Indemnity Corporation, the massive conglomerate Rosenzweig owns,
was founded in 1984. The incorporators were Elliot Rosenzweig,
Robert Hart, and Carl Schaeffer. This gets complicated—I'm going
to trace the history of Rosenzweig's empire going backward in
time—so listen carefully. Columbia was formed for the sole purpose of acquiring the assets of two other existing insurance companies: Franklin Life and the Dorchester Companies. Franklin Life
was owned by Rosenzweig, Hart, and Schaeffer. Dorchester was in
the reinsurance business in Philadelphia, and as far as I can tell, it
was owned by somebody else. Franklin Life was created in 1967
and was the result of a consolidation between American Mutual

and Youngstown Life. American was owned by Rosenzweig and Youngstown was owned by Hart."

"So Rosenzweig kept acquiring his own companies?"

"Well, he kept merging them. And buying others."

"Where did you get all this information?" Catherine said.

"It's all in the public records. Some came from the Illinois Department of Insurance, some from the Illinois Secretary of State corporate division, some from the Federal Trade Commission. It's all there, you just have to dig.

"Here's the juicy part: American Mutual was founded in 1948. Its sole incorporator was Elliot Rosenzweig of 1450 Lake Shore Drive. At that time the state required a life insurance company to post an indemnity bond and a minimum requirement for cash reserves, both of which were met by Rosenzweig. He satisfied the reserve requirement with cash and a letter of credit from the Midwest Bank and Trust Company of Chicago."

"How does a penniless camp survivor post a multimillion-dollar cash reserve? And how does he get a letter of credit?" Catherine said.

"Exactly. He would have to have had security for the Midwest letter of credit."

"What was his security?"

"Well, now that's a problem. Midwest was bought out by National Union Bank in 1988. The files of the obsolete loans and letters of credit no longer exist."

"So we don't know who or what provided security for Rosenzweig's letter of credit?" Catherine said.

"That's right. But I'm still digging."

Liam stood and slipped on his jacket. "I have a statement to record this afternoon, so I'll see you later. What time do you want me on Thursday?"

"Dinner's at four. Come early for a cocktail. Ben's coming, too."

"Excellent. I can taste the turkey already."

"Wait, Liam," said Catherine. "We have news for you, too. Rosenzweig says he's found the real Otto Piatek."

"What?" Liam sat down. "Where is he?"

Catherine smiled. "That's the rub. They believe they found his home, and they're staking it out, but the elusive Otto Piatek has yet to show his face."

"You believe this?"

"I don't know. On the basis of that representation, Jenkins asked that I stop working on Ben's case."

"Right," said Liam. "I'm sure." He shook his head. "What's the address? I'll check it out."

"We don't know."

"Sounds like a cock-and-bull story to me. When you get an address, let me know."

Liam left. While sitting in the living room, a fire crackling in the brick fireplace, Ben said, "These financial transactions, showing that Rosenzweig formed his insurance empire right after he settled in Chicago, is that evidence we can use?"

"It's a piece of the puzzle. It's one brick in the construction of a trial. It certainly creates an inference, but it doesn't *prove* that Rosenzweig used stolen property to form his business. There are all sorts of alternative explanations. He could have found a backer who helped him arrange for the loan, or he could have had a business associate put up security. And it still doesn't link Rosenzweig with Piatek."

"When we file our lawsuit, when we're before the court, don't we have the right to demand that he produce all of his records? Can't we ask him at a deposition how he got his money? And how he came to America?"

"Yes. That's called discovery, and we have a right to subpoena documents and take depositions."

"He'd have to answer all the questions, wouldn't he?"

"He would."

"Well, then, those pieces, those other bricks, will come in time, Catherine. Just have faith."

She reached for her pen and pad. "What did the good Father Janofski have to say when you woke up?"

Kraśnik, Poland, 1942

"I went looking for him the next morning and found him outside, walking in the quadrangle, his hands clasped behind him, saying his morning prayers. He quickly shooed me back into the building, where I waited for him in my chamber. Sometime later, he knocked on the door. 'You must stay out of sight,' he snapped. 'Until we figure out what to do with you, your presence here is a danger to our entire operation.'

"'What has become of my family?' I asked.

"'They are well. We'll talk about them after you've fixed my window. Come with me.'

"He gave me glass, a cutter, and putty and left me to figure out how to fix a broken window. Needless to say, it was a learning experience. After I finished, he invited me for breakfast.

"I followed him through the church into the vestry. Soon, plates of eggs, potatoes, and meat were brought and laid on the desk by Sister Mary Magdalena, who bowed and softly closed the door as she left.

"'Your father is a very talented man,' Father Janofski said at long last. 'His engraving skills are valuable assets.'

"'I'd like to see my wife.'

"'How much do you know about our operations?'

"'Only what Lucyna told us: that you assist people in leaving the country. Obtaining visas and travel papers. Not much more than that.'

"He took small forkfuls of food. He was a delicate eater. 'We do what we can,' he said. 'It has become increasingly difficult to move people out of harm's way. Germany now controls all of Europe from the English Channel to the Volga, from the Balkans to North Africa. All of the Mediterranean Sea is German water. With America in the war and the Russian armies massing, that may change, but for the moment . . .' He shrugged his shoulders and took another bite of meat.

"'I'd like to see my wife,' I repeated.

"Again he nodded, but did not answer me. 'Next year will be critical for this war. Until sanity returns, we must do what we can to combat the ungodliness. We are called upon to do so.'

"'My wife,' I repeated.

"'She is with the sisters. Do you think this is a hotel?' He patted his mouth with his napkin and walked to the vestry door, which he opened, peeked out into the church, and then locked. He walked directly to the large closet where the altar linen and clerical vestments were hanging. Sliding them aside, he pushed on the back wall, which opened to reveal a passageway. We descended a staircase into a windowless basement area. There sat my father at a long oak table on which magnifying glasses, microscopes, and documents were laid.

"Father Janofski held up two visas, examined them closely, and smiled. 'You can't tell the original from the copy. Brilliant.'

"'Father,' I said, figuring that now, at last, I'd get some answers, 'what's going on with Mother and Hannah?'

"'It's a long story.'

"'I'm listening.'

"'The first night we arrived and you left for Zamość, the girls were cared for by the sisters, and Father Janofski brought me down to this cellar. I was famished. He brought me a bowl of soup and some bread and we talked through the night. He's a remarkable man, Ben. Our original plans were to wait for you and then leave. St. Mary's does not house refugees.'

"'The church is under constant surveillance,' added Father Janofski, 'and the Gestapo barges in at unexpected times looking for fugitives. If any lay people were found hiding in the church, we'd all be arrested and the church destroyed.'

"'Anyway,' my father continued, 'when I spoke of my background, my engraving, Father asked if I was able to copy travel documents. So here I sit. I have a little bedroom in the corner of the cellar and I'm doing my part to help people escape the death camps.'

"Father Janofski walked over to my father and put his hands on his shoulders. 'Our last angel—I call them all angels because they are doing God's work—was a calligrapher. A beautiful artist, she was. But she received news that her mother was ill, and she left for Gorlice. That was two months ago. We were unable to process any new travel documents until your father came along.'

"'And Hannah?' I asked again.

"'Hannah, Lucyna, and your mother are living in the convent,' my father said. 'When necessary, they put on habits and pretend to be nuns. They're doing their part too: sewing suits, uniforms, dresses, and other articles of clothing needed by people traveling the resistance underground. We're welcome to stay here as long as we wish. Father Janofski has been very generous.'

"'What about me? What am I to do? I don't think I'd look good in a habit.'

"'I have need for a strong, young body,' answered Father Janofski. 'I think God is overly ambitious with these old bones. This noble church demands a lot of care. It would be acceptable to me if I never had to climb another ladder.' He paused with a wry smile. 'With the possible exception of Jacob's.' He chuckled at his joke. 'There are also occasions when we need a courier, and there are nights I must make contact with the resistance. If you are willing to take on these responsibilities and abide by our restrictions, you may stay in the cellar.'

"'I would like to stay with my wife. We just got married.'

"'Shall I reserve the honeymoon suite?' Father Janofski said. 'She's in a convent. There are no men allowed. The doors are locked at night.'

"My father winked at me. 'The nuns file into the chapel in the morning and for vespers. That's when I talk to your mother.'

"I didn't want to appear ungrateful, but the prospect of living separately from Hannah and seeing her only a few minutes a day was disheartening.

"'Keep your conversations to a minimum,' snipped Father Janofski. 'And don't talk to her when lay worshippers are present. We cannot control who walks into our church. Our services are open to all, including the Germans, and there's always a Nazi or two on Sunday morning. I don't know if they're worshipping or watching, but we don't take any chances.'"

"So you came to live at St. Mary's?" Catherine said.

"Yes, I did, and a more generous, heartwarming group I have never met in my life, although it was agonizing to be so close to Hannah, yet so far, to see her dressed in a postulant veil, filing into church in the morning and the evening, trying to catch a moment alone."

"As a Jew, did it trouble you to see Hannah dressed as a nun?"

"Hannah and Lucyna were dressed as postulants—they were young enough—my mother was dressed as a professed nun. And no, it didn't trouble me at all; these people were saving our lives. I was concerned that the sisters would resent a non-Catholic wearing a holy habit: the veil, the white head covering, the collar, the cord from the belt. These are all deeply religious symbols and it took great beneficence for these nuns not to consider the masquerade offensive. But, they were strongly supportive of Father Janofski and his work."

Ben stood to stretch his legs. He walked to the fireplace, repositioned the logs, and poked the embers. "During the day, I stayed in the cellar with my father, assisting him in whatever way I could, or I did odd jobs around the church. I longed for the masses and my brief moments with Hannah. Out of respect, Hannah would sit through the service, but during communion, when the other nuns were receiving the host, she'd slip into the corner of the transept, out of sight, where I'd kiss her a thousand times and tell her how much I loved her and how I wanted to be with her. She'd say, 'Dance with me, Ben, like we did in Zamość,' and for a few brief moments we'd waltz in the darkened recesses of the old church. We had only moments, the length of the communion, before she'd hurry back to her pew and file back into the convent."

"Father Janofski had mentioned that he needed you to make contact with the resistance," Catherine said. "Were you given those assignments?"

"Not initially. The man who made deliveries of milk and eggs twice a week was really a messenger for the resistance. He would pass along the information about persons needing forged papers, who they were, what sort of clothing they needed. A few days later we would covertly pass the forged papers and suits of clothes to him and he'd hide them in his wagon. In January 1943, he was randomly interrogated by the Gestapo. Although nothing came of it, he felt threatened and would no longer serve as an intermediary. Father Janofski then asked if I would transport documents and clothing, and my service as a resistance courier began."

"You look tired, Ben. Do you want to stop for the day?"

He took a deep breath and nodded. "I think so. It's been a long day. Shall I come tomorrow?"

Catherine walked Ben to the door. "Not tomorrow or Wednesday. I'll be shopping and cooking—turkey, stuffing, sweet potatoes, and pumpkin pie. I'll see you Thanksgiving Day. Bring a big appetite."

THIRTY-FOUR

...

Chicago, Illinois, November 2004

THANKSGIVING DAY BEGAN WITH rain and wind. The temperature hung in the low forties and was forecast to drop throughout the afternoon with measurable snow toward evening. In contrast, Catherine's home was warm and festive. Her china and crystal were set upon a lace tablecloth, embroidered in browns and oranges. A wicker centerpiece, shaped like a turkey, held cut flowers. A fire crackled and danced in the living room fireplace.

Catherine's sister Deirdre and her husband Frank, Catherine's Aunt Ethel, Ethel's son Charles and his pregnant wife Jessica, Catherine's brother Stephen and his second wife Jeanette, and Liam all mingled about in the living room enjoying cocktails and hors d'oeuvres set out on Catherine's antique rosewood chiffonier.

"Who's the extra place setting for?" asked Frank, checking out the dining room. He was a stout man with a bald head, a double chin, and a perpetual smile.

"It's for Ben Solomon," Catherine said. "He's a client of mine, a sweet old man who doesn't have a family, so I invited him to share our Thanksgiving."

"That's charitable of you," Aunt Ethel said.

"It's not charity. I've become very fond of him. He's a remarkable man, although he does have some idiosyncrasies."

"What kind of *idiot*-syncrasies?" Frank snickered. "What, does he drool or something?"

"Frank, I know you don't mean any harm, but can I ask you not to tease Ben? You'd be doing me a favor," Catherine said.

Deirdre added through clenched teeth, "Frank, for once, behave yourself."

"Okay, okay," he said with a chuckle. "Take it easy. I won't tease the sweet old man. But tell me, what idiosyncrasies?" he said, pouring himself another cocktail.

"He has very intense memories and sometimes he sort of zones out. His eyes'll glaze over and . . . I think he experiences scenes from earlier times in his life. And he'll talk to his deceased wife."

"So what you're telling me is . . . he's daffy."

"Frank, stop!" Deirdre said.

"No," Catherine said quietly. "I'm telling you to be nice. He lost his whole family in World War II. If he wants to talk to them, it's his business."

The doorbell rang. "That'll be him. Be nice, Frank."

Catherine opened the door and greeted Ben, who stood on the stoop in a raincoat, folding his umbrella.

"I brought this," he said, handing her a box of Frango Mints.

"Why, thank you, Ben, you didn't have to do that."

As she helped him with his coat, he held out a CD, wrapped in striped paper. "And this is specially for you."

"How thoughtful. Thank you so much. Should I open it now?"

"Sure. With all the time we've spent talking about Poland the last few weeks, I thought you should experience some of her more noble aspects. It's Chopin's 'Krakowiak.' The pianist is Bella Davidovich."

"Terrific. I'll put it on later," she said. "Come with me and I'll introduce you to everyone."

She took Ben's arm and led him into the living room where she made the introductions. Frank, a multicolored wool sweater covering his paunch, walked over with a smile and stuck out his large hand. "Frank Gordon. Nice to meet you. Lemme get you a cocktail." Walking to the chiffonier, he said, "Whaddya drink?"

"A glass of that red wine would be just fine, thank you."

Frank turned and winked playfully at Deirdre.

Twilight brought freezing rain that changed to snow by dinner, but the townhome was cozy and the turkey was plump and golden brown. Frank had refilled his cocktail glass several times before the group took their places around the table.

Aunt Ethel, the family matriarch, said grace and mentioned in her prayer how grateful she was for health and family.

"Amen," Frank said, glancing at Ben, who seemed disengaged, staring at the centerpiece, moving his lips.

"It's been a tradition in our family," Ethel pronounced, "to go around the table and for each of us to share something that we're thankful for in the past year. Liam and Ben, you're certainly welcome to participate if you like, but it's not a requirement. You'll still get your turkey."

One by one, the guests offered a short recitation, often about companionship, good health, or business success. When it came to be Catherine's turn, she said, "I'm thankful that everyone has come to help me celebrate the holiday."

"Hear, hear," the group echoed, toasting their hostess.

"I'm also thankful for my new friend, Ben, and for his helping me to realize that practicing law can have a higher calling, one of principle and moral significance. And that once again I can be passionate about my work."

"Whoa," whistled Frank. "That's deep stuff."

"Clam up, Frank," snapped Deirdre.

"How about you, Ben?" Frank said. "Do you want to tell us what you give thanks for?"

"Frank, if you don't shut up, I'm taking you home," Deirdre said.

"It's okay," Ben said. "I have a lot to be thankful for. Catherine, for one. She's a strong, intelligent woman, and I could not have found a better attorney or a better listener. In many ways she reminds me of my wife, Hannah."

"Is that who you were talking to a few minutes ago?" Frank said with a grin.

"That's it!" Deirdre said. "Get your coat, you buffoon."

"Honey, I didn't do anything."

Deirdre stood and put her napkin on her plate, but Ben said, "Please, Deirdre, sit down. I'll answer his question. Frank, did you ever hear a song on the radio, and it brought back vivid memories of something, maybe high school or a summer romance?"

"Of course. Everybody has."

"And you could feel something in your senses, couldn't you, Frank? It was more than just pinging a memory, wasn't it? It was like you could once again experience a piece of the past—feel a summer breeze, smell a fragrance in the air, a drive with your friends, maybe feel an emotion like joy, sadness, or affection. Didn't it feel like part of you was going back in time a little bit to when the song was popular?"

Frank nodded. "Yep."

"A few days ago, Liam stood in this room and said he could taste the Thanksgiving turkey already. Did you ever have that sensation—where you could taste something just by thinking about it?"

"Yep."

"Senses are funny that way, aren't they, Frank? It's not entirely cognitive, it's more than that. Something we can't really explain. And how about dreams? Did you ever have a dream about someone, maybe even someone close to you who had passed on, and it was intensely real for you, as though you had actually been with them? Even after you woke up, did you still have that feeling?"

Frank's expression turned serious. "Yes."

"I'm sorry, I just struck a chord, didn't I?" Ben said.

Frank nodded.

"Frank's mother," Deirdre said. "She died last year."

"I'm very sorry for your loss," Ben said. "I don't know the extent of your religious beliefs, Frank. Are you a religious man?"

"Well, I go to church."

"Right," said Deirdre, "maybe twice a year."

Frank shrugged.

Ben continued. "Do you accept the church's concept of the human soul? For example, do you believe that the soul is a portion of the living God, that it has a spark of divinity?"

Frank swallowed. "Um, yeah . . . I guess I do." He looked around the table, but no one was bailing him out.

"Can I ask you, then, what is your concept of the relationship between the body and the soul? And I'll tell you in a minute why I'm asking that question."

He shrugged and looked at Deirdre. "Answer him, Frank," she said.

"Well, I don't know. I guess I think that the soul is eternal and it's in your body and when you die, I don't know, I guess that maybe it returns to God."

"That's what I believe, too," Ben said. "The book of Genesis tells us that God blew the breath of life into Adam, and many scholars believe that to be a metaphor for Adam's eternal soul. It's spiritual, isn't it, Frank? It's not tangible, not physical, maybe not even logical, but you believe it's there, don't you?"

Frank nodded and took a sip of his drink.

"Some feelings, some visions, come to me. There is no rational explanation. When you saw me moving my lips, I was talking to my Hannah. She was there for me. I believe her soul is eternal and as vibrant today as it was sixty years ago. In fact, I am certain of it. Do you think that makes me crazy? Maybe just a little strange?" Ben smiled.

"No, I don't," he said softly, looking around the table. Everyone was quite still, and a few moments passed with only the sweet strains of the "Krakowiak" on the stereo. Finally, Frank said timidly, "Can I ask you a question, Ben? These visions that you have, do you think they come from the afterlife? Is there a life after we die?"

Ben raised his eyebrows. "That's the jackpot question, isn't it? I guess we won't know for sure until we're dead. I have my beliefs, and to some extent they're based upon my studies—the Bible, the Talmud. The Bible tells us that Abraham went to rest with his father. Each time one of the Patriarchs dies—Isaac, Jacob, Aaron, and Moses—the Bible recites, 'He was gathered to his people.' Those passages say to me that the essence of our loved ones still exists, and when we die we'll be gathered to them. The Mishnah says the world is like a lobby before the *olam ha-ba*—the world to come—and one prepares himself during life in the lobby so that he may enter the banquet hall."

"Is that just in your religion? Your people?"

"No," Ben said with a smile. "Maimonides taught that the righteous of all nations have a share in the *olam ha-ba*. And the Zohar tells us all that our ancestors are watching over us."

"And my mother and father? Are they . . . ?"

"I believe they're waiting for you, Frank. In the *olam ha-ba*, watching over you right now."

"How do I . . . ?"

"Open your heart."

Frank sat still for a moment, then looked at Catherine, flipped his thumb in Ben's direction, and said, "He's a pretty smart guy."

She laughed. "Liam, it's time to carve the turkey."

AFTER DINNER, WHILE THE guests were enjoying coffee in the living room, Ben called Liam over to the window.

"I don't want to disturb anyone," he said softly, "but do you see that gray Camry across the street?"

"Yes," Liam said. "The motor's running and there are two people in the front seat."

"It was there when I arrived. Same two guys sitting in the car. And I think I've seen that car on the block before, maybe Monday."

Liam nodded. "Stefan Dubrovnik said he was driven in a gray Camry." He motioned for Catherine to join him in the kitchen.

"Do you have a camera I can borrow?" he said. "I think we have some visitors outside."

With Catherine's digital camera in his hand, Liam walked boldly out of the front door, down the steps, directly to the Camry, and tapped on the window. The driver, a stocky man with a buzz cut and a barbed-wire tattoo on his neck, lowered his window.

"What do you want?"

Liam leaned on the driver's door. "Are you guys waiting for an invitation to dinner? Because if you are, I regret to inform you that the turkey's all gone."

"Very funny, asshole. Get lost."

"What are you doing out here?"

"Listening to the radio. Is there a law against sitting in my car?"

Liam snapped a picture of the driver and the passenger. "Smile," he said. Then he stepped back and took a picture of the side of the Camry, the back, and the license plate before returning to the driver.

"Tell Rosenzweig that you and this piece-of-shit car have been made. If anyone has an accident, or is bothered in any way, these pictures go straight to the state's attorney."

"You don't scare me, tough guy."

"Feeling's mutual," Liam said. "Tell your boss to let you use his limo next time. It's the least he could do for a couple of fine gentlemen like yourselves." He turned and walked back in to the house as the car pulled away.

"What were they doing?" Catherine said.

Liam shook his head. "I don't know. Ben said he's seen them before. Ben's building super, Stefan Dubrovnik, gave me a description of a man with a tattoo—matches the driver. I think it's time to revisit Mr. Dubrovnik."

"Why are they watching my house?" Catherine said.

"I don't know. Ben's here, you're here. Keep your eyes open. If you see the car again, call me. We've blown their cover, so they may not be back."

"I'm scared, Liam. For myself and for Ben. Maybe you're wrong. Maybe Rosenzweig would arrange for an accident. Maybe it's not Rosenzweig at all, and the real Piatek would try something."

"Do you want me to stay here tonight?"

Catherine nodded. "The guest room's all made up, if you wouldn't mind."

Liam started to return to the living room but suddenly stopped, held Catherine by the arm, and said, "They didn't deny it."

"What?"

"They didn't deny Rosenzweig had sent them. When I said, 'Tell Rosenzweig that you've been made,' they didn't say, 'Who's Rosenzweig?' or anything like that. They didn't deny they were watching your house. All they said was, 'You don't scare me.' If we can tie the driver to Rosenzweig, Dubrovnik can put him in Ben's apartment."

"It's him, isn't it, Liam? Piatek. He's out there. And it's really Rosenzweig."

THIRTY-FIVE

...

I'M STILL STUFFED FROM Thursday's dinner," Ben said, sitting in Catherine's winged chair and waving off a breakfast pastry. "You're a wonderful cook."

"Thank you. I don't cook often but I enjoy it." Catherine picked up her yellow pad and reviewed the previous session's notes. "I think you had just signed on as a caretaker and courier for the good Father Janofski," she said. "Tell me about your time in the church."

Kraśnik, Poland, 1942

"Father Janofski had a radio in the cellar. A wire, used as an antenna, stretched from the top of the church steeple, down the back of the church, and through a hole in the transept wall. It was powerful enough to pick up the Allied stations, and with that radio, we kept up with the progress of the war. I didn't know it at the time, but the radio was also a source for coded messages. At certain times Father Janofski would exclude my father and me from the basement to receive these messages. We were never privy to the code or the information.

"In the fall of 1942, the tide began to turn against Hitler's Germany. Up to that time, the German army had seemed unstoppable. Rommel's Afrika Corps was in command of North Africa and the German Sixth Army, using Romanian, Hungarian, and Italian divisions for support, was about to take Stalingrad. But Hitler's objectives were too ambitious and he had overreached himself.

"We listened in early November as the British under General Montgomery broke through Rommel's lines west of Cairo at El Alamein, forcing the Germans back seven hundred miles, and we listened as American and British troops under Eisenhower and Patton landed in Morocco and Algeria to begin their sweep across North Africa.

"More important for us, however, was the Russian counteroffensive at Stalingrad, which began on November 19. Father Janofski spoke Russian, and we followed the broadcasts closely. More than a million German troops were lost in Russia. The Soviet victory in Stalingrad in January 1943 turned the tide on the eastern front. The Russian army started marching west toward Poland, while the British and Americans were storming across North Africa and then to Sicily. From that point on, Hitler was doomed to fight a defensive war, but his grip on Poland and central Europe would not loosen for a long time.

"Meanwhile, our work at St. Mary's continued. Hannah, Mother, and Lucyna tirelessly sewed garments and helped out in the convent. My father meticulously processed travel documents. I maintained liaisons with the underground resistance groups, shuttling papers and bundles of clothing between St. Mary's and the safehouses."

Catherine interrupted. "What about you and Hannah? Tell me about the two of you."

Ben blushed. "Well, you know, we couldn't room together, and I was limited to the briefest of encounters, once or twice a day, but . . . there were a few times when the locked convent doors were conveniently left unlocked. The nuns, especially a couple of the younger women, were partial to Hannah and sympathetic to our situation. They'd giggle at our dilemma and find ways to promote our romance. Despite the strict rules laid down by Mother Superior, there were nights when they would forget to bolt the courtyard door. On those prearranged occasions, Hannah and I would meet on the lawn and dance beneath the stars, then curl up in a blanket. Sometimes we'd find a bottle of wine and two glasses by the fountain."

"And Mother Superior never caught you?"

"Well, I wouldn't say that. She never confronted me, but she gave me a look every now and then that kind of told me she knew more than she was supposed to."

Catherine smiled and retrieved a pot of tea from the stove. She poured two cups and set them on a table before the hearth with the pastries. Ben continued.

"Spring turned to summer and summer to fall with our lives in relative balance. The women never left the grounds. My father spent most of his time in the cellar, and I split my time between church maintenance during the day and my courier duties at night.

"My rendezvous point with the Polish underground was a small brick house on the eastern part of Kraśnik, about a mile and a half from the church. My contacts would let me in the back door. I would deliver the forged travel documents and articles of clothing I'd carried in a backpack. They'd hand me a sealed envelope for Father Janofski.

"I learned to find my way in the dark of night. There were no streetlights. There was only the moon. I came to know which streets were patrolled and which were not. Which backyard garden gates were locked and which were open. And which homes had barking dogs that could alert the neighborhood. It was a zigzag journey from the church to my contact and it took more than three hours round trip.

"As for Father Janofski, I grew to respect and admire him deeply. He was an extraordinary man who lived his ideals. He risked his life for Catholics and non-Catholics alike, people outside his pastorate, acting in defiance of the most intolerant penal code ever decreed, at a time when most non-Jewish clergy shut their eyes. The nuns adored him and held him in esteem. They followed him willingly, putting their own lives on the line, too.

"He also took an interest in my salvation. By the time I arrived at St. Mary's, religion was on the back burner for me. I hadn't thought much about God or Judaism in any way other than the obvious—the realization that being a Jew targeted me for extinction.

"One day Father Janofski invited me to join him in the quadrangle for morning prayers. 'It would do you good to reconnect with God,' he said.

"'Where is God?' I asked. 'Why is he letting this happen?'

"Father Janofski raised his eyebrows. 'That would be a good question to ask him. Seeking those answers is an exercise in faith. Morning prayers are a solid way to begin each day.'

"Above all, Father Janofski was a man of faith who saw that my soul was starving. We spent many an hour discussing religious philosophies, for he had great knowledge and drew from many religions. He didn't try to proselytize me, he just wanted me to be a God-fearing man, and I credit him for the comfort I now receive from my faith. You know, our philosophies are not so different. The Kabbalah teaches that the goal of man is to bring God into the world.

"We also followed the progress of the war. Father Janofski and I had prepared a map of Europe which we kept in the cellar by the radio, and as we listened to the broadcasts we tried to plot the positions of the armies. So, for example, when Hitler launched his last offensive thrust against Russia in July 1943, we plotted the battles and held our breath. Within two weeks, the German armies had been repelled at Kursk and by October the Russian army was at the gates of Kiev, just a few hundred miles from Poland."

"You must have been heartened."

"We felt that liberation was near. I was confident that my family would survive the ordeal and that we'd return to help rebuild Zamość. We knew of the death camps, but we had no way of knowing the extent of the murders or the extermination of our people. We didn't know, for example, that by May 1943 every last Jew in Zamość had been deported, almost all to the death camps. Even as I sit here today, it's beyond comprehension.

"As the Allied armies closed in on Hitler, he increased his fanatical pursuit of the Final Solution, by which he planned to murder eleven million Jews, including five million in Russia, three million in Poland, a million in Romania and Yugoslavia, three-quarters of a million in France, and a third of a million in England. To this end, he stoked up the ovens at Auschwitz, burning six thousand bodies a day, and at Treblinka, Sobibor, and Chełmno, too."

"You didn't mention Belzec."

"Belzec closed in December 1942 because it was inefficient compared to Auschwitz. The Germans were concentrating their efforts at Auschwitz and Birkenau.

"In December 1943, it was on the Feast of the Immaculate Conception, the radio broadcasts told us that the Russians were nearing the Polish border. News of the advance raced through the church and plans were made for a celebration. That night, after mass, Sister Mary Magdalena locked the church doors and brought out a tray of wine. A small glass of wine was poured for each of us. And then another. Prayers of thanksgiving were offered. Giggles and songs filled the halls.

"Father Janofski and I stood watching the sisters, Hannah, my mother and father, and Lucyna all smiling and giddy. He took me aside. 'See how happy they are, Ben. They're rejoicing for the first time in years. There's an expectation of freedom, but sadly, it's premature. I don't want to burst their bubble, but this war is far from over.

"'We've all taken refuge in this house of God,' he said, 'but there's a false sense of security here. My Christian brothers are being expelled or killed throughout Poland. Half of the Catholic priests in Chełmno have been murdered, a third have been killed in Łódź and Poznań. Of the thirty churches and forty-seven chapels that existed in Poznań, only two churches remain. We live on borrowed time here in Kraśnik.'

"'But the Russians are on our doorstep,' I said. 'Freedom is near.'

"'They could be months away, Ben. The German army may be backpedaling, but it hasn't been defeated. There is danger in a wounded animal. We must continue our efforts.

"'The Polish underground is increasing its activity,' he said, 'and I want to assist in any way I can. We'll continue processing our documents, but I've been asked to transmit information to the

British underground and I'd like your help. The message I decoded yesterday told me that microfilms, pictures of German armament factories in occupied territories, will be delivered soon. They're to be passed on to the Allies through a contact in Rzeszów. If you're willing, you can take my car, but it'll be dangerous.'

"I savored the opportunity to handle important missions and readily agreed. Three days later, after evening vespers, I took Father Janofski's car, a ten-year-old two-seater with a long metal shifter in the center of the floor, and drove out on the road to Rzeszów. It putted along noisily, shaking like it had the palsy, and wouldn't make more than thirty miles per hour. The passenger seat was filled with religious articles, and my cover story was well rehearsed—I was delivering the articles to or from a church in Rzeszów, depending on which direction I was headed. Father had prepared a set of phony papers to use if I was stopped, but we all knew that if the ruse failed, the car would be readily connected to the church and an arrest would mean death for us all.

"Among the religious items was an old, leather-bound Polish Bible. A hole had been cut out of the center pages, large enough to conceal a four-inch canister containing microfilms for the British. I was to deliver the book to a store in Rzeszów that sold antique books and ask for a man named Poulus. My password was, 'The good father returns this gospel with his compliments.'

"When I got there, the shop was crowded. Mr. Poulus was a burly man with a large, square-shaped head and a close-cut black beard. His reading glasses hung from his neck on a silver chain. When it was my turn to be waited on, he asked me gruffly what I wanted. I mumbled the password.

"'Ah,' he said. 'I'm glad he liked it. I have another version that the good father is sure to enjoy. One moment and I'll fetch it.' He disappeared into the rear of the store and returned with another old book, which he handed to me and quickly shooed me out the door.

"Although I was nervous as all hell, the pass was ridiculously easy and I carried the book to the car and put it on the seat with the other articles. The return trip to St. Mary's was similarly uneventful. All in all, the assignment was accomplished smoothly, and I relished the prospect of another opportunity.

"From then on I would deliver books or envelopes to contacts in nearby villages and, on occasion, all the way to Lublin. The city trips were the most dangerous. Father Janofski's car was unreliable, and I was told to travel in the middle of the day when traffic was the heaviest and it was easiest for me to blend in."

"Were you ever stopped?" Catherine said.

"Twice. The first time as I drove into Lublin. There was a blockade searching for weapons being smuggled north to Warsaw. They looked at the religious items and opened the trunk, but since they were looking for weapons and they didn't see anything like a rifle, they waved me on. The second time I was stopped, I was walking to the car after delivering the canister to Poulus. I was shoved up against a building and searched. The book fell to the ground. Since I had nothing incriminating on my person, I was released. They never picked up the book or opened it. I don't know if anything was inside, but that search scared the heck out of me. I mentioned it to Father Janofski, who shrugged and told me that he had another delivery ready, and did I want to take it or not. Of course I agreed, knowing that our work with the underground network was important to the war effort. Did you know, Catherine, it was a Polish underground message that alerted the British to Germany's rocket base in Peenemünde?"

"Peenemünde?"

"Hitler was developing the V1 rocket, an unmanned guided missile that could carry a bomb in its warhead. Peenemünde was destroyed by Allied bombs before Hitler could get his rockets off the ground."

Ben sat back and laced his fingers behind his head. "And so the winter passed into the spring of 1944. Every day the radio news was more encouraging and we could sense the day of liberation was coming. In May, the rumors were rampant that the Americans were planning to land in Europe and the radio gave us the news that the Russian army had crossed the Polish border.

"Finally, on June 8, we received word that joint American and

British expeditionary forces had landed in Normandy and were pushing east. The news was so exciting I couldn't wait to see Hannah. I paced impatiently all day waiting for the communion service. When Hannah finally came to meet me in the corner of the transept, I whispered, 'The Americans have landed. The Russian army is on Poland's doorstep. Our rescuers are coming soon, Hannah. We're going to make it.'

"She nodded. But her face was flushed and she seemed unsteady on her feet. I felt her forehead and it was burning. 'You're sick,' I said.

"'The sisters have been attending to me.' Her voice was thin and it took effort for her to speak. We held each other tightly and she put her head on my chest. 'I hurt inside, Ben.'

"I helped her back into the main sanctuary and brought her to Sister Mary Magdalena. 'We told her not to come tonight, to stay in bed, but she said she had to see you. She needs a doctor,' the sister said. 'The care we're giving isn't helping her. She's failing.'"

Catherine wrung her hands. Tears welled in her eyes. "Oh, no," she said.

"I asked Father Janofski for the name of a local doctor. I told him I'd go into Kraśnik and fetch him immediately, but he was fearful of sending me to summon a doctor for a nun. My presence at the church would be difficult to explain, and there were no doctors in Kraśnik that could be trusted with information about our operations. Since Hannah needed a doctor, he would go himself.

"Late that night he returned with a portly middle-aged man dressed in a tweed sport jacket. He introduced himself as Doctor Groszna and I was introduced as the church caretaker. Father Janofski and I led him back into the convent to where Hannah lay in a single bedroom.

"'What is the patient's name?' he asked.

"I answered quickly. 'Hannah.'

"'Sister Hannah?'

"'No. Just Hannah.'

"He looked at her cheeks flushed with fever and the pale area around her lips. Her eyes were half closed and she shivered, though she was burning to the touch. She was barely conscious. Loudly, he called, 'Hannah. Hannah. I'm Doctor Groszna. Show me, where does it hurt you?'

"She weakly pointed to her throat and her lower abdomen. He probed deep into her throat with a tongue depressor, all along nodding his head and repeating 'Uh-hmmm.' Finally, he turned to Father Janofski and me and said, 'You'll have to excuse us, please. I need to examine her more fully.' I was reluctant to leave her, but Father Janofski pulled me out of the room and into the hall.

"A few minutes later, the doctor came out to see us. 'I examined her chest and abdomen. As I expected, there were bumpy red rashes.' He took the stethoscope from around his neck and placed it in his black bag. 'Unusual for a woman her age. I'm afraid it's scarlet fever.'

"'Can you cure her?' I asked. I'm sure there was panic in my voice.

"He eyed me curiously and then shook his head. 'There is no cure, young man. I have advised the sisters to keep her cool with cloths, to feed her liquids so she does not dehydrate, and to pray that her immune system is strong enough to overcome the disease. Whoever attends to this woman must wash very carefully. We believe the disease is transmitted by saliva and mucus. It's quite contagious.'

"'Will she be okay?' I asked.

"He bent down to take a small bottle from his black bag and answered in a disinterested tone, 'Some recover and some do not. Those who recover often have permanent damage to their heart or organs.' He gave us the bottle of medicine and left the church. He never returned.

"The next morning a black sedan pulled onto the gravel drive and two Gestapo agents walked to the door. Sister Mary Magdalena alerted us, and I quickly ducked through the closet and down to the cellar. Father Janofski was told that Doctor Groszna had reported something unusual at the church: a woman named Hannah lay ill in the convent. He suspected that she was not a nun and by law was required to report such a finding to the Gestapo. They demanded to see her.

"'Of course, you may do as you please,' Father Janofski said, 'but that would be unwise. She is a young postulant and under quarantine, as I'm sure the doctor told you. She has the plague. We do not expect her to live.'

"'We were also told of a young man who showed an unusual interest in the sick woman. Where is he?'

"'A local farm boy, I'm not sure where he lives. He comes around from time to time to do maintenance work in exchange for food and a few złotys. If you come next Friday, you'll probably see him.'

"'You don't mind if we look around, do you?' they asked.

"'Not at all.'

"They inspected the church and convent, inside and out, but when they came to Hannah's room with its quarantine sign on the door, they shook their heads and kept walking.

"Days went by slowly and Hannah suffered greatly with the disease. Pain and nausea were her constant tormentors. I sat by her bedside every day holding her hand and urging her to take her liquids, but she had no appetite and her condition worsened. Father Janofski and I prayed together several times a day. The entire convent prayed for her." Ben's eyes glassed as he stared at the fireplace. "She was so pale.

"The following Friday brought the return of the Gestapo. Again I hid in the cellar while Father Janofski shooed them away. This time they insisted on seeing Hannah. Holding a cloth over their nose and mouth, they stood at the doorway and briefly looked into her bedroom. Then they demanded to see the caretaker.

"'He didn't show up today. He's not very responsible, but in these times, what could you hope for?' Father Janofski said.

"'It would be a mistake to lie to us,' they said. 'Your priestly garb will not protect you.' With an arrogant smile they turned and left the church.

"Three or four days later, I was summoned by Lucyna and told to come immediately. I rushed to Hannah's room to see her propped up on pillows and taking a bowl of soup. Her fever had broken. Color had returned to her face. She smiled at me. So pretty. I hugged her tightly and whispered, 'I was so afraid . . .'

"'You're stuck with me,' she said. 'I'll never leave you.' I don't mind telling you that I bawled like a baby. I spent the rest of the day sitting on her bed, just watching her.

"We knew the Gestapo would return, so we decided to dig a fresh grave in the church cemetery and report that she had died. That night I took a shovel into the graveyard. It gave me the chills to turn up the dirt, even though it was a deception.

"Hannah grew stronger day by day. Soon she was walking the hallways and chatting with the nuns. With the British and American armies on the continent, we had every reason to believe that the Nazi scourge was in its final hours. We were going to survive this madness. The Russian army was driving westward, Allied forces were dropping bombs on German cities, and the radio reports were enthusiastic.

"Two weeks later, on a Friday, as we expected, the Germans returned—the same two Gestapo officials, one tall and thin like Ichabod Crane, the other squat and stout with a Hitler mustache. They banged on the church door in a most insolent way. They demanded to see Hannah. Father Janofski took them outside to the cemetery and to the freshly dug grave. They nodded, took a walk around the church, and left. After they pulled away, Father Janofski came down to the cellar.

"'Well, they're gone, the vermin.' He picked up a set of travel documents my father was preparing and examined them with a magnifying glass. 'Remarkable work,' he said.

"But as he paced around, he looked uneasy, and my father noticed it too. 'Is something wrong?' my father asked.

"Father Janofski nodded. 'Abraham, this recent visit troubles me. First, I was afraid they would order me to exhume the body. Then, when they were walking around, there was a lot of hush-hush talking between these two Gestapo snakes. They kept eyeing the church. Nodding and pointing. Whispering.' He shrugged. 'Ach, maybe I'm getting old.' As he turned to climb the stairs, he added, 'Anyway, be on your guard. It never hurts to be too careful.'

"Nothing out of the ordinary happened for the next two days. I was making plans to deliver a microfilm canister to my British contact in Lublin. It was due to arrive at the church on Tuesday.

"Early Monday, after morning prayers, as my father and I were having breakfast with Father Janofski, we heard the sound of tires rolling over the gravel drive. I ran to the window and saw the black Gestapo sedan followed by two canvas-covered trucks pull to a stop at the front of the church. I waved at my father and Father Janofski, signaling danger. My father quickly descended into the cellar.

"Loud knocks reverberated throughout the church, and as Sister Mary Magdalena unlatched the large wooden door, she was pushed aside by the rush of German soldiers. I didn't have time to make it to the cellar, so I stood with a mop in my hand in the dark of the western transept. A dozen soldiers in full uniform stormed into the church, automatic weapons in their hands, their jackboots clacking on the stone floor. The two Gestapo officers followed and demanded to see Father Janofski. Sister Mary Magdalena hurried to find him.

"Without an ounce of fear, Father Janofski boldly strode into the nave. 'What is the meaning of this?' he snapped. 'How dare you bring weapons into my church. This is a house of God.'

"'Does God listen to the radio, Father?' the tall agent said.

"'Is that a crime now, to listen to music? Is Beethoven an enemy of the Reich?'

"'Does Beethoven need a fifty-foot antenna?' He pointed to the cupola. 'Show us the radio.'

"'Is that what this is all about? The radio is broken. We have sent it for repairs.'

"A helmeted soldier whispered into the fat Gestapo officer's ear. He pointed first toward the ceiling and then traced a line down the back of the west wall toward the rear of the church.

"The officer smiled. 'What is behind the altar?' he said.

"'Only the vestry,' Father Janofski said, 'where my robes and vestments are stored.'

"'Take us there.'

"Father Janofski shook his head. 'That is a holy room meant for ordained clergy. It would be a sacrilege to take you there.'

"'I care nothing about your sacrileges.' He advanced in the direction of the altar. 'Bring him along.' The barrel of a German rifle prodded Father Janofski forward.

"The vestry door was opened and the two Gestapo officers entered, followed by Father Janofski and several uniformed soldiers. They were out of my range of vision, but I heard the fat one say, 'There are several dishes here. Who are the ordained holy men who eat their breakfast in this forbidden room?' He laughed. 'Search the room,' he ordered. 'Find the radio.'

"I heard the sounds of cracking wood and smashed ceramics, and I knew that the soldiers were tearing up the vestry.

"'This is an abomination,' Father Janofski hollered. 'You are defiling holy ground. You are all committing mortal sins.'

"'Spare me your superstitions, priest. What is at the back of this closet?' he said, and I heard hollow, knocking sounds. 'Tear it down,' he said and I heard more sounds of cracking wood. Moments later, I heard the fat man's sickly laugh and his comment, 'Why, look at this. These must be stairs to heaven, only they're going the wrong way, eh, Manfred? What will I find down there, priest? Do you suppose Beethoven is giving a piano recital in your hidden cellar?'"

Ben stopped his narrative. He stared into the fireplace and breathed deeply. His jaw was tense and it quivered. His hands closed into fists, opened and closed again. He began to talk in monotones, a few words at a time. "This was a day the demons scorched the earth."

Ben started to rock slowly, back and forth. Catherine walked over and put her arm around him. He spoke softly. "Soon I hear the sound of footsteps coming up the stairs. My father and Father Janofski are forced into the nave, prodded ahead by the tips of rifle barrels, soldiers at their backs. They are followed by more soldiers, their helmets held in place by leather chin straps below their tightly closed lips. They show no emotion. They obey blindly. They are pawns of the devil. Slowly, the two Gestapo officers in their black leather trench coats walk into the sanctuary. In their hands, they have visas, travel documents, and identification papers seized from the basement. They look around the church interior and take in the scene. They laugh—a jackal's laugh from hell itself.

"'Where are the rest of your holy people, old man?' the tall one says to Father Janofski. 'Where are your women in their black sheets? Where are the brides of Christ?' He points at Sister Mary Magdalena. 'Summon the rest of your flock. I want everyone here, in this room. Now!'

"Soon all of the nuns, Hannah, my mother, and Lucyna are collected, and they huddle together in the nave. They are all frightened. I can't let Hannah face this ordeal without me. I walk quickly to her side.

"'Who is this?' The fat one points at me.

"'He is the caretaker,' Father Janofski answers. There is no fear in his voice. He is solid and secure in his beliefs. He will not back down. If this is his moment, he will go out proudly.

"We are told to sit in the pews while the Gestapo and the soldiers search the church. They smash statues with their rifle butts. They kick over altars. They defile the church. We are guarded by four young soldiers. Father Janofski tries to converse with them in German. He tells them they are desecrating a house of God, that it is an apostasy. They pay no attention to him. We sit silently for quite a long time, and then we are ordered to rise and walk to the front vestibule.

"Finally, a voice behind me says, 'Are you now a convert, Ben?'

"I spin around and look directly into the steely eyes of Otto Piatek. He shakes his head at me as a parent would to a disobedient child. 'Tsk-tsk. You should have stayed in Zamość. You should have obeyed the rules. I warned you.'

"'Stayed in Zamość to be slaughtered? Transported to Belzec to be gassed? Is that what I should have done?'

"He shrugs and slaps a riding crop against his black pantaloon, a mannerism he must have picked up from Dr. Frank. Turning to the SS guards he says, 'Take them all out into the yard and shoot them.'

"'Wait! Wait!' I scream. 'How can you do this? These are your parents. Hannah is like a sister to you. These nuns are all good people. What have you become?'

"'These nuns,' he sneers, waving his arm at the sisters huddled together, 'have been helping this criminal priest to violate the law. As to Abraham Solomon, he's your father, not mine, and he's an enemy of the Reich.' He turns to my father. 'What did you think would happen when you were caught forging documents, *Abe*? Did you think you'd get a medal from the führer?'

"My father, pinning his hopes on the belief that there remains a vestige of filial affection, takes a few steps slowly toward Otto, past the Gestapo officers who have deferred to Otto and are now smiling. He is halted by the point of a soldier's bayonet. 'Otto,' he says from several feet away, 'this is not the boy I knew. This is not the man we raised you to be, the man who stood shoulder to shoulder with us on Belwederski Street. The Otto Piatek I know has principles and compassion. He's intelligent and honorable.'

"There is a moment of hesitation, a touch of softness in Otto's steely mien, and he waves the soldier away. 'Let him come.'

"My father approaches with tentative steps. 'Please, Otto. Leah brought you up with love and kindness, she nurtured you. Don't repay her with cruelty. And the children, Ben and Hannah . . .'

"Otto curls his lip and leans into his words. 'Do you remember when you stood in my office and I asked you to bring Ben to me, that he was killing German officers with his band of freedom fighters? It was the day you came to beg for the life of Weissbaum the doctor. You refused me then, didn't you?'

"My father stands mute.

" 'Didn't you?' he screams.

"My father hangs his head, as I'd seen others do, hoping that meekness will be perceived as contrition, that Otto will be satisfied to have made his point, and that humiliation will engender a less severe response. 'I begged for the life of my friend, a good doctor. I stood solid for the life of my son, as I would have done for you, Otto.'

" 'Really? Then get down on your knees and beg me. Beg me for the life of your wife and children.'

"My father drops to his knees. He will do anything. 'Please, Otto,' he says with tears in his voice, 'please don't hurt Leah and the children.' He looks up at Otto. 'This is an opportunity for you to stand on the side of goodness. Let them live.'

"Otto looks around the church. The Gestapo officers and the

uniformed soldiers are staring at him, awaiting his decree of life or death. Otto locks eyes with the Gestapo. Then he turns to look at my father, still on his knees, pleading for his family.

"Slowly and calmly, Otto places his jackboot on my father's shoulder and kicks him over. He lies sobbing, cowering on the stone floor. 'Please, let them live,' he cries.

"'You Jewish slime, you are where you belong, on the floor, on the bottom of my boot.'

"'Otto,' I say quietly, a few feet behind him, 'the war is almost over. The Allied armies are closing in from every direction. The Russians have taken Zamość. It's only a matter of time until they're in Berlin. You know it's true. Then all of you will be held to account. If you have no regard for your family, think of yourself. What will you say to the Allies when Germany is vanquished? This is an opportunity . . .' I am slapped in the face with Otto's riding crop.

"'Shut up,' he says, and he turns to me, inches from my face. 'Always the smart one, the privileged one, who could talk his way out of everything. Not this time, Ben. Now it's the son of a woodcutter, not the coddled child of Jewish wealth, who's calling the shots. You are an enemy of the Reich in a time of war.'

"'Then take *me*, shoot *me*, do anything you want to me—*I* was the one who left you in Izbica. I was the one who joined the freedom fighters. Let Hannah and my parents and these good people go. Please, Otto.'

"'Please, Hauptscharführer Piatek,' he says with a grin.

"'Please, Hauptscharführer Piatek,' I repeat.

"'Very touching, Ben. You're breaking my heart.' He turns to the Gestapo and the assembled guards and holds out his hands in a begging gesture. 'I'm moved by his emotional appeal. Load the nuns and the other women into the trucks and drive them to Auschwitz. Maybe Mengele has use for them.' Turning back to me he says, 'There, you see, I let them live. I'm a humanitarian. I have compassion and goodness.' Slapping his leg and walking to the door, his voice echoing off the walls, he says, 'Hang the priest from the bell tower so all of Poland can see this papist traitor.' Turning his head in the direction of my father lying on the floor, he says, 'Shoot the forger in the courtyard.' Pointing at me, he says, 'Bring him along. He has information.'

"'No!' I scream. I am berserk. I see only Otto. I lunge for his throat but something hits me in the back of the head and I black out."

Catherine froze. She swallowed hard. Her nails dug into Ben's shoulder. "Did he do it? Did he shoot your father?"

Ben nodded.

"Oh my God, he shot your father! And he hanged Father Janofski?"

"From the steeple."

"Were your mother and Hannah and all of the nuns sent to Auschwitz?"

"They were." He paused to rub his eyes. "I regain consciousness in time to see them herded into the trucks. I am bound hand and foot. I scream and I feel the steel toes of German jackboots slam into my ribs and my back as the truck drives away.

"But Otto isn't finished with me. He saw the forged identity papers and he knows we are tied to the resistance. He is determined to get the names of our connections and is prepared to flay me open if that'll do it. I am driven to some building in Kraśnik, where I am tortured for the names of my contacts. For three days I am interrogated. They strip me naked and spray me with a hose. They burn my chest with cigarettes. They break my jaw with a nightstick. They hold my head back and force me to look at pictures they've taken of Father Janofski hanging from the church tower and of my father lying in his blood on the church steps. And at the end of each session they throw me into a locked storage closet.

"But they never break me. I have no reason to go on living and no amount of pain or threats can induce me to talk. I welcome death. At the end of the third day, Otto receives an urgent message that the Germans are pulling out of Kraśnik in advance of the Russian army. He spits on me and tells his adjutant, 'Take this *Saujude* to Majdanek. Maybe they can get him to talk before he dies.' So I am dragged from the building and driven to Majdanek. I arrive there in July 1944."

While listening to the narrative, Catherine's breaths are short and shallow and catch in her throat. It takes effort for her to speak. She shivers. "Yet . . . you survived."

Ben shrugs. "They didn't have time to kill me. Majdanek was liberated by the Russian army on July 23, 1944, shortly after I got there."

"I have to stop," Catherine says. She quavers unsteadily, like a vase in an earthquake, teetering on the edge. She clenches the sides of her wool skirt and squeezes until her hands are white. "I have to stop now." And then her walls crumble.

"I'm sorry," Ben says, wrapping his arms around her and smoothing her hair as she cries onto his shoulder. "I . . . it was all part of the story. It was the end of the story. The last time I saw Otto Piatek. I'm sorry. It's taken a toll on you and I'm sorry."

"I had to know. I needed to know." She sits up and looks into the tearing eyes of Benjamin Solomon. "Tell me again, Ben. Tell me you're sure. Tell me that Rosenzweig is Piatek."

"I'm sure."

She grabs a handful of tissues. "We'll have a meeting—Liam, you, and I—and we'll get this case going, I promise you. I will help you bring this man to justice. I won't rest until it's done. What was it you said with your freedom fighters? Never surrender?"

Ben nods. "*Nigdy się nię poddamy.*"

III

...

THE
LAWSUIT

THIRTY-SIX

...

Chicago, Illinois, December 2004

L IAM AND CATHERINE SPENT all Sunday and the better
part of Monday converting her aunt's former sewing room
into a litigation office, a "war room" as Catherine called it.
Reams of paper were stacked in the corner. A dry-erase board stood
on an easel along the wall next to the fax/copier. A bookcase held
pens, Post-its, envelopes, file folders, and other supplies.

Liam sat cross-legged on the floor and struggled with the assembly of a hutch-style computer desk purchased earlier in the day
from an office supply store. He grumbled loudly. "The least they
could do is design these parts to fit together without gaps. The damn
sides aren't even square."

Catherine smiled.

"I went out to Dubrovnik's Saturday," Liam said, twisting an
Allen wrench. "I thought I'd have a little talk with Stefan, but he
was gone. The house was empty and a For Rent sign hung in the
window. A neighbor told me that the family went back to Croatia.
She forwards his mail to a Zagreb post office box."

"Did you find out anything about the Camry that was parked
outside our house?"

Liam nodded. "It's registered to a Carl Wuld on West Argyle.
I haven't yet had an opportunity to do a search on him. And I'm

trying to follow a lead on the car. I don't suppose you've heard anything about the great stakeout on Piatek's house in Cleveland."

"In fact, Jenkins called yesterday. He told me that Jeffers left a message that no one has been seen in the Cleveland home for a couple of weeks. They continue to watch the house. They're sure they'll catch Piatek soon."

"After they locate Amelia Earhart? Doubt there's anything to it, but I've got a contact in Cleveland. Let's see what he can find out. On a more realistic note, I'm working on a few ideas. I don't want to get your hopes up, but a couple of them might pan out."

Catherine walked over to Liam. "Did I ever tell you how grateful I am for your help . . . for your friendship? More than you can know. It's one thing for me to jump into the fire with my career, but it's quite another for me to drag you in. If we end up in litigation against Rosenzweig, all your big-firm clients—Lawrence McComb, Fisher Longworth, all of them—will shun you like the plague. You may not get any more work from any of them."

"That's interesting coming from you, Cat. Wasn't it just a couple of months ago that *I* was trying to talk *you* into taking this case? Wasn't it *me* who made you promise to evaluate Ben's case?"

"It's different. I made a professional choice to represent a client. I got wrapped up in his story. I committed a lawyer's blunder— I became emotionally invested in a client's case. You, on the other hand, were back-doored into it. And I happen to know that you've given up profitable assignments over the past couple weeks in order to gather information about Rosenzweig. Not to mention the hours you've spent with Ben and me."

"Cat, do you think you're the only one affected by Ben's story? I feel as deeply as you do." Liam fished through a plastic bag of corner connectors. "Let's stop this conversation. It's going nowhere."

The doorbell rang and Catherine said, "The pizza's here. How about we quit for the night? We'll do more work tomorrow. Tonight, let's just relax."

Liam tightened his lips and shook his head. "I'm going to finish this first. It's me and the desk—mano a mano. I won't go down without a fight. According to the easy-assembly instructions I have only three sections to go."

Catherine left to set the pizza in the warmer. From time to time she winced as Liam's curses echoed through the building.

Half an hour later, Liam walked into the kitchen and said, "Do you have a Band-Aid?" He held his hand out like a little boy to show Catherine that he had skinned two of his knuckles.

"I have a Band-Aid and a glass of wine," she answered. "Which do you want first?"

T HE LAST FEW PIECES of pizza sat in the box on the coffee table next to a bottle of Chianti. The fire blazed and Oscar Peterson played "Porgy and Bess" on the stereo. Catherine raised her wine glass. "Here's to our efforts. May we have the strength to see this case through to the end."

"And some luck."

Catherine nodded. "Some luck and some evidence." She stared at the fire and then at Liam, who had a faraway look in his eyes. "What are you thinking about?" she said.

Liam shifted uncomfortably. "About high school—the Fleetwood Mac concert at Alpine Valley."

Catherine smiled at the recollection. "That was the one and only time we double-dated. You were with Janet Morgan. What made you think of that?"

"We went for pizza afterward."

Catherine leaned back against the couch pillow and pondered the memory. "God, that was a long time ago. I was so uncomfortable that night, did I ever tell you?"

"No. How come?"

"Just being out on a date, the two of us, and I was with someone else and you were with someone else."

Liam quietly chuckled. "When I took Janet home, she wouldn't even kiss me good night. She was pissed at me. She said all I did was talk to you all night and didn't pay any attention to her."

"After that concert, I was sure you were going to call me and ask me out, but you never did."

Liam reached out, lifted the bottle of wine, and poured another glass for each of them. "I was afraid."

"Of what?"

"Of not having a good time. Of not meeting your expectations. I don't know. We could've dated and sooner or later, like all high school romances, we'd have broken up. I guess I didn't want to risk messing up our friendship. Maybe if I had asked you out, we wouldn't have been friends for all these years. You never know."

They sat on the couch long after the pizza was gone and the fire had settled into a glow. Catherine, her wine glass in her hand, her stocking feet tucked under her, sidled closer to Liam, leaning her head on his chest. He put his arm around her.

"I don't deserve a friend like you," she whispered. "You've always been in my corner, since day one."

She took another sip of wine and stared at the embers. "Why did you let me marry Peter?" she said at last. "Why didn't you stop me?"

Liam shook his head. "If only I could have. It was the saddest day of my life."

"Damn the choices we make that change our lives forever," Catherine said. "The doors of decision are one-way only. You can never go back. I'll never be the same person again."

"Let it go, Cat. None of it was your fault. You've got to give life another chance."

Catherine finished her wine and set the glass on the table. She turned and faced him with a soft and gentle gaze and cupped his face with her hands.

"You're right," she said. "I know you're right. Maybe we should take that chance we should have taken years ago. Will you stay with me tonight?"

He hugged her tightly. His hand found the small of her back beneath her sweater and he rubbed her back as he kissed her. "I've loved you forever, Cat."

"I know."

THIRTY-SEVEN

...

Chicago, Illinois, December 2004

AFTERNOON SUNSHINE POURED THROUGH the windows and onto the printouts of Illinois appellate decisions, statute books, manila folders, and notepads that lay strewn about on Catherine's dining room table. Crumpled balls of yellow notepaper lay on the floor beside the wastebasket—errant hook shots, missed free throws. A stack of library books, annals of Polish history, were piled on the table in front of Liam. Ben had arrived earlier that morning.

"I still need a more definitive list of the stolen property," Catherine said to Ben. "You've given me fourteen items, including your father's bundle of currency, with a total present-day value of $850,000. The nonmonetary property, the items of jewelry and silver, need to be described with more particularity." She looked at Ben and tilted her head. "For example, item eight, 'A Silver Watch,' is not descriptive enough. Can you remember what it looked like, the name of the manufacturer?"

Ben just nodded and tapped the point of his pencil on his notepad.

"Liam, anything further on Otto Piatek? Your ideas? Your leads?" Catherine said.

"There is no one named Piatek in Cleveland. My buddy has verified that there are no phones, real estate records, licenses, or listings for a Piatek anywhere in the Cleveland area. He did come across a Pia*cek*, but so far, no one answers the phone. I've still got some lines in the water. At the library I dug up some info from historical journals. There are scattered references to Piatek in the German military archives. Nazi administrative records, produced at the Nuremberg trials, confirm the elevation of Piatek from Scharführer to Hauptscharführer in 1941. His rank and an increase in pay were reported in the audited General Government accounting journals in 1943. His posting in Zamość is noted."

"Are there any references to Piatek after 1943?"

"Not that I've seen yet."

Catherine stretched her arms. "We've been at this for five hours today. Why don't we take a break? Anybody want some lunch?"

Ben stood. "I'm going for a walk. I need some air."

"It's cold out," Catherine warned.

Ben smiled. "Not really. It's in the thirties. When I was a starter, sitting in that golf cart out on the first tee, many an April morning that wind would whip off the lake and chill me to the bone." He struck a boxer's pose. "I'm tough."

Left alone in the townhome, Liam approached Catherine and gently placed his hands on her shoulders. Catherine tensed, patted his arm, and turned away to walk to the kitchen.

"What's the matter?" Liam said.

"Nothing."

"Nothing? Last night, was that a problem for you, because for me it was heaven."

Catherine shook her head but averted her eyes. "No, it was wonderful, Liam. It's not that."

"Then, what?"

"Let's not talk about it now," she said, opening the refrigerator and sliding out the meat drawer. "We have a lot to do. How about a turkey sandwich?"

Liam slid back a kitchen chair, reversed it, straddled it, and watched Catherine gather the makings for a turkey sandwich. "White or whole wheat?" she said.

"I'm not okay with this, Cat. I don't get it."

"Let's just leave it for now," she answered without turning around. "You have to respect my wishes. That's just the way it is. I've got to work my way through this. White or whole wheat?"

"Catherine, don't put me off. I have a stake in this, too."

She turned to face him. Her face was flushed. "Damn it, Liam! White or whole wheat?"

Liam blinked. "Whole wheat."

I⸝T WAS AN OMEGA pocket watch," said Ben, returning from his walk. "Made in Switzerland in the early 1900s. My father bought it in Zurich." He hung his coat in the hall closet and returned to the kitchen. "It had a model name—Labrador, I'm pretty sure. Silver case, with an intricate design. Inside, the face had roman numeral hour markers. My father kept it on a silver chain clasped to his belt loop. I expect it would be worth quite a handsome sum today. Descriptive enough?"

Catherine nodded. Unmoved. She obviously had other things on her mind.

"Something wrong?" Ben said.

"No," said Catherine and Liam in unison.

"I'm going to add that description to the lawsuit," Catherine said, walking to the dining room. "I still need more details on your mother's bracelet."

"Did I do something?" Ben whispered to Liam.

"No, it's not about you."

The phone rang and Catherine answered it in the kitchen. A few minutes later she returned to the dining room.

"That was Jenkins. He wanted to know if I had reconsidered his offer. He says Rosenzweig's investigator is watching the Piatek house in Cleveland, but that it's actually owned by a man named Piacek. He tells me that's the English pronunciation of *Piatek*. Isn't that the name your friend came up with?"

"It is," Liam said.

"Well, Jenkins said there's nobody home. The house is dark. Rosenzweig's investigator now thinks he might be in Europe. He surmises that Piatek heard about the Rosenzweig incident and fled for Poland or Germany."

"Nobody home. What a surprise," Ben said.

THE BALANCE OF THE afternoon was spent doing research, Catherine questioning Ben, and Liam poring through chronicles of the German army campaigns in Poland and western Russia.

"Are we going to work into the evening?" said Liam at five o'clock. "Because that little sandwich isn't going to hold me—I'm getting hungry."

"If you don't need me," Ben said, "I've been invited for dinner at Adele's. She's going to pick me up."

Catherine set her pen down on the table and turned to face the two. She had her palms flat on the table and leaned forward. "Gentlemen, this is the bottom line: we need to have more evidence before I can file a lawsuit. I just don't have enough factual support. I don't want to file it on Ben's ID alone. We need more than mysterious circumstances—more than a false immigration date, more than unexplained wealth. Something that will tie Rosenzweig directly to Piatek. Otherwise, we'll get bounced on a motion and lose our opportunity forever."

Liam poured three glasses of wine. "Trust me on this. I will have something soon, maybe in a day or two. I'm about to catch a fish." He winked.

"What do you have?"

"Trust me."

Adele stopped by at six, and she and Ben left shortly thereafter.

"Having second thoughts about the lawsuit?" Liam said as he walked over to put his arms around Catherine.

"Nope. Not about the cause, anyway. Just about myself. I'm not sure I'm the right girl for the job."

"He couldn't have a better advocate," he said and kissed her on the forehead. "Let me take you to dinner."

Catherine shook her head. "Not tonight. I want to work a little more."

"What is it, Cat? What's wrong here? Have I done something?"

"No, it's not you, it's me. Don't worry about it." She kissed him lightly on the cheek and walked into the kitchen.

"Hold on," said Liam, who followed her, grabbed her hand, and led her back to the couch. "Sit down, please. I've got something to say." Reluctantly, she took a seat beside him. "Twenty years, Cat. I've been waiting around for twenty years. And all that time, I've loved you every day. I've laughed with you, I've cried with you, and yet, I was always resigned to just being your friend because I knew that's all it'd ever be. Then last night happens and now everything has changed. At least it has for me. I know I'm just a hard-nosed Irishman, but, believe it or not, I've got feelings. I can't go back to some dispassionate friendship. You've got to level with me. What's going on?"

Catherine, her eyes tearing, grabbed a fistful of tissues. "I'm sorry, Liam. I truly am. It's a crisis of confidence. It's all about me and my doubts. I doubt my judgments. I doubt my competence as a lawyer. I doubt my ability to sustain a relationship." She turned to face him and gripped his wrists. "Don't you get it? Ever since Peter, it's all a façade. I'm a fake. I'm putting up a false front here, Liam, and I know that sooner or later everyone is going to find out. No one of sound judgment could make the mistakes I've made in my life. I'm a goddamn failure." She shook her head. "And it's not just my bad judgment. When my marriage crashed and burned, I swore I'd never let myself be that vulnerable again. I'd never get hurt like that again. I built myself a nice, strong, protective wall. I rebuilt my career. I put some money in the bank. That's just the way I wanted it. Then along comes Ben. My career craters. When I file against Rosenzweig, it'll hit every paper in town and I'll be so overmatched it'll make David and Goliath look like a fair fight. And now, on top of all that, I go and throw my heart out on the line like some stupid teenager. It's overwhelming me. I can't do this right now." She broke into sobs and squeezed his forearms. "I can't do this!"

Liam nodded and hugged her. "It's all right. It's okay."

"If our relationship falls apart," she said, "like all my other love affairs have my entire life, then I've lost the only friend I've got. I can't afford for that to happen. I need you, Liam. Especially now. Please. Let me work this out my way."

"Okay, Cat," he said, drawing her head to his chest. "Okay."

After a few moments of silence, she lifted her head and said, "Let me do a little work, a few more minutes, finish up, and then you can take me to dinner. Okay?"

"Sure," Liam said.

THIRTY-EIGHT

• • •

Tinley Park, Illinois, December 2004

CARL WULD HEARD THE doorbell ring at 8:00 A.M. He stumbled down the stairs in his underwear and opened the door a crack. "Whaddya want?" he said to Liam standing on the front stoop.

"I want to talk about Carl Henninger."

"Never heard of him."

"Really? Have you heard of Samantha Green? I believe she was sixteen at the time. Am I jarring your memory? What about *State of Arizona v. Carl Henninger?*"

The door opened and Wuld stepped back to let Liam in. He led him to the small living room and took a soiled sweatshirt off the back of a chair. He pointed. "You could sit here."

Wuld sat on the sofa. "What do you want?" he said.

"Does your wife know about Carl Henninger? Does Rosenzweig?"

"Nobody does. How do you know?"

"I'm a great detective. I also have a friend in Arizona."

"That was fifteen years ago. I paid my debt."

"I didn't come across your State of Illinois registration, you know, as a sex offender. I didn't see your name online, either. Let's see, your jurisdiction of registration would be the city of Chicago.

My, my. You must've forgotten to file your notifications. Damn, how those things can slip your mind."

"What the fuck do you want? You want money? I don't have much."

Liam smiled. "I want you to tell me about Piatek."

"Can't do it."

Liam rose. "So long, Henninger." He walked to the door.

"Wait. Wait. Maybe we can work something out. What do you want to know?"

"I want you to tell me about this bullshit stakeout story and why you were sitting outside in your car at Thanksgiving."

"Okay, it's a bullshit story. Okay? I gotta make a living just like you. Rosenzweig calls me to his fancy office and hires me to find out anything I can about Otto Piatek, a Polish Nazi. Find him if he's still alive. If he's dead, find his grave. Any information I can dig up, I'm to come directly to him. For that, he's willing to pay me big bucks. I'm getting checks for twenty, thirty grand. It's sweet. Only trouble is, there ain't shit to find. This guy was some minor Nazi and he disappeared. Totally. I saw a giant payday walking out on me.

"So I decide to run a number and milk Rosenzweig for a little money. Shit, he'd never miss it. You'da done it too. I find this guy in Cleveland, through the phone book, a guy named Piacek. What a fuckin' coincidence. He lives in a little house in a blue-collar neighborhood. It's perfect. So I visit the guy. He's a retired metalworker. On a pension. Doesn't even speak good English. All his family's in the old country—Lithuania or something. I couldn't believe my luck. I say how would you like to go visit your family for a few months? I'll give you the money. He's not too keen on it. He don't wanna go. It takes some convincing on my part, if you follow me. I don't really leave him no choice. So he leaves and I tell Rosenzweig I found Piatek's house, but he's out of town. I show him the listing in the Cleveland phone book. Piacek, Piatek—it's gotta be."

Wuld spreads his hands like a showman. "Bada boom."

Liam is not amused. "Go on."

"I tell Rosenzweig I'm going to watch the house for a while.

Sooner or later, we'll get him. I tell him he split for Europe. After a while, I figure I'll plant a Nazi flag and some Nazi medals in the house. Come on. Who gives a rat's ass if I run a number on a billionaire? Like you wouldn't do it. You're no different from me. We're in the same business, you know, like brothers-in-arms. So cut me a break here, will ya?"

"Rosenzweig didn't know?"

Wuld shook his head. "He don't know shit. You wonder how the prick got to be so rich when he's so fuckin' simple."

"Why were you out in the street on Thanksgiving?"

"Surveillance, man. Rosenzweig told me to find out everything I could on Solomon."

"Did he tell you why?"

Wuld rubbed the stubble on his face. "Nah, he didn't have to."

"What did you find out?"

"Nothin'."

"What did you find out when you busted into his apartment?"

Wuld grinned and shrugged his shoulders. "Just some papers. There wasn't shit. Just like Piatek. There's just nothing on these two guys."

"What did you do with the papers?"

"Gave 'em to Rosenzweig. Didn't even make a copy."

Liam rose and walked to the door.

"Hey," Wuld said. "You gonna cut me a break, you know, one dick to another?"

"Sure. One dick to another. Brothers-in-arms. You stupid bastard, you're an embarrassment. I should blow the whistle and have your ticket pulled." Liam stuck his finger in Wuld's face. "But here's the deal, brother. I won't say a word. You run your games. But I want to know every time Rosenzweig talks to you about Piatek or Solomon. You keep me in the loop, I'll keep my mouth shut. Screw up and I crow like a rooster."

"Yeah, yeah. No problem. Thanks, bud."

Liam opened the door and stepped out onto the stoop. Wuld called after him, "How d'ya know? I mean about the Arizona thing?"

"The Camry. It's ten years old with an Arizona dealer sticker on the trunk. I took a picture of the registration number, remember? You should've bought a new car."

"Shit."

Chicago, Illinois, December 2004

"So the whole story about Piatek living in Cleveland in a bungalow was a lie?" said Catherine.

"Yep." Liam twisted the cap off a bottle of beer.

Ben smiled and brushed off his invisible chest medals. "Told you so."

"Was that one of your fishing lines in the water?" Catherine said.

Liam nodded. "I got one more, and I think I'm getting a bite. I'm supposed to meet Brad Goodlow this afternoon. He says he's got something for me."

"Who is he?" Catherine and Ben said in unison.

"Do I have to reveal my sources?"

Catherine narrowed her eyes and put her hands on her hips.

"Okay, okay, you win. He's a researcher at NBC News and an old buddy of mine."

"What's he got?" asked Catherine.

"For that, you'll have to wait and see."

Ben mumbled something and Catherine turned her head. "What?"

"I said maybe Wuld wasn't running a number on Rosenzweig," said Ben. "Maybe it's the other way around."

"Explain."

"Rosenzweig's not simple and he's not stupid. I find it hard to believe that a thug like Wuld could pull the wool over Rosenzweig's eyes."

"Do you think Rosenzweig knows—that he's going along with the story?"

Ben shrugged. "Maybe. Maybe it's Otto who's running the number on all of us."

* * *

LIAM RETURNED TO CATHERINE'S shortly after sunset. He had a broad smile on his face and a large envelope in his hand.

"Why are you smiling?" she said. "What do you have? Did you catch a fish?"

"You mean, like, maybe a killer whale?" He opened the envelope, pulled out a five-by-seven photograph, and laid it on the table.

"That's him!" shouted Ben. "That's Otto! In full Nazi regalia. Where did you get that?"

"Goodlow. Naturally when he Googled Piatek, he came up with nothing, just like all of us. All the obvious sources were dead ends. But one of his young interns was a wizard in searching old European periodicals. He found this picture in a Nazi propaganda piece titled 'Germany Re-cultures the General Government.' It's a story about how German efficiency was bringing culture to the backward cities of Poland. Piatek is pictured in front of some building talking to a well-dressed woman."

"It's the town hall," Ben said. "I would guess it's 1942, maybe later, given the uniform. The woman is obviously not Jewish."

Catherine stared long and hard at the picture. "There's no doubting the resemblance to Rosenzweig." She turned to Liam. "Do you realize the importance of this find? Convictions have been upheld on the basis of a picture coupled with eyewitness testimony."

Liam looked very pleased with himself. "As some entertainer use to say, 'You ain't seen nothing yet.'"

Ben shook his head. "No."

"What?"

"It was Al Jolson. And he said, 'You ain't *heard* nothin' yet.'"

Liam stuck out his chin, "Well, maybe I'm talking about Bachman-Turner Overdrive. Ha!"

Catherine interrupted. "Liam, will you please tell us what else you have in the envelope. The suspense is killing me."

"Well, when the intern found the old magazine article, that gave him the idea of searching old American magazines for pictures."

He dug into the envelope and spread out several more photographs on the coffee table. "Here's one of a young Rosenzweig in *Life* magazine taken in 1953. Rosenzweig is standing next to Senator Griffen. The likeness between that and the German picture is uncanny."

Catherine and Ben studied the two pictures side by side. "Wow," she said over and over. "Wow."

Ben hung his head and covered his face with his hands. "That's enough, isn't it? To justify a lawsuit, to withstand a challenge? To get us all into court?"

Catherine nodded. "It sure is!" She threw her arms around Liam. "Wow."

THIRTY-NINE

...

Winnetka, Illinois, December 2004

ELLIOT ROSENZWEIG, DRESSED CASUALLY in a cream silk shirt and brown wool slacks, walked down the hall of his gracious home and into the north sitting room, where his wife, his granddaughter, and another young woman were seated around a glass table leafing through piles of booklets and brochures.

"Popi," said Jennifer, rising and indicating her guest, "I want to introduce you to Andee Grattinger. She's our wedding consultant, the best around. She did the Chadwick wedding in Kenilworth last summer, the one that made the cover of *Northshore Magazine*."

Andee stood and extended her hand. "I'm honored to meet you, sir, and delighted to be given the privilege of coordinating Jennifer's wedding. I've brought along some albums, some of our more spectacular occasions. Please let me know if they meet with your expectations."

"My expectations are entirely in my granddaughter's hands. If she's happy, then I'm happy."

They all took seats around the table and paged through the albums. "I love this setting, Nonna," Jennifer said, holding up a page in a pink quilted album. "See how they have the orchestra silhouetted against the sunset."

"Sunset won't work for us," said her grandmother, lovingly. "We face east, darling. But what about the moon shining off the lake? It would make a lovely backdrop."

"Are there other family members who should be singled out throughout the evening?" Andee said, making notes.

Elliot shook his head. "My daughter and her husband died in a car accident many years ago, when Jennifer was just a baby, and she has no brothers or sisters. Neither my wife nor I have any family other than Jennifer. We came from Europe, you know. Jennifer's father was an only child, so there are no aunts or uncles. No, I'm afraid there's just the three of us, as far as family is concerned. I think you'll find no shortage of friends, however."

In his gray butler's jacket, Robert walked to the doorway, politely cleared his throat, and said, "Excuse me, Mr. Rosenzweig, may I see you for a moment?"

"Pardon me," Elliot said with a smile. "I leave it all to you ladies. I'm a bull in a china shop, as they say."

In the hallway, Robert whispered, "There is a gentleman, a uniformed officer from Cook County, at the gatehouse. He says he must see you about official government business."

Elliot looked puzzled. "On a Saturday? Why do they bother me at home?" He shook his head. "Have Russell bring him to the front door. I'll meet him there."

A few minutes later, a man in a brown bomber jacket, a Cook County Sheriff's Department patch on his sleeve, delivered a manila envelope to Elliot. "I've been ordered to personally hand this to you, sir. It's a lawsuit."

"A lawsuit? Why would this come to my house?"

"I'm not sure, sir," said the deputy and he left to return to his car.

Elliot tore open the top of the envelope, just enough to see the caption, *Benjamin Solomon v. Elliot Rosenzweig a/k/a Otto Piatek*, and turned white.

"What the hell is this?" he said as he rushed to call his lawyer.

FORTY

• • •

JEFFERS FINISHED READING THE lawsuit, removed his half-glasses, and turned to face his client.

"It's like I told you on the phone," Elliot said, sitting in his leather chair, his back to his bay windows. "It's Solomon, the same damn lunatic that's been stalking me since last September. Now he's sued me in Cook County Court for all the world to see. He's sued me for being a Nazi executioner."

A *Chicago Sun-Times*, early edition, sat on the desk with a banner headline reading: "Prominent Chicagoan Sued over War Crimes." A three-column picture of Elliot sat above a caption posing the question: "Elliot Rosenzweig: Nazi or Victim?"

"Actually, he's sued you for taking his property. It's a suit for money damages."

"I can read, Gerry."

"The lawsuit says he made a demand for return of specific property and you failed to return it. Do you have any idea what he's talking about?"

Elliot nodded. "About a week ago I got a letter demanding that I deliver a whole list of things to Solomon. It was bullshit. I threw it away."

"Why didn't you call me?"

"Because it was bullshit. Look, we need to counter this as strongly as possible, both in the courts and in the media. Look at this newspaper," he said, holding up the front page and furiously rattling the pages.

"Settle down. I've called a press conference for this afternoon at my office. These allegations concern things that happened sixty years ago. They're probably all time-barred by the statute of limitations. I'll express our outrage, announce our intention to immediately move for a dismissal, and file a countersuit against this money grubber for defamation."

"Are you nuts? Dismiss the case on a technicality? That's like saying I'm guilty but you didn't sue me in time. No, he either has to withdraw this case and make a public apology or we have to beat him on the merits of the case. And forget about suing him for defamation. What's the public going to think when a billionaire sues some poor crazy old man?"

"Okay, calm down, we'll take care of it."

Elliot rose from his chair and walked to the windows. The December skies, a persistent, dispirited blanket of low-hovering gray that wouldn't snow and wouldn't go away, mirrored Elliot's mood. He stared at the silver-gray lake. The reflection of the clouds made the horizon imperceptible. He took a deep breath and turned to face his lawyer. "This man threatens to eradicate an entire legacy. All a man has is his reputation. Everything that's gone before—my work, my charities, my foundations—everything that I've accomplished in my life will be tarnished if these accusations continue to find safe harbors. They must be recanted! He must concede he has made a mistake and that in his confusion he has misidentified me."

"You shouldn't have interfered in September. If you hadn't urged the state to drop the charges, Solomon'd still be behind bars. What's happening with your stakeout of Piatek's house in Cleveland?"

"Nothing. The house is vacant. Wuld thinks Piatek split for Europe. He wants me to send him to Poland. I may do that."

"Earlier this month," Jeffers said, "I used all my influence to persuade Jenkins and that woman lawyer, what's her name, Lockhart, to drop Solomon as a client. Jenkins saw the light and agreed, but Lockhart left the firm, and now I understand she's working out of her house."

"Then you should be able to make it go away quickly. The longer it continues, the more damage it causes. Rumor feeds upon itself. The public loves to see successful people trashed; that's how the tabloids were built. Gerry, I know I don't have to remind you how much business we throw your way. This has to be, right now, the most important case in your office."

"I understand perfectly. I'll put half a dozen lawyers on it. We'll bury her with court time and paperwork. She's on her own and there's no way she can keep up. We'll smash her in court."

"It's not just a matter of beating someone in court. Why do you lawyers always think like that? Why do you fail to see the big picture? I am accused of being a Nazi. The world is my court. It wants to know, 'Is this man a Nazi?' We have to show the public that I am wrongfully accused. If we can't get him to retract, we have to make a public fool of Solomon in court, show him to be a madman possessed. That's the only way to clear my name. I got a call this morning from Carol Mornay at NBC. She wants a televised interview."

"I'm advising against it, Elliot."

"I'm going to give her the interview. I've sat with her before. I've known her for some time. It'll go well. Don't worry."

"If you insist, but I want to go with you. They'll have legal questions."

Elliot shook his head. "It gives the whole matter too much credence. If I sit there with my lawyer, the public will think I have something to hide. If I go on by myself and show I'm willing to answer questions, just her and me, it'll create a more informal atmosphere. It'll have the desired effect."

"I'm not happy about this, Elliot. You never know what these journalists will dig up. I've had clients burned by the media."

"I'll have to take that chance. I need to fight the battle of public opinion. You need to fight the battle in court. If Solomon won't recant, I need for you to prove that I am not Piatek."

"It's not your burden to prove you're not Piatek. It's Solomon's burden to prove his case—that you are, in fact, Piatek. He's the one who has to have the evidence in court."

Elliot nodded and together they walked to the portico where

Jeffers' car was waiting. "Of course, you're right, Gerry, I shouldn't have had him released after the opera incident, but I took pity on him. So many of us survived the war physically but not emotionally. I don't wish anybody any harm, but this guy has to be stopped."

Jeffers slid into the driver's seat. "Call me after you've spoken to Carol Mornay. Meanwhile, we're going to kill a lot of trees and paper Lockhart to death."

FORTY-ONE

• • •

Chicago, Illinois, December 2004

CATHERINE WAS IN THE midst of making her morning coffee when her phone rang. Two weeks until Christmas and she still hadn't started her shopping. Despite the demands of the lawsuit, this was a day she had set aside for Michigan Avenue. She had her eye on a digital camera for Liam. She thought she'd shop for a warm sweater for Ben.

"Catherine, it's Walter Jenkins. I need to talk to you about this Rosenzweig lawsuit."

"I'm listening."

"Can you come by this morning?"

"Why, Mr. Jenkins? Why would I come by? So that you can pressure me again?"

"Please, Catherine, would you just show me the courtesy of stopping in to talk to me? This firm was good to you. You owe me."

"Charming. You certainly have a way of ingratiating yourself," she said.

"Please, Catherine. I'm asking you."

"Very well. I'll come in around eleven."

No sooner had she set down the phone than the doorbell buzzed. A FedEx driver delivered a box from Jeffers' office. Inside was a stack of legal papers and clipped to the top was a letter from Jeffers.

Dear Ms. Lockhart:

Pursuant to the Illinois Code of Civil Procedure and the Rules of the Supreme Court, we are enclosing the following discovery demands, and we expect compliance within 28 days:

1. Notice for the deposition of Benjamin Solomon

2. Notice for the depositions of government offices of vital statistics in Warsaw, Frankfurt, and Zamość

3. Request for production of documents, objects, and tangible things

4. Defendant's first set of interrogatories to plaintiff

5. Defendant's request for admissions of fact

We are also enclosing herewith three motions which we have set for hearing before Judge Ryan on December 20, 2004:

1. Motion to accelerate case for trial

2. Motion to produce medical and psychiatric records of Benjamin Solomon

3. Motion for an independent psychiatric examination of Benjamin Solomon

We remain open to discuss amicable resolution of this matter at any time.

> Very truly yours
> E. Gerald Jeffers
> Storch & Bennett

I GUESS I SHOULD HAVE realized this was coming, Liam," Catherine said into the phone. "Of course, it's physically impossible for me to cover all these demands within the time they've scheduled. But that's their game plan."

"Won't the judge give you relief? You're only one person."

"I'm sure he will, but as to how much leeway he'll give to me, I won't know until Wednesday. That's when Jeffers' motions are scheduled to be presented to Judge Ryan. Meanwhile, I'd like to do some brainstorming. Would you bring Ben here tomorrow morning?"

"I'll call him."

Catherine bundled herself up for the winter cold and headed

downtown for what she hoped would be a very brief meeting with Jenkins.

T HE OFFICE RECEPTIONIST, DRESSED in a red sweater adorned with sequined reindeer, smiled broadly as Catherine walked into the reception area. "Why, hello, Miss Lockhart, it's so good to see you again," she said. "Mr. Jenkins is waiting for you in his office and he said to send you right back. I'll tell him you're on your way."

Jenkins rose and greeted Catherine with a smile and a warm handshake. He shut his office door and gestured toward the couch.

"May I offer you a cup of coffee?" he said. She politely declined and sat on the edge of the leather couch, her legs together, her hands on her knees, as though she expected to leave at any moment.

Jenkins took a seat behind his desk. "Let me get right to the point. Just as I predicted, this Solomon case has become a disaster for us. In the past week we've lost three of our insurance clients and there are threats from others. They don't want to offend Rosenzweig, so they're taking their business elsewhere. It's a damn row of dominoes."

"Why? This isn't J & F business. I'm no longer with the firm."

Jenkins parried with a quick wave. "Yesterday, Judge Miller called me. 'What the hell is Lockhart doing? Why can't you stop her?' And you know what, Catherine? We have several cases on his docket. He can hurt us."

"Judge Miller? What does Judge Miller have to do with it? Judge Ryan's got Ben's case."

"It's all over the courthouse."

"Did you tell him I quit a month ago?"

"Of course I did. He didn't care. Like everyone else, he still associates you with Jenkins & Fairchild. Let's face it, Catherine, you were working up the case in this office on my time before you left the firm. It's not like we weren't involved."

"Well, Mr. Jenkins, I don't know what you want me to do about this. I'll call Judge Miller and tell him I'm not with the firm. I'll tell him that you insisted I decline the case but I refused, and that was the reason I left the firm. Is that what you want?"

"What I want? I want you to drop this madness. Non-suit the case."

"You know I won't do that."

Jenkins leaned back and took a breath, ready to play his hole card. "I'm prepared to make you a generous offer. I'll give you your job back, increase your salary by two hundred thousand dollars, and give you a fifty-thousand-dollar bonus, payable upon dismissal of the Solomon suit. And we never had this conversation."

Catherine rose and walked to the door. She stopped and turned to face Jenkins. "Thank you, Walter. You did me a favor."

"I did? You accept?"

Catherine shook her head. "No. You've set my mind at ease. No second thoughts now. You're entirely unprincipled. Your unethical, illegal, and immoral offer is rejected. Nice try, though."

"Damn it, Catherine," he called after her, "you'll be sorry. There won't be a firm in Chicago that'll touch you."

FORTY-TWO

...

"THERE ARE THIRTY THOUSAND lawyers in Chicago. Neither Jenkins nor Jeffers speaks for the entire legal community," Liam said, unfolding a long collapsible table in Catherine's home office.

"I know, but I thought about it all afternoon. I couldn't get him off my mind," Catherine said. "It's not so much that Jenkins has influence. I'm not worried about my position; I've already burned that bridge. And it's not that I care whether any big firms like J & F will hire me. I don't want a mega-firm environment anymore. All they care about is the numbers—billable hours, realization, contribution to partnership. Do you know that Kincaid & Rothschild has thirty-five hundred lawyers? They don't even know who's working for them; they buy books of business. And if your book declines, you're gone. They care nothing for who you are and what you are or what you bring to the profession.

"What troubles me the most is the magnitude of Ben's case. I'm worried about my ability to handle this case solo. I fear that I'm simply inadequate, that I'm not a good enough lawyer, and that, at the end of the day, I'll fail my client because of it."

She lifted a color printer from the shelf and set it on the table. "I'm going into battle hopelessly outmanned and outstaffed. Jeffers is pushing hard with depositions, some of them to take place in Europe, dozens of interrogatories, and now he's starting with the motions. And it's all scheduled to happen within a month."

"Don't worry. Judge Ryan will give you time. It's routine to extend the time to complete discovery."

"I'm sure he'll give me some time. I've appeared before him on several occasions and he's always been reasonable. But Jeffers has filed a motion to expedite the case, so I don't know how much time he'll give me."

"What right do they have to send me to a psychiatrist?" Ben said, walking into the room. "Is that normal for a lawsuit?"

"No, but your testimony is the cornerstone of our case, and they've raised the issue of your mental capacity."

"Well, relax. There's nothing wrong with me."

Liam took a deep breath. "Ben, as Catherine's brother-in-law said so eloquently at Thanksgiving, you got some 'idiot-syncrasies.' My suggestion would be not to mention Hannah or any of your visions if you go for an evaluation."

"I'm not stupid, Liam, but I got news for both of you. We wouldn't have a case if I hadn't been told to watch that program on public television. Do you think I routinely watch documentaries on rich benefactors? I'd have *no* interest in such a program. I watch very little television, maybe the Cubs and some news shows. There's no way I ever would have recognized Otto unless I watched that show and saw the close-up of his face."

"And you were told to watch that show?"

"That's right."

"Who told you?"

"Don't worry about it. I watched it, didn't I?"

"All I'm saying," Liam said, "is keep your cosmic conversations to yourself. There's no need to tell some shrink about them."

Catherine waved her hands. "When I appear before Judge Ryan next Wednesday, I'm going to oppose this psychiatric examination. I don't think they have the right to do it. It's just for intimidation."

"Am I supposed to go to court with you?" asked Ben.

Catherine shook her head. "It's a morning court call, a courtroom full of lawyers arguing motions. There won't be any clients there."

FORTY-THREE

. . .

STANDING PATIENTLY BEFORE THE bench of the Honorable Charles J. Ryan, Catherine and E. Gerald Jeffers waited while Judge Ryan read Jeffers' motions and made his notes on a yellow pad. When he was finished, the veteran jurist set the papers down, nodded at each of the attorneys, leaned back, and spoke softly.

"I sure get the assignments, don't I? Twenty years on the bench and I've never had a case like this one. Not even close. Well, I can see why you want to push this along, Mr. Jeffers, and I can't say I blame you. What's your response to the motion to accelerate, Ms. Lockhart?"

"It's unreasonable. I'm entitled to adequate time to prepare my case. I'm not trying to delay the proceedings, but Mr. Jeffers is asking you to compress six months of discovery into four weeks. It's not humanly possible for me to cover it all. They're double- and triple-tracking me—they've scheduled depositions in different countries on the same day. They've filed extensive interrogatories, requests for production, and requests to admit, and they want answers in three weeks. They know I'm a sole practitioner. This is just a tactic to overwhelm me. It's unfair. There's only one of me."

Jeffers, in his gray tailored suit, looked smugly at Catherine and then back at Judge Ryan. "Why should Mr. Rosenzweig be penalized because the plaintiff is understaffed? These allegations are scandalous and must not be allowed the slightest tinge of legitimacy by lingering on the court's docket. We intend to file a motion for summary judgment at the earliest possible juncture."

"He has a point, Ms. Lockhart. Your client has accused the defendant of belonging to the most evil criminal enterprise in modern history. He's entitled to nip it in the bud. That is, if he can. I'll give you an extra two weeks to answer the written discovery and I'll prohibit double-tracking—no simultaneous depositions—but beyond that, I'm going to accelerate the case. Motions are due in forty-five days and trial will be set for April 14 at 9:00 A.M."

"But, Your Honor," protested Catherine, "that's less than four months away."

"Well, that's my ruling. Call the next case," he said to his clerk.

"Just a minute, Your Honor," said Jeffers. "I still have two more motions. We've moved for plaintiff's medical records and an independent psychiatric examination of Mr. Solomon."

Judge Ryan picked up the papers. "Is his mental condition in issue?"

"Certainly not," Catherine said. "The only conduct in issue is that of the defendant sixty years ago."

Jeffers smiled. "We think the plaintiff is . . . how shall I say . . . non compos mentis. Since we anticipate that they will have no tangible evidence and will proceed on the uncorroborated testimony of Mr. Solomon . . ."

"I object to this, Your Honor."

The judge raised his eyebrows, wrinkling his forehead. "Do you have tangible evidence: photographs, writings, war records?"

"I'm not prepared at this time to disclose our evidence," Catherine said.

Judge Ryan nodded and scratched his head. "Would you agree, Ms. Lockhart, that Mr. Solomon will be offering eyewitness testimony?"

"I'm sure he'll testify, but his mental or physical condition is not an element of this case."

"Oh, it will be," interjected Jeffers. "Of that you may be sure."

The judge gathered his papers and stuffed them into the file jacket. "I'm going to reserve ruling on defendant's motion for medical records or a psychiatric examination. At this time I don't see a basis for it. Take his deposition and if you think there are grounds, we'll revisit it. Otherwise, get your work done; we're going to trial April 14."

Jeffers stopped Catherine on the way out of the courtroom. "Tell your client, if he drops the suit immediately and issues a public apology, there'll be no repercussions. And that offer is open until noon tomorrow. Otherwise, the two of you are going to spend a lot of money, and when our motion for summary judgment is granted and this case is over, we're coming after both of you for attorney's fees and fines, and you can expect it to be well in excess of a million dollars."

"Goodbye, Mr. Jeffers. You got the rulings you wanted."

Jeffers pointed his finger in Catherine's face. "Not yet, I didn't. There's not the slightest doubt in my mind that this is nothing but a bullshit lawsuit, just a shotgun to the head of a wealthy, elderly man to extort money. And what makes it more outrageous to me, Miss Lockhart, is that Mr. Rosenzweig was himself a victim of Nazi terror."

"Goodbye, Mr. Jeffers."

"It's your professional obligation to convey my offer to your client," he called after her as she walked toward the elevator. "You tell him: noon tomorrow."

FORTY-FOUR

. . .

"WHAT DID JEFFERS MEAN, he'd come after *us* for a million dollars?" Ben said, sitting on the edge of the stuffed chair by Catherine's fireplace.

"The signature of an attorney on a lawsuit constitutes a certification that she believes, after reasonable inquiry, that the suit is well grounded in fact and is warranted by existing law. If we lose the case, especially on a motion in its early stages, and the court determines that the suit was interposed for an improper purpose or was frivolous, the judge can impose financial sanctions on you and me, including an order to pay the defendant's legal bills."

"I'm confused. What rights does Rosenzweig have to get my case dismissed? Didn't we ask for a jury? Aren't we guaranteed our day in court?"

"I'm afraid not—not by a long shot. It's common practice in civil suits for the defendant to file a motion to dismiss or a motion for a summary judgment. Those are motions that allow a judge to decide whether a case is substantial enough to proceed to a jury or whether it should just be dismissed. If Rosenzweig were to file a motion for summary judgment, he would be saying, in essence, that there isn't enough evidence to justify a jury trial. If we can't come forward and show the judge that there is a reasonable amount of evidence in support of our claims, Judge Ryan has the discretion to enter judgment for Rosenzweig. The case would not get to a jury."

"Would Ryan do that?"

"Who knows? It happens. Maybe you should consider Rosenzweig's offer. Our case is based largely upon your personal identification, your memory of your family's property, some photographs, and some pretty circumstantial facts—Rosenzweig's background, his sudden fortune, the inconsistencies in his immigration stories. At this stage it would be touch and go. And a summary judgment would certainly vindicate Rosenzweig. It's the same as a final judgment."

"We didn't come this far to be frightened off," Ben said. "I told you that the evidence will be there. I've been assured of that."

"By whom, Ben?" Catherine said wearily.

"Never mind. I've promised you and I'll keep my promise."

Catherine shook her head. "I don't know why I believe you, but I do."

"Scary, isn't it?"

Liam entered the foyer and brushed the snow from his shoulders, singing, "It's Beginning to Look a Lot Like Christmas."

He walked over and rubbed his hands before the fire. "There must be four inches out there and it's still coming down."

"Were you able to find out anything more about Rosenzweig's finances?" Catherine said, pouring a cup of coffee into a mug and walking it over to him.

"Nothing more than we knew. My guess is that he stuffed his stolen riches into a Swiss bank account before he left Germany, like the other Nazis. We'll have to subpoena the Swiss banks for further information."

"You can forget about that," Catherine said. "I've already looked into it. Swiss banks won't recognize an American subpoena, only subpoenas issued by the Swiss courts, and then only for criminal activity, not civil property cases. Besides, it takes months to get a response and I have less than one hundred and twenty days."

FORTY-FIVE

...

ELLIOT ROSENZWEIG RECEIVED WARM greetings at the NBC studios, friendly handshakes from the station's news director, the producer of *NBC Nightly News*, and Carol Mornay. He was dressed in a dark blue suit set off with a patterned plum tie—not overly elegant or fashionable, as had been so often written about him at prior society events, but certainly put together, a solid and compact presentation befitting a man in total control.

"How are you, Carol? It's so nice to see you again."

It was Elliot's request to be seated in an armchair for his interview rather than side-by-side at the anchor desk, a setting which he thought would lend itself to cordiality, not confrontation. He consented to a small amount of makeup—he remembered Richard Nixon—and clipped the microphone to his lapel.

"Elliot, we're going to tape this segment now for replay on the six o'clock and ten o'clock programs," said Carol, "and we're going to run the promotions all day. You'll have your chance to tell your story before a considerable TV audience."

Elliot smiled and nodded.

LIAM ALERTED CATHERINE TO the telecast, and just before six o'clock, Ben joined them to watch the news. Catherine held the remote tightly as NBC's introductory fanfare and video came on.

"Are we recording this?" asked Ben.

Catherine nodded, unable to take her eyes off the screen.

"Good evening, Chicago," said co-anchor Bill Douglas. "Today NBC News has obtained an exclusive interview with Elliot Rosenzweig, popular Chicagoan and prominent philanthropist, who has been accused in a lawsuit of being Otto Piatek, a Nazi officer during World War II. Our Carol Mornay spoke with him here in our studios this afternoon, and in a moment, we will play that interview for you." He turned to Carol, who was seated to his right. "I was able to preview it before our broadcast, Carol. Remarkable piece of journalism."

She smiled. "I called Elliot Rosenzweig earlier this week, after the lawsuit was filed, and asked if he would consent to a videotaped interview. You know, I've done taped segments with him in the past. But frankly, this time I didn't expect him to agree. Normally, I can't get defendants to speak with me on the air because their lawyers won't let them. But Mr. Rosenzweig had no hesitations. He said he didn't need his lawyer involved and agreed to answer all of my questions with no preconditions. He said he had nothing to hide. The interview took place here at the station earlier today."

"Let's roll the tape," said Douglas.

As the video commenced, Carol and Elliot were seated across from each other on a set that resembled a cozy living room. Elliot smiled confidently as Carol made the introduction, in which she recounted many of Elliot's civic achievements. Then she gave a detailed account of the lawsuit and said, "Tell us, Elliot, with this lawsuit pending and the scathing allegations made against you, why have you decided to sit for a television interview? It's quite courageous of you."

Elliot leaned forward and spoke with an air of sincerity. "Not at all. I have nothing to hide and I have a reputation to protect. Carol, you know I care deeply about our city and the people who live here. I have spent the major portion of my adult life and a pretty fair amount of money in service to this great community. What the people think about me and about my family means everything to me. Now, because this baseless suit has been filed, and it's made a splash in the media, there may be some out there who are saying, 'Can this be true? Can Elliot Rosenzweig really be a Nazi?' So I'm here to answer any questions you may have and let the city know how absurd these allegations are."

"Whoa, he's good," Liam said. "This guy has to be the world's best bullshitter."

Ben looked dispirited. "That's Otto. He could charm the sparkle off a diamond."

Catherine was mesmerized. "He's so self-assured. He'll be magnificent in front of a jury."

Carol, a warm smile on her face, lifted an eight-by-ten document from an end table.

"Oh, oh. Here it comes," said Liam. "She's going to show him the picture."

"NBC has obtained a photograph of Otto Piatek, taken during the war some sixty years ago," Carol said, as she handed the copy to Elliot. NBC displayed the photo as a split-screen shot. Elliot stared for quite a while at the picture without talking and then returned it to her. He shrugged his shoulders. "It doesn't mean anything to me," he said.

"Well, look at this, Mr. Rosenzweig. We dug up a magazine picture of you from 1953." The screen showed the pictures side by side. The facial features were practically identical. "You must admit, there's a remarkable resemblance," she said.

"Pause it, back it up," said Liam. Catherine froze the picture and rewound it. She played it forward in slow motion.

"Look at Rosenzweig's face. For just a second, he's shocked! Then he recovers. He's smooth."

Catherine ran the short segment a few times and then resumed the playback. Elliot quickly regains his composure. "Well," he says. "I suppose I can see why some misguided person could accuse me. On the basis of these photographs, the likeness is striking." He volleys his gaze from one to the other. "I'll grant you, a troubled man like Mr. Solomon could jump to conclusions and confuse me with this Nazi, Piatek."

Liam laughed. "Nice try, asshole. Why didn't you make that

connection when she showed you the picture for the first time instead of saying it didn't mean anything?"

On the screen Elliot continued to shake his head in disbelief. "A picture," he said. "All this over a picture. A facial likeness. Carol, all I can say to you is that physical similarities do not make me a Nazi. Nor do they make me Otto Piatek, whoever he is. I stand by a lifetime of accomplishments. I have given millions to Jewish charities, even though I no longer practice the faith."

"We know that, Mr. Rosenzweig, and that you were voted Israel Bond Man of the Year in 1976. And we also know it will take more than a photographic likeness to prove you are Otto Piatek, the Butcher of Zamość."

"Look!" Liam said. "He winced again."

Elliot replied in a muffled voice, "The Butcher of Zamość? I've never heard that phrase. Now I'm a butcher? It's not in the lawsuit."

"No," Carol said, "that comes from our research. It's an epithet we uncovered when investigating Piatek through the Jewish Documentation Center in Vienna."

Elliot was somber. "Simon Wiesenthal."

"Correct."

Again he took a breath and regained his composure. "Well, it's not me and I'm not him. And I'll prove it in court, if it comes to that."

With his head held high and his shoulders back, Elliot rose to shake the hand of Carol Mornay and the interview ended.

Ben sat quietly, staring deeply into the fireplace. The news went on to the next story. Catherine and Liam spoke, but Ben did not hear them. He was mumbling, conversing with his visions. "Even when face-to-face with indisputable truth, he credibly and convincingly denies it," he mumbled.

"He doesn't convince me," Liam said.

Ben sadly shook his head. "Catherine may be right. He may be too powerful, too likable to defeat in court."

"Ben, it's my job to bring out the truth," Catherine said. "He won't have an easy time with me."

Ben looked up. "His wife," he said softly.

"What?"

"Can you question Rosenzweig's wife?" he said, more alert.

"Yes, of course, and in a case like this it would make a lot of sense to depose her. But we are under a tight schedule and I don't know if that would be time well spent."

"I think you should take her deposition," Ben said.

"What's on your mind, Ben? Why should she take it?" Liam said.

"Maybe she can identify property. Maybe tell us how they got into the country. I'm not sure why, but I know we should get her testimony."

Catherine tilted her head. "And why do you know this?"

"It's just an idea that came into my head. An inspiration. You may discover something."

Catherine sighed and walked to the window with her coffee to stare at the blowing snow. The brief December daylight had vanished and the streetlights had come on illuminating the falling snowflakes. The neighborhood holiday lights twinkled through the veil of the storm. But for Catherine, the impressionistic setting did little to evoke seasonal cheer. The massive task before her bent her spirit like the snow bent the tree boughs. "How was it I got all tangled up in this snare?" she asked herself aloud.

"It's not a bad idea, Cat," Liam said from the couch. "There were no other Rosenzweigs listed on the *Santa Adela* manifest. No Mrs. Rosenzweig. Other than Elliot, I didn't find any Rosenzweigs who came through Ellis Island."

Ben folded his arms and said, "There's something else. We need to look at the numbers."

"What numbers?" Catherine said.

Ben frowned. "I don't know."

"Another inspiration?"

Ben nodded. "Yes."

She shook her head. "I've handed over my career to a man who receives litigation strategies from the ether—a paranormal paralegal. I'm the one that needs a psychiatric evaluation."

She turned around to find Ben with a crestfallen expression.

"I'm sorry. I shouldn't have said that. It was a joke," she said. "What numbers are you talking about?"

"I don't know, Catherine. I just know that somehow numbers will be important in this case."

"And you know this because . . . ?"

"Because I know it, that's all." Ben stood up and walked to the windows. He stood face-to-face with Catherine. "Did you ever get an idea, a fabulous idea, and you thought, How in the world did I ever think of that?"

She nodded.

"At the time, weren't you amazed that such a great idea just came to you out of the blue?"

"Okay. I guess everyone has."

"Right, and how about inspirations. Do you think Mozart was inspired when he wrote a symphony at age six? Who put that music in his head? What about Jonas Salk and Thomas Edison and Frank Lloyd Wright? What about Shakespeare and Socrates? Who planted those incredible concepts in their minds? Where'd they come from? These people were inspired, wouldn't you agree?"

"Okay, I agree."

"Ideas came to them, like ideas come to all of us from time to time, but the difference is—they were receptive to their inspirations. They were better listeners. They took hold of them, embraced them, and developed them."

He put his hand on her shoulder. "Catherine, the word *inspiration* comes from the Latin and means 'to breathe into.' I believe that inspirations are divine revelations. In some way, they come from beyond. The biblical prophets were inspired. Poets are inspired. I dare say that even lawyers, on occasion, are inspired—I'm sorry, that too was a joke. Ask any writer; they thrive on inspirations, like waiting for the next bus."

Ben shrugged. "Like everyone else, ideas come to me. One of those ideas says, 'Look at the numbers.' It's still not very clear to me what that's all about. I'm sure it's my fault, maybe I didn't listen well enough, but I would like us to think about numbers and how they relate to this case."

"Okay," Catherine said, "we'll think about numbers. In the meantime I have to respond to Jeffers' discovery demands. I want you to give me the names and addresses of any witnesses that you can call."

"Well, there aren't many. Mort Titlebaum, an old friend of mine, might be a witness. He lived in a small Polish village and was sent to Zamość for resettlement. He saw Piatek in the square. Then he was sent to Auschwitz."

"Really," Catherine said. "Another eyewitness. Could you bring Mr. Titlebaum over? I'd like to talk to him."

"Well, he only saw Otto that one time. The day he was sent to Auschwitz."

"He might remember the face of the man who sent him to a concentration camp."

"He might, but he's in Florida. I don't think he's planning on coming back here until June. Maybe I can talk him into coming up here. I'll call."

FORTY-SIX

...

THE IRON GATE SLID open and Jeffers drove slowly onto the grounds of the Rosenzweig estate. Heavy snows had blanketed the lawn and flocked the trees, creating a picturesque landscape in the days before Christmas. It was fit for a holiday card, minus the seasonal decorations of which Elliot would have no part.

Seated in the den, Jeffers set his folder of papers on the desktop.

"Why the hell didn't you tell me about Piatek's picture," Elliot sneered. "Mornay caught me totally by surprise."

"I didn't know about it."

"That's great. My hotshot lawyer can't keep up with NBC."

"I told you not to go on TV. The reporters can be murder."

"The two pictures look identical, Gerry. Christ, he could be my twin brother. I could get convicted just because I used to look like some Nazi."

"It'd take more than that. Other than that picture, they have no tangible evidence of any kind connecting you with Poland or the Nazis."

"Other than that picture. Shit. 'Other than that nasty incident, Mrs. Lincoln, how did you enjoy the play?'"

"What I'm saying is, they don't have any other evidence that puts you in Poland."

"Well, what did you expect?" Elliot said. "I've never been to Poland." Elliot paced furiously. "What other surprises am I going to find?"

Jeffers shook his head. "In response to our requests, Lockhart has produced copies of your immigration papers from 1947, public records of the formation of your companies, and a page from the 1948 telephone directory showing your address on Lake Shore Drive."

"That's it?"

"Well, there's a bunch of newspaper photographs taken over the years: one from 1951, a few from the late 1950s, and a few photos from magazines. Same stuff. Nothing incriminating. Just photos of you with the mayor or your business partners."

Elliot snorted. "Photographs."

"They disclosed a witness, a Morton Titlebaum, who they say will testify to the physical description of Otto Piatek."

"Never heard of him. Do they have any other pictures of Piatek?"

"They've disclosed no other pictures."

"Damn that Mornay. Smiley little bitch stabbed me in the back."

"I also received a notice to take your deposition and a subpoena to take the deposition of your wife."

"Elisabeth?" Elliot jumped up and grabbed the subpoena. "What the hell do they want with her? She's never had a part in my business. She rarely goes out in public, she doesn't attend the functions. She hates to be in the spotlight." He quickly read it over. "Quash this thing. I don't want my wife involved. You hear me, Gerry?"

"I'm not sure I can. They could argue that she has information leading to relevant evidence. Property in your house? And you've established her as an officer of several multimillion-dollar corporations."

"She knows nothing about those corporations. I made her the president so we could qualify as a minority-owned business. And what does that have to do with accusations of war crimes?"

"Maybe nothing. Maybe they're trying to trace money. Or property. I don't know."

"What about the marital privilege? A wife can't be forced to testify against her husband, can she?"

Jeffers shook his head. "The privilege only covers private, confidential communications between a husband and wife. They can ask her about anything else."

Elliot threw the subpoena back at Jeffers. "This bastard is causing me no end of grief and now he wants to upset my wife. This is extortion, can't you see it?" He circled around his desk, making wild arm gestures. "I'm not even going to tell her about this. She's in the middle of planning a wedding. You get this subpoena thrown out, do you hear me, Gerry?"

"I hear you. I'll do what I can. They didn't put me in charge of the court system yet. Meanwhile we're scheduled to take Solomon's deposition January 6. I think you should be there to confront him."

"Not interested. Besides, I thought you were going to Poland."

"Not personally. I'm sending Dennis the second week of January to examine the official county records. He's verifying that there are no records pertaining to you in Warsaw or Zamość. He'll also look for any records regarding Otto Piatek. If we find some, we can use them to prove that you're two different people."

"Is Lockhart going too?"

"No. She's sending her investigator, Liam Taggart."

Rosenzweig slammed his fist on his desk. "I want this case over, Gerry, and I want it over now!"

"It'll be over by April, that's for sure."

"It's not soon enough."

FORTY-SEVEN

• • •

Chicago, Illinois, December 2004

EARLY CHRISTMAS EVE, AS though on the director's cue, large snowflakes began to drift down, lightly at first and then much more heavily. With the temperature hovering around the freezing mark, the thick snowflakes had formed more slowly and smoothly, with long, fat dendrites, and soon the city shimmered under a fresh white frosting. Liam arrived at Catherine's shortly after eight.

"Mmmm. What smells so good?" he said, removing his shoes in her foyer.

"That, my good man, is rack of lamb," she answered from the kitchen.

Liam stepped out of the hallway and took in the scene. The dining room table was set for two, with fresh flowers, votive candles, and a decanted bottle of Châteauneuf-du-Pape. Catherine's Christmas tree twinkled in the corner of her living room. Aperitifs were set on a folding table by the tree.

Catherine, in a curve-hugging black cashmere dress with a plunging neckline, walked in from the kitchen with a tray of appetizers.

"Wow. You look fabulous," Liam said. "You didn't tell me to dress up." Looking meekly down at his wool sport coat and turtleneck, he added, "I'm totally underdressed."

"You're fine. I just felt like getting a little spiffy."

Her meal, all four courses, was culinary perfection. Finishing his dessert of apple tartlets and patting his belly, Liam said, "This was extraordinary! When you asked me to come for dinner . . ." He stopped short. "Well, I mean I didn't . . . well, it's not that I think you *couldn't* . . . or that you would just make . . ." He shrugged. "There's no gracious way out of this, is there?"

Catherine laughed. She covered Liam's hand with hers and said, "I wanted to make us a nice dinner. I'm sorry for the way I've been treating you."

Liam waved her off. "It's okay."

"No. I've been distant since the night we spent together. I know you thought we had turned a corner, and you had a right to think that. You *do* have a right to think that. But this is such a crazy time in my life. I'm working through some tough issues. Don't give up on me."

"I'm okay with it."

She stood and smiled brightly. "I have something for you under the tree." She took his hand and led him to the living room, where she reached beneath the tree and held out a gaily decorated box with both hands.

"Merry Christmas."

She stood over him while he carefully unwrapped the gift that she had purchased two weeks earlier. Like a child, his entire face broke into a smile and he looked up at Catherine. "What a thoughtful gift. I've been lusting for a new camera. How did you know?"

"I thought you could take this with you to Poland next month," she said. "You can return it if it's not what you would buy."

"Why do people always say that? It's ideal. It's exactly what I would buy, if I was reckless enough to splurge on myself."

Catherine smiled proudly. "I'm happy you like it."

"I have something for you, and don't say, 'Oh you shouldn't have.'"

"Okay. I promise," she said, sitting down and crossing her hands in her lap.

Liam walked to the front hall closet and retrieved a small square box, unmistakably from a jewelry store. He handed it to Catherine, who tensed noticeably and turned quite serious.

She shook her head and held out the box. "Liam, I can't . . ."

"Wait a minute," he interrupted. "I don't know what you're thinking, but it's not that. Open it."

With an anxious look on her face, Catherine slowly opened the box. Inside was a set of designer gold drop earrings.

"They're beautiful!" she exclaimed, with joyous relief. "I was thinking . . . oh, never mind. I love them."

They sat together by the tree, had an after-dinner cordial, and laughed at a few funny memories. After a while, Catherine looked at her watch.

"Liam, it's eleven o'clock. I would very much like to go to midnight mass. Would you take me?"

"Seriously? I mean, sure, if you want to. Is this a regular thing for you?"

"No. But I really would like to go tonight."

"Okay." He smiled and shrugged. "Where is your neighborhood church?"

"I want to go downtown. To Holy Name Cathedral."

"Whoa. That's big time. Doesn't the cardinal serve the mass? I think you have to have tickets."

"You don't have to have tickets; you can stand in line. After the people with tickets are seated, they let the general public in."

"Have you done this before?" he asked as they grabbed their coats. "Holy Name on Christmas Eve?"

"I never have. But given everything that's gone on recently, I feel a need to go tonight."

CHICAGO'S AMBER STREETLIGHTS SET the snow-coated city aglow. Filled with holiday spirit, Liam and Catherine approached the cathedral, arm in arm. A long line snaked from the cathedral door around the corner and alongside the large, Gothic structure with its two-hundred-foot spire.

Slowly shuffling forward, they entered through the massive

bronze doors, where they were ushered into one of the side pews. The interior was a feast for eyes and ears. Lights and candles sparkled brightly. The choir and brass ensemble mixed sonorously with the buzz of fifteen hundred worshippers, irreverently discordant but joyfully Christmas. Visiting Holy Name for the first time, Liam took in all its visual majesty—the bronze sculptures lining the walls, the red and black altar with its bronze bas-relief scenes from the Old Testament, and high up, above the cathedra, the five red galeros, the wide-brimmed tasseled hats of Chicago's five deceased cardinals. "If you're going to do midnight mass," he said quietly, "no sense going halfway."

Throughout the mass, Catherine seemed to be deeply involved in her prayers, but during the homily, Liam noticed that she kept turning around to look at the front vestibule. She appeared to be upset and shivered sporadically. Finally, he whispered, "What are you looking at?"

"At ghosts, Liam," she said sadly. "I'm looking at Abraham Solomon and Father Janofski. I'm looking at a group of frightened, huddled nuns. They're all here. Over there in the vestibule. I can see them. It's just like St. Mary's Ascension Church."

Liam patted her leg. "No it's not, Cat. It's long ago and far away. A whole different world. This is Chicago and it's 2004, and that criminal insanity will never happen again."

"It's not so far away." She shook her head. "Not for me. And like Ben says, don't think we're ever immune to such insanity." Her eyes were misted. "You don't know—I haven't told you everything." Her lips quivered. "Piatek and the others. What gave them the right? All those innocent people."

Liam squeezed her hand and held it tightly throughout the remainder of the mass, which concluded at 1:30 A.M. with the singing of "Joy to the World." With their hefty portions of spiritual nourishment, the worshippers filed out into the bright, clean winter night.

At the bottom of the steps, Catherine stopped short and pointed across the street.

"Liam, that man selling chestnuts from his cart—that vendor—it's Ben!"

Liam peered through the snow. "I'm sure it's not Ben. You're seeing things tonight." He took Catherine's hand and led her across the street, where they took their place in the small line waiting for roasted chestnuts. The vendor wore a coat layered over two sweaters and his head was covered with a wide-brimmed Italian fedora. Catherine stooped to get a glimpse of his face. He winked at her.

"Evenin', missy," he said.

"We'll have two bags, please," Liam said, placing a ten-dollar bill in his coffee can. "Your name wouldn't be Solomon, would it?" he added with a smile.

The vendor handed two bags to Liam. "No, sir. It's Andolini." His face curled in a wide grin. "You and the pretty lady, you have a merry Christmas. Be thankful for each other. I'm sure your Christmas wishes will come true."

Catherine whispered to Liam, "Why did he say that? What does he know about my Christmas wishes? Liam, this is ethereal. It's ghostly. I'm looking through windows to another world."

"Stop. He meant nothing more than Merry Christmas. Relax, Cat. You're suffering from emotional overload."

"I'm not so sure."

BACK AT HER TOWNHOME, Catherine made some Irish coffee and served it by the fire. After a bit, Liam set down his cup and loudly cleared his throat. He grabbed an invisible microphone and, in a rough imitation of Dean Martin, sang, "'Ah, but in case I stand one little chance.'"

He stopped and raised his eyebrows. Catherine laughed. "Kinda late to ask a girl out for New Year's, don't you think? Did you expect me to wait around forever?"

"It snuck up on me."

She kissed him. "I accept. What do you have in mind?"

"I thought we'd go back to Ambria, where this whole thing got started last fall."

Catherine laughed. "Liam, they've been booked for weeks, maybe months."

"I've got connections."

She put her hands on her hips. "I have to buy a dress. You didn't give me much time."

"I think the stores are all closed tonight, Cat. Besides, I have a more enticing alternative, if I can interest you."

"You want to tempt the fates again?"

"I'm a risk-taker."

He took her hand and led her toward the stairs. She kicked off her shoes and flipped off the lights. Arms around each other, they climbed the stairs singing "What Are You Doing New Year's Eve?"

FORTY-EIGHT

...

Chicago, Illinois, January 2005

THE MIDWINTER WINDS MADE a howling noise outside Catherine's study, rattling the windows and creaking the walls as she sat staring at her computer screen. Her long Internet research session and preparation for Rosenzweig's deposition were blurring her eyes. Her mind drifted to thoughts of the holidays, which had been pleasant for the first time in years. But now the holidays were over and Liam was gone and she felt the pressure of the lawsuit. There was a lot she'd wanted to say to him before he boarded the plane to Poland and it troubled her that it remained unsaid.

The ring of her telephone interrupted her reveries. "Morning, Cat. It's your on-the-scene world traveler."

Her face brightened at Liam's upbeat greeting.

"You should see Zamość," he continued. "It's just like Ben described, a little pastel village. It bears few scars from the war. From Ben's story, I feel like I've been here before. I went to the town hall, I even went by Ben's old house on Belwederski, but I gotta tell you, it's eerie.

"And the language," Liam said. "I'm in big trouble here—hardly anyone speaks English. I bought a Berlitz phrase book, but it's totally useless—I can't pronounce or understand a single word. There are way too many consonants and not enough vowels."

"It's good to hear your voice," she said. "Things have been kind of rough for me. I wish you were here."

"I wish I was there too. Do you need a friend to commiserate with?"

"More than just a friend, Liam," she said softly. "It's way more than that, and you know it." She paused. The line was silent.

"Cat? Cat, are you there?"

"When do you get back, Liam?"

"Wednesday night, January 12. What's wrong?"

"I don't know . . . I need you. I really miss you. I can't wait until Wednesday."

"That's good to hear. I miss you, too."

"I don't know if it's good or not. I just know I do. Liam, I just want us to be together."

"It's what I want too. Only today, I'm four thousand miles away. And don't forget it was you who sent me."

"I meant to tell you the other night before you left that I was sorry about how I pushed you away after Thanksgiving. I worry that you think I'll do it again."

"Cat, you don't need to apologize again. Remember Christmas Eve? New Year's Eve? Things are good."

"But I don't want you to lose faith in me. All my old insecurities are getting in the way and, well . . . I just want you to know I don't have any more hesitations. Liam, I want a love like Ben and Hannah's. One for all time. We can do that, Liam. I want you to come home and dance with me."

"You are in a bad way if you want me to dance with you."

"Stop joking, I'm serious."

"I'm sorry. It's what I want too, Cat. It's what I've always wanted. I'll come home as soon as I can. Wednesday night."

"I'll pick you up at the airport. Liam, I love you."

"I love you, too."

"I guess I should ask, how did the records depositions go?"

"We checked the Zamość records this afternoon, but either the Russians or the Germans destroyed all the old records, so all we have is birth, death, marriage, and burial records since 1946 and there's no mention of Piatek or Solomon."

"I didn't expect you to find anything."

"Before we came here we were in Warsaw and, as anticipated, there were no records there, either. The city was leveled by the Germans in October 1944 at the end of the Warsaw uprising right through to January 1945 while the Russians were standing on the banks of the Vistula. So all of our examinations in Poland have come up with a big zero."

"Are you finished with the document depositions?"

"Nope. We still have to go to Frankfurt on Tuesday. In the meantime, I'm going to poke around Zamość and see what I can dig up. How did Ben's deposition go?"

"Not good. Jeffers kept coming at him, like a boxer, backing him into the ropes, demanding that he produce proof of his allegations. He took him through his story, stopping him every few minutes, asking, 'What the heck does that have to do with *my* client?' At the end, it all boiled down to Ben's uncorroborated belief that Rosenzweig is Piatek."

"That's tough. Was Rosenzweig present?"

"No, just Jeffers and his two assistants. Come back soon, will you?"

"As soon as I can. By the way, what was the name of the family that moved into Grandpa Yaakov's farm?"

"Zeleinski. Say, that's not a bad idea, Liam."

"Maybe it was an inspiration, huh, Cat? I'll see you Wednesday. Love you."

She hung on to the silent phone for a few minutes before returning to her work.

FORTY-NINE

• • •

ON THURSDAY MORNING, THE day of Rosenzweig's deposition, the mercury sank below the zero mark. In the grips of a January deep freeze, Liam sat and waited with a Styrofoam cup of coffee and a jelly donut, double-parked in front of Ben's apartment building, still jet-lagged from the transatlantic flight the day before. Ben was uncharacteristically tardy. Finally, Liam picked up his cell phone and called him.

"Hey, sleepyhead, it's eight fifteen already. I've been out here for twenty minutes."

"Sorry. I'm moving kind of slowly this morning. I had a rough night, thinking about Otto's deposition and facing him again. I'll be down in a minute."

Ben walked stiffly out to the car and Liam noticed a slight limp. "You okay, buddy?"

"It's these creaky old bones, Liam. Sometimes I feel like Methuselah. But you look chipper today." He winked.

Liam had a sheepish grin. "How do you always seem to know things before I tell you?" He pulled away from the curb. "It's Catherine, of course. Your case seems to have brought us together. Actually we've even begun talking about the future, you know, maybe when your case is over."

Ben smiled. "*Mazel tov*," he said. "It's not a bit surprising. Only that it took you two so long to discover the obvious."

Liam slowly proceeded down Bittersweet. The engine seemed

to agonize in the bitter weather. "You matchmakers work in peculiar ways."

THE CLOSEST PARKING PLACE to Catherine's townhome was two blocks away, and by the time they reached the front door the frigid morning wind had chilled them to the bone. They quickly shuffled into the living room to stand before the warm fire. Ben couldn't stop shivering and he took his place in the overstuffed chair, rubbing his hands together.

"He's not looking well, Cat," Liam said quietly in the kitchen. "His breathing seems short and it's an effort for him to walk."

"Liam, why didn't you drop him off?"

"I tried to. You know Ben."

"It could be the cold—it's freezing today," she said. "Or it could simply be nerves. He's going to face Rosenzweig today for the first time since the opera. I'd expect him to be anxious. I hope he's not coming down with something."

Catherine carried a tray to the living room. "Here's a cup of nice hot tea and a muffin for you, Ben."

Liam leaned against the wall and paged through a folder. "You know, there's something puzzling about these records. There was no Cook County marriage license issued to Elliot and Elisabeth Rosenzweig in 1947 or at any time thereafter. Either they're not legally married or they got married before they immigrated. But the name Elisabeth Rosenzweig does not appear in the NARA immigration records. Not at any time that I can find."

"They could have been married in some other state," Catherine said. "She could have immigrated under her maiden name."

"True. Still, it's another curious aspect to this case."

"I'll ask him about it today during his deposition. Do you have the records produced in Frankfurt?"

Liam held out an envelope. "Birth certificate for Elliot Rosenzweig, born in 1921 to Joshua and Mildred Rosenzweig in Frankfurt, Germany. And here's a copy of Otto Piatek's birth certificate I obtained when I side-tripped to Leipzig. The certificate says he was born in 1921, and it lists Stanislaw and Ilse Piatek as the parents."

"A birth certificate from Frankfurt proves nothing," Ben said weakly from his chair. "When the Nazis were fleeing in the face of certain defeat, they used the names and identities of Jewish families from the cities where the Jews had all been killed. They used these fake identities to immigrate to Britain, South America, and the United States. That's a well-known fact and any World War II historian can give you the details."

Liam nodded. "I found Zeleinski, the six-year-old boy who cared for Buttermilk. His first name is Vitak and he still lives in Zamość, although no longer on a farm. He's seventy now but he remembers Otto Piatek and Ben's family."

"Can he help us?" asked Catherine.

"He was very young at the time and he doubts he could recognize either Ben or Otto. I asked him if there were any pictures or other items that might identify Piatek. Wouldn't that be great if he had a picture of Ben and Otto together? He said there was a trunk in storage, packed by his father after the war, which no one has been into for many years. He promised to take a look. I gave him your email address and he said he'd drop us a note."

"Where are we going for this deposition today?" Ben said.

"Jeffers' office and it's just about time to leave. Ben, are you all right or do you want to stay here?"

"Nothing on earth could keep me away."

THEY TAXIED DOWN TO Jeffers' office and were shown into an empty conference room. A few minutes later, a young court reporter wheeled her equipment into the room and set up her stenograph machine at the end of the walnut table. Finally, precisely at 10:00 A.M., Rosenzweig, Jeffers, and the two young Storch & Bennett associates filed into the room and took their seats. Rosenzweig stared icily at Ben and then at Catherine with a look that broadcast how offended he was at the colossal impertinence of the proceeding and the public assault upon his character.

"Do you solemnly swear to tell the truth," the reporter said, "so help you God?"

"I affirm, I do not swear to God," replied Rosenzweig. "And although it seems to have been in short supply recently, you will hear nothing but the truth from me."

After the requisite preliminaries, Catherine asked, "Where were you born?"

"Frankfurt, Germany. In 1921."

"Where did you go to high school?"

"In Frankfurt."

"What was the name of the high school?"

Elliot's eyes were fixed contemptuously on Catherine. "I can't recall."

"Did you attend a Jewish synagogue?"

"Is there any other kind?"

"Did you attend a Jewish synagogue?"

"Yes."

"What was the name of your synagogue?"

Elliot looked around the room, studied the table in front of him, and said, "I don't remember, something Talmud."

"Do you remember the name of your rabbi?"

"I do not."

"Can you give me the name of a teacher, *any* teacher, that you may have had in religious school or high school?"

"I'm not sure. Perhaps there was a Mrs. Stein."

"Perhaps? And in all your schooling, that's the only name you can remember?"

"That's quite enough," interrupted Jeffers. "I'm going to object to this line of questioning. Not only is it seventy years ago, but it's completely irrelevant and immaterial. Get on to something meaningful, young lady."

"Let me ask an easier question," Catherine said. "Do you have any brothers or sisters?"

"None that are living."

"What are the names of your siblings that are now deceased?"

Rosenzweig tensed, rose suddenly from his seat, and announced,

"I wish to confer with my lawyer." Together they abruptly left the room, followed by the two young associates, writing pads in hand.

Left alone in the room, Liam said to Ben and Catherine, "I found no other birth records for children born to Joshua and Mildred Rosenzweig. As far as I could tell, he was an only child."

"Hmm," Catherine said. "Then what kind of an answer is, 'None that are living'? No wonder he wants to talk to his lawyer."

Rosenzweig and his three attorneys reentered and took their seats. Jeffers spoke. "For the record, Mr. Rosenzweig and his family suffered greatly during the war. Mr. Solomon has no monopoly on wartime tragedy. As you know, Mr. Rosenzweig was himself a prisoner in the Auschwitz concentration camp until rescued in 1945. Personal questions about his life and family in prewar Germany are extremely upsetting to him. He refuses to answer any more such questions. He will confirm that he is not Otto Piatek and he has never been to Poland. We are limiting the scope of your personal questions to post-1945."

Catherine unfolded her hands and pointed at Jeffers. "I don't accept that and I'm prepared to adjourn the deposition right now to put the matter before Judge Ryan. Mr. Rosenzweig has no right to select which questions he will answer, nor does he have a right to avoid questions about his life pre-1945 because they are upsetting. In case you haven't noticed, pre-1945 is the gravamen of our lawsuit. Furthermore, you do not have the right to limit the scope of my deposition, unless of course your client is taking the Fifth. Are you asserting your rights against self-incrimination, Mr. Rosenzweig?"

Elliot looked to Jeffers for an answer.

"Nice try," Jeffers said sharply. "Asserting the privilege against self-incrimination can be construed against him in a civil case. He's not taking the Fifth. He just doesn't want to be harassed by you any further. Personal questions about what happened during the war are intensely disquieting to him. You wouldn't know, Ms. Lockhart; you never endured such conditions."

"What he did or didn't do during the war is the subject of our lawsuit and I'm going to put the matter to him, disquieting or not.

If you direct him not to answer, we'll seek an immediate hearing before Judge Ryan."

"What possible relevance does the name of his high school teacher have in this proceeding?"

"I'll be the judge of that. I wish to examine his memory."

"Memories of his family are painful and cause him mental and emotional distress. They bear no relevance to your claims. I'm telling you that he is not Otto Piatek and he's never been to Poland."

"Is that right?" Catherine asked Elliot directly. "Do you agree with what your attorney has said?"

He nodded. "Of course."

"Auschwitz is in Poland, Mr. Rosenzweig." Catherine leaned forward and stared confrontationally. "Do you want to change your answer?"

"You little smart-ass, I know where Auschwitz is. I was talking about Zamość. I've never been to any of the Polish cities."

"The numbers," Ben said to himself with a look of astonishment. "Of course." He cupped his hand over Catherine's ear and whispered, "I think I know what 'Look at the numbers' means. Ask him to show you his left arm."

She nodded and resumed her questioning. "Mr. Rosenzweig, now that you've had a chance to confer with your lawyer, do you remember the names of your siblings?"

Elliot stared venomously. "I refuse to talk about my family. It has absolutely nothing to do with your lawsuit. It's too painful. Take me to court if you want to."

Catherine flipped a page. "We'll come back to that line of questioning. Right now I'd like to ask you about the day you arrived at Auschwitz. First of all, how did you get there?"

"In a limousine with a bottle of champagne." Turning to Jeffers, he said, "Gerry, do I have to put up with this crap?"

"Just give her the answer, Elliot. If she continues to ask stupid questions, we'll stop the deposition and get a protective order."

"I arrived, along with the other resettled Jews, in a train. We were unloaded at the Auschwitz station and told to get in line. The men were led in one direction and the women in another. It was very orderly. We were all issued uniforms and given haircuts. Then each of us was assigned a number for identification that was tattooed on our arm. I resided at the Auschwitz II Camp at Birkenau until the Russian army arrived. Now, are you satisfied?"

"Tell me, Mr. Rosenzweig, what date did you arrive at Auschwitz-Birkenau?"

"It was in December 1943. The exact day, I don't remember."

"May I see your tattoo, please?"

Again, Elliot looked to his lawyer. "Why?"

"Just show her, Elliot. Let's get this over with."

Elliot rolled back his left sleeve to reveal the blackened A93554 on the inside of his left forearm. Ben and Catherine each wrote down the numbers. Below the tattoo, nearer his wrist, was a four-inch scar. On either side of the scar were surgical spots where the cut had been stitched.

"Happy now?" he said.

"Where did you get the scar on your arm?"

He shrugged. "I got injured as a kid."

"Did a doctor stitch it up?"

"Right."

"Did you get sliced by a razor blade on the streets of Zamość?"

"I don't know what you're talking about. I was cut with a piece of metal on a playground. I've never been to Zamość. I've never been to Poland, except for the internment. How many times do I have to tell you that?"

"Did you get that scar protecting Beka?"

"Beka who?"

Catherine glared. She leaned sideways and whispered to Ben, "Is that where the cut was?"

Ben nodded.

"Were you forced to work while imprisoned at the Auschwitz-Birkenau camp?"

"Everyone had a job, of course. I helped in the kitchen preparing the meals for the prisoners. They had a reasonably functional kitchen, considering there was a war going on."

"When the Russian army liberated Auschwitz and Birkenau, where did you go?"

"Oh, no, you don't. You're not going to trip me up with a cheap lawyer's trick." He laughed. "Oh yes, I was in *Poland*, because we were released in Poland. But I didn't stay there. I made my way to Italy and sailed to Argentina. I lived there for a couple of years before coming to the United States."

Catherine quickly shifted gears. "What is your wife's name?"

"Why don't you leave my wife out of this?"

"What is your wife's name, please?"

"Elisabeth."

"What is her birth date?"

"March 21, 1922. And why does that matter?"

"Where was she born?"

"In Germany. Does that make her a Nazi too? Do you want to accuse her? Do you have some picture of Eva Braun that looks like Elisabeth? You have no reason to involve my wife, other than to piss me off. And I'm getting damn tired of it."

Catherine continued without hesitation. "What was her maiden name?"

"None of your damn business!" He stood up and shook his head. "Gerry, let's go. She has nothing and all she's trying to do is get under my skin."

"Settle down, Elliot. Just answer her question. Give her the maiden name."

Elliot sat down, leaned back, and folded his hands on his stomach. "I don't want to answer any more irrelevant questions. Ask me about who I am, ask me about the time Mayor Burton gave me the key to the city, ask me about the time I had dinner at the White House, ask me about the millions of dollars I've contributed to charities, including all the Jewish charities, ask me about the thousands of people I've employed in my businesses."

"With all due respect, Mr. Rosenzweig, let me clarify our roles here. I ask the questions and you give the answers. What is your wife's maiden name?"

"Okay, we're going to play games; then my answer is: I don't know," he said.

"You don't know your wife's maiden name? Where were you married?"

"I don't know. And that's my answer to the rest of your questions."

"Did you get married before or after you were imprisoned at Auschwitz?"

"I don't know."

Catherine laid her pen on the table. "Mr. Jeffers, this is ridiculous. I'm going to get Judge Ryan on the phone. I'll put it on the speaker. You can participate if you choose."

"Hold on," Jeffers said. He took Elliot's arm and led him to the door. "Give me a few minutes. It's obvious that you've upset him. We've spent forty minutes and you've yet to pose an intelligent question."

When the door had closed, Catherine asked, "Why would someone get upset about his wife's maiden name? What's this all about? Did you notice his emotional demeanor in response to the prewar questions, the ones that supposedly caused him emotional distress? I saw some anger, maybe confusion."

"But no grief," Liam said.

"Exactly. No *emotional distress*."

"Why did you write down his tattooed numbers?" Catherine asked Ben. "Are they important?"

"I don't know. My friend Mort was at Auschwitz. I think his job had something to do with the identification numbers. I want to send these numbers down to him."

Elliot and his lawyers filed back a few minutes later. Elliot looked directly at Ben and said, "You'll get what's coming to you."

Catherine jumped to her feet. "Put that on the record. Put those threats on the record. I want the judge to see that."

Then she turned to Jeffers. "If anything happens to Mr. Solomon, if he gets any threatening telephone calls, if someone bumps into him on the street, if he gets jostled on the bus, I mean *anything*, I'm taking this transcript to the state's attorney."

Jeffers was calm. He smiled. "You're out of line, Ms. Lockhart. Mr. Rosenzweig didn't mean anything more than to tell you what he was going to do to Mr. Solomon in a court of law. He intends to seek fines and sanctions after your case is dismissed. That's what's coming to him. Financial disaster and embarrassment. Nothing more. Ask your next question."

Catherine scowled at Elliot. "What was your wife's maiden name?"

"Cohen."

"Elisabeth Cohen?"

"That's right."

"What were her parents' names?"

Elliot put his hand to his forehead. He rubbed his bald head. "Selma and . . . and Aaron."

"What was the name of the town they lived in?"

"Now, that I don't remember; it was a small town in northern Germany."

"What were your parents' names?"

The question startled Elliot. He stammered, "Mildred and . . . J-Jonathan."

"Jonathan?"

He nodded. Catherine glanced at Liam, who raised his eyebrows. He leaned over and whispered, "It was Joshua and Mildred." Catherine smiled.

"When did you purchase Columbia Indemnity?"

"At the end of 1948."

"How much did you pay for the company?"

"I don't remember exactly. Around a million dollars."

"Where did you get the money?"

"I had money."

"Where did you get it?"

Elliot's teeth were clenched and his face was red. "I had it!"

"Where did you get it?"

Elliot turned to his lawyer. "Just answer her as best you can," Jeffers said with an air of nonchalance.

"I made money in Argentina raising horses. After I arrived in

Buenos Aires, I took a job with a breeder. I sold a few and bought a few and got lucky with a few. I left Argentina with over two million dollars."

"From the sale of horses?"

"More or less."

"Mr. Rosenzweig, I believe you said that you came to America as a penniless refugee after the war. Is that right?"

Elliot smiled and shook his head. "I never said that. That's what newsmen have reported."

"But you never denied it?"

He shrugged. "Why should I? Let them reach their conclusions. My money is none of their business."

"So you came to America with two million dollars?"

"Give or take."

"Did you meet your wife in Argentina?"

"Oh, are we back to the wife now?"

"Can you answer the question or did you forget where you met your wife?"

"You little snot. I met her in Frankfurt."

"Did she immigrate with you in 1947?"

Elliot stood up and leaned on the table. "You'll have to excuse me, Miss Lockhart, but I'm not used to answering personal questions from little nobodies like you, and it makes me sick to my stomach."

Unflustered, Catherine said, "Did she immigrate with you in 1947?"

"She came afterward."

"When?"

"The exact date? I don't remember. Afterward."

"What name did she use to enter this country?"

"I wasn't there."

"Did you see her immigration papers at the time? Did you know at the time she entered the country what name she was using?"

"I don't recall."

"There seems to be a lot of information you don't recall, Mr. Rosenzweig. Is there something wrong with your memory? Are you on medication today?"

"Fuck you!" he shouted, tipping over his chair. "This case is bullshit. You have no evidence against me. There *is* no evidence against me. You've been fishing all day and you've come up empty. Don't blame it on my memory, young lady."

In the midst of the tense exchange Ben exclaimed, "*Co zrobiłeś z pudełkiem z biżuterią?*"

Elliot snapped his head in Ben's direction. "Wouldn't you like to know!" he screamed.

"Wait a minute, wait a minute!" said the court reporter, throwing up her hands. "What did you say?"

"All right, all right, gentlemen," said Jeffers, rising and stretching out his palms like a referee. "Let's stop the bickering and get on with the deposition. You may proceed, Ms. Lockhart."

"Would you be seated, please, Mr. Piatek?" Catherine said.

"Oh, aren't you cute. The name is Rosenzweig and I prefer to stand."

"You're going to get tired, Mr. Rosenzweig. I have twenty-five pages of questions. You're going to be here all afternoon."

"I'll stand. And you're crazy if you think I'm putting up with this all day."

Catherine looked to Jeffers. "Will you talk to your client, please?"

Jeffers nodded and led Rosenzweig from the room. The two young associates scrambled after.

Liam turned to Ben. "A moment ago, when that court reporter threw up her hands, did you say something in Polish?"

Ben nodded.

"What did you say to Rosenzweig, Ben?" asked Liam.

Ben smiled. "I said, 'What happened to the box of jewelry?' His answer, if you recall, was, 'Wouldn't you like to know.'"

"Did you get any of that?" Catherine said to the reporter.

She shook her head. "Sorry. I don't speak Polish. All I got was, 'Wouldn't you like to know.'"

A few minutes later, Jeffers returned to the room alone. "Put this on the record," he said to the court reporter, pointing to her stenograph. "Mr. Rosenzweig is unable to continue with this deposition. Although I warned Ms. Lockhart about harassment, she chose to pursue an abusive course of conduct, delving into irrelevant personal matters, driving a vulnerable, elderly man to the brink of hysteria. I am terminating this deposition and advising all present that I intend to move the court for a protective order, sanctioning Ms. Lockhart and protecting Mr. Rosenzweig from further abuse."

"The questions I asked were proper and germane," Catherine said. "Your client's responses were evasive and, frankly, dishonest. His testimony was ludicrous—he couldn't remember the names of his siblings? When his wife came to America? What name she used? We'll see what his wife has to say next week."

"There will be no deposition next week. I will not submit Mrs. Rosenzweig to a similar inquisition. Until the judge rules on my motion for a protective order, all discovery is suspended."

Jeffers turned and strode from the room.

FIFTY

...

W E'RE JUST WEEKS FROM trial, Elliot, and I don't have to tell you, they have nothing," Jeffers said, rocking back in his leather desk chair. "They've disclosed no witnesses other than Solomon and a guy named Morton Titlebaum, who I understand is out of the city."

"They have a Nazi picture. They have newspaper pictures of me from the 1950s," Elliot interrupted. "They have that crazy old man. What if they drag up some other lunatic, some senile camp survivor, to come to court and testify that they saw Piatek in Poland and they recognize me from the newspaper photo? Maybe this Titlebaum, for all I know, will say he had dinner with me and Adolf Hitler. Damn it, I don't want any surprises."

"It would take more than that. Look, Elliot, this is still a civil case. They have to prove you took Solomon's property, the stuff he testified to at his deposition: jewelry, money. Solomon has no proof that his family even owned that property."

Elliot shook his head. "I want to meet with him. Set it up."

"A four-way settlement meeting with attorneys and clients? I suppose it couldn't hurt."

"No, Gerry. Just me and Solomon, alone in a room."

"Oh, I don't know, Elliot. Maybe that's not such a good . . ."

"I'm not asking you. I'm telling you. Set it up. Here at your office as soon as possible."

"They might object. Maybe they fear for Solomon's safety."

"Funny, Gerry. He's the one with the gun, remember? Besides, I need him alive to beat him in court. If he died now, the world would always harbor the suspicion that I really was a Nazi."

Jeffers nodded. "Okay. Okay. If that's what you want."

Jeffers reached behind him and picked up a thick bound volume entitled "Defendant Rosenzweig's Motion for Summary Judgment" and slid it across his desk to Elliot. "I want to show you something my staff has been working on for a while. Take your time and read this motion. We filed it yesterday. This could be the end of the road for Ben Solomon."

Elliot read slowly and carefully, nodding his head every now and then. It took him thirty minutes to read the motion and the attachments. "Very good piece of work, Gerry. What happens now?"

"As you can see, the motion asks Judge Ryan to throw the case out of court for lack of material evidence. It's a summary judgment motion—time to put up or shut up. Solomon has to come forward now and show the court he has material evidence to take the case to trial. If he can't, then judgment should be entered for you and this case will be over."

"Legally speaking, would this have the same effect as a jury verdict in our favor?"

"It would be even better. It would show the world that there wasn't even enough evidence to take the case to the jury. It would say there's no triable evidence."

"Hmm. Isn't Solomon's testimony evidence? What about the pictures?"

Jeffers shrugged. "We've argued that they are de minimis, insufficient to sustain a verdict. Without further corroboration or physical evidence Judge Ryan can exercise his discretion and dismiss the case."

Elliot frowned. "I'm not optimistic. Set up the meeting."

FIFTY-ONE

...

"CAN YOU CHECK THE NARA records for Elisabeth Cohen in 1947?" Catherine said to Liam. She stood behind the folding table in her makeshift war room. Ben and Liam sat on metal chairs. "She might even be listed on the same manifest as Elliot Rosenzweig."

"I'll go this afternoon."

Catherine turned on her computer. "There's an email here from Vitak Zeleinski."

"What does it say?" Ben said.

Catherine smiled. "I have no idea. It's in Polish."

Ben looked over Catherine's shoulder and read the note. "'Hello, Ben. It is good to talk to you again, my friend. Life has so many odd turns. As Mr. Taggart requested, I retrieved my father's trunk from storage. There were many pictures, but none of them showed Otto Piatek. I have no pictures of anyone in a German uniform. I did find a picture of your grandfather and I am attaching it to this email. I am the little one standing behind him. Nothing else was in the box. Just some of my mother's things—her wedding dress and a couple of blouses. I guess they were special to my father. He died in 1970. I am sorry I cannot help you. Long life to you, my friend. Vitak.'"

Catherine frowned. "That's disappointing. I had hoped we'd find a smoking gun."

The doorbell rang and Catherine excused herself to answer it.

"Don't worry," Ben said. "We'll have plenty of guns at trial. I'm certain of it."

Catherine returned to the room with a thick envelope. She sliced it open and pulled out a bound document running fifty-three pages entitled, "Defendant Rosenzweig's Motion for Summary Judgment." Liam and Ben sat quietly while Catherine skimmed through the motion.

"Well, they didn't waste any time," she said. "They've moved for judgment alleging that we have no material evidence. They attach affidavits, birth certificates, and immigration records all showing that Elliot Rosenzweig was born in Frankfurt and immigrated to Chicago in 1947."

"I'll bet the birth certificate doesn't list Mildred and Jonathan as his parents," Liam said.

"I expect he'll just say he was under emotional distress at the deposition and said 'Jonathan' by mistake," Catherine answered.

Ben and Liam looked at each other and then back at Catherine, with schoolboys' expressions that waited for an answer to the un-asked question.

"Don't worry," she said, "this motion will be denied. I'm positive. It would be a total abuse of discretion for Judge Ryan to dismiss your case. All the law requires of us at this stage is to have *some* evidence. The judge is not permitted to weigh or evaluate the evidence. That's for the jury. The photos, Ben's testimony, the immigration records, even Elliot's erroneous identification of his father—they're all evidence. They're inferences from which a jury can draw conclusions. Judges are not permitted to draw factual inferences on a motion. They're all we need to get us by the motion at this time."

"When will Judge Ryan rule on the motion?"

"I have twenty-eight days to answer. Then Jeffers has a right to file a reply, if he so chooses. Sometime after that, maybe in six weeks, Judge Ryan will rule. Or he may defer his decision until the trial."

Ben stared at the motion. "We have to get to trial. The world has to know."

The telephone rang and Catherine excused herself. She returned a moment later.

"It's Jeffers. He's proposing a meeting between Ben and Rosenzweig to take place at his office next Monday."

"What's this all about?" Ben said.

"All he said was that Rosenzweig wanted to meet with Ben. No lawyers. Just the two of them."

Ben smiled. "The weasel's on the run."

"We don't have to meet. There are no requirements. I don't see how anything positive can come out of such a meeting. But if you want to attend, I think I should go with you," Catherine said.

"No. He said no lawyers. I'll meet with him. I want to hear what he has to say."

"On one condition, Ben. Liam and I will drive you there and sit in the outer office until the meeting is over."

Ben nodded.

FIFTY-TWO

• • •

LIAM, CATHERINE, AND BEN arrived promptly at 10:00
A.M. and announced themselves to the Storch & Bennett
receptionist. Moments later Jeffers walked briskly into the
room, but he stopped short, casting an irritated look in Catherine's
direction.

"I thought we agreed there'd be no lawyers," he said.

"Then what are you doing here?" Liam said.

"It's my office, Mr. Taggart."

"We're here to wait for Ben and make sure there's no funny
business."

Jeffers curled his lip. "I'm offended by that remark. I'm an attorney and, unlike you, bound by strict rules of ethics and honor."

Liam brushed him off with a wave of his hand. "Spare me. If
your client's here, let's get the meeting going."

Jeffers laid a printed document on the reception room table. "A
few ground rules, if you please. Before you is an agreement that today's meeting is absolutely confidential. With the exception of your
lawyer, Mr. Solomon, and," he sneered, "perhaps Mr. Taggart here,
nothing you say or Mr. Rosenzweig says in this meeting may be
disclosed to anyone, nor may anything be repeated or used in any
way by either party in any proceeding. As you can see, Mr. Rosenzweig has already signed it."

Ben looked to Catherine, who nodded her approval. He signed

the bottom of the page and handed the paper to Jeffers. "We'd like a copy," Catherine said.

"Of course."

Jeffers left and returned a moment later with a burly man. His blue blazer fit snugly over his large chest and shoulders. He carried a security wand.

"Mr. Kruk is here to verify that Mr. Solomon is not wearing any eavesdropping devices."

"Bring out Rosenzweig," Liam snapped. "We want the same verification."

Jeffers nodded, rolling his eyes with a theatrical show of ennui. "As you wish." He left to fetch Elliot. "Petulance," he muttered under his breath.

Elliot followed Jeffers slowly into the reception room. Elliot's blue eyes, like those of an aged jungle cat, settled first on Ben and then on Catherine and Liam. He stood with his arms out while Kruk waved the metal detector. When the muscular security guard finished, he turned to Ben. After wanding him with no beeps, Kruk shook his head. "No guns this time, Mr. Rosenzweig," he said.

"Let's get this started," Liam said.

The two were led into a small conference room and the door was closed behind them. In the center was a round glass table surrounded by four black, webbed chairs. Elliot sat directly across from Ben. For a long moment, they sat in silence, their eyes locked upon each other's face.

Finally, Elliot took a breath, leaned forward, and folded his hands on the tabletop. "Mr. Solomon, you have sued the wrong person. I want you to dismiss the lawsuit. And in exchange I am prepared to pay you whatever you think was stolen from your family during the war. I'll write you a check today. All you need do is concede you have made a mistake."

"Is that all?"

"Correct. Giving you the benefit of every doubt, and valuing your property at its highest and best amount, I am willing to pay you twenty million dollars. Today."

"Twenty million? That's five times more than I've claimed."

"Call it generosity. Call it the price of peace. It's worth it to me, Mr. Solomon, to preserve my reputation and be done with you."

"Just concede my mistake?"

"That's all. You don't even have to apologize. Just admit you've made an error and withdraw your lawsuit."

Ben raised his eyebrows. "I'd be a fool not to agree."

"Excellent. In anticipation of your response, I have taken the liberty of having my attorney draft a settlement agreement and I'll ask him to bring it in." Elliot stood.

Ben leaned back in his chair. "Fuck you, Otto."

"What?"

"You and your bullshit façade. You can't buy me off."

Elliot remained unflustered and retook his seat. "Twenty million dollars, Mr. Solomon. That's an extraordinary amount of money. You can live comfortably for the rest of your life. You can give it away to charity. Think of the good that you can do. Give it to your Jewish causes."

"Will twenty million dollars wash your hands, Otto? Will it cleanse you from the thousands you condemned?"

"I have condemned no one, sir. My name is Elliot Rosenzweig."

A sardonic smiled twisted Ben's lips. "You are truly without conscience. A soulless envoy of the devil. But I will never relent, so you can forget the offer."

"This mad pursuit of yours, will it bring back your family? Will it change the past?"

"Nothing can change the past, Otto, but your conviction and public condemnation will serve to keep mankind mindful of the evil that snakes like you are capable of."

Elliot lifted his hands to his forehead. He spoke softly.

"Give it up, Ben."

"Never. Not as long as I have breath."

Elliot swallowed hard and spoke plaintively. "I had no choice. Don't you understand? It was you and your father who forced me to join the National Socialists. I didn't want to. I stood in your living room and begged not to become involved. It was your father who insisted I take a posting. What did you expect me to do? If I didn't follow orders, if I wasn't an obedient soldier, I would have been killed. They were ruthless people. Don't you see, I had no choice?"

"Are you looking for mercy? Do you dare petition me for absolution? For a man who murdered with enthusiasm? What kind of a man executes the only family he ever had without a second thought?"

"They were already dead, Ben. The Gestapo would have killed them in the church if I hadn't. You saw them all looking at me for my pronouncement. Do you think I could have freed them? I did your father a favor, a quick death rather than torture in a camp."

Ben sat tall in his chair. "I will not recant. You will get what you deserve. This case will be your judgment day."

Elliot's jaw quivered in anger. He scoffed, "Don't be a fool. You can't win this case. Do you think we'll ever let you get to trial? Are you so simple that you think our judicial system is about evidence and justice? Ha! It's about money and power and politics. This case will never come to trial. You'll never get a public platform. In the end you'll be humiliated and disgraced. Take the money, Ben. It's your last chance."

"I'll die first."

Elliot shrugged and walked from the room. "Just another dead Solomon."

TWENTY MILLION DOLLARS?" CATHERINE pursed her lips and made a soft whistle.

"I had the feeling he'd pay much more than that," answered Ben. "You know, as we sat there, I kept wanting to ask him questions, to make some sense of the unfathomable, maybe to satisfy a macabre curiosity. Like those who interview serial killers—what made you do it, how can you live with yourself? I wanted to know how he could sleep at night with the wails of thousands of innocents screaming in his head. But I already knew his answer."

* * *

Y OU OFFERED TWENTY MILL and he turned it down? Christ, Elliot, what the hell does he want? Did he give you a counter?"

"It's not about money, Gerry. He's a fanatic on a mission. He's carrying the banner for six million Jews and he's chosen to make me his paschal lamb."

Jeffers looked down at his suit jacket, smoothed his lapel, and bloused his azure pocket square. "Everyone has his price. If it's not currency, then it's something else. What would it take to purchase Solomon? What does he really want?"

Elliot shook his head and wrinkled his forehead. "Why can't you get it through your thick skull? He *is* getting what he wants. An audience. A platform. World attention."

Jeffers crossed his legs and, with the back of his fingers, brushed a speck of dust from his highly polished shoes. "Well, that certainly complicates matters."

"Gerry, we cannot give him a podium. As much as I hate to place myself in the hands of others, especially lawyers, I am relying on you to do everything in your power to prevent a public hearing. This case must not go to trial. We cannot give the public free access to his maniacal rantings. Use every resource available. Money is no object. Do I make myself clear?"

"Crystal, Elliot, crystal."

FIFTY-THREE

• • •

Chicago, Illinois, February 2005

IT WAS THE BAR Association's custom on committee meeting nights to schedule an intermission for coffee and cookies at
the halfway point, so at eight thirty there was a pause in the
proceedings of the Court Rules Committee to enjoy the refresh-
ments. Jeffers found an opportune moment and approached Judge
Ryan as he was filling his cup at the coffee urn.

"Hello, Chuck, how have you been?"

"Just fine, Gerry. Although your fifty-three-page motion sure
makes for a long workweek."

Jeffers laughed. "I apologize for the length. We just had a lot to
say."

"Understood. When is Lockhart's brief in opposition due?"
Judge Ryan said quietly.

"Fifteen more days by court rules. How soon can we expect
your decision?"

Ryan shrugged. "Haven't finished reading and researching. This
is a high-profile case. Who knows?"

Jeffers leaned forward and whispered quickly to the judge.

He smiled, nodded, and replied, "Tomorrow is Wednesday. I
have some time after my calendar call. Come see me then."

The committee meeting was called to order and the committee
members took their seats.

FIFTY-FOUR

• • •

CATHERINE WALKED INTO THE Gavel shortly before noon on a busy Friday. The old Chicago watering hole, kitty-corner from the courthouse, had borne witness to countless deals, settlements, and trade-offs, not to mention thousands of post-verdict whiskeys in celebration of victory or in consolation of defeat, and Fridays started early. Catherine struggled to adjust her eyes to the dark of the bar. A raised hand in the corner caught her attention and she nodded.

In a burgundy vinyl booth set into the darkest part of the room sat a thin man in a short-sleeve white shirt and narrow black tie. His suit coat was neatly folded on the seat beside him. A half-empty highball glass held an amber liquid. No ice. Sunglasses hid the red in his jaundiced eyes. A porcelain ashtray was filled with the detritus of chain smoking, testimony to the morning's passage of time.

"Hello, Mickey."

He patted the booth. "Slide in, Cat." He pointed to his drink. "Can I get you something?" He raised his eyebrows and, seeing Catherine's hesitation, said, "Coffee, maybe?"

"Coffee'd be fine." He lifted an index finger and a waitress materialized from the darkness, took the order, and disappeared.

"Damn, Cat, you're looking good."

"You too, Mickey."

A wry smile appeared along with a short nasal chuckle. "Don't kid an old bullshitter, I look like the wrath of God."

Catherine's eyes misted and she turned to face him. "It's been a long time, Mickey, and I tried to pick up a phone so many times, find the words to tell you how sorry I was that I walked out on you. That I left you with all my baggage. That I trashed our relationship. I tried to find some way . . ."

He held up his hand like a stop sign. "Don't go there. You did what you could do at the time, baby. You were sinking, and we all saw it, but like the *Titanic*, the rift was too big to fix. We couldn't save you. All we could do was watch." He took a swig and finished his drink. A fresh one replaced it moments later.

"It's all ancient history, Cat. You've come back stronger than ever."

She shook her head. "If you only knew. The hurt I caused you and others still haunts me. Every day. . . ."

"Let it go, Cat."

Catherine nodded slightly and sipped her coffee. "I was surprised to hear your message on my voice mail." She mimicked his gravelly voice. "'Hey, Cat. Meet me at The Gavel tomorrow at eleven thirty. It's important.' So what's up?"

Mickey swirled his drink. "The fix is in."

Catherine felt the bile rise in the pit of her stomach. "The Rosenzweig case?"

"Yep."

"How do you know this?"

He shrugged his right shoulder slightly. "Doesn't matter. Old Mick's still got his contacts." He took a swallow and stared into the darkness. "Ryan's always been for sale. He's due to step down at the end of the year and peddle his influence to some big firm. He and Jeffers struck a deal Wednesday. Cash now, partnership later."

"And my case?"

"He'll pitch it. Jeffers has a motion for summary judgment. After you file your answer, Ryan'll toss the case."

Catherine's heart thumped hard in her chest. "Shit, Mickey."

"Sorry, Cat."

"What if I SOJ Ryan—get the case away from him before he decides the motion?"

"Substitution of judges? You can try. But you know the law as well as I do. An SOJ has to be brought at the earliest possible time after the alleged prejudice is discovered. He's had the case for weeks. Besides, if he's made any substantive decisions, he doesn't have to grant your motion. He'll fight hard to keep the case. It's a big payday."

"There have been no substantive decisions. He's only ruled on procedural matters."

Mickey shrugged again, as if to say, "Like that'll really matter."

Catherine banged her fist on the table. "Damn! What can I do, Mickey?"

"You can start drinking at ten in the morning, like I do. It's a great cure for disillusionment."

Mickey lit another cigarette; Catherine gazed into her coffee cup. Conversations and laughter in the bar raised the background noise.

"What about Murphy?" Catherine said finally.

"The chief judge? He's honest but he's no crusader. He didn't get to his position by rocking boats."

"Can you help me, Mickey?"

He sadly shook his head. "I've passed along the bad news. It's all this old drunk can do." He raised his hand to signal the cocktail waitress, and Catherine knew the meeting was over. She gave him a peck on the cheek.

"Cat. If you have to, and it does you any good, you can use my name."

"Take care of yourself, Mickey," she said and walked out into the glare of the noonday sun.

FIFTY-FIVE

• • •

CATHERINE KNEW THE ONLY chance they had was to get the case away from Ryan. She immediately began to draft a motion to transfer the case to another judge. She was aware that according to Illinois law, such a motion was routine and was usually granted without a hearing. Judges were not permitted to inquire into the basis for the claim of prejudice. It was only necessary that the litigant allege that he could not get a fair trial because the judge was prejudiced against him.

However, Catherine also knew that Illinois disapproved of flagrant forum shopping. Appellate case decisions held that if a judge had made a substantive ruling, a decision based on the merits of the case, such a motion should be rightfully denied. The line between substantive and procedural decisions was often blurred. If a judge wanted to deny the transfer, he'd likely claim there had been substantive rulings.

Catherine filed the motion and set it to be heard as an emergency Monday morning before Ryan's regular call.

JUDGE RYAN PLACIDLY READ the motion while Catherine and Jeffers stood before his desk in his chambers.

"What makes you think I'd be prejudiced against Mr. Solomon, Catherine? I've given you a fair shake every time you've appeared before me."

"You know you can't make that inquiry, Judge."

Ryan nodded and looked over at Jeffers. "Gerry, what's your position on this motion?"

"We oppose it. I think it's outrageous that, at this late date, after the matter has been pending before you for weeks, Ms. Lockhart suddenly wants to go judge shopping. We have a trial setting and a motion for summary judgment pending. Our recent settlement conference was unsuccessful, and now Ms. Lockhart wants to delay the inevitable. It's as plain as the nose on her pretty little face."

Judge Ryan wagged his finger in reproach.

"The bottom line, Your Honor, is that you've made substantive rulings," Jeffers continued. "It's too late to bring this motion. It's no longer timely."

"What substantive rulings, Gerry? I think they've all been procedural, haven't they, Catherine?"

Shocked at Judge Ryan's amenability, at the thought that he might actually grant the SOJ, and that Mickey might have had bad information, Catherine harbored second thoughts. But she responded, "That's correct. The only matters before you have concerned settings."

"Oh, not true," Jeffers said. "On December 20 we appeared before you with four motions, one of which was to accelerate the case for trial. At the time, we examined the heinous allegations of the complaint, and I think you stated that we were entitled to 'nip it in the bud' if we could. It was for that reason you gave us an early trial date. Now Ms. Lockhart is seeking to have you reverse yourself and buy more time to fabricate a case against my client."

Ryan raised his eyebrows and looked to Catherine for her reply.

"A trial setting is procedural," she said. "There have been no substantive rulings."

Ryan set the motion down on his desk and looked thoughtfully at Catherine. "On most occasions, I'd be inclined to agree with you. But here, I'm afraid I view this motion as a delay tactic. There were good reasons for me to accelerate the case for trial. Illinois law cautions me not to grant a substitution where its main purpose is to effectuate a delay. I'm going to deny your motion. The trial date will stand. I advise you to have your answer to Mr. Jeffers' motion for summary judgment filed on time. I will grant no extensions."

CATHERINE MET LIAM FOR lunch.

"Can't you appeal Judge Ryan's decision?" he asked.

Catherine sighed. "Not at this time. I'd have to wait until the case is over, until after Ryan has granted Jeffers' motion and dismissed the case. By then the newspapers and television stations would be having a field day, ridiculing Ben and praising Rosenzweig, 'Chicago's Treasure.' I think the appellate courts would be pressured to leave the case alone. Besides, any appellate rulings would be years away."

Liam watched Catherine as she took a bite of her salad. She should have looked defeated. But, on the contrary, Liam saw no despair.

"What's going on in that head of yours? You're not admitting defeat?"

"Nope," she said.

He smiled. "What?"

She put her napkin down and rose from the table. "I'm going sky-diving without a parachute. Do me a favor, have some bail money ready this afternoon. I'll call you." With his heart full of admiration, Liam watched her stride confidently from the room.

FIFTY-SIX

...

THE OFFICES OF THE Chief Judge of the Chancery Division of the Circuit Court of Cook County were located on the twenty-third floor of the Richard J. Daley Center. The large, well-appointed chambers afforded a southeast corner view: Monroe Harbor, Millennium Park, the museum campus, and Soldier Field. His privacy was guarded by his secretary of twelve years, a humorless woman named Glenda Szabortusz, nicknamed "Saber Tooth" by the litigation bar. She sat in the outer office like a watchdog. Catherine entered her domain shortly after 2:00 P.M.

"Please tell Judge Murphy that Catherine Lockhart is here to see him on an emergency matter," Catherine said.

Glenda did not look up from her crossword puzzle. Her gray hair was tied up in a bun. "I don't have you scheduled for an appointment."

"No, ma'am. It's an emergency."

Glenda put down her pencil and looked up at Catherine in annoyance. "Judge Murphy does not see anyone without an appointment. Does this concern a pending matter?"

"Yes, it does."

"Then Judge Murphy will not see you without all attorneys being present. He does not permit ex parte communications. You'll need to contact your opponent and schedule an appointment, in writing, setting forth the reasons that you seek to involve the Chief Judge. In detail. Follow the rules, Ms. Lockhart." She lowered her head and returned her attention to her crossword puzzle. "Good day."

Catherine stood for a moment, then quickly walked behind Glenda, opened the door to the Chief Judge's chambers, and marched in. James Murphy was seated at his desk reading a report from the Courts Commission and was taken aback by the sudden intrusion. Although his football days at Notre Dame were only memories, the stocky, white-haired judge still cut an imposing figure. Behind him on the wall hung a photograph signed by the Irish coach, his arm around a lanky Jimmy Murphy.

Glenda came scrambling in after Catherine. "I tried to stop her, Judge. I told her to make an appointment. She just barged right in. Want me to call security?"

Murphy swiveled his head and looked at Catherine.

"I'm sorry to bother you, Your Honor," she said, "but I need to speak to you privately. It's most urgent."

Murphy sighed and waved Glenda back to the outer office. She left and shut the door.

"What's this all about, Counselor?" he snapped at her.

"It's about Judge Ryan. I want you to remove him from a case."

"A case you're working on?"

She nodded.

Murphy looked puzzled. "Did you file an SOJ?"

"I did. It was denied."

"Well, you have your appellate rights. This conversation is most improper, Ms. . . ."

"Lockhart."

"I cannot, nor would I, intercede. Goodbye, Ms. Lockhart."

Catherine didn't move. "Your Honor, I want you to pull him off the case. Reassign it. Ryan's on the take and I'm not about to sit by and see my client sold out by a dirty judge."

"What!" Murphy bellowed. "Chuck Ryan?" His face turned red. "You better damn well have a videotape or you're finished practicing law in this county. What's your evidence?"

"I've been informed by someone who knows."

"Who?" Murphy shouted.

"I can't say. I can only tell you that Ryan's taken money and been promised a cushy job when he retires, all in exchange for pitching my case."

"Get the hell out of here. Do you care that little about your license?"

"No, sir," Catherine said calmly. "I care that much."

"Where'd this information come from?"

Catherine took a step forward, wondering how she still had the strength to stand. "Someone I respect very much. And I'm not leaving until you reassign the case. Because if you don't, I'll have the U.S. Attorney check every dollar Ryan spends and if it's ten cents more than his judicial salary, or if he ends up working for Storch & Bennett next year, he'll be indicted. And I'll squawk to every paper in town that I was in here trying to get him off the case."

Murphy stared. Catherine's brash determination had made its impression. "What case is this?"

"*Solomon v. Rosenzweig.*"

He raised his eyebrows and leaned forward. "Come here, young lady."

Catherine inched closer to the front of the desk. Her jaw was set. Her heart was resolute but her hands were shaking.

The judge spoke slowly and firmly. He pointed his finger. "You tell me here and now: *where* did you get this information?"

Catherine bit her lower lip. "Michael Shanahan."

The judge nodded and rocked back in his chair. He stroked his nonexistent beard. "Do you have a copy of your motion for substitution?"

Catherine reached into her briefcase and handed a copy across the desk.

"What rulings has Judge Ryan made in the case?"

"It's all in the motion. Nothing substantive." Catherine recounted the rulings.

Murphy took several deep breaths while he studied the motion and contemplated his decision. Finally, he reached behind him, picked up the telephone, and dialed a three-digit extension.

"Chuck? Murph. Great, yourself? Listen, I'm doing a little

administrative housekeeping. I'm reassigning the Rosenzweig case to DiGiovanni." Pause. "I understand. Fifty-three pages and you've already researched it. Yes, it's a lot of work for nothing, but I need to even out the assignments." Pause. "No, you can't, Chuck. I'll send Glenda down for the file. Thanks for your understanding."

He set the phone down and stared menacingly at Catherine. "Not a word of your slanderous accusations leaves this office."

Catherine nodded. "Yes, sir."

"This conversation never took place. He's retiring at the end of this year. Let the man go."

"Yes, sir."

Murphy nodded. He gestured for Catherine to leave and buzzed Glenda. "Ms. Lockhart," he said to Catherine as she left his office, "tell Mickey that Jimmy sends his best."

Catherine walked shakily into the hallway and into an empty courtroom. She sat down hard on a back spectator bench. Her knees were rattling like aspen leaves.

ELLIOT TOOK OFF HIS coat and hung it on Jeffers' antique coat rack. "What the hell was so important that I had to drop everything and come directly to your office? I hope you're going to tell me that Ryan granted your motion for judgment."

Jeffers somberly shook his head. "Ryan lost the case."

"What do you mean 'lost the case'? What's that supposed to mean?"

"I mean the case was reassigned to Judge DiGiovanni. I just got notice."

"I thought Ryan denied Lockhart's motion to transfer. That was a done deal. He cost me two hundred grand. How the hell did you let this happen?"

"It wasn't Ryan. It was an administrative shuffle from the chief judge. I don't know, Murphy might have smelled a rat. Maybe he just had a hunch."

Elliot pinched his lower lip and paced in Jeffers' office. "How much is DiGiovanni gonna cost me?"

"I can't get to him. He's acting chairman of the Judicial Ethics Board. He's unapproachable. That's what makes me think Murphy knew something."

"Can't we file a motion, like Lockhart, and get the case assigned to someone else?"

"It wouldn't do us any good. All reassignments come from the chief judge. We're stuck with DiGiovanni."

Elliot clenched his teeth. "Then, I guess you're just going to have to win this case. We need to pull out all the stops."

FIFTY-SEVEN

• • •

LIAM DIDN'T RECOGNIZE THE caller ID, but he knew the voice. It was Carl Wuld.

"Say, Taggart. This is your brother-in-arms. I got news for you."

"Go ahead, Carl."

"I'm being sent to Poland and France to find Piatek. Brian Cunningham, he's Rosenzweig's right-hand guy, gave me twenty grand to fund my trip."

"Congratulations on your good fortune. Your scam seems to be working out well."

"Thanks, bro. But that ain't why I'm calling you. Remember when you stood in my house and told me to call you if Rosenzweig was doing anything with Solomon?"

"Yeah, go on."

"Well, you didn't bust me, so I owe you. I was just a front all along, so Rosenzweig could say he was searching for Piatek. He used me and I used him. Now I'm off to Europe so he can tell the media that he's funding a worldwide search for Piatek. But Rosenzweig's got another muscle man. It's the other guy, Pickens, that you got to worry about. He's the one who set up the break-in at the apartment."

"Why do I have to worry?"

"There's a contract on your boy. We're all square now, bro." And the phone went silent.

* * *

LIAM DIALED BEN AGAIN and again, but the calls went un-answered. "Stay in your apartment," Liam warned on his voice mail. "I'm on my way over. Stay away from the windows and double-lock your doors."

As he sped down Addison Street, his call was returned. Ben was out of breath and spoke between gasps. "There are people after me, Liam. They know where I live. Two of them are downstairs."

"Where are you?"

"In my apartment, but I had to take the stairs. They're watching for me in the lobby. It's one of the guys who was sitting in the car outside Catherine's. He's in the picture you took. I'm worried they'll get in here. The doorman's got a pass key. So does the super."

Liam floored his car. "Block the door. Put a chair under the doorknob. I'll be there in a few minutes. I'm calling 911."

"There's a gunman at 620 Bittersweet," he said to the 911 opera-tor. "He's trying to break into an apartment on the seventeenth floor. I believe the gunman's name is Pickens."

There were three squads parked in the turnaround, lights flash-ing, when Liam reached the building. "I'm the one that made the call," he said to CPD Lieutenant Silas Brown, flashing his Illinois PI license. "It's Ben Solomon's apartment on the seventeenth floor."

Four police officers, guns drawn, dashed out of the elevator on 17 followed by Liam and the building's doorman. The hall was empty. Liam ran down to the apartment door. "Ben, it's me. It's Liam. Ben?" He rapped on the door. No answer.

Waving the doorman over, Brown said, "Give me the keys." He unlocked the door, but it still wouldn't open. It was jammed. He was about to kick in the door when Liam stopped him. "Hold on. I told him to put a chair against the door. Ben? Are you in there?"

No answer.

Brown and Liam looked at each other and Liam nodded. He smashed into the door with his shoulder, breaking the doorjamb and splintering the dining room chair propped beneath the doorknob. They entered the apartment and found it empty. Looking around, Liam noticed that the bathroom door was shut. "Ben, are you in there? It's Liam."

"Thank God," Ben said as he opened the door. "Liam, there were people after me. I'm not hallucinating." Ben was still out of breath.

"I know you're not. I got an anonymous call this afternoon warning me that there would be people looking for you."

"I was coming home from the grocery store, almost at the building, and I saw these two guys. I recognized the tall one. But they didn't see me." Ben was breathing hard. "You know me. I hear voices. They alerted me. Maybe it was my Hannah. I held the bags to block my face and snuck into the lobby. But the elevator wouldn't come and they were turning to come into the lobby. I had to take the stairs. Seventeen floors."

Liam walked Ben over to a chair. He couldn't catch his breath and he was sweating. "What's your doctor's name, Ben?"

"Dr. Kevin Chou. But I'll be all right. Just give me a few minutes."

"Was there anybody here looking for Mr. Solomon?" Lieutenant Brown said to the doorman.

He nodded. "Couple guys. Never saw them before. They said they had business with Mr. Solomon. They were delivering an insurance policy. They wanted to know if he was in. I saw him a couple minutes earlier, but you know, I can't give out that kind of information. I told them that they could buzz him, announce themselves, and maybe he'd authorize me to let them in. They stood around outside and then the squad cars pulled up and they walked west on Bittersweet."

Lieutenant Brown stayed to get a description and a statement from the doorman. Liam told Ben to pack a suitcase. "I'm going to put you up at my place for a while until we figure this thing out," he said.

"He knows he's defeated, doesn't he?" Ben said on the way to Liam's house.

"I don't think he does. He's like a cornered wolverine and just as dangerous. I got a call today from Wuld. He told me Rosenzweig's put a contract out on you."

Ben smiled broadly. "That's great news."

"It is?"

"Is there clearer proof of guilt? Now it's just a matter of convincing the jury."

FIFTY-EIGHT

...

Chicago, Illinois, February 2005

IT WAS ANOTHER BITTER morning, affording no relief from the succession of below-zero days and nights. Ice and crusted snow blanketed the lawns and parkways. Chimneys breathed columns of white steam into the clear blue sky. Catherine, warmly dressed in a cream, bulky-knit turtleneck and camel slacks, stopped her research session to answer her door at 10:00 A.M. Liam, Ben, and a third gentleman entered the foyer. Ben's breathing was labored and he stood slightly bent, fatigued from his short walk from Liam's car.

"This is Morton Titlebaum," he said. "Mort, this is my lawyer, Catherine Lockhart. She's the one I've been telling you about."

They gathered in the kitchen where Catherine passed around mugs of tea and coffee.

"Mort was a prisoner at Auschwitz," Ben said. "He has something interesting to tell you."

Mort sat upright, posture-perfect, a gray mustache and goatee giving his thin frame dignity. "Rosenzweig was never at Auschwitz. His tattoo's a fake. I know, because for a while in 1944 I was assigned to work in the tattoo line."

"How do you know it's a fake?"

"At Auschwitz more than four hundred thousand inmates were tattooed. They were the ones who were registered and sent to work. Other poor souls were marched directly into the gas chambers without registration or identification. Before I got there, Jews were identified by tattooing triangles below their numbers. Starting in the spring of 1944, the SS decided to start over and precede the numbers with letters. So they tattooed an A before the numbers until they reached twenty thousand for the men and thirty thousand for the women. Then they started the numbers with a B."

"Rosenzweig's number is A93554."

"Right. It's a fake."

"Will you come to court and testify to that?"

Mort nodded. "You bet your babushka."

"Show him Rosenzweig's photos," Ben said.

Catherine handed the newspaper photo of Rosenzweig and NBC's photo of Piatek to Mort. He placed them side by side on the table. "That sure looks like the same guy. But I only saw him the one time and just for a moment. Sixty years ago. I don't know how strong my identification will be. I'm going to have to leave that eyewitness thing to Ben." He shrugged. "But it looks like him."

Ben smiled, but his complexion was pallid. Catherine thought for the first time that he looked older than his eighty-three years, that he had aged considerably since Thanksgiving. It was obvious the recent stress had taken its toll.

"Do we need anything more to defeat Rosenzweig's motion?" Ben asked. "We can always add Mort's affidavit."

"Sure, we can add it. Everything helps. I expect Rosenzweig will counter with some excuse about the tattooer making a mistake, but the erroneous tattoo casts further doubt upon his credibility and raises yet another factual issue. We're in good shape though, Ben. Especially since Judge DiGiovanni's got the case," Catherine said. "Jeffers' motion doesn't stand a chance."

"What about the scar, the cut he got protecting Beka?"

Catherine nodded. "They're all pieces of evidence. Stack them up. One by one they drop on the scales of justice."

"Liam," Ben said in a raspy voice, "I want you to check your immigration records for me. Look up the name Krzyzecki. I'll spell it for you: K-r-z-y-z-e-c-k-i. See if that name appears around the time that Rosenzweig entered the country."

Liam watched Ben weakly write the name on a pad and hand it to him. The paper fluttered in Ben's shaking grip.

"Who is that, Ben?"

"Elzbieta."

Catherine looked stunned. "Oh my God! He married Elzbieta! Your two inspirations. Rosenzweig's wife and the numbers."

"Right. I'll make a believer out of you yet." Ben grinned, then suddenly grimaced and grabbed his left arm.

"Are you all right?" Catherine said. "Ben?"

He started to speak and his eyes rolled up into their sockets. Liam caught him as he fell sideways from his chair.

When the paramedics arrived four minutes later, Liam was still administering CPR. Ben was hooked up to an IV and wheeled unconscious into the ambulance. Liam, Mort, and Catherine scrambled into Liam's car and followed the EMS van. On the way, Liam called Adele, who said she'd meet them at the hospital.

An hour later, Adele burst into the emergency room's waiting area, where Mort and Liam were sitting vigil on the plastic chairs. Catherine was pacing by the Coke machine.

"How is he?" Adele said.

"We don't know anything," Catherine said.

"Has Dr. Chou been called?"

The three looked at each other and shrugged.

"He's Ben's cardiologist—he's been seeing him for some time," Adele said. She walked over to query the admitting nurse. The nurse checked her records, left for a moment, and returned to whisper to Adele, who nodded and walked over to the others.

"She told me that Dr. Chou was called earlier and he's attending to him in the ER," Adele said. "She didn't have any further information for us. Ben's had a heart condition for some time. This is not the first time he's put me on pins and needles in the waiting room." She took off her hooded parka, gloves, and scarf and set them on a connecting chair. "The last few months have been very hard for him."

Eventually a blue-gowned doctor, youthful and slight, with intense black hair, emerged through the double doors and into the area where the four anxious friends were waiting. "I'm afraid Ben's suffered a myocardial infarction—a heart attack. He's alive, thanks to your CPR and the paramedics, but he's not awake. We're keeping him sedated and helping him to function."

Adele swallowed and nervously inquired, "What's the prognosis, Dr. Chou?"

He shook his head. "His heart's taken a beating and this is the third time I've seen him in the ER—of course, nothing this severe. I just don't know. He's a scrappy fighter. I wouldn't have given you a nickel for his chances a few months ago, but he's a driven man—he's got a real strong will to live."

Liam and Catherine eyed each other. "We know."

"There's no reason for you all to stay here," he continued. "I mean you're welcome to, but we'll call you if there's any change in his condition. We're going to transfer him to the cardiac care unit." They shook his hand and he disappeared back into the ER.

"You might as well go home," Adele said, picking up her winter gear. "I'll stay with Ben for a while and I'll call you if anything changes."

"I'll hang around for a bit," said Mort.

Liam and Catherine departed into the midday freeze with plans to meet everyone back at the hospital at ten the next morning.

The drive home was quiet. Catherine stared over her shoulder and out of the passenger window, too upset to talk. She held a handful of tissues, periodically dabbing her tears. Off and on, her chest heaved with insuppressible sobs.

Back in her townhome, Catherine went straightaway to her office and printed out a subpoena directed to Elzbieta Krzyzecki, commanding her to appear for deposition in four days and demanding that she produce all documents in her possession pertaining to her marriage, her immigration, and her naturalization. She held the subpoena out for Liam. Her cheeks were flushed, her eyes were red, and her facial muscles were clenched in a struggle to hold it all together. "How fast can you serve this on Mrs. Rosenzweig?"

"Catherine . . ." he said softly.

"I want it served today." Her voice was breaking. "Here, take it!"

"Catherine. We don't know for sure that Elisabeth Rosenzweig is Elzbieta."

"Take it, damn it, I know my job. I can't stand here arguing with you, I have research to do. I have to prepare affidavits and I have lots of work to do to get ready for trial."

He grabbed her arms. "Catherine, if Ben doesn't regain consciousness, the case is over. You can't go to trial without Ben. You won't have a plaintiff. Only Ben can tell his story, make his identification. You can't even win the motion without Ben. He has to sign the affidavit. He has . . ."

"Stop! Stop talking like that. Please. He's going to be all right. This case is keeping him alive, you heard the doctor. Please, Liam. He'll get better. He'll recover. I know he will. Now I have to get ready for trial. Please serve the subpoena. Please . . ."

He threw his big arms around her and cradled her while she dissolved into tears.

"Oh, Liam, what am I supposed to do now? Why have I been chosen?" she said through uneven breaths. "I'm so damn inadequate."

"No, you're not. You're a good lawyer. And a good friend to Ben."

"Compared to Ben, I'm nothing. What have I ever done? What have I accomplished in my life? I've represented insurance companies and big corporations in cases that have no social significance. What kind of a lawyer have I been? Were I to die tomorrow, Liam, what footprints have I left on the earth?"

"Cat, why are you beating yourself up?"

"This case means everything to me, Liam. Don't you understand? It's not just Ben's case, it's mine, too. It validates me—as a lawyer, as a human being. I will have done something. I will have made a contribution."

"Don't. You're a good woman and a damn fine lawyer. And besides that, I love you."

"I love you, too," she said, her arms around his waist, a fistful of Liam's sweatshirt clutched tightly in her hands. "Please, Liam. I can't let this go. Not now. Will you serve the subpoena?"

"Of course," he said softly. "Don't worry. I'll serve the subpoena.

You go and do your research. You prepare for trial and I'll get her served."

She sniffled and looked up into his eyes. "She has to be served today; I set the deposition for Monday."

"I'll get her."

FIFTY-NINE

• • •

Winnetka, Illinois, February 2005

ROBERT WALKED INTO THE east parlor where Elisabeth Rosenzweig sat needlepointing a throw pillow.

"Madam, there is a delivery for you from Bloomingdale's."

"Oh, how nice. It must be the engagement present I ordered for Jennifer. Bring it in."

Robert stood with his hands clasped behind his back and said, "I'm sorry, madam, but the delivery man is requiring that you personally sign for the package."

She completed the stitch and set the pillow on the couch. "Very well." She followed Robert to the front door, where a tall man in a brown uniform, a brown cap sitting on top of his rusty red hair, stood holding a large white box wrapped in a gold ribbon. He held out a clipboard.

"If you're Mrs. E. Rosenzweig, you can sign right here."

"I don't remember having to sign for Bloomingdale's packages before," she said, taking the pen and signing her name to the delivery log.

Handing her the box, the delivery man said, "Homeland Security, ma'am. Never can be too careful. See you Monday."

"Monday? What are you talking about?"

He tapped the bill of his cap, smiled, and walked out to the

UPS van. Climbing into the passenger seat, he said, "Thanks, Gordon, I appreciate the help."

"No problem, Liam."

Inside the house, Elisabeth had a puzzled look. "'See you Monday'? Did you hear him say that, Robert? Do you suppose he has another package he didn't give me today?"

"Very odd, madam."

She took the package into the parlor and unwrapped it. Inside was a white envelope from the law offices of Catherine Lockhart. Her hands started to shake. She ripped open the envelope and read the name on the subpoena. Her face turned white.

Elliot returned home later that afternoon. "Where is Elisabeth?" he asked Robert.

"She went for a walk, sir. A couple of hours ago she received a package from Bloomingdale's. Whatever it was, it upset her. She said she was going to take a walk."

"It's freezing outside. What's wrong with her? Why didn't you call me?"

"Sir?"

"Never mind. Have my car brought around."

Elliot was driven slowly through the neighborhood, up and down the side streets. Finally he saw Elisabeth on a sidewalk. Her gait was unsteady.

"Elisabeth," he called. She looked, turned her head, and kept on walking. Elliot jumped out of the car and quickly caught up to her.

"What are you doing out here?"

Elisabeth's eyes were red. She twisted a handkerchief in her right hand. With her left, she handed the tear-stained subpoena to Elliot.

"Son of a bitch," he said as he crumpled the paper. "Don't worry, Jeffers'll get it quashed."

"They know, Otto. They know about us."

"They know nothing! They have no proof."

"What am I supposed to do? What will I say?" she cried.

Elliot hustled her back to the car. "I won't let them question you."

"I'll have to go to court. How will you stop them?" She raised her voice. "This is a subpoena to Elzbieta Krzyzecki! I thought we left those identities in Europe. You promised me!"

"Stop whining, Elisabeth. Get a damn backbone. If they get to question you, you'll tell them you never heard of Elzbieta Krzyzecki. Or Otto Piatek. You'll lie, Elisabeth, like you've been doing for fifty years."

She shook her head. "I'm not a good liar. Ben will see right through me. It's over, Otto. I'm going to get deported, sent back to Poland. Or worse. I don't want to go to jail."

Elliot grabbed her face. "You listen to me, Elisabeth," he said sternly. "You'll do exactly as I tell you. You'll give the answers I tell you to give them. You won't fuck this up, do you hear me?" He squeezed hard on her cheekbones.

Elisabeth sobbed. She nodded her head.

"You've done pretty damn well, Elzie, from a simple apartment in Zamość to a mansion on Sheridan Road. Take a look around. I've given you the life of a queen. I've taken you from nothing to respectability. If you fuck this up, it'll be the last thing you ever do."

Elzbieta hung her head and cried.

SIXTY

...

A T 2:00 A.M., CATHERINE was abruptly shaken from a deep sleep by the ring of her telephone. "Oh, no," she cried, grabbing Liam, digging her nails into his arm. "I don't want to answer it—it'll be the hospital." She folded her hands in prayer. "Oh, please God, please don't let him die. Please don't take him now."

Liam lifted the phone off its cradle and held it out. She reached over the pillow, hesitantly accepted the handset, and took a deep breath. "Hello?"

The answer was just a whisper. "Is this Catherine Lockhart?"

"Who is this?" Catherine demanded.

"It's Elisabeth Rosenzweig," was the whispered response. "I'm calling from my kitchen. My husband is asleep."

"What do you want at this time of the night, Mrs. Rosenzweig, or should I say 'Elzbieta'?"

"I want you to leave me alone. I didn't have anything to do with Ben's property. I never took a thing. Leave me out of this."

"I'm afraid we can't do that, Elzbieta. You're going to testify whether you like it or not. You're going to tell us all about you and Otto and how the two of you snuck into the country under phony identities. You're going to tell us how the two of you got all your money from Otto's Swiss accounts—how the two of you have lived a life of luxury on the confiscated property of murdered Jews."

"Stop saying 'the two of you.' It was Otto, it was Otto. I never took anybody's property. Back in Poland, I was the one who tried to help Ben and his family. I was never a Nazi. Ask Ben. He'll tell you to leave me alone."

"It's over, Mrs. Piatek. Whether you were a Nazi or not, you're going to be deported. Immigration fraud, assisting a Nazi war criminal in sneaking stolen money into the country, a whole host of offenses."

"I can't—I won't—go back to Poland. You don't understand. My granddaughter needs me, I'm all she has. And she's getting married. Can't we talk about this? Maybe we can work something out."

"Does Otto know you've received the subpoena today?"

"Yes. He's very upset. He spent the evening at his lawyer's office. When he came back, he went right to bed."

"Mrs. Piatek, I can't make you any promises, but if you're willing to cooperate, I will try very hard to help you to stay in the country."

Pause. "What would I have to do?"

Catherine put her hand over the phone's mouthpiece and said to Liam, "Get me Richard Tryon's home telephone number."

"How the hell am I supposed to get that?" he whispered.

"I don't know. You're the PI. Just do it."

"Mrs. Piatek," she said into the phone, "I want you to meet me in the lobby of the Dirksen Federal Building tomorrow morning at eight o'clock. Adams and Dearborn streets."

"What are you planning to do?"

"We're going to meet with the U.S. Attorney."

"Oh no. I can't do that. Otto will kill me."

"We're going to pitch a deal. Your testimony against Otto in exchange for protection and immunity from prosecution. You don't have to say a word. If I can't get the U.S. Attorney to make a deal, to promise not to prosecute you or deport you, you can go right home."

"I don't know. I have to think about it," she said.

"Mrs. Piatek, if you're not there at eight o'clock, the deal's off."

"I have to think about it. He's a very violent man." She hung up.

Liam came back into the room and handed Tryon's phone number to Catherine. "It's in the damn phone book under 'R. Tryon.' You're not seriously going to call him now, are you? At this hour?"

"Liam, this'll be the biggest case of his life. He'll jump at it."

While Catherine was dialing, Liam said, "How did you know she assisted Otto in bringing Nazi money into the United States?"

Catherine smiled. "I didn't. I took a shot. It was an inspiration."

Six hours later, as a midwinter thaw was lifting the temperatures into the forties, a well-dressed woman in sunglasses and a full-length mink coat slid out of a yellow cab and walked into the Federal Building. Liam, Catherine, and Richard Tryon were waiting for her in the lobby.

"Mrs. Rosenzweig, my name is Richard Tryon. Thank you for coming. I want you to know that I've spoken with my superiors at the Justice Department, and I have authority to talk to you about your cooperation. Will you accompany us to my offices?"

She nodded.

The interview was conducted in the U.S. Attorney's corner office overlooking Federal Plaza. Elisabeth kept shifting her eyes, as though she expected Otto to appear at any moment, peering at her through the fifth-floor windows.

"I'm going to need protection," she said, "for myself and my granddaughter. You have no idea how ruthless my husband can be."

"I think we have some idea," Richard said. "Ms. Lockhart has given me a brief summary of your anticipated testimony. On the basis of what I have been told, we are prepared to offer you a grant of derivative use immunity, which means that in exchange for your cooperation, now and at trial, we will agree not to prosecute you for any of the facts you provide to us or testify to. This assumes, of course, that you had no involvement or participation in persecution under the Nazi regime."

"I was never a Nazi. I didn't hurt anybody. I never took anyone's property. At the end of the war, Poland lay in a pile of rubble. My life was in shambles. Otto was my only way out; he had money and connections. My only crime was becoming his wife."

"Well, not exactly. You helped him access resources stolen by Nazi officers and held in postwar Switzerland. You conspired to assist your husband in the concealment of his true identity. You lied on your immigration application. We have more than enough to commence deportation proceedings," Tryon said.

Elzbieta sat speechless.

"Can you give us precise information about his wealth, his bank accounts, and the property he confiscated?"

She nodded slowly. "Can you assure me that I won't be deported or prosecuted?"

"Will you testify about his role in the persecution of Zamość and its citizens?"

"I want it all in writing. I get to stay in the country."

Richard nodded. "You'll have immunity."

"And I want protection for Jennifer and myself."

Richard nodded.

The interview lasted three hours. A nine-page statement was prepared, and Elzbieta Krzyzecki Rosenzweig, having received a written grant of derivative use immunity, signed her name before a witness. The statement contained a detailed narrative and disclosed, inter alia, the true identity of Elliot Rosenzweig, the number and location of Swiss bank accounts established sixty years ago in the name of Otto Piatek and subsequently transferred by her into the name of Elliot Rosenzweig, and enough factual data to firmly establish Elliot as Hauptscharführer Otto Piatek, the Butcher of Zamość. A warrant for the arrest of Otto Piatek, n/k/a Elliot Rosenzweig, 455 Sheridan Road, Winnetka, Illinois, was issued and handed to the U.S. Marshals Service. There would be no bond.

CATHERINE AND LIAM TAXIED directly to the hospital from the Federal Building. Adele was sitting by Ben's bedside. A wall of machines was blinking and beeping—oxygen tubes, intravenous tubes, and electrocardiograph wires came out of Ben like spaghetti. Ben lay still, his eyes closed, his skin pale.

"Has Doctor Chou been in?" Catherine said.

"Several times. He's totally noncommittal. He just keeps saying, 'Let's wait and see.'"

"I have such good news for Ben. Otto is being arrested. With the testimony of Elzbieta and the subpoenaed bank records, he'll be deported and sent overseas to be tried as a war criminal. Better than anything we could have accomplished in civil court. He'll finally pay his debt to all the innocent people he tortured or sent to die, and Ben will have avenged the murder of Hannah and his family."

Adele stepped away from the bed. She put her arm around Catherine's shoulders. "There are some things I'd like to tell you," she said to Catherine. "This is Friday and I have a promise to keep. I'd like you to come with me." She turned to Liam and Mort. "Call us if anything changes, please."

Catherine and Adele drove out of the downtown area and onto the Kennedy Expressway. "How far did Ben get in his story?" she asked Catherine.

"To the end of the war. He got to the part where the Russian army had liberated the Majdanek camp."

"That's as far as he went?"

Catherine took a deep breath. "That day, when he told me what had happened, I'm afraid I broke down. I was overwhelmed. Otto had ordered the execution of Ben's father and Father Janofski. Hannah, Ben's mother, Lucyna, and the sisters of St. Mary's were sent to die at Auschwitz. I was so upset that I stopped him and spent the rest of the night curled up in the chair."

Adele nodded and patted Catherine on the leg. "Well, there's more."

"Really? Please, Adele, tell me."

"Ben and the other Majdanek prisoners were not actually liberated in the sense that they were free to go anywhere. Stalin was a distrustful anti-Semite and didn't want to release the Jews behind his lines, so the Russian army sent the survivors to a detention camp in Siberia. They were interned there for several months. Those who didn't perish from the cold or their weakened condition were finally released. It was late in the spring of 1945.

"Ben had no family and nowhere to go. He was a DP, a displaced person, one of thousands who wandered Europe after the war. Although the Allies had established displaced persons camps where people could go waiting to emigrate to the United States, or perhaps to Israel, they held no interest for Ben. He was sick at heart and felt a need to reconnect with his memories.

"He decided to return to Poland, but Zamość had changed. The people that he knew, all his personal connections, all the Jews, were gone. The Jewish ghetto had been razed, and his old neighborhood was full of strangers. He was unwelcome. He was an outcast in his own town.

"He left Zamość and started walking south along the country roads, drawn to Uncle Joseph's cabin because intuitively he knew that's where he should go, if for no other reason than to spend his time with the memories of Hannah and Beka."

Adele exited the expressway and turned her car onto Old Orchard Road. "The return was painful for Ben. The mountain tranquillity, the peace he craved, eluded him and the wilderness gave him no comfort. The valleys around the cabin were abandoned, even Krzysztof was gone, but in truth, Ben had no desire for companionship. A recluse, he fished the streams. He hunted in the forest. He talked to the memories of Hannah and Beka. Weeks went by and the mountains blossomed into summer.

"Then one night in early July, a U.S. army jeep pulled up to the cabin. Ben watched it from his front porch. An African American corporal got out of the driver's seat and walked a few steps toward the cabin.

"'Mr. Solomon?' he called.

"Ben nodded.

"The corporal walked around the car and held out his hand to assist his passenger. Ben stood. He knew even before he saw her legs slide out of the passenger seat."

"Hannah!" Catherine whispered.

Adele smiled. "Yes, dear. It was Hannah. And no moment was ever sweeter."

Catherine wiped her eyes with the back of her hand. "No matter where he ended up, she promised she'd be there."

"That's right." Adele pulled her car into the parking lot of Henderson's Florist. "We'll stop here for the flowers."

The bouquet, a standing order of red and white carnations, was wrapped and ready. Adele took the bouquet and drove across the street into Memorial Park Cemetery. Together they walked down the pathway till they came to a rose-colored granite marker. Adele set the flowers gently into the holder on the stone above the inscription:

Hannah Solomon
Dance Through All Eternity
1921–2001

Catherine stared at the stone in silence, feeling strangely connected. "You knew Hannah?" she asked Adele, after a few moments.

"Oh my, yes. She was my best friend."

"Wasn't she sent to Auschwitz?"

"Indeed she was, just as Ben described, on that terrible afternoon in 1944 when the women were loaded onto the truck in the courtyard of St. Mary's and driven from Kraśnik to Auschwitz. Upon arrival, Leah Solomon and the sisters of St. Mary's were separated from Hannah and were never seen again. Hannah and Lucyna, young and strong, were assigned to work in a nearby armaments factory. Hannah's beautiful auburn hair was shaven and she was issued a striped uniform.

"Every day they were marched out of the Birkenau camp with the other women laborers in columns of five, four miles to the factory. At the end of a twelve-hour workday, they marched back. In a drafty wooden stable, meant to hold forty-eight horses, Hannah and eight hundred other poor souls slept on bare wooden platforms, three compartments high. No blankets, no pillows. There were holes in the floor for human waste. There was no heat or running water. As the weeks went by, many succumbed to the ordeal. Malnutrition, disease, madness, or the sheer exhaustion of the daily labors claimed those that the gas chambers did not consume.

"In October 1944, they began to hear the distant guns of the Russian army. To Hannah and Lucyna the artillery blasts were the drums of freedom. As they grew louder, they knew they would be freed if they could only hang on a little while longer.

"But Lucyna was failing. Although a tough little woman, she was losing her mental and physical stamina. Hannah urged her on, found extra food and water for her, and encouraged her to keep going. 'We're survivors,' she told her. 'When this is over, we'll all be together again.'

"Just as the prisoners anticipated the advance of the Red Army, so did the Germans. In October and November they dismantled and destroyed the crematoriums. Gassings stopped. The SS did whatever they could to cover up the evidence of mass executions. Finally, on the morning of January 18, 1945, the women were roused by the kapos and told to gather in the yard. It was the final roll call.

"Snow blew over the frozen ground, yet Hannah, Lucyna, and the women stood outside in their threadbare clothes. They were each given a piece of bread and a slab of margarine and then they were marched out of the gate. Fifty-eight thousand prisoners, in columns of five, began what was to be known as the Auschwitz Death March. You see, Catherine, even in the face of defeat, the Nazis continued to pursue their Final Solution.

"The prisoners were marched at night and slept in barns or in the open during the day. This was the dark of the Polish winter, the rivers were frozen and the snowdrifts were at times as high as their knees. If a prisoner fell, became ill, complained, or was unable to walk, she was shot and her body left in the snow.

"Lucyna's strength was all but gone, but Hannah commanded her to keep walking. Leaning on each other, and on Hannah's in-domitable will to live, they reached the railroad station in the town of Wodzisław.

"There the women were stuffed into unheated railroad boxcars for transportation to other concentration camps deep in Germany. They were so tightly crammed that there was little or no room to sit and the train moved with agonizing slowness, often sitting on a side rail to allow the military trains to pass.

"Once each day the train would stop. The women would be given a pail of water and a ladle, although the water was insufficient to serve everyone, even with minimal portions. It was during this ghastly transport that Lucyna gave up the fight. Dehydrated and weakened, she slipped away in Hannah's arms.

"Eventually the doors slid open and the women, blinded by the bright sunshine, were prodded down the ramps and into the Buchenwald concentration camp. There they found conditions just as bad as at Auschwitz, if not worse.

"Hannah was assigned to the Dora-Mittelbau subcamp where women labored, some of them in caves, assembling munitions. The work was so strenuous and the conditions so foul that many women did not survive, but for Hannah, she had made a promise and she intended to keep it.

"On April 11, 1945, in the midst of her ordeal, weak and barely able to endure another day, she awoke to a chaotic scrambling in the camp. The guns that she heard were those of the U.S. Army 104th Infantry, the Timberwolf Division, which had landed in France and advanced eastward through the Rhineland. Some of the Dora SS had fled. Some guards had taken prisoners and marched them north. The other guards were left behind to execute the remaining inmates, but they were foiled when the American troops overran the camp.

"Hannah, weighing less than eighty pounds, was helped to a stretcher, carried out, and driven to an American field hospital. She was in the hospital when Hitler took his life on April 30 and when Germany unconditionally surrendered to General Eisenhower on May 7.

"There was a medic at the hospital, a corporal who cared for Hannah every day. He was a sweet man named William Porter, from a small town in Mississippi, and he patiently nursed her back to health. Through broken English and over many days, Hannah told him her story. Bit by bit. The story of Zamość and of her family. The story of Ben Solomon.

"Through it all, she never lost faith and hung tight to the vows she and Ben had made. She always knew she'd find him and she came to believe it would be at the cabin. 'He'll be there,' she said to Corporal Porter one day. 'He's waiting for me, I'm sure of it. I promised I would come to him.' And Corporal Porter gave her his word, he'd help her get there when she regained her strength.

"In July, almost a year to the day after she was sent to die, a year since she'd seen Ben, Corporal Porter borrowed a jeep and drove her south to the mountains."

Catherine kneeled on the frozen grass and gently touched the headstone. She whispered a prayer and stood up. "What is it, Adele? Why do I feel so close to her? Why do I feel like I know her?"

Adele smiled.

"Remarkable people," Catherine said. "Such determination. How did they get to Chicago?"

"Cousin Ziggy. After the war, there were thousands of displaced people: survivors of the camps, war refugees. But there were strict immigration quotas in the United States. It was eventually possible for U.S. citizens to obtain visas for displaced European relatives, provided the citizens signed a document agreeing to be financially responsible. After a tangle of red tape, Ben and Hannah came to Chicago in 1949."

Adele's cell phone buzzed. She pulled it out of her coat pocket and held it to her ear. "It's Liam. Ben's condition is unchanged."

Catherine stared at the flowers. "They're already frozen."

Adele smiled. "Of course. But they're here. It's an unbroken link. A promise kept."

"Tell me about their life in Chicago," Catherine said on the ride downtown.

"Just plain old Chicago folks, I guess. They lived in an apartment on Cornelia Street for many years. Hannah took a job at a hospital and enrolled in DePaul's School of Nursing. When she got her degree, she worked at Children's Memorial Hospital until her retirement. Ziggy got Ben the job with the Chicago Park District, where he worked at the golf course until 1996. He was a voracious reader and never stopped educating himself. He pursued a degree through the evening program at Northwestern and later accepted an adjunct position teaching evening courses in European history."

"No children?"

Adele shook her head. "Hannah couldn't have children, whether it was the scarlet fever or the abuse her poor body took in the concentration camps . . . no, it was just the two of them, but they had a sweet life. Almost every Saturday night he would take her dancing.

"Ben retired eight years ago and they talked about moving to Florida, but they loved the city and all their friends were here. About three years ago, Hannah came down with heart disease—maybe that too was a result of the scarlet fever. She was bedridden for weeks. Her heart finally gave out on August 25, 2001. To Ben, it was as though half of him had left. Maybe more than half."

"But she didn't really leave, did she, Adele. All these years since she died, she's still here, right? I mean, he's still in touch with her, isn't he?"

Adele looked at Catherine, one to another, keepers of a mystical secret, and shrugged. "Who knows for sure, honey. He says he is. If you ask me, I believe him. If any two people could stay connected through all eternity, it's Ben and Hannah."

Catherine's cell phone buzzed. "Okay. I'll be there," she said, then, turning to Adele, she said, "That was Richard Tryon at the U.S. Attorney's office. They're going out to arrest Rosenzweig. If it wouldn't be too much trouble, can you drop me at the Federal Building? I owe it to Ben to be there when they bring him in."

SIXTY-ONE

· · ·

ELLIOT TURNED THE PAGE of the *Wall Street Journal*, which lay open on the marble breakfast table, and took a spoonful of fresh grapefruit, a pleasant start to his early afternoon brunch. He loved grapefruit but disliked the effort required to struggle with the rind, not to mention the occasional squirt on his French-cuffed shirt, so his kitchen staff neatly segmented the grapefruits for him each day. One of the perquisites of enormous wealth enjoyed by the Grand Benefactor.

Robert entered the breakfast room followed by four men.

"Excuse me, sir."

"What is it, Robert? Who are these men? What's this all about?"

Richard Tryon handed Elliot a paper and said, "These men are U.S. deputy marshals and this is a warrant for your arrest. The government intends to revoke your citizenship and deport you under Title 8 of the United States Code, section 1182 (a)(3)(E), otherwise known as the Holtzman Amendment; that is to say, participating and assisting in persecution under the Nazi regime."

Elliot scoffed and flipped the warrant onto the table. "This is bullshit. Just more of Ben Solomon's bullshit. I'll have my lawyer call you later this afternoon." He returned his eyes to the *Wall Street Journal* and picked up his spoon.

"You have the right to remain silent . . ."

"I said my lawyer would call you. Robert, show them to the door. Goodbye, Mr. Tryon."

"Anything you say can and will be used against you in a court of law."

Elliot bellowed, "Do you know who I am?" To Robert, he barked, "Get me the phone. I'm calling Mayor Burton. This young fellow doesn't know who he's dealing with. On second thought, get Congressman Douglas on the line."

Tryon snapped, "Leave the phone where it is. He'll have the opportunity to make a call after he's booked."

Elliot looked shocked.

"My, my, things seem to be unraveling, don't they, Mr. Piatek?"

Elliot's face turned purple. He pointed his finger at Tryon. "Rosenzweig! The name's Rosenzweig, and it's on buildings all over this town." The marshals moved around the table and stood on either side of Elliot's chair. "Look here, sonny, I know every big-time politician in this country. I don't know who the hell you think you are." He curled his lip. "Are you Jewish? You don't look like a Jew."

"I am Richard Tryon, assistant U.S. Attorney. And you are Otto Piatek, and you're under arrest. Cuff him."

The marshals lifted Elliot by his armpits, put his hands behind his back, and slapped on the handcuffs.

"Elzie," he yelled. "Elzie, get in here."

"She left early this morning, sir," Robert said.

Tryon continued, "You have the right to consult with an attorney and have an attorney present during all questioning. If you cannot afford an attorney . . ."

"'Can't afford'? You little shit. My pinky ring's worth more than your whole family."

". . . one will be appointed for you. Do you understand each and every right as I've explained them to you?"

"Go to hell. I'll have your job. You'll be on the streets by dinnertime."

Elliot was led out of the house and into the waiting patrol car. By the time he arrived at the Federal Building, a crowd of reporters, alerted by Tryon, had gathered to watch the perp walk. Elliot scowled as he shuffled forward, hands cuffed, past the photographers, through the lobby, and into the elevators.

"I want my lawyer," he snipped. "I know my rights."

"You can call him as soon as you're booked," Tryon replied.

The staff of the U.S. Marshals Service was ready and waiting for Elliot when he was led through the doors, a strong grip on each arm. His head and shoulders twisted from side to side like a wild coyote on a choker leash. Then he saw Catherine standing quietly in the background.

"You!" he sneered. "I don't get it. What's all this to you? You couldn't have made any money. You lost your job. Your career went to hell. Where will you be tomorrow?"

Catherine shrugged. "I won't be in prison."

Catherine watched Elliot as he was processed. Then her cell phone buzzed.

"Cat, it's Liam. Dr. Chou just called. Ben's awake. Adele and I are heading over. We'll meet you in the lobby."

SIXTY-TWO

• • •

BEN LAY IN ROOM 3 at Northwestern Memorial's cardiac care unit. Mort, two nurses, and Dr. Chou were standing at the foot of the bed as Catherine, Adele, and Liam rushed up. The young cardiologist stepped away to talk to them in the hall.

"He's very weak and under strong medication, but he's awake. We're doing everything we can to control the arrhythmia, but . . ." He shrugged. "Don't stay too long."

Ben smiled as the two women approached his bed, one on either side. "Here I am again," he said to Adele, so softly that she had to lean far over the bedrails to hear him.

He turned his head. "How's our case, Counselor?"

Catherine fought back her tears. "You already know, don't you? Somehow, you cantankerous old bird, you already know."

"Elzbieta." He coughed a puff of air. "She was the key."

Catherine squeezed his hand and blinked the water from her eyes. "They arrested him this afternoon, Ben. I just came from the U.S. Marshals office."

A smile stretched the weakened skin on his face as Catherine re-created the scene.

"After he was fingerprinted, photographed, and booked, they let him call his lawyer. That was the coup de grace. Jeffers cut him loose—he refused to represent him. Rosenzweig screamed into the phone, 'What do you mean I'm too hot to handle? I've paid you a fortune! I own you!' But Jeffers wouldn't budge and left Rosenzweig adrift.

"And then it all finally hit him, that there would be no bail, that he would be considered a flight risk, that they were never going to release him. Ever. All the color drained from his face. His entire bearing changed. Gone was the arrogant swagger. What remained was just a frightened, defenseless old man looking plaintively into the faces of his keepers, begging for mercy. What a turnabout."

Catherine shook her head. "All his wealth won't buy him another day of freedom. He'll ultimately be sent overseas for trial. And it's already hit the media. It'll be on every TV station and in papers all over the world. Everyone will know."

With great effort and in a raspy voice, Ben spoke. "You did a great job. You're a first-rate attorney." He motioned for her to come close, and she leaned far over the rail. "Let go of those self-doubts now," he whispered to her. "God doesn't ask you to be Ruth or Sarah. He only asks you to be Catherine."

She nodded.

"The Catherine I know, she's there." He pointed to her chest. "Inside. Find her and be true to her."

She nodded.

"Remember: *nigdy się nię poddamy*. Never surrender."

Catherine swallowed and nodded her head.

He turned his head slowly back to Adele. "Did you take Hannah her flowers?"

"I did. Catherine went with me."

"I'm going to see her soon, she's waiting for me."

Catherine put her finger on his lips. "Shh. Dr. Chou says you're going to be fine."

He squeezed her hand. There was a twinkle in his eyes. "Not this time. Besides, I can't keep Hannah waiting. I promised her the next dance."

Catherine glanced over at Liam, who stood at the foot of the bed, his arms folded before him. He nodded gently.

Ben closed his eyes. A beatific peace settled on his smiling face. A single tone sounded on the electrocardiograph and Ben loosened his grip on Catherine's hand. Several nurses quickly entered and started for the bed, but Dr. Chou shook his head. Catherine leaned over the rail and kissed Ben on his forehead. "She says you're a very good dancer. Goodbye, Ben. I love you."

EPILOGUE

...

SUMMER HAD GIVEN WAY to a glorious fall, the turn of another season in the Midwest, though Catherine felt a hint of winter in the northerly breeze as she pulled out of Henderson's Florist and into Memorial Park. She carried two bouquets and knelt to set them into holders between the adjoining stones, pausing to chat for a while as had become her habit on Friday afternoons.

"I opened my new office this week, Ben, on Fullerton Avenue in a storefront we passed on the way to lunch at Rocco's. My little practice is coming together and I feel good about it."

Gently, she arranged the flowers in their vases. The petals fluttered in the autumn breeze.

"I've had time to do a lot of thinking—sometimes wondering: where are my inspirations? What will they say? Where will they come from? And I've come to realize—you were my inspiration, Ben. It was you all along."

She brushed a blade of grass from the marker. "One thing I'm sure of—I've found Catherine. She was inside, like you said, hiding for so long behind insecurities, large law firm anonymity, and self-doubt. I'm happy with the person I'm becoming and I owe that to you.

"My practice is people-oriented and very satisfying. I've even volunteered at a neighborhood legal clinic. I want to do something significant with my life, something to make you proud."

Her tears fell upon the stone and she spread them with her fingertips. Beneath Ben's name was an inscription in Hebrew, which read: "Light is sown for the righteous, joy for the upright in heart." It was an excerpt from a psalm that Catherine and Adele thought was fitting. A stiff gust of wind tore red and yellow leaves from the maples and tumbled them along the grass.

"Otto's trial has been set for next month in Tel Aviv. At his extradition hearing, he showed no remorse. Like so many before him, he denied responsibility and had no self-reproach. I understand that the Israeli court has developed quite a case against him. Liam and I are going to attend the trial." She smiled. "We're good for each other. You were right about that, too. I've asked Adele to go with us, but she's not feeling too well these days."

A single red leaf floated down and came to rest in the center of Ben's headstone. She picked it up and held it in her hand. Its color was pure, its five points elegant in their symmetry. She smiled and held the soft leaf to her cheek. "'And there was morning and there was evening, the third day,'" she said.

She stood. "I have to leave now."

She brushed off her skirt, took a few steps toward Liam, who stood patiently waiting at the car, and then turned around to stare at the landscaped serenity.

"The music beckons, Ben. Enjoy the dance."

ACKNOWLEDGMENTS

Although *Once We Were Brothers* is a work of fiction, it was my intention to portray the story in a historically accurate setting. Several persons assisted me in researching and writing this novel. A treasure trove of information was and is available in the individual stories of those who lived through the Holocaust and had the courage to open their wounds and chronicle their experiences, and to whom I express my deepest gratitude. Many of their narrations may be found through the multiple doorways of the Internet. The staff members of the United States Holocaust Memorial Museum in Washington, D.C., and the Illinois Holocaust Museum and Education Center in Skokie, Illinois, were very helpful. United States case law concerning claims brought by survivors against sovereign nations; against the commercial entities that sought to and did profit from their business arrangements with the Third Reich; and against those persons who participated in, lent support to, and enabled the Nazi regime is available in law libraries and through the online research venues. I am deeply indebted to my dear friend Rabbi Victor Weissberg, who gave me the privilege of studying with him, who reviewed my manuscript, and generously gave me encouragement. My thanks to all those who read, reviewed, and edited my work, including Sara Flynn; my literary agent, Maura Teitelbaum; my son Dave, a brilliant grammarian; and my son Matt, who helped me through the technological minefield. Thanks also to Jolanda Krawczyk, who provided information on all things Polish, including the Polish phrases used herein. Finally, my heartfelt thanks to my support group: my wife, Monica; my children; my sister, Linda; and my good friend Richard Templer.

DISCUSSION QUESTIONS FOR
ONCE WE WERE BROTHERS

1. Does it trouble you to think that remnants of the Nazi era may remain? Of the six hundred thousand SS members alive at the end of the war, only a few thousand were actually brought to justice. Most escaped, some to America. Only one hundred or so have been found and deported. Was Ben's quest after all these years, in spite of Rosenzweig's civic contributions, justified?

2. Responding to someone who said, "I can't believe anybody cares about those events of so long ago," Eli Rosenbaum, former head of the U.S. Office of Special Investigations, stated, "I think there's particular value in showing would-be perpetrators that if one dares to perpetrate such crimes, there is a chance that he or she will be pursued for the rest of his or her life to locations thousands of miles from the locations of their crimes." Where do you stand? Do you think we should continue to seek out and prosecute now-elderly Nazi war criminals?

3. It is said that "first impressions are lasting ones." What were your first impressions of the principal characters? At what point did your opinion change? Why?

4. Ben's family had the opportunity to leave Europe at certain times in the story. When cousin Ziggy told them of the persecution in Germany and when Uncle Joseph came from Vienna, they could

have all escaped through the mountains into Slovakia. Why didn't they take advantage of each of those opportunities? Why did Jewish families remain?

5. From the diaries of survivors, there are many stories of extraordinary heroism, of ordinary people who, in the darkest moments, find unbelievable strength and courage. Have you known such people? Where do you think they find such courage?

6. If you had the opportunity to speak to any of the characters at any moment in the story, to whom would you choose to talk, what advice would you give, and what would you say?

7. Ben was a religious person, as was Catherine. If religious doctrine preaches that God is all-knowing and omnipotent, how does a religious person accept the existence of the Holocaust in God's world?

8. Ethnic slaughter, the oppression of minorities, did not cease with the end of World War II. Does the world community today do enough to respond to the oppressors? What should be done?

9. Why did Elisabeth decide to turn against her husband? Did it have anything to do with her fear of facing Ben?